Enhancing
Reading Comprehension

英文閱讀
加深加廣

MP3下載引導頁面

https://globalv.com.tw/mp3-download-9789864544035/

掃描QR碼進入網頁並註冊後，按「全書音檔下載請按此」連結，可一次性下載音檔壓縮檔，或點選檔名線上撥放。
全MP3一次下載為zip壓縮檔，部分智慧型手機需安裝解壓縮程式方可開啟，iOS系統請升級至iOS 13以上。
此為大型檔案，建議使用WIFI連線下載，以免占用流量，並請確認連線狀況，以利下載順暢。

PREFACE

本書不僅助您打穩英語檢定考試的閱讀基礎，更讓您的閱讀能力加深加廣！

從我多年教學和出版書籍的經驗中，我深刻地感受到，學習英語並非僅僅是詞彙與文法的累積，而是如何在閱讀中構築語言能力。舉例來說，30年前的TIME雜誌通常會使用許多艱澀字彙，而且句型複雜，這樣的英文在以前被認為是高端的語言運用，但是現代的英文並不是如此，這些年TIME雜誌的用字越來越平易近人，使用的句型也比以前簡短俐落許多，這樣的趨勢也顯示在美國大學的入學考試。舉例來說，SAT 一直是以艱澀單字文法著稱，但是2016年SAT改制之後，明顯減少艱澀詞彙和刁鑽文法，轉向要求考生的閱讀理解力。在台灣，108課綱也將高中單字從過去的7000必學字彙降低為4500字，目的是希望減少死記硬背的學習方式，鼓勵學生花更多時間閱讀文章，增進閱讀理解效率。

然而，許多學習者往往因為基礎文法的不穩固或閱讀練習不足，在重要的英語測驗中感到挫折。因此，為了幫助學習者有效突破這些瓶頸，本書的目標是讓每一位讀者都能在系統化的訓練中，逐步提升自己的英語能力，並在重要的英語測驗中取得理想成績，尤其是多益測驗。多益成績一直是求職者證明自己英語水平的重要條件，近年來多益成績也已經被大專院校列為畢業門檻之一，其重要性不可言喻。

無論是初學者，或是希望提升測驗分數的進階學習者，幾乎都會面臨相似的問題：文法基礎不穩、句型理解不足、閱讀速度緩慢、應對題型的策略不靈活。針對這些問題，本書設計了這套分為三大部分、共 18 週的完整學習計劃，目標是幫助讀者及考生在有限的時間內，系統性地解決這些困難，並獲得具體的成效。

第一部分為文法基礎訓練（8 週的訓練）。文法是語言的根基，在台

灣沒有英語母語環境，因此扎實的文法學習是必要的，就像在美國上中文課，一樣要學習中文的文法。多益測驗是將文法知識運用到實際情境中的最佳範例之一，因此，這部分內容不僅涵蓋了句子結構、詞性、動詞時態與語態等基礎，還特別加入了多益測驗中常見的考點解析，希望藉由這部分的訓練，幫助讀者理解句型背後的邏輯，靈活運用。

　　第二部分聚焦多益閱讀測驗中的題型訓練（7 週的訓練）。多益測驗的閱讀部分涉及各種商務情境，例如電子郵件、公告、通知、備忘錄、報導、廣告、網頁資訊…等，這些題型對考生的時間管理與資訊提取能力有極高的要求。本書由淺入深的設計，幫助讀者提升閱讀效率，並理解閱讀測驗的底層邏輯。

　　第三部分為多篇閱讀題組綜合攻略（3 週的訓練）。雙篇與三篇閱讀題組是多益測驗中最具挑戰性的部分，雙篇閱讀題組也是全民英檢、托福、雅思等測驗的必考題型。許多考生在面對這類題型時，往往會因為內容龐雜而感到不知所措。本書提供不同題型的高效解題技巧，教會考生如何快速抓住每篇閱讀的關鍵資訊。在最後三週的多篇閱讀題組訓練，讀者不僅能突破最高的難關，更能將所學的技巧靈活應用於考試中。

　　本書最後附上前面各單元的關鍵字彙、片語及慣用語列表，並搭配線上音檔，方便讀者隨時隨地練習聽力與學習詞彙。希望每一位學習者都能善用零碎時間，在日常生活中逐步提升英語能力。本書不僅是一個學習工具，更是對於每一位英語學習者及考生的期許。希望藉由本書的練習，每位學習者都能找到屬於自己的進步節奏，並在英語能力提升的過程中收穫成就感與自信。無論您是為了準備多益測驗，還是希望全面提升英語能力，本書都能成為您的最佳夥伴。讓我們一起踏上這段學習旅程，迎接挑戰，突破自我！

周昱翔 2025 年於台北

本書特色與使用說明

WEEK 03　英文裡的動詞

▶ 穩固基礎

必備 Point 1

對於**動詞**的基本認知,要以「**五大基本句型**」為基礎。因為,五大句型就代表著五大類動詞的運用。

❶ **及物動詞**:運用在「**S + V + O**」的句型。例如:
Sarah enjoys working with children and finds it fulfilling.
莎拉喜歡處理小孩子的工作,並認為這是一件令人滿足的事情。
☞ enjoys、finds 是及物動詞,後面分別接受詞「working with...」以及 it。但此句的動詞 find 是「不完全及物動詞」(請見以下 ❸)

❷ **不及物動詞**:運用在「**S + V**」的句型。例如:
The study group meets once a week.

第 1~8 週,每週 1 個必考文法主題:藉由一開始的「穩固基礎」,除了把學過的文法以及句型結構的觀念找回來,也能再進一步推升英文實力!

「多益會怎麼考」針對前述「穩固基礎」內容,給自己來個牛刀小試,同時熟悉一下 TOEIC 閱讀 Part 5 考題與考點。

多益會怎麼考?

多益會考選擇適當動詞類型的題目。

1. The jury --------- him guilty of all charges related to the embezzlement case.
   (A) found　　(B) founded　　(C) determined　　(D) appraised

▶ 關鍵概念

必備 Point 1

動詞時態:一個句子所表達的動作、事件或狀態,通常也伴隨著不同時間點的概念。例如「現在」、「過去」、「未來」…等不同時間點,而在這 3 個時間點中,可能表達**單純的動作、事件或狀態**,也可能表達**正在進行、正在發生**,或**已經完成、已經發生**等狀態。

時間 狀態	簡單式	進行式	完成式	完成進行式
現在式	現在簡單式	現在進行式	現在完成式	現在完成進行式
過去式	過去簡單式	過去進行式	過去完成式	過去完成進行式
未來式	未來簡單式	未來進行式	未來完成式	未來完成進行式

「關鍵概念」延續「穩固基礎」的文法要點:將先前提及的文法概念深入與延伸說明,進一步統整出關鍵考點!然後再熟悉一次 TOEIC 考題。

多益會怎麼考?

多益 Part 5 會考選擇適當動詞形態的題目。

1. Concerns about data privacy --------- discussions in the tech industry for years.
   (A) permeate　　　　　　　(B) are permeating
   (C) have been permeated　　(D) have been permeating

翻譯 對於數據隱私的擔憂已經在科技業界的討論中滲透多年。
解析 從四個選項來看,空格要填入一個正確的動詞形式,而根據句尾的 for years 可知,應填入完成式,故原形動詞 (A)、現在進行式 (B) 可直接刪除。permeate(滲透)

TOEIC 閱讀 Part 5 的實戰演練：
總結本週所學文法概念與考點，藉由 TOEIC 閱讀的 Part 5 模擬試題，驗收一下自己在 15 題的文法考題可以答對幾題，解答解析就在書本最後面喔！

▶ Week 05

01 (B)　02 (B)　03 (C)　04 (A)　05 (D)　06 (A)　07 (C)　08 (B)
09 (C)　10 (D)　11 (D)　12 (A)　13 (D)　14 (D)　15 (C)

01.
翻譯 我追求的不是僅僅是成功，而是當下的滿足。
解析 本題考的是「相關連接詞：not... but...」（不是…而是…）」。空格要填入一個連接 success 和 fulfillment 這兩個名詞的連接詞，前面有 not 所以與其搭配的是 but，為固定用法，答案是 (B)。

04.
翻譯 這項決策被延後至所有數據都能被徹底分析為止。
解析 本題考「表「時間」的連接詞 until」用法。句意是「決策被延後，直到…為止」，所以正確答案是 (A) until。

05.

▶ TOEIC 實戰演練

Part 5　請在以下四個選項中選出正確的答案

01　Experienced nurses know how to --------- the discomfort of patients after surgery.
　　(A) soothe　　(B) prevail　　(C) thrive　　(D) vanish

02　Her gaze --------- for a moment on the old photograph before she put it away.

第 9～15 週的課程，主要針對 TOEIC 閱讀的 Part 6-7 進行題型訓練： 從「選出正確句子」到「信件／電子郵件／廣告／公告／通知／備忘錄／報導／資訊…」等各類型篇章題型介紹。

WEEK 09　選出正確句子的題目

▶ 出題模式

必備 Point 1
選出正確句子是多益 Part 6 的題型之一，有點類似學測的「篇章結構」題型。考生必須根據空格的前後文、上下文甚至整篇文章的意旨，在四個「句子選項」中找出一個與前後文**語意連貫、符合文意**的句子。在 Part 6 中的四篇文章中各有 1 題這樣的題型。此題型給你 1 分鐘的時間，其餘 3 個選項加起來也是 1 分鐘，所以通常 Part 6 的 1 個題組要在 2 分鐘內解決掉（總共 8 分鐘解決這個 Part）。

▶ 解題步驟

解題 Step 1
先不看選項，只看空格前後句子，推測空格可能出現的內容。了解要填入的句子與其前後文的連接關係，非常重要。如果從空格前後部分無法推測可能的內容，再往下多看一些內容。例如：

WEEK 15　備忘錄&說明的題目

▶ 出題模式

必備 Point 1
備忘錄（memo）有點像電子郵件的編排方式，通常用來傳達公司內部政策或設施相關、工作通知、公司舉辦活動等。**說明**（information）是提供資訊的文本，其涵蓋範圍很廣，可能是產品、飯店設施或各種活動的使用說明，也可能以**網頁**（web page）的形式呈現。

必備 Point 2
常考問題類型：尋找主題／目的、5W1H 問題、Not/True 問題及推論問題。例如：
❶ **尋找主題／目的**：可能詢問備忘錄／說明的目的或主要關於什麼。例如：
① Why was the memo written?
② What is mainly disclosed in the memo?
③ What is the information about?
④ What is the purpose of the information?

熟悉「問題類型」也很重要：
不同的問題類型（詢問主旨、詢問意圖、Not/True、細節推論、插入句子、同義字詞…等）都可以在題目句本身得到確認。

哪個位置通常是「解題線索」來源？ 比方說，郵件的收件人、寄件人欄位、日期、表格中的數字⋯等，都要特別留意！

▶ **實用策略**

備忘錄或說明的內容編排通常具**條理性**和**結構化**。因此表現在各類題型上，比較有跡可循。其中常有**條列式**的具體訊息、指示或細節，通常也是答題線索的來源。另外，特別留意與「**期限**」、「**聯絡方式**」有關的敘述。

 備忘錄或說明的「**尋找主題／目的**」問題，就是在詢問這篇「備忘錄」要傳達的主要訊息或這篇說明的核心目標。通常解題線索集中在備忘錄的主題（subject）行或開頭段落，以及「說明」內容中的第一段文字。例如：

> MEMORANDUM
> To: All R&D Engineers
> From: Michael Chen, Department Manager
> Subject: Project Update Submissions
> Date: November 15

多益會怎麼考？

多益會考一張票券中所不包含的資訊問題：

> **Ocean Breeze Park**
> Ticket for Adults (16 and above): $40
> Operating Hours:
> Mondays to Fridays: 8:00 A.M. ~ 6:00 P.M.
> Weekends and public holidays: 8:00 A.M. ~ 7:00 P.M.
> Parking: $3 per hour (applies to weekdays, weekends and holidays)
> Date: September 12, 2024

第 16～18 週主要針對 TOEIC 閱讀的 Part 7 的多篇文章題組進行訓練： 先學會辨認哪一題是「可鎖定單篇解題線索的題型」、「以題目關鍵字詞或關鍵語句來鎖定搜尋範圍的題型」、及需要看兩篇文章才能解的「連結問題」吧！

WEEK 16 雙篇文章題組

▶ **出題模式**

 信件／電子郵件／通知／公告 是 TOEIC 雙篇文章題組出題比例較高的文本，通常出 2 個題組，各 5 小題，出現在第 176-185 題。每一個題組有 4 題是**可以根據題句的關鍵字詞或語句，直接從其中一篇找到答案**，只有 1 題是必須**綜合兩篇的線索才能解題**（又稱為「連結問題」）。「雙篇文章」難度較高的是「**文章＋文章**」（例如「article 報導＋letter 信件」、「advertisement 廣告＋email 電郵」…），而最常配在一起的就是「**信件＋信件**」。此外，雙篇文章的連結問題在 GEPT 或 TOEFL 等閱讀測驗考試中，也必然會出現，因此學習此類題型的解題技巧是不可或缺的！

 可鎖定單篇解題線索的題型：雙篇題組可能出現先前提及的「5W1H 疑問詞」問題、「NOT/true」問題、推論問題、同義字詞…等，但不會考「插

 以題目關鍵字詞或語句來鎖定答題線索：這裡針對上述「**詢問特定細節**」進一步說明。當題目句沒有明顯指出要你在哪一篇中找答案，這時候就得**在題目句中找出關鍵訊息**。例如，當第 1 篇是 advertisement，第 2 篇是 email，第 3 篇是 invoice 時，有題目這麼問：

❶ How can customers obtain a discount?
☞ 廣告內容都會有產品說明、折扣優惠等內容，因此可直接在 advertisement 那篇找答案。

❷ What is mentioned about Mr. Smith?
☞ 「關於某人」的事，不會出現在廣告中，所以可以在 invoice 和 email 當中找線索。

 必須對照 2~3 個文本才能解答的題型：即所謂「**連結問題**」，通常針對其中兩篇的相關內容來出題，只有少數題型是必須綜合三篇內容（必須找到三個線索）才能解題的。同樣地，要先抓住題目句的**關鍵字詞或語句**，判斷要先看哪一個文本。接著，找出相關的第一個線索，然後判斷第

掌握解題的節奏,輕鬆破解最棘手的「連結問題」:在「多益會怎麼考」的示範例題中,以顏色標示解題線索,搭配底下的中譯和解析,多加練習,熟悉題目的設計。

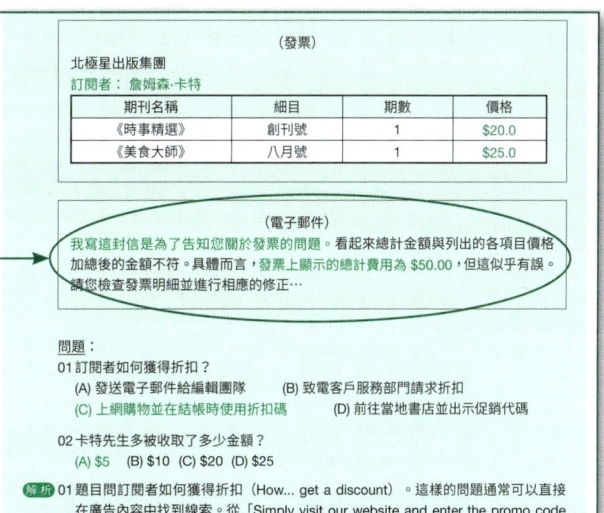

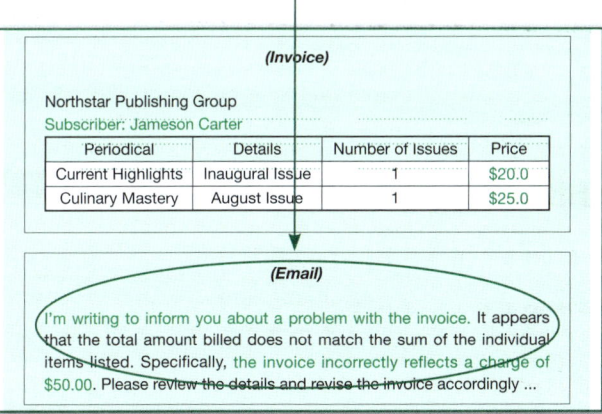

附錄的單字片語及慣用語列表:前面 Week 01～18 各單元出現過的、TOEIC 常考的中高程度以上的單字、片語、慣用語一併收錄。您可以用手機掃描 QR Code 聆聽正確的發音,讓自己的詞彙實力隨時隨地大幅提升!

CONTENTS

目錄

Prelude 2
本書特色與使用說明 4

Week 01	構成句子的基本元素	9
Week 02	八大詞類	18
Week 03	英文裡的動詞	28
Week 04	動狀詞	37
Week 05	連接詞與子句	46
Week 06	關係詞與子句	55
Week 07	假設語氣	64
Week 08	特殊句型	72
Week 09	選出正確句子的題目	81
Week 10	信件／電子郵件的題目	90
Week 11	訊息對話的題目	102
Week 12	表格＆單據的題目	111
Week 13	新聞＆報導的題目	122
Week 14	廣告＆通知的題目	133
Week 15	備忘錄＆資訊的題目	144
Week 16	雙篇文章題組	155
Week 17	三篇文章題組（1）	167
Week 18	三篇文章題組（2）	177

TOEIC 實戰演練解答／解析／翻譯......191
附錄—多益常考字彙、片語、慣用語......233

WEEK 01 構成句子的基本元素

▶ 穩固基礎

必備 Point 1

主詞是動作或狀態的主體。任何一個句子都要有主詞和動詞，否則無法成為一個完整的句子。例如：

In some cultures, disciplinary practices may vary significantly.
在某些文化中，紀律懲戒的做法可能會有顯著的差異。

> **補充**
>
> 有些句子，尤其是在口語會話中，可能有看不到主詞的情況，像是祈使句、感嘆句等，但那並不表示這個句子沒有主詞，而是主詞被省略掉了！例如：
>
> ❶ Do not disclose classified information to unauthorized individuals.
> *請勿將機密資訊透漏給未經授權的個人。*
>
> ❷ What an absent-minded student (he) is!　*他真是個心不在焉的學生！*
> ☞ 感嘆句中主詞擺放的位置不同！有時也會被省略。

必備 Point 2

動詞代表**主詞**所執行的動作或呈現的狀態。例如：

❶ The engine coughed and died.　*引擎噗噗響了幾聲後就熄火了。*

❷ The coach seemed doubtful about his own ability to lead the team to victory.　*教練似乎懷疑自己能否領導該隊獲得勝利。*

❸ After some questioning, he elicited what really happened from the young girl.　*在數次詢問後，他從這年輕女孩身上誘出了事情的真相。*

必備 Point 3

受詞意指承受某動作的對象。對於要有受詞才能表達完整意義的動詞而言，受詞也是句中必要的元素。例如：

After a long flight, I was relieved to finally retrieve my luggage from the carousel.
經過一段長途飛行後，我終於鬆了一口氣，從行李輸送帶上取回了我的行李。

必備 Point 4 **補語**對主詞或受詞做補充說明。對於要有補語才能表達完整意義的動詞而言，補語也是句中必要的元素。例如：

❶ He is a bachelor who enjoys traveling the world and immersing himself in different cultures.
他是一位單身漢，喜歡周遊世界並深入體驗不同的文化。

❷ He makes himself indispensable by consistently delivering innovative solutions. 他藉由持續提供創新的解決方案而讓自己變得不可或缺。

必備 Point 5 **修飾語**（modifier）**不是句中必要元素，但可以為必要元素或整句添加意義**，因此沒有修飾語也不影響**句子結構的完整**。其功能在於提供更多的描述性資訊，使句子更豐富、更具鮮明性或更精確。它可以修飾名詞、動詞、形容詞或副詞，進而增加句子的表達能力和清晰度。修飾語可以是單一字彙、片語或子句。例如：

The rollout of the new product without proper testing and preparation was a catastrophe that led to significant financial losses for the company.

新產品的推出沒有經過適當的測試和準備，是對公司造成重大財務損失的一場災難。

☞ 底線部分即為修飾語

多益會怎麼考？

多益會考在主詞／動詞／受詞／補語等必要元素的位置選出正確形態的題目。

1. The large government --------- aims to improve infrastructure across the region.

   (A) projects (B) projecting (C) to project (D) project

   翻譯 這個大型政府專案旨在改善整個地區的基礎設施。

   解析 空格後面 aims to... 是句子的動詞，所以「The large government ---------」整個是主詞，要填入的正確答案是可以做為動作（aims to improve...）主體的 (D) project。aims 是第三人稱單數動詞，所以複數名詞的 (A) 錯誤。

2. The research paper --------- the impact of social media on modern communication.

   (A) analysis (B) analyzes (C) analyzer (D) analytical

   翻譯 這篇研究論文分析了社交媒體對現代溝通的影響。

   解析 空格前後都是名詞，且句子沒有動詞，所以要填入的就是句子的動詞，正確答案是 (B)。

▶ 關鍵概念

主詞的位置：可以當名詞用的，都可以擺在主詞的位置。包括名詞（片語或子句）、代名詞、動名詞（片語）、不定詞（片語）。

❶ 單一名詞：The cemetery is a place of quiet reflection and remembrance for those who have passed away.
墓地是一個靜靜的地方，讓人們反思和紀念已故者。

❷ 名詞片語：The census data provides valuable insights into demographic trends and population dynamics.
人口普查資料提供有價值的見解，讓人了解人口趨勢和人口動態。

❸ 名詞子句：What the organization needs is a team of certified professionals to handle the complex project.
這個組織需要的是一支認證專業人士的團隊來處理這項複雜的專案。

❹ 代名詞：He will need to obtain certified qualifications before he can apply for the job.
他需要獲得認證資格才能申請這份工作。

❺ 動名詞（V-ing）：Using this new software is easy once you familiarize yourself with its interface and features.
熟悉了這新軟體的介面和功能後，用起來很容易了。

❻ 不定詞（to-V）：To accelerate the project timeline requires allocating additional resources and streamline the approval process.
要加快專案進度就得分配額外的資源並簡化批准流程。

動詞的位置：可以擺在動詞位置的，包括「be 動詞」、「**動詞（片語）**」、「**（助動詞 + 原形動詞）**」、「**be 動詞 +（現在／過去）分詞**」、「**have/has/had + 過去分詞**」。

❶ be 動詞：The concert was quite satisfactory, as the performers showcased their talents perfectly.
這場音樂會是相當令人滿意的，因為表演者完美地展現出他們的才華。

❷ 動詞（片語）：She nervously fiddled with her pen during the meeting, a sign of her anxiety.
她在會議期間神經兮兮地擺弄著她的筆，顯示她的焦慮情緒。

❸ 助動詞＋原形動詞：Learning effective time management techniques can help you balance work and personal life more effectively.
學習有效的時間管理技巧能幫助你更有效地平衡工作與個人生活。

❹ be 動詞＋現在分詞（Ving）：The security team is monitoring the building's entrances and exits closely to ensure safety.
安全團隊正嚴密地監控著大樓的出入口，以確保安全。

❺ has/have/had ＋動詞過去分詞（p.p.）：The aliens have abducted several cows from the farmer's field.
外星人已經從農夫的田地裡綁架了幾頭牛。

❻ 祈使句：Call off the meeting scheduled for this afternoon.
取消今天下午安排的會議。

☞ 祈使句沒有主詞（或者說省略主詞 You），沒有時態的考量，須以原形動詞為句子開頭。

> 注意
>
> 務必確認動詞位置的**數**、**時態**、**語態**要正確。例如：
>
> ❶ The principal (~~commend~~ / commends) the students for their outstanding academic achievements.
> 校長讚賞學生們在學業上的傑出成就。
>
> ❷ My cousin (~~emigrates~~ / emigrated) to Canada last year to pursue higher education.
> 我表弟去年移民到加拿大，去追求更高等的教育。
>
> ❸ I (was distracted / ~~distracted~~) by the noise outside this morning.
> 今早我被外面的噪音分心了。

受詞的位置：可以當名詞用的，都可以擺在受詞的位置。包括名詞（片語或子句）、代名詞、動名詞（片語）、不定詞（片語）。

❶ 名詞：Sarah and her daughter have a striking resemblance, often mistaken for sisters.
莎拉和她的女兒長得非常像，常常被誤以為是姐妹。

❷ 名詞子句：They don't understand that practicing consistently is key to improving their skills.
他們不明白，持之以恆地練習是提升他們技能的關鍵。

❸ 代名詞：The fascinating documentary about marine life made him interested.
那部關於海洋生物且迷人的紀錄片讓他產生了興趣。

❹ 動名詞 (V-ing)：She studied diligently to avoid failing her exams.
她努力唸書，以免考試不及格。

❺ 不定詞 (to-V)：The politician promised to implement sweeping reforms to address systemic inequality.
這名政客承諾實施全面性的改革以解決系統性不平等問題。

> **注意**
>
> 動詞、形容詞、副詞都不能當受詞。例如：
>
> ① She stopped (~~worry~~, worrying) about the things she couldn't control.
> 她不再擔憂自己無法掌控的事情。
>
> ② The research team has received (recognition, ~~recognizable~~) for their groundbreaking discoveries.
> 研究團隊以其破天荒的發現而獲得認可。
>
> ③ The beauty of nature never fails to inspire (awe and wonder, ~~awfully and wonderfully~~) in those who spend time appreciating it.
> 大自然的美總能在那些花時間欣賞它的人們心中引起敬畏和驚嘆。

必備 Point 4

補語的位置：可以當名詞或形容詞的，都可以擺在補語的位置，包括名詞（片語或子句）、代名詞、動名詞（片語）、不定詞（片語）。形容詞包括形容詞片語、形容詞子句及分詞（片語）。補語分為「**主詞補語**」及「**受詞補語**」兩種。以下列舉：

❶ 主詞補語：

① The environmental degradation in the region is an aftermath of unchecked industrial expansion.
該地區的環境惡化是工業擴張不受控的餘波。

☞ 主詞補語是名詞的話，代表「**主詞補語 = 主詞**」。

② His mastery of the intricate software algorithms **was** impressive.
他精通複雜軟體的演算法真是令人印象深刻。

☞ 主詞補語是形容詞的話，代表主詞補語「**用來修飾或說明**」該主詞。

❷ 受詞補語：

① Despite his potential, many **consider** his recent performance a disappointment.
儘管他有潛力，許多人認為他最近的表現是令人失望的事。）

☞ 受詞補語是名詞的話，代表「**受詞補語 = 受詞**」。

② The researcher **found** the correlation between cultural heritage preservation and economic development particularly interesting.
研究人員發現文化遺產保護與經濟發展之間的相關性特別有趣。）

☞ 受詞補語是形容詞時，代表受詞補語用來「修飾或說明」該受詞。

> **注意**
>
> 動詞、副詞不能放在補語的位置：
>
> ① Her proposal for the project timeline is (~~accept~~, acceptable).
> 她對於專案時間表的提議是可以接受的。
>
> ② Understanding cultural nuances is (helpful, ~~helpfully~~) for navigating global business environments effectively.
> 了解文化細微差異對於有效地應對全球商業環境是有幫助的。

必備 Point 5　**修飾語**：就是指形容詞與副詞。形容詞用來修飾名詞，而副詞用來修飾動詞、形容詞或副詞：

❶ **形容詞**：可能以**單一形容詞**、「**介系詞片語**」、「**不定詞（片語）**」、「**動名詞（片語）**」、「**（現在／過去）分詞（片語）**」、**形容詞／關係子句**等型態出現。：

① The company implemented new safety protocols for employees working in hazardous environments.
公司為在危險環境中工作的員工實施了新的安全協議。）　分詞片語當形容詞用，修飾前面 employees。

② The board of directors decided to adopt the plan to streamline operations and improve efficiency.
董事會決定採納這個精簡操作並提升效率的計畫。）

☞ 不定詞片語當形容詞用，修飾前面 plan。

❷ **副詞**：可能以**單一副詞**、「**介系詞片語**」、「**不定詞（片語）**」、「**分詞構句**」、**副詞子句**等型態出現。但也有少數「**現在分詞**」當副詞用的情況。以下列舉：

① **After the initial data analysis**, it became evident that further experimentation was necessary.
在進行了初步的資料分析後，顯示出進一步的實驗是必要的。

☞ 介系詞片語當副詞用，修飾後面整句。

② Feel free to stop by our office **to register** for the upcoming workshop.
歡迎隨時來我們辦公室報名即將舉行的工作坊。

☞ 不定詞當副詞用，表示目的，修飾前面動詞 stop by。

③ **Listening to** the keynote speaker's insightful analysis, I gained a deeper understanding of the industry's current challenges.
聆聽著主講者深刻的分析，我對此產業目前面臨的挑戰有了更深入的理解。

☞ 分詞構句作為副詞，修飾後面整句。

④ **Because the weather deteriorated unexpectedly**, all flights scheduled for departure were grounded indefinitely.
由於天氣突然惡化，所有預定出發的航班都無限期停飛了。

☞ 副詞子句修飾後面整句。

> **注意**
>
> 形容詞／副詞子句皆由一個**連接詞**來**引導**；相反地，形容詞／副詞片語不會有連接詞。
>
> ① (~~Despite~~, **Even though**) negotiations stalled repeatedly, the president remained steadfast in pursuing diplomatic solutions to the crisis.
> 儘管談判屢次陷入停滯，總統仍堅持追求外交解決危機的方案。
>
> ② (**Due to**, ~~Because~~) the heavy rain, the couple decided to postpone their outdoor picnic until the following weekend.
> 因為下著大雨，這對夫妻決定將戶外野餐延後到下個週末。

多益會怎麼考？

多益會考填入主詞／動詞／受詞／補語等主要元素的位置。

1. The analysis of the historical data --------- that socioeconomic factors have a profound impact on the patterns of migration.

    (A) revealing (B) to reveal (C) revelation (D) reveals

    翻譯 這項歷史數據的分析揭示了社會經濟因素對於移民模式產生了深遠的影響。

WEEK 01 構成句子的基本元素

15

解析 空格前是句子的主詞「The analysis of the historical data」，空格後面是「that 引導的名詞子句」，所以應填入的是句子的動詞，故正確答案是 (D)。

2. Any evidence presented in the trial that adheres to procedural rules will be considered -------- by the court.

(A) valid　　　(B) validity　　　(C) validate　　　(D) validation

翻譯 在審判中，任何符合程序規則的證據將被法院視為有效。

解析 「Any evidence presented in the trial that adheres to procedural rules」這部分是這句子長長的主詞，動詞是被動式的「will be considered」（將被視為 ...），所以空格應填入主詞補語，故正確答案是形容詞的 (A)。

▶ TOEIC 實戰演練

Part 5　請在以下四個選項中選出正確的答案

01 The experienced mountain -------- reached the summit of the high mountain.

(A) climb　　　(B) climbing　　　(C) to climb　　　(D) climber

02 The software --------- that New-Tech offers remove security risks and improve the performance of computers.

(A) to enhance　　(B) enhancing　　(C) enhancement　　(D) enhancements

03 The CEO may --------- from the company after a series of financial scandals.

(A) oust　　　(B) be ousted　　　(C) have ousted　　　(D) was ousted

04 The police --------- the suspect to prevent them from causing further harm.

(A) restrained　　(B) restraining　　(C) to restrain　　(D) was restrained

05 The proposed merger is expected to receive --------- from regulatory authorities.

(A) approve　　(B) approving　　(C) to approve　　(D) approval

06 --------- on the new budget proposal will be held next Monday.

(A) Discuss　　(B) Discussions　　(C) Discussed　　(D) Discusses

07 Because of their busy schedules, they often find it difficult to schedule regular family dinners, which can prevent --------- from spending quality time together.

(A) they   (B) their   (C) them   (D) themselves

08 Many teenagers find themselves --------- to social media due to its constant availability and engaging content.

(A) addict   (B) addicts   (C) addicted   (D) addicting

09 Recent studies --------- that regular exercise can significantly improve cardiovascular health.

(A) revealed   (B) revealing   (C) to reveal   (D) revelation

10 --------- consensus on the new policy, the committee decided to implement it starting next month.

(A) Achieve   (B) Achieving   (C) Achieved   (D) Achievement

11 Mr. Chang advocated for expanding the sales team, --------- Ms. Wang proposed improving customer service instead.

(A) except   (B) while   (C) besides   (D) which

12 The project launch was postponed --------- unforeseen technical issues.

(A) while   (B) because   (C) in spite of   (D) due to

13 Although the --------- had differing opinions on the proposal, the chairman emphasized the need for consensus before proceeding.

(A) representation   (B) representatives   (C) represent   (D) representing

14 The new policy initiative --------- a crucial step toward achieving environmental sustainability goals.

(A) deemed   (B) was deeming   (C) to be deemed   (D) was deemed

15 The hiker --------- by a venomous snake is receiving urgent medical treatment.

(A) bites   (B) biting   (C) bitten   (D) to bite

WEEK 02 八大詞類

▶ 穩固基礎

依據一個單字／片語在句子裡的「作用」或「功能」，分為**名詞／代名詞、動詞、形容詞、副詞、介系詞、連接詞、感嘆詞**等八大類。學習一個單字或片語的不同詞類（或詞性）變化，才能夠精準使用並將其放在句子裡的正確位置上。除動詞（Week 03）與連接詞（Week 05）之外，以下將進一步說明。

必備 Point 1

名詞可以放在**主詞**、**受詞**以及**補語**的位置：

❶ The indigenous people have maintained their cultural traditions.
這些原住民一直堅持著他們的文化傳統。
☞ 名詞片語 The indigenous people 作為句子的主詞。

❷ The general ordered the artillery to target the enemy's stronghold at dawn.
將軍命令炮兵在黎明時分鎖定敵方據點。
☞ 名詞 artillery 作為及物動詞 ordered 的受詞。

❸ The soldiers were trained to defend against any threats from hostile forces.
士兵們接受訓練，以防範任何來自野蠻侵略者的威脅。
☞ 名詞 threats 作為介系詞 against 的受詞。

❹ Tom's primary role is a courier responsible for urgent deliveries.
Tom 的主要職責是一名負責緊急送貨的快遞員。
☞ 名詞 courier 作為主詞 Tom's primary role 的補語。

> **補充**
>
> ❶ 名詞會出現在冠詞（a / an / the）、所有格（his / her…）或形容詞的後面。
>
> ❷ 名詞分為「可數名詞」與「不可數名詞」，不定冠詞（a / an）或數量詞（one / two / three…）只出現在可數名詞前。
>
> ❸ 能放在可數名詞前的數量表達用語：
> one / each / every + 單數可數名詞
> (a) few / many / both / numerous… + 複數可數名詞

❹ 能放在不可數名詞前的數量表達用語：
(a) little / much / less + 不可數名詞

❺ 可數／不可數名詞前皆能放的用語：
some / more / most / all + 可數／不可數名詞

代名詞主要有**人稱代名詞**、**指示代名詞**、**反身代名詞**、**不定代名詞**及**關係代名詞**。

❶ The sudden news left him speechless.
這個突如其來的消息讓他無言以對。

☞ 人稱代名詞 him 當受詞用。

❷ The quality of this fabric is much better than that of the previous batch.
這種布料的品質比前一批好得多。

☞ 指示代名詞 that 代替 the quality。

❸ She proved herself capable of leading the team through difficult challenges.
她證明她自己有能力帶領團隊度過困難的挑戰。

☞ 當主詞與受詞是同一人時，受詞要用反身代名詞。

❹ Some of the staff expressed concerns about the new company policy.
一些員工對新的公司政策表達了擔憂。

☞ 不定代名詞 some 就是指 some staffers / employees。

補充

❶ 人稱代名詞除了有不同的「人稱」（第 1 / 2 / 3 人稱），還有不同的「格」，即主格、受格、所有格、所有格代名詞。

❷ 指示代名詞主要是指 that / these / that / those；that 用來代替前面出現過的單數名詞，those 用來代替前面出現過的複數名詞。另外，this / these / that / those 也可以作形容詞用，一般稱為「指示形容詞」。

❸ 不定代名詞主要是指 one / some(thing) / any(thing) / (the) other(s) / another；同樣，也都可作形容詞，一般稱為「不定形容詞」。

❹ 關係代名詞主要是指 who / whom / which / that，因為它們會帶出另一個子句，具有連接詞的功能（牽涉到關係／形容詞子句），將一併於 Week 05 進行解說。

必備 Point 3

形容詞用來修飾名詞，通常擺在**名詞前面**，但有部分形容詞必須放在名詞後面作「**後位修飾**」，例如，修飾「something / anything / nothing...」等代名詞的形容詞，必須擺在後面作修飾。另外，形容詞也可以擺在**補語的位置**。

❶ The hurricane caused a devastating impact on the coastal communities.
這場颶風對沿海社區造成了毀滅性的影響。

☞ 形容詞 devastating 放在冠詞 a 後面，名詞 impact 前面。

❷ She is dubious about the effectiveness of the new training program.
她對新培訓計劃的效果持懷疑態度。

☞ 形容詞 dubious 擺在主詞補語的位置。

❸ There are limited seats available for the concert.
演唱會的座位有限。

☞ 不可寫成 ...available seats...。

❹ There is nothing more invigorating than the crisp air of an early autumn morning.
沒有什麼比初秋清晨的涼爽空氣更令人精神振奮。

☞ 不可寫成 ...more invigorating nothing...。

❺ The movie was nothing short of spectacular.
這部電影簡直令人嘆為觀止。

☞ nothing short of 是指「完全沒有缺少…」，也就是指「簡直就是…」。

補充

「be 動詞 + 形容詞 + 介系詞／to-V」的慣用語在各大英文考試中都會出現，重要的是形容詞和什麼介系詞的搭配。例如：be eligible for / to-V（有資格取得／做…）、be (un)familiar with...（熟悉…／對…不熟悉）、be responsible for...（對…負責）、be subject to...（受制於…）…等。

必備 Point 4

副詞用來**修飾形容詞、副詞、動詞、動狀詞**，也可以修飾片語、子句或整個句子。副詞通常擺在形容詞或副詞前面、動（狀）詞的前面或後面、be 動詞／助動詞與 –ing / p.p. 之間。副詞可以表示時間（時間副詞），需搭配相應的動詞時態。例如：before、ago、later、yesterday、next week…；副詞也可以表示頻率、習慣（頻率副詞），例如 sometimes、always、 usually、often、seldom / rarely / hardly / barely / scarcely（幾乎不）、never（從不，絕不）等，通常搭配動詞現在式。另外，有些副詞常與動詞完成式搭配，像是 already、yet（尚未）、sofar 等。

❶ The typhoon is extremely unpredictable, so we should stay prepared.
這颱風相當難以預測，所以我們應該保持戒備。

☞ 副詞 extremely 放在形容詞 unpredictable 前修飾。

❷ She completed the project rather quickly, surprising everyone.
她相當迅速地完成了這個項目，讓大家感到驚訝。

☞ 副詞 rather 放在副詞 quickly 前修飾。

❸ The organization will flourish immensely with the new funding.
有了新資金，該組織將會大大地茁壯。

☞ 副詞 immensely 放在動詞 flourish 後修飾。

❹ She has consistently performed above expectations in her role.
她在自己的角色中一直表現超出預期。

☞ 副詞 consistently 放在助動詞 has 與分詞 performed 中間。

必備 Point 5

介系詞可以用來表示時間、地點、空間、方向、目的、所呈現的狀態…等多種意義。介系詞不一定只有 1 個字，兩個字以上的介系詞（<u>或稱作「**片語介系詞**」</u>，像是 due to, in spite of, for the purpose of...）非常多，也是考題中的常客。重點在介系詞與相關動詞或名詞搭配而成的<u>片語或慣用語</u>，以及<u>應搭配的動詞時態</u>。另外，「**易混淆介系詞**」（例如 beside 與 besides）也是令考生頭痛的一大重點。

❶ The company has implemented sustainable practices for several years.
這家公司已經實施永續性措施好幾年了。

☞ 「介系詞 for + 一段時間」應搭配完成式動詞。

❷ There's no smoke without fire.
無風不起浪。

☞ 介系詞 without 常用於雙重否定（負負得正）的句型。

❸ Whether he likes the decision is beside the point.
他是否喜歡這個決定並不重要。

☞ beside 表示「在…旁邊」，而 beside the point 是個慣用語，表示「離題，偏離重點」。

❹ No one knew the answer besides me, so I had to speak up.
除了我之外，沒有人知道答案，所以我只好發言。

☞ 這裡的 besides = in addition to，表示「除…之外」。

❺ They are still searching for a solution to the complex problem.
他們仍在尋找解決這個複雜問題的方案。

☞ 這裡的 to 是介系詞，搭配特定名詞形成慣用語。「a solution to + N./Ving」表示「…的解決方案」

❻ In the event of an emergency, please follow the evacuation instructions carefully.
若發生緊急情況，請仔細遵循疏散指示。

☞ In the event of 是（片語）介系詞，表示「在…情況下，萬一…」。

必備 Point 6

感嘆詞可以獨立存在，也可以是句子的一部份，用來表達開心、興奮、失望、無奈、憤怒等情緒，像是 Wow! / Hooray / Hurrah / blah, blah, blah / Er...。雖然感嘆詞比較不會直接出現在考題中，但在電子郵件或對話類型等文章中不時會出現。感嘆詞本身沒有特定意義，必須跟著前後句來解讀其真正含意，對於解題也會有幫助。例如：

❶ Gee! What on earth were you thinking?
天啊，你當時到底在想什麼？

☞ Gee! 有不耐煩的語氣，偏向負面。

❷ Gee! That sounds interesting!
哇！那看聽起來挺有趣的！

☞ Gee! 帶有讚嘆的語氣，偏向正面。

多益會怎麼考？

多益會考在名詞和其他不同詞類（動詞、形容詞…等）的選項中，選擇名詞填入空格的題目。

1. Despite the long hours of work, they received little -------- for their efforts.

(A) compensation
(B) compensations
(C) compensative
(D) compensating

翻譯 儘管工作時間長，他們的努力卻只獲得了微薄的報酬。

解析 空格前面是形容詞 little，要填入一個不可數名詞，所以正確答案是 (A)。

多益會考選擇符合句意的介系詞。

2. ---------- the challenges, she managed to complete the project on time.

(A) In the event of
(B) Instead of
(C) In addition to
(D) In spite of

翻譯 儘管面臨挑戰，她還是按時完成了這個專案。

解析 句意是「------ 挑戰，她準時完成了這個專案」，所以應填入表示讓步的「儘管…」，故正確答案是 (D)。

▶ 關鍵概念

必備 Point 1

一般來說，具體或有形體的名詞為**可數名詞**，而沒有形體的抽象名詞為**不可數名詞**，其他像是 rice、sugar、salt 等小物體組成的物件，以及沒有固體形狀的 gas、smoke，還有相似物件的統稱，像是 furniture、bread、fruit 等，也都只有不可數名詞的用法。不過實際仍應根據實際狀況判別。例如 approach（方法）、profit（利潤）、request（要求）、success（成功）、compliment（恭維）…等，都有可數名詞的用法。例如：

The proposal needs (approval, ~~approvals~~) from the board before it can be implemented.
這項提案在實施前需獲得董事會的批准。

☞ approval 只有不可數名詞的用法。

必備 Point 2

複合名詞是指「名詞 + 名詞」，所以在考試中如果有空格前面是及物動詞，後面是名詞的情況，那麼要填入的可不一定是形容詞喔！多益常見的複合名詞像是 customer satisfaction（顧客滿意度）、contract negotiation（合約協商）、keynote speaker（主講人）、office supplies（辦公用品）、retail sales（零售額）、standard procedure（標準程序）…等。

必備 Point 3

指示代名詞 those 後面常接關係子句 who…，those who… 表示「**…的人們**」。例如：

Opportunities often come to (~~these~~, those) who are prepared to

seize them.
機會常常降臨在那些準備好要把握的人身上。

☞ who are 可省略，變成「Opportunities often come to <u>those prepared</u> to seize them.」。

必備 Point 4

不定代名詞 one / another / others / the other 表示**特定範圍內指定的人事物**。例如：

❶ Some of the students prefer online classes, while (~~other~~, others) enjoy learning in person.
有些學生喜歡線上課程，而其他人則喜歡面對面學習。

☞ others = other students，表示**已經提到的學生以外的其他學生**。

❷ One of the main goals is to improve efficiency, and another is to reduce costs.
其中一個主要目標是提高效率，而另一個是降低成本。

☞ one 表示非特定的單數可數名詞；another 表示「（已經提到的人事物以外的）另一個」

必備 Point 5

形態相似而容易混淆的形容詞也是頻繁出現的考題之一。常考的像是「advisable（明智的）與 advisory（建議性的）」、「beneficial（有益的）與 beneficent（行善的）」、「comparable（相當大的，重要的）與 comparative（比較性的）」、「considerate（考慮周到的）與 considerable（相當大的，重要的）」、「economic（經濟上的）與 economical（經濟的，節約的）」、「responsible（負責的）與 responsive（有反應的）」、「successful（成功的）與 successive（連續的，後繼的）」等。例如：

❶ Her skills are (comparable, ~~comparative~~) to those of a professional, despite her limited experience.
儘管她經驗有限，她的技能可媲美專業人士。

☞ 如果選 comparative，意思會變成「她的技能與專業人士的是相對性的」的奇怪句意。

❷ The new policy is (successive, ~~successful~~) to the previous one, building on its foundation.
這項新政策承襲前一項政策的基礎而制定。

連接性副詞是連接前後句意的副詞，常考有 besides / also / in addition（此外，再者）、moreover / furthermore（而且）、therefore / thus / consequently / hence（所以，因此）、however（然而）、meanwhile（與此同時）、(or) else / otherwise（否則）、then（然後）、nevertheless / nonetheless（儘管如此）、likewise（同樣地）、instead / conversely（相反地，反而是）。例如：

❶ They had planned to finish the project by Friday. (Therefore, However), unforeseen delays pushed the deadline to next week.

他們原計劃在星期五前完成專案。然而，不可預知的延誤事件導致截止日期延後至下週。

❷ The proposal is cost-effective, and (furthermore, otherwise), it aligns with our sustainability goals.

這項提案具成本效益，此外，它還符合我們的永續發展目標。

多益會怎麼考？

多益會考依句意選擇適當的不定代名詞。

1. Mr. Lin agreed with the new strategy, but ---------- were hesitant to accept it.

(A) another   (B) these   (C) the other   (D) the others

翻譯 林先生同意了這項新策略，但其他人對接受它感到猶豫。

解析 空格要填入一個正確的不定代名詞形式，而句意是「林先生同意…，而其他人…」，應填入表示「參與決策的其他人」的 the others，所以正確答案是 (D)。

多益會考選擇符合句意的形容詞題目。

2. The team is highly ---------- to customer feedback, constantly making improvements.

(A) responded   (B) responsive   (C) responsible   (D) response

翻譯 這個團隊對顧客的回饋意見反應迅速，且不斷進行改進。

解析 空格要填入一個形容詞，所以 (D) 直接刪除。而句意是「對顧客的回饋意見反應迅速」，所以答案是 (B) responsive（反應積極的）。respond 如果要當及物動詞（可改為被動式 responded），意思應為「回應說出…」，如果要表示「回應某人」，正確說法為 respond to，所以 (A) 錯誤。(C) responsible 是「負責任的」的意思，後面通常接介系詞 for。

▶ TOEIC 實戰演練

Part 5 | 請在以下四個選項中選出正確的答案

01 The cozy cafe had a warm ambiance, enhanced by the soft ---------- melodies playing in the background.

(A) acoustic　　　(B) tangible　　　(C) disgusting　　　(D) appalling

02 It is --------- to consult a financial expert before making any major investments.

(A) advice　　　(B) advising　　　(C) advisable　　　(D) advisory

03 The quality of this product surpasses --------- of its competitors in both durability and design.

(A) this　　　(B) these　　　(C) that　　　(D) those

04 We need to challenge ---------- if we want to achieve greater success.

(A) yourself　　　(B) ourselves　　　(C) themselves　　　(D) itself

05 If you have --------- of the required documents, please submit them by the end of the week.

(A) any　　　(B) that　　　(C) others　　　(D) something

06 The new marketing strategy is appealing --------- younger consumers who value sustainability.

(A) for　　　(B) to　　　(C) with　　　(D) from

07 The project was finally completed two months --------- than originally planned.

(A) ago　　　(B) before　　　(C) later　　　(D) rather

08 After the long hike, I was so exhausted that I can --------- keep my eyes open.

(A) even (B) lately (C) mostly (D) barely

09 I would like to thank everyone on --------- of the entire team for their hard work and dedication.

(A) behalf (B) account (C) top (D) condition

10 The hikers found themselves --------- the sudden storm that rolled in without warning.

(A) in the event of (B) at the mercy of
(C) in accordance with (D) with respect to

11 Learning --------- management is essential for ensuring the long-term success of any organization.

(A) risk (B) risky (C) risking (D) risked

12 The project faced numerous setbacks. ---------, the team remained focused and committed to its success.

(A) Therefore (B) Moreover (C) Otherwise (D) Nevertheless

13 Some students thrive in a traditional classroom setting, but --------- prefer online learning for its flexibility.

(A) others (B) the other (C) the others (D) one another

14 --------- who seek knowledge will always find opportunities.

(A) One (B) Others (C) Those (D) These

15 Many find solace in writing and reciting --------- during difficult times.

(A) a poetry (B) the poetry (C) poetry (D) poetries

WEEK 03 英文裡的動詞

▶ 穩固基礎

對於**動詞**的基本認知，要**以「五大基本句型」為基礎**。因為，五大句型就代表著五大類動詞的運用：

❶ **及物動詞**：運用在「**S + V + O**」的句型。例如：
Sarah enjoys working with children and finds it fulfilling.
莎拉喜歡處理小孩子的工作，並認為這是一件令人滿足的事情。

☞ enjoys、finds 是及物動詞，後面分別接受詞「working with...」以及 it。但此句的動詞 find 是「不完全及物動詞」（請見以下❸）

❷ **不及物動詞**：運用在「**S + V**」的句型。例如：
The study group meets once a week.
這個讀書會小組每週見面一次。

☞ 這裡的 meets 是不及物動詞，後面沒有受詞，once a week 是副詞修飾語。

❸ **不完全及物動詞**：運用在「**S + V + O + OC**」的句型。例如：
In a fair trial, it's crucial to consider the suspects innocent until proven guilty.
在一場公正的審判中，重要的是在罪刑確定之前將嫌疑人視為無罪。

☞ consider 是不完全及物動詞，其受詞 the suspects 後面接形容詞 innocent 作為受詞補語（OC）。

❹ **不完全不及物動詞**：運用在「**S + V + SC**」的句型。例如：
John remained silent as he listened intently to the discussion.
約翰保持沉默，專心聆聽討論。

☞ remain 是不完全不及物動詞，其後 silent 是主詞補語（SC）。

❺ **授予動詞**：運用在「**S + V + IO + DO**」（或「**S + V + DO + 介系詞 + IO**」）的句型，通常有「給」、「傳遞，傳送」等意思的動詞都是授予動詞。例如：
She brought me a thoughtful gift for my birthday.
她帶給我一份體貼的生日禮物。

☞ bring（過去式是 brought）是個授予動詞，後面接 me（間接受詞）和 a thoughtful gift（直接受詞）兩個受詞。這句也可以寫成「She brought a thoughtful gift to me.」

> **補充**
>
> ❶ 所謂「**及物**」，就是「**後面一定要接受詞**」，那麼「**不及物**」當然就是「**後面不能再接受詞**」。
>
> ❷ 所謂「**不完全**」，就是「**句意不完整**」，那麼如果「不完全」加上「及物」，亦即「**不完全及物動詞**」，就表示這個動詞接了受詞之後，句意還是不完整，那怎麼辦呢？這時候受詞後面就必須再加上一個「必要元素」，那就是「補語」，在此稱之為「**受詞補語**」。
>
> ❸ 如果「不完全」加上「不及物動詞」，亦即「**不完全不及物動詞**」，就表示這個動詞雖然可以不必接受詞，但句意卻是不完整的，這時候不及物動詞後面必須再加上一個「必要元素」，那就是「補語」，在此稱之為「**主詞補語**」。另外，大家所熟知的「連綴動詞」，例如 be 動詞、「感官動詞」（look / feel / taste / sound...）都屬此類。
>
> ❹ **授予動詞**的核心意義就是「給予（某人某物）」，所以**後面要接兩個受詞**，一個是「間接受詞（人）」，一個是「直接受詞（物）」，缺少任一個受詞的句意都是不完整的。

必備 Point 2

在學習動詞的過程中，**助動詞**是不可或缺的一部分。**分為「一般助動詞」和「情態助動詞」兩種**，後面必須接原形動詞。

❶ **一般助動詞**是指 do 和 have，主要用於否定句及疑問句。一般助動詞當然也有人稱和時態的變化。例如：do → does → did；have → has → had。另外，have / has / had 也用於構成「完成式」的動詞時態。

❷ **情態助動詞主要有** will / would / can / could / may / might / shall / should / must / have to / need（用於疑問／否定句）/ ought to / had better / used to 等。情態助動詞沒有人稱的變化，但也有時態的變化。例如：will → would；can → could，不過這樣的變化不一定與時態有關（不一定表示過去式），也可能與「語氣的強弱」有關。

多益會怎麼考？

多益會考選擇適當動詞類型的題目。

1. The jury ---------- him guilty of all charges related to the embezzlement case.

   (A) found   (B) founded   (C) determined   (D) appraised

翻譯 陪審團判定他在挪用公款案件中所有指控都成立。

解析 從四個選項來看，要填入一個文法正確，或符合句子結構的動詞。空格後面是「him guilty of」，顯然要表達的是「判決他有…罪」，所以要填入 find 這個動詞的過去式 found，正確答案是 (A)。find 在「find + O + OC (adj.)」的句型中，是個不完全及物動詞，而其餘選項動詞都沒有這種用法。

2. I will demonstrate the process in detail to --------- you how the algorithm optimizes data retrieval.

   (A) unveil　　　　(B) show　　　　(C) indicate　　　　(D) reveal

翻譯 我將詳細示範這個過程，讓大家看看演算法如何優化數據檢索。

解析 雖然四個選項的動詞都有「拿東西給某人看看」的意思，但只有 show 有「show sb. sth.」的授予動詞用法，所以正確答案是 (B)。

▶ 關鍵概念

動詞**時態**：一個句子所表達的動作、事件或狀態，通常也伴隨著不同時間點的概念。例如「現在」、「過去」、「未來」…等不同時間點，而在這 3 個時間點中，可能表達**單純的動作、事件或狀態**，也可能表達**正在進行、正在發生**，或**已經完成、已經發生**等狀態。

時間＼狀態	簡單式	進行式	完成式	完成進行式
現在式	現在簡單式	現在進行式	現在完成式	現在完成進行式
過去式	過去簡單式	過去進行式	過去完成式	過去完成進行式
未來式	未來簡單式	未來進行式	未來完成式	未來完成進行式

❶ **現在（簡單）式**：表示**常態**的行為、習慣，或**例行**公事的作為，或陳述**事實、真理**。例如：
They meet once a month to discuss their progress on the project.
他們每個月會見一次，討論他們在項目上的進展。

☞ 動詞的時態經常搭配特定時間副詞，此即所謂**「時態的一致性」**，例如這裡的 once a month（每月一次）表達「頻率」的概念，因此必須搭配現在簡單式。

❷ **現在進行式**：表示**此刻正在進行**的行為、動作，或**短暫持續**的事件，或近期**即將發生**的事件，以「is / are + 動詞 -ing」的形態出現。例如：

My father is sleeping in the living room now.
我爸爸現在正在客廳睡覺。

❸ 現在完成式：

① 從**過去**某時間點**持續到現在**的動作或狀態，常與「持續一段時間」的副詞搭配。例如：She (~~worked~~, has worked) in the field of environmental engineering for 5 years.

她在環境工程領域已工作了 5 年。

☞ 底線部分就是「持續一段時間」的副詞。

② 從過去某時間點到現在**已完成**的動作，通常伴隨著一個過去的時間點。例如：
The organization has completed several groundbreaking initiatives since it first adopted its new strategic framework.

自從首次採用新的戰略框架以來，該組織已經完成了幾個突破性的倡議。

☞ 底線部分表示一個過去的時間點。

❹ 現在完成進行式：從過去某時間點開始的動作或狀態，一直**持續**到現在且**正在進行**中，或是**反覆進行**的動作。例如：

They have been looking for a solution to the problem for several months.

幾個月來他們一直在尋找解決問題的方案。

❺ 過去（簡單）式：單純敘述發生在過去的事件或狀態，經常伴隨著表過去的時間副詞。例如：

The manager addressed the concerns of the team regarding the pending decision on the project yesterday.

昨天經理解決了團隊對於該專案中待決定事項的擔憂。

❻ 過去進行式：

① 在**過去某個時間點正在進行**的動作，通常伴隨著一個過去的時間點。例如：
At 8 o'clock last night, I was reading a thought-provoking novel that kept me captivated until the early hours of the morning.

昨晚八點鐘的時候，我正在看一本引人深思的小中，這本小說讓我一直陶醉到凌晨。

② **過去某段時間內持續**進行的動作。例如：
She was meticulously organizing the event all week, ensuring every detail was perfect.

她整個星期都在精心籌辦這個活動，確保每個細節都完美無缺。

❼ **過去完成式**：

① 在過去某時間點之前已經完成的動作。例如：
By the time the meeting started, she had already prepared an extensive report.
等到會議開始時，她已經準備了一份詳盡的報告。

☞ 底線部分就是「過去某時間點」。

② 用來表達過去的兩個動作中，先發生的那一個。例如：
He had completed the project before the deadline approached.
在截止日期到來之前，他已經完成了這個項目。

☞ 先發生的動作是 had completed，後發生的是 approached。

❽ **過去完成進行式**：

① 一個過去的動作在另一個過去事件之前持續了一段時間。例如：
She had been practicing the piano for hours when the electricity suddenly went out.
她練了好幾個小時的鋼琴，這時突然停電了。

② 用來表達在某個過去的時間點之前的持續狀況或動作。例如：
By the time the storm hit, they had been preparing the emergency supplies all day.
等到暴風雨來襲時，他們已經準備了一整天的應急物資。

❾ **未來（簡單）式**：單純敘述發生在未來的事件或狀態，經常伴隨著表未來的時間副詞。例如：
The government will liberalize trade regulations to boost the economy.
政府將會放寬貿易法規以促進經濟發展。

❿ **未來進行式**：

① **未來**某個時間點**正在進行**的動作。例如：
Next Saturday morning, the committee will be discussing the new policy proposals.
下週六早上，委員會將正在討論新的政策提案。

② 表達一種**預計**或**推測**的**未來持續**狀態。例如：
They will be launching the new product line when the conference begins.
當會議開始時，他們將會推出新的產品線。

☞ 表示未來的副詞子句要用**現在式代替未來式**。

⓫ **未來完成式**：
用來描述未來某個時間點之前已經完成或已持續進行的事情，通

常伴隨一個未來的時間點。例如：
By tomorrow morning, they will have traveled for 12 hours straight.
到明天早上，他們已經連續旅行了十二小時。

☞ 底線部分就是「未來某時間點」。

⓬ 未來完成進行式：

描述未來某個時間點之前，已經開始並持續到該時間點的動作，強調動作的持續性和持續的時間。例如：
When you finally get here, we will have been discussing the project for hours.
當你終於到達時，我們已經討論了這個項目幾個小時。

必備 Point 2

動詞**語態**：用來表達動作的承受者和執行者之間的關係。主要有**主動語態**和**被動語態**兩種：

❶ 主動語態：句子的主詞是動作的執行者，動詞直接描述主詞所做的動作。例如：
His constant lateness aggravated his manager's dissatisfaction.
他常態性的遲到加重了他經理不滿的情緒。

❷ 被動語態：主詞是動作的承受者（而非執行者），動詞的形式是「be 動詞 + 過去分詞（P.P.）」通常會有一個 by 引導的副詞片語來表示動作的執行者，但有時這部分可以省略。例如：
The suspect was extradited by the authorities to face charges in his home country.
嫌疑犯被當局引渡回他的祖國，以面對指控。

補充

只有及物動詞有被動式，**不及物動詞沒有被動式**，而一個句子的被動語態有以下的使用時機：

❶ 當執行者不重要或不知名時。例如：The cake was eaten.
蛋糕被吃掉了。

☞ 誰吃掉蛋糕不重要。

❷ 當要強調動作的結果或受害者時。例如：The building was destroyed in the fire. *這座建築在火災中被毀壞了。*

☞ 強調建築被毀壞了。

❸ 當執行者已知但不重要，或者顯而易見時。例如：Research findings were published last year. *研究結果去年已經發表了。*

☞ 執行者應該就叫作 researchers 或是 the researcher，所以不需要再重複一次了。

多益會怎麼考？

多益 Part 5 會考選擇適當動詞形態的題目。

1. Concerns about data privacy --------- discussions in the tech industry for years.

    (A) permeate
    (B) are permeating
    (C) have been permeated
    (D) have been permeating

    翻譯 對於數據隱私的擔憂已經在科技業界的討論中滲透多年。

    解析 從四個選項來看，空格要填入一個正確的動詞形式，而根據句尾的 for years 可知，應填入完成式，故原形動詞 (A)、現在進行式 (B) 可直接刪除。permeate（滲透）是及物動詞，句意是「.. 已在業界的討論中滲透多年」，動詞應為主動而非被動，所以正確答案是 (D)。

2. The rumors about the company's financial troubles ---------- easily by the official statement.

    (A) squashed   (B) were squashed   (C) were squashing   (D) have squashed

    翻譯 關於公司財務困境的謠言被這份官方聲明輕易地破除了。

    解析 句子大意是「…的謠言被破除」，動詞應用被動式，所以答案是 (B)。

▶ TOEIC 實戰演練

Part 5 請在以下四個選項中選出正確的答案

01 Experienced nurses know how to --------- the discomfort of patients after surgery.

   (A) soothe   (B) prevail   (C) thrive   (D) vanish

02 Her gaze --------- for a moment on the old photograph before she put it away.

   (A) undermined   (B) lingered   (C) endangered   (D) massaged

03 The board of directors --------- him manager of the new project team.

   (A) abandoned   (B) alleged   (C) appointed   (D) abolished

04 After the long journey, she --------- tired but relieved to be home.

(A) broadened　　(B) disregarded　　(C) correlated　　(D) appeared

05 After several attempts, they finally --------- how to solve the complex equation.

(A) marveled at　　(B) figured out　　(C) settled down　　(D) involved in

06 After the meal, please --------- me the bill so I can settle the payment.

(A) hand　　(B) foot　　(C) collect　　(D) exchange

07 Her initial concerns about the project proved --------- when the delays started piling up.

(A) truth　　(B) true　　(C) truly　　(D) trued

08 The technical issues with the software --------- for months despite numerous updates.

(A) assisted　　(B) consisted　　(C) insisted　　(D) persisted

09 The company holds a meeting every Monday --------- new strategies.

(A) will discuss　　　　　　(B) discussed
(C) to discuss　　　　　　(D) will be discussing

10 After receiving the surprising news, he --------- the best course of action to take, and weighed the potential risks carefully.

(A) contemplate　　　　　　(B) contemplated
(C) will contemplate　　　　(D) will be contemplating

11 The small campfire, left unattended, kindled a devastating wildfire that --------- rapidly through the dry forest.

(A) spread　　(B) spreads　　(C) spreaded　　(D) was spreading

12 The company's annual expenditures on research and development --------- to several million dollars.

(A) is amounting (B) has amounted (C) amounts (D) amount

13 When the project is finally completed, we --------- one of our most challenging goals to date.

(A) are achieving
(C) will have achieved
(B) have achieved
(D) should have achieved

14 Jane felt --------- due to the constant, unsolicited feedback she received from her colleagues.

(A) harassing (B) harassed (C) to harass (D) harassment

15 This innovative new restaurant --------- the best dining experience in the city for three consecutive years.

(A) will be voting
(C) is voted
(B) will have voted
(D) has been voted

WEEK 04 動狀詞

▶ 穩固基礎

必備 Point 1

動狀詞僅**具有動詞的特性**，沒有動詞的功能。所謂**動詞特性**就是有及物（後面要接受詞）、不及物、主動／被動…之分，或是可以被副詞修飾等特性。動狀詞在句中可以當名詞、形容詞、副詞等 3 種不同詞類。

必備 Point 2

動狀詞有 3 種：**不定詞（to-V）**、**動名詞（Ving）**以及**分詞（現在／過去分詞）**：

❶ **不定詞（to-V）**：在句中有名詞、形容詞及副詞3種功能。

① The authorities launched an investigation <u>to prevent</u> any attempts <u>to abduct</u> children in the area.
   當局展開一項調查，<u>以阻止</u>該地區任何<u>綁架</u>兒童的企圖。

   ☞ 不定詞 to prevent 當**副詞**，<u>表示目的</u>，修飾動詞 launched；不定詞 to abduct 當**形容詞**，修飾其前名詞 attempts。<u>「any... area」這整個名詞詞組作為 to prevent 的受詞</u>。

② <u>To defy the order of the court</u> will set a dangerous precedent that could encourage others <u>to disregard</u> legal authority.
   <u>違抗</u>法庭命令將造成一個鼓勵其他人<u>無視</u>法律權威的危險先例。

   ☞ 不定詞片語「To defy the order of the court」當名詞，作為句子的主詞；後面的不定詞片語「to disregard legal authority」作為受詞 others 的補語。

③ He made efforts <u>to ensure</u> his team <u>adhered to</u> the new safety protocols.
   他努力使團隊<u>有遵守</u>新的安全規範<u>的義務</u>。

   ☞ 不定詞 to ensure 當形容詞，修飾名詞 efforts。

> **補充**
>
> in order to（可以變形為 in order that 的連接詞用法），後面接原形動詞，等同於表示「目的」的不定詞用法，也可以寫成 so as to (+ V)，有些考試喜歡把具有相同意思的「with <u>a view</u> / <u>an eye</u> to + Ving」測驗考生對於片語認知的廣度，應特別注意！

❷ **動名詞（Ving）**：為「描述動作狀態」的**名詞**，可作為句子的主詞或受詞。

① Going astray in life can result in a sense of regret over time.
在生活中偏離正軌會隨著時間過去而帶來懊悔的感覺。

☞ 動名詞片語 Going astray in life 是句子的**主詞**，表示「在生活中偏離正軌」這件事，因此視為第三人稱單數。

② The government decided to postpone dismantling the old factory until a more comprehensive plan is in place.
政府決定延後拆除舊工廠，直到有一個更全面的計劃。

☞ 動名詞 dismantling 作為不定詞 to postpone 的受詞。

③ The heavy rain inhibited the workers from completing the construction on time.
大雨使得工人無法按時完成施工。

☞ 動名詞 completing 作為介系詞 from 的受詞。

❸ **分詞（V-ing 或 V-ed）**：有**現在分詞**和**過去分詞**兩種，在句中可當「形容詞」或「副詞」。

① The new technology seems promising, but more research is needed to fully assess its potential.
這項新技術看起來很有前景，但還需要更多研究來全面評估其潛力。

☞ 現在分詞 promising **當形容詞**，作為主詞 The new technology 的**補語**。

② The company provided an extended deadline for the project to ensure higher quality work.
公司為此專案提供延後的截止日期，以確保更高品質的工作。

☞ 過去分詞 extended 當形容詞，修飾名詞 deadline。

③ Despite the freezing cold, the hikers continued their journey up the mountain.
儘管天氣寒冷刺骨，登山者們仍繼續他們的攀登旅程。

☞ 現在分詞 freezing 當副詞，修飾其後形容詞 cold，表示「非常地」。類似用語還有 scorching hot、tiring long、astonishing tall、blinding bright…等。

多益會怎麼考？

多益會考選擇適當動詞形態的題目。

1. I traveled to Japan ---------- its rich culture and history.

   (A) experience　(B) will experience　(C) experiencing　(D) to experience

   翻譯 我前往日本以體驗其豐富的文化和歷史。

   解析 空格前面已經是個完整的句子，所以 (B) 可直接刪除；句意是「為了體驗…而去日本」，所以正確答案是 (D)。

2. The secret to good health is ---------- a balanced diet.

   (A) maintain　(B) maintained　(C) to maintain　(D) maintaining

   翻譯 保持均衡飲食是健康的祕訣。

   解析 句子已經有動詞 is 了，所以 (A) 直接刪除，(B) 是被動式，但空格後面是名詞（a balanced diet），所以也錯誤；(C) 和 (D) 在文法結構上都是正確的，但關鍵在「健康的祕訣」是一種真理、科學上的事實，不適合用不定詞作為其補語，所以答案為 (D)。

▶ 關鍵概念

必備 Point 1

意義上的主詞：因為動狀詞，尤其是不定詞與分詞，表現的是某個動作或呈現某種狀態，所以當然也有「動作的執行者」— 也就是「意義上的主詞」。了解動狀詞的意義主詞可以幫助我們在相關考題中迅速找到正確答案。例如：

❶ The notice (informing, ~~informed~~) all employees of the upcoming changes to the company policy will be posted on the bulletin board tomorrow.

這份通知所有員工公司政策即將進行變更的公告，將於明日張貼在公告板上。

☞「通知所有員工」這個動作是主詞 The notice 主動執行的（員工是被通知），也就是「informing all employees...」意義上的主詞是 The notice。

❷ The sculpture (~~unveiling~~, unveiled) in a ceremony yesterday was inspired by the city's rich cultural heritage.

昨天在典禮上揭幕的雕像塑受到該市豐富文化遺產的啟發。

☞ 雖然「揭幕」這個動作的執行者不明（也可能不重要），但絕不會是這座雕像自己去執行的，所以必須用被動式的 unveiled。

必備 Point 2 **一定要接不定詞（to-V）或動名詞（Ving）的動詞**：幾乎所有英文檢定考試一定會考不定詞與動名詞的使用判別。有一些及物動詞後面的受詞，如果要以動狀詞來表現的話，一定要用不定詞：

❶ Despite facing numerous challenges, the team <u>managed</u> (~~completing~~, to complete) the project ahead of schedule.
儘管面臨許多挑戰，團隊仍設法提前<u>完成了</u>這個計畫。

❷ She didn't <u>bother</u> (~~explaining~~, to explain) her decision, leaving everyone confused about her motives.
她不想大費周章去<u>解釋</u>自己的決定，讓每個人對她的動機感到困惑。

有一些及物動詞後面如果要以動作來表現的話，一定要用動名詞：

❸ The teacher <u>suggested</u> (reviewing, ~~to review~~) the material thoroughly before the final exam to ensure better understanding.
老師建議在期末考試之前徹底<u>復習</u>這些資料，以確保更深的理解。

❹ He devoted several hours each week to practicing (blending, ~~to blend~~) colors and creating textures.
他每週花幾個小時練習<u>混合</u>顏色和創造質感。

> **補充**
> ❶ 常見須接<u>不定詞</u>的動詞有：agree、fail、refuse、aim、hope、wish、bother、manage、want、decide、plan、need、expect、promise…等。
> ❷ 常見須接<u>動名詞</u>的動詞有：admit、finish、practice、avoid、keep、quit、delay、mind、suggest、enjoy、postpone…等。
> ❸ 可接<u>不定詞或動名詞且意義不變</u>的動詞有：begin、like、propose、continue、love、start、hate、prefer…等。

必備 Point 3 **可接不定詞（to-V）或動名詞（Ving），但意思不同的動詞**：一般來說，不定詞帶有「**目的／計畫／期望／未來**」（意味「非同時發生」），而動名詞帶有「**習慣性**」、「**持續性**（意味「同時發生」）」等意義。例如：

❶ Stop (complaining, ~~to complain~~)！Just take action and you won't regret it.
別再<u>抱怨</u>了！只要付諸行動，你不會後悔的。

☞「stop doing something」表示「停止做某事」，而「stop to do something」表示「停下來去做某事」，所以這句若改成「Stop to complain...」顯然是不合常理的。

❷ My grandpa forgot taking medicine this morning.
我爺爺今天早上忘記吃過藥了。

My grandpa forgot to take medicine this morning.
我爺爺今天早上忘記吃藥了。

☞ 以上都是正確的句子，但意思不同。

> **補充**
> 常見可接不定詞或動名詞但意思不同的動詞有：remember、forget、stop、try 等。

必備 Point 4

分詞片語簡化自**形容詞子句**；**分詞構句**簡化自**副詞子句**，或**對等子句其中之一**：通常在英文寫作的訓練中，為了修辭及美化句子，會利用這兩種結構來增添句子的靈活度，而且在英文考試裡，它們也是經常出現的考點。例如：

❶ Allen, walking through the vibrant market, felt excited to discover new flavors and unique crafts.
走在熱鬧市場中的艾倫，期待發現新的風味和獨特的手工藝品。

☞「walking through the vibrant market」可以還原成形容詞子句「who was walking... market」。

❷ Walking through the vibrant market, Allen felt excited to discover new flavors and unique crafts.
艾倫走在熱鬧的市場時，他期待發現新的風味和獨特的手工藝品。

☞「Walking through the vibrant market」可以還原成副詞子句「When Allen walked... market...」。

❸ After (being) promoted, she took on new responsibilities with enthusiasm.
在晉升之後，她以熱情承擔新的責任。

☞「After (being) promoted」可以還原成副詞子句「After she was promoted」。

❹ She enjoys painting landscapes, capturing the beauty of nature with every brushstroke.
她喜歡畫風景，透過每一筆捕捉自然的美。

☞「capturing the beauty of nature with every brushstroke」可以還原成「and captures the beauty of nature with every brushstroke」。

必備 Point 5

獨立分詞構句：當主要子句的主詞與副詞子句的**主詞不同**時，或兩個對等子句有不同的主詞時，其中一句亦可簡化為分詞構句，但此**分詞構句必須保留原主詞**。例如：

❶ The sun setting over the horizon, the sky transformed into a canvas of vibrant colors.
當太陽在地平線上沉落時，天空變成了一幅充滿活力色彩的畫布。

☞ 整句可還原成「As the sun set over the horizon, the sky...」。

獨立分詞構句還有一種「變體」，通常以介系詞 with 引導，用來表示「原因、附帶條件或附加說明」。例如：

❷ With the rain pouring down, we decided to stay indoors.
由於雨水滂沱，我們決定待在室內。

☞ 底線部分可還原成「Because the rain poured / was pouring down」。

❸ James stood at the entrance, with a bouquet of flowers held in his hand.
詹姆斯站在入口處，手裡握著一束花。

☞ 底線部分可還原成「and a bouquet of flowers was held in his hand.」。

補充

❶ 部分文法書籍或教材並無「分詞構句」的說法，而是將分詞片語分為形容詞與副詞兩種，只是擺放的位置有所不同。

❷ 副詞子句簡化成分詞構句時，原則上可以省略副詞連接詞，但若省略了連接詞之後語意模糊（通常與時間順序有關），則不宜省略。
例如：
Before starting the engine, he adjusted the driver's seat and rearview mirror.
在開始發動引擎前，他先將駕駛座與後照鏡調整好。

☞ Before 不宜省略

多益會怎麼考？

多益會考依句意，在修飾語的位置填入現在分詞或過去分詞的題目。

1. An ---------- version of the software will be available for download next week.

   (A) update   (B) updated   (C) updating   (D) updates

   翻譯 更新後的軟體版本將於下週供下載。

   解析 空格要填入一個正確的分詞形式，而句意是「已更新的軟體版本⋯」，應填入表被動的 updated，所以正確答案是 (B)。「更新版」的英文說法只有「updated version」，沒有「update / updates version」這種講法。

2. The company is facing difficulties and challenges due to ---------- sales in its key markets.

   (A) decline   (B) declined   (C) declining   (D) declines

   翻譯 公司正面臨著困難與挑戰，由於其主要市場的銷售下滑。

   解析 空格要填入一個正確的分詞形式，而句意是「由於其主要市場下滑的銷售量」，所以答案是 (C)。decline 當及物動詞是「拒絕」的意思，當不及物動詞是「下跌，衰退」的意思。現在分詞 declining 表示「下滑中的」。

▶ TOEIC 實戰演練

Part 5 　請在以下四個選項中選出正確的答案

01 She submitted a résumé ---------- her extensive experience in project management and her ability to lead cross-functional teams.

   (A) emphasize   (B) emphasizing   (C) to emphasize   (D) emphasized

02 The new product will be available exclusively at ---------- retailers starting next month.

   (A) authorized   (B) authorizing   (C) authorize   (D) authorization

03 During the meeting, he lightened the mood by sharing an ---------- story from his recent travels.

   (A) amusement   (B) amuse   (C) amused   (D) amusing

04 The engineer was called in --------- the machinery after it showed signs of malfunctioning.

(A) inspecting   (B) inspected   (C) to inspect   (D) to inspecting

05 She proved to be the best candidate --------- the project, thanks to her strong leadership skills.

(A) to lead   (B) to leading   (C) leading   (D) leader

06 We need to gather more data in order for us --------- an informed decision about the next steps.

(A) making   (B) and make   (C) to make   (D) to be made

07 The quiet nod from the committee allowed the proposal --------- without further debate.

(A) approving   (B) approval   (C) to approve   (D) to be approved

08 --------- your boss for a raise requires careful preparation and a clear presentation of your achievements.

(A) Approach   (B) Approachling   (C) Approaches   (D) Approached

09 The new interns are expected --------- several tedious tasks during their first few weeks on the job.

(A) to complete   (B) to completing   (C) completing   (D) completion

10 Preparing for so many presentations in such a short time --------- in increased stress and fatigue.

(A) result   (B) resulting   (C) to result   (D) results

11 The weather was --------- hot, and I struggled to find any shade.

(A) scorching   (B) scorched   (C) scorches   (D) scorcher

12 They decided to delay --------- the report until they had gathered all the necessary data.

(A) submit (B) submitted (C) to submit (D) submitting

13 She stopped --------- the beautiful sunset before continuing her walk along the beach.

(A) admiration (B) admiring (C) to admire (D) and admired

14 The children were shrieking at the sight of the clown, their excitement --------- the air as he began to juggle colorful balls.

(A) filled (B) filling (C) was filling (D) was filled

15 After the meeting concluded, I headed to the office, --------- my laptop from the conference room.

(A) retrieving (B) retrieved (C) retrieve (D) retrieval

WEEK 05 連接詞與子句

▶ 穩固基礎

可以帶出另一個子句，並且讓一整個句子有兩個以上動詞的詞類，稱為連接詞。以基礎程度來說，可分為三大類：**對等連接詞**、**相關連接詞**和**從屬連接詞**。**對等連接詞**主要是指 and、but / yet、or 這四個。**相關連接詞**的考題在 TOEIC 等英文測驗中也相當熱門，像是「not only... but (also)...」、「either... or...」、「neither... nor...」…等。**從屬連接詞**是涵蓋範圍最廣的連接詞，亦稱**附屬連接詞**，可引導「**名詞／形容詞／副詞子句**」。請見以下繼續說明。

必備 Point 1

對等連接詞連接兩個單字、片語或子句（此時稱為「**對等子句**」），原則上前後動詞時態也必須對等：

❶ She studied hard but failed the final exam due to nervousness.
   她努力用功了，但因為緊張而未能通過期末考試。

   ☞ but 前後動詞必須時態相同。

❷ We can focus on solving the problem, or we can continue to blame each other.
   我們可以專注於解決問題，或者繼續互相指責。

   ☞ or 前後連接兩個對等子句。

❸ It is a simple task, yet it requires careful attention to detail.
   這是一個簡單的任務，但卻需要細心注意細節。

   ☞ yet 前後動詞皆為現在式。另外，yet 雖然與 but 意思差不多，但通常帶有驚訝或出乎意料的事。

❹ We were uncertain about the plan, but we decided to take the risk, and now we are seeing positive results.
   我們對這個計劃感到不確定，但我們決定冒險，而現在我們正看到正面的結果。

   ☞ 有時兩個對等連接詞會同時使用在一個句子中。另外，當出現特定時間副詞（例如 now）時，該子句時態也必須跟著調整。

> **補充**
>
> ❶ 對等連接詞前後結構必須對等，因此像是「I like basketball, playing football, and to go swimming.（✗）」是錯誤的句子。
>
> ❷ 對等連接詞 but 常與 not / never... 等否定副詞連用。例如，「I haven't begged for her forgiveness, or have I regretted it.（✗）」是錯誤的句子，其中 or 應改為 but 才符合句意。

必備 Point 2

相關連接詞是指「固定搭配在一起」、可用來連接兩個對稱的單字、片語或子句的連接詞。常見的有 either... or（不是…就是…）、neither... nor...（既不是…也不是…）、not only... but (also)（不但…而且…）、both... and（…和…兩者都）。而有些相關連接詞用來連接的是「句子裡的兩個部分」。例如 so / such... that...（如此…以致…）、whether... or（不論…或…）、not so much... as...（與其…不如…）、would rather... than...（寧可…而不願…）。

❶ You can either submit the report by email or hand it in personally at the office.
你可以透過電子郵件提交報告，或親自交到辦公室。

☞ either 後面的「submit the report by email」與 or 後面的「hand it in personally」形成對稱結構。

❷ He said that they not only improved the system, but we also benefited from the new features.
他說他們不僅改進了系統，我們也從新功能中受益。

☞ not only 後面的「improved the system」與 but also 後面的「benefited from the new features」形成結構與時態的對等。

❸ The presentation was so engaging that the audience remained attentive throughout the entire session.
這場簡報如此吸引人，以至於觀眾在整個過程中都保持專注。

☞ so 後面可以接形容詞或副詞，後面帶出一個 that 子句，通常主要子句與 that 子句的動時態一致。

❹ The actual issue is not so much about the budget as it is about the lack of clear communication.
真正的問題與其說是與預算有關，不如說是缺乏明確的溝通。

☞ as 是連接詞，前後動詞皆為現在式（is），且「about the budget」與「about the lack of clear communication」形成對等結構。

必備 Point 3

廣義來說，在一個句子中，主要子句之外的子句，皆可稱為從屬子句，而能夠引導或帶出從屬子句的詞類，稱為**從屬連接詞**。其中，**引導副詞子句的連接詞**，有表「**時間**」的 before / after / when / while / since / until / once / as soon as...；表「**原因、理由**」的 as / because / since / for、表「**結果**」的 so、表「**條件**」的 if / only if / unless / as long as...、表「**類比**」的 as / as if / as though、表「**讓步**」的 although / though / while / even though / despite of the fact that。

❶ As soon as the meeting ended, she started working on the next project.
會議一結束，她就開始著手進行下一個專案。

☞ as soon as = once（一…就…）用來表示一個短暫的時間點，比起用 when，它更強調動作的積極性。

❷ As long as we maintain open communication and mutual respect, the collaboration will continue to thrive.
只要我們保持開放的溝通和相互尊重，合作就會繼續蓬勃發展。

☞ as long as = if（倘若，如果…）用來表示條件，不過 **as long as 並沒有假設語法**（Week 06）**的適用**。

❸ He would navigate the complex situation as if he were an experienced diplomat.
他處理這個複雜情況的方式，彷彿他是一位經驗豐富的外交官。

☞ **有些副詞連接詞不可置於句首**，as if（= as though 就如同…）就是其中之一。另外，as if 有**假設語法**（Week 06）**的適用**。

❹ Despite the fact that the project faced numerous challenges, it was completed on time with impressive results.
儘管該專案面臨許多挑戰，但它仍準時完成，且成果令人印象深刻。

☞ Despite the fact that = though / although（雖然，儘管…）。

補充

❶ 有些介系詞與連接詞具有相同意義，但介系詞後面要接名詞，而連接詞後面要接子句，因此在考題中應特別注意。例如：「in spite of / despite + 名詞」與「despite the fact that + 完整句」、「because of + 名詞」、「because + 完整句」。

❷ 副詞連接詞 since 具有雙重意義：「自從」與「因為」。前者通常搭配主要子句的完成式動詞時態。例如：

① Since the new policy was implemented, employee productivity has significantly increased.
自從新政策實施以來，員工的工作效率顯著提高。

② **Since** the market conditions have improved, we decided to expand our operations.
因為市場狀況好轉，我們決定擴大業務。

多益會怎麼考？

多益會考依句意選擇正確的對等連接詞題目。

1. Customers demand quality service, --------- they will look for alternatives.

   (A) and　　　(B) but　　　(C) or　　　(D) then

   翻譯 顧客要求優質的服務，否則他們會尋找其他選擇。

   解析 空格前後都是完整句，所以要填入一個連接詞，(D) 可直接刪除。前一句是「顧客要求優質的服務」，後一句是「他們會尋找其他選擇」，顯然要填入的是「或者，否則」，所以正確答案是 (C)。

多益會考選出與相關連接詞搭配的字詞。

2. The project requires --------- excessive funding nor unrealistic deadlines to succeed.

   (A) as much　　(B) not only　　(C) either　　(D) neither

   翻譯 這個計畫的成功，既不需要過多的資金，也不需要不切實際的截止日期。

   解析 句意是「既不需要…也不需要…」，這是 neither... nor... 的相關連接詞運用，所以正確答案是 (D)。

▶ 關鍵概念

必備 Point 1

若以「**對等連接詞連接對等結構**」的文法觀點來說，其實前述提及的相關連接詞 both... and...、either… or...、neither… nor... 以及 not only… but (also)...，也都是對等連接詞的一種，不過這裡要複習的重點是，當這些相關連接詞連接 A 和 B 兩個主詞時，其動詞的單複數問題。也就是說，除「both A and B」當主詞時，動詞恆用複數形之外，其他三者動詞必須隨最近的主詞 B 變化。

❶ **Both** this book **and** that movie *inspire* creativity and provoke

deep thoughts in me.
這本書和那部電影都能激發我的創造力及深入的思考。

☞ 句子主詞是「Both this books and that movie」，應用複數行動詞 inspire。

❷ **Either** the teacher **or** the students <u>dictate</u> the pace of the discussion, depending on the situation.
不是這位老師就是學生們來決定討論會的進行速度，視情況而定。

☞ 句子主詞是「Either the teacher or the students」，動詞應跟隨較近的 the students，所以用複數形 dictate。

❸ **Not only** my colleagues **but also** my boss <u>was</u> impressed by the thoroughness of the report I presented.
不僅是我的同事們，還有我的老闆也對我提交報告的詳盡程度印象深刻。

☞ 句子主詞是「Not only my colleagues but also my boss」，動詞應跟隨較近的 my boss，所以用第三人稱單數 was。

> **補充**
>
> ❶ 對等連接詞 as well as 的意思等同 and，但**不能用來連接子句**，且應連接**對等結構**。此外，「A as well as B」當主詞時，動詞單複數應以 A 為主。例如：
> The man <u>as well as</u> his two kids <u>enjoys</u> hiking in the mountains every weekend.
> 那位男子以及他的兩個孩子每個週末都喜歡去山裡健行。
>
> ☞ 「A as well as B ...」當主詞時，其實可以視為「A, <u>as well as B</u>, V...」= 「A, <u>together with B</u>, V...」，將畫線部分視為插入語，這樣來理解為什麼動詞要跟著 A 而不是 B 就很清楚了。
>
> ❷ 表示「越…越…」的「The + 比較級 ..., The + 比較級 ...」也可形成兩個對等子句。例如：
> **The more** challenges we face, **the stronger** our resolve becomes.
> 我們面對的挑戰越多，我們的決心就越強。

必備 Point 2

能夠**引導名詞子句**的從屬連接詞，常見的有 **that**、**疑問詞 5W1H**、**複合關係詞 wh-ever**（whatever, whoever, whichever、whatsoever）、**whether / if** 以及 **because** 等。

❶ The professor <u>believes</u> **that** critical thinking is essential for academic success.
教授認為思辨能力對於學術成功相關重要。

☞ that 引導名詞子句作 believes 的受詞。

❷ The fact that he remained calm under such immense pressure speaks volumes about his character.

他在如此巨大的壓力下依然保持冷靜，這一事實充分展現了他的性格。

☞ that 引導名詞子句（that he remained... pressure）作 fact 的同位語。

❸ Whether the intricate balance between tradition and innovation could ever be truly achieved is not the point.

傳統與創新之間的微妙平衡是否能真正實現並非重點。

☞ whether 引導名詞子句作整句的主詞。

補充

whether 和 if 都可以和 or not 連用，但兩者有以下差別：

① whether or not = whether... or not = if... or not，但沒有 if or not 的用法。例如：I don't know whether / if she's telling the truth or not. = I don't know whether or not she's telling the truth.，但 I don't know if or not she's telling the truth. 是錯誤的句子。

② whether 名詞子句可以當主詞或受詞，但 if 名詞子句不可當主詞。例如，「Whether you'll come or not isn't important.」這句的 Whether 不可用 If 來取代。

❹ The reason for his sudden resignation was because he no longer aligned with the company's ethical stance.

他突然辭職的原因是因為他不再認同公司的道德立場。

☞ because 引導名詞子句作主詞補語。

❺ Whoever fails to adapt to the rapidly changing environment is not likely to thrive in this industry.

任何無法適應環境迅速變化的人，都不太可能在這個行業中蓬勃發展。

☞ Whoever 引導名詞子句（Whoever fails to... environment）作主詞。

必備 Point 3

有一些**帶有 that 的副詞連接詞**也是多益考題中的常客，像是 given that（考慮到）、provided that（如果，倘若）、on condition that（條件是⋯）、so that / in order that（目的是⋯，如此一來⋯）、now that（既然⋯）、except that（除了⋯之外）、for fear that（以免⋯）⋯等。

❶ The project was delayed, given that key stakeholders failed to meet their deadlines.

這項計畫被延遲了，這是考量到主要利益相關者未能按時完成任務。

☞ given that 引導的副詞子句可以放在句首或句中。

❷ **Provided that** everyone agrees, let's proceed with the new strategy.

若大家都同意，我們就採取新策略。

☞ provided that 引導的副詞子句可以放在句首或句中。

❸ They adjusted the schedule **in order that** everyone could attend the meeting.

他們調整了時間表，為的是讓每個人都能參加會議。

☞ in order that = so that（目的是…，為了…）用來表示做某事的目的。只不過 in order that 可置於句首或句中，而 so that 只能放在句中，不可放在句首。考試最喜歡考一些特例情況，應多加注意！

多益會怎麼考？

多益會考有兩個主詞時，選出正確動詞型態的題目。

1. Neither Jack nor his two attorneys ---------- aware of the unexpected turn of events.

    (A) was　　　(B) were　　　(C) had　　　(D) has been

    翻譯 傑克和他的兩位委任律師都對意外的事態發展毫不知情。

    解析 空格前有「Neither... nor...」這個相關連接詞構成的主詞，所以動詞應跟著 nor 後面的名詞（his two attorneys）來變化，所以 (A)、(D) 可直接刪除。空格後是形容詞 aware，所以應填入 be 動詞，而非一般動詞，故正確答案是 (B)。

多益會考依句意選出適當連接詞的題目。

2. ---------- they approve the proposal or not is none of my concern.

    (A) If　　　(B) What　　　(C) That　　　(D) Whether

    翻譯 他們是否批准該提案，我都不在意。

    解析 全句的動詞是 is，因此「---------- they approve the proposal or not」這個名詞子句是句子的主詞。(A) If（是否）引導名詞子句時，不可當主詞，所以錯誤；approve 已經有受詞 the proposal 了，所以前面不能用 (B) What；而從子句句尾的 or not 來看，應與 Whether 搭配，所以正確答案是 (D)。

▶ TOEIC 實戰演練

Part 5　請在以下四個選項中選出正確的答案

01　I seek not merely success --------- fulfillment now.
　　(A) as　　　　(B) but　　　　(C) yet　　　　(D) than

02　It was such a compelling argument --------- the audience was left in silence.
　　(A) than　　　(B) that　　　 (C) but　　　　(D) or

03　I would rather embrace uncertainty --------- settle for mediocrity.
　　(A) and　　　 (B) but　　　　(C) than　　　 (D) nor

04　The decision was delayed --------- all the data could be thoroughly analyzed.
　　(A) until　　 (B) unless　　 (C) because　　(D) so that

05　He spoke with such confidence --------- he were the expert in the meeting room.
　　(A) even though　(B) as long as　(C) only if　(D) as though

06　--------- I appreciate the feedback, I can never compromise my core values.
　　(A) While　　(B) Because　　(C) Despite　　(D) Unless

07　--------- we adapt to the changing environment, or we risk becoming obsolete.
　　(A) Even　　 (B) Rather　　 (C) Either　　 (D) Neither

08　Not only the participants but also the organizer --------- transparency in the process.
　　(A) value　　(B) values　　 (C) have valued　(D) was valuing

09 The leader as well as the team members --------- for innovative solutions.

　　(A) advocate　　(B) are advocating　(C) advocates　　(D) have advocated

10 It's a pity --------- such talent remains unrecognized in the industry.

　　(A) when　　(B) why　　(C) if　　(D) that

11 The reason for the delay is --------- the stakeholders require more data before proceeding.

　　(A) how　　(B) whether　　(C) since　　(D) because

12 I wondered --------- the recent changes would truly enhance our productivity.

　　(A) if　　(B) that　　(C) as if　　(D) as though

13 --------- leads the initiative is responsible for its success or failure.

　　(A) He　　(B) That　　(C) Those who　　(D) Whoever

14 The project will proceed as planned, --------- that we secure the necessary funding.

　　(A) believing　　(B) as such　　(C) for fear　　(D) provided

15 You can achieve --------- goals you set for yourself with dedication and hard work.

　　(A) those　　(B) what　　(C) whatever　　(D) whenever

WEEK 06 關係詞與子句

▶ 穩固基礎

雖然我們在 Week 02 提到過**關係代名詞**屬於代名詞的一種，不過因為關係代名詞會帶出另一個子句（即**關係子句** or **形容詞子句**），所以也具有連接詞的功能；也就是說，它既是代名詞，也是連接詞。以代名詞的角度來說，當然就有**主格、受格、所有格**之分了；而以連接詞的角度來說，因為它在子句中已扮演主詞或受詞的角色，所以關係代名詞（及其所有格）後面必然是不完整的句子。

必備 Point 1

關係代名詞有代替「人」的 who / whom / that，以及代替「事物」的 which / that。關係代名詞前面若加逗號，為補述或非限定用法，但 that 前面不可加逗號。關係代名詞當主詞時，關係子句的動詞單複數應與先行詞一致。

❶ She gave me a book which explains the basics of philosophy.
她給了我一本解釋哲學基礎的書。

☞ 主格的關係代名詞 which 帶出了「which explains the basics of philosophy」這個關係子句。

❷ He is the professor that / whom I admire the most.
他是我最敬佩的教授。

☞ 受格的關係代名詞 whom 帶出了「whom I admire the most」這個關係子句，此時的 that / whom 可省略。

❸ I have two sisters, who both excel in their respective fields of work.
我有兩個姐姐，她們在各自的工作領域都表現優異。

☞ 非限定用法的關係代名詞 who 前面需有逗號（,）。此句可等於「I have two sisters, both of whom excel in their respective fields of work.」

❹ I have two sisters who / that both excel in their respective fields of work.
我有兩個在各自的工作領域都表現優異的姐姐。

☞ 限定用法的關係代名詞 who 前面沒有逗號。這句暗示「我不是只有兩個姊

姊」，而前一句表示「我只有兩個姊姊」。

❺ He is a diligent and hard-working man, which is widely known.
它是一位勤奮且努力工作的男人，這是大家都知道的事。

☞ 可別以為 which 前面不可能是「人」喔！關係代名詞 which 可以用來代替前面整句或前句中部分概念，但 which 前面必須有逗號。

❻ The only solution that addresses the issue effectively is a comprehensive policy change.
唯一有效解決這個問題的方案是全面的政策變更。

☞ 關係代名詞的先行詞前面有 only 時，關係代名詞只能用 that（不能用 which），且不能有逗號。

> **補充**
>
> 一般情況下，that 可以取代 who / whom / which，但是當先行詞之前有以下情況時，只能用 that：
>
> ❶ 先行詞前有「**絕對性字眼**」，像是 the only、the very、the first、the last、最高級形容詞時，關係代名詞只能用 that。例如：
> The most unforgettable experience (~~which~~, that) shaped my career was my internship abroad.
> 塑造我職業生涯的最難忘的經歷是我在國外的實習。
>
> ❷ 先行詞為 all、everything、nothing...，或先行詞被 all、every、any、no 等修飾時。例如：
> I have learned everything (~~which~~, that) is necessary to excel in this field.
> 我已經學會了成為這個領域佼佼者所需的一切。
>
> ❸ 先行詞為「人 + 動物」或「人 + 事物」時。例如：
> I can see the dog and his master (~~who~~, ~~which~~, that) enjoy their daily walks in the park.
> 我能看到那隻狗和他的主人，他們在公園裡享受每日的散步。

必備 Point 2

關係代名詞所有格：無論先行詞是人或事物，皆用 whose 表示，它後面會緊跟著一個名詞，看似關係子句的主詞，但這個主詞無法獨立存在，因為缺少了冠詞或其他限定詞。

❶ The man whose ideas revolutionized the industry was invited to speak at the conference.
那位其想法徹底改變了整個行業的男人被邀請在會議上演講。

☞ whose 的先行詞是「人」，後面的「ideas revolutionized the industry」看

似「S + V + O」的完整句子，但 ideas 本身不能當主詞，所以前面要有關係代名詞所有格。

❷ We must address this issue whose impact affects the entire community.
我們必須解決這個問題，其影響波及整個社區。

☞ whose 的先行詞也可以是「事物」。這個句子也可以變成「We must address this issue of which the impact affects the entire community.」或「We must address this issue, the impact of which affects the entire community.」。

❸ The company launched several new projects, the success of which remains suncertain.
該公司推出了幾個新專案，但其成功與否仍然不確定。

☞ 當關係代名詞所有格是「the + N + of which + 先行詞」此種特殊形態時，關係子句動詞應跟著這個 N. 作變化，而非跟著先行詞。

多益會怎麼考？

多益會考依句意選出適當的關係代名詞題目。

1. That was the very moment --------- changed the course of his entire career.

   (A) who　　　(B) which　　　(C) that　　　(D) when

   翻譯 那正是改變他整個職業生涯的關鍵時刻。

   解析 空格後不是完整句，所以 (D) 可直接剔除。而從其餘 3 個選項來看，要填入一個正確的關係代名詞。因為先行詞是 moment，所以 (A) who 也錯誤，接著看到前面有 very 這個限定詞，所以關係代名詞只能用 that，故答案是 (C)。

2. The museum houses a vast collection of ancient artifacts, some --------- date back thousands of years.

   (A) which　　　(B) whose　　　(C) of whom　　　(D) of which

   翻譯 這座博物館收藏了大量的古代文物，其中有些可追溯至數千年前。

   解析 空格前雖有可作先行詞的 some，但其前並無連接詞，所以 (A)、(B) 皆不可選。如果 some 不是先行詞，那麼先行詞肯定就是 artifacts，「some---------」這部分構成 是關係代名詞所有格的特殊用法，因為並非「人」，所以 (C) 也錯誤，故答案是 (D)。

▶ 關鍵概念

能夠帶出關係子句的，可不只有關係代名詞喔！**關係副詞** where、when、why、how 也具有此功能。此外，在整個**關係詞**的大家族中，還有**複合關係代名詞** what、whatever、whoever、whichever，可引導名詞子句與副詞子句。複合關係代名詞 = **先行詞 + 關係代名詞**，故其前不能再有先行詞了。**複合關係副詞** whatever、wherever、whenever、however 引導的是副詞子句。最後，關係形容詞與準關係代名詞，雖然在考題中並不多見，但為強化考生們文法知識的廣度，本單元中也將為您略作介紹與複習。

必備 Point 1　**關係副詞**其實就是從關係代名詞的概念延伸而來的，因為「**關係副詞 = 介系詞 + 關係代名詞 which**」。

❶ We visited <u>the restaurant</u> <u>where</u> (= in which) the chef is renowned for creating innovative fusion dishes.
我們去了那間餐廳，那裡的主廚以創新融合不同菜餚而聞名。

❷ She received the prestigious award <u>last month</u> <u>when</u> (= in which) her groundbreaking research was finally recognized by the scientific community.
她上個月獲得了那項殊榮，當時她的突破性研究終於獲得了科學界的認可。

　　☞ 表時間的關係副詞 when 最容易被誤以為是引導副詞子句的 when。

❸ <u>The reason</u> <u>why</u> (= for which = that) he succeeded is his unwavering determination.
他成功的原因是他堅定不移的決心。

　　☞ 就文法觀點來說，reason 後面的子句由 why 或 for which 引導時，稱為形容詞子句。但也可以用 that 來引導一個子句，此時的 that 子句則是名詞子句（為 reason 的同位語）。如果覺得文法觀念太複雜，只要記住 <u>reason 後面可能接 for、that、why 這三個字</u>就可以了。

❹ They were shocked by <u>how</u> / <u>the way (in which)</u> she handled the crisis with such composure.
他們對她*如此冷靜地處理危機*感到震驚。

　　☞ how = the way (in which)，但<u>沒有 the way how 的用法</u>。此時 how 引導的是名詞子句。

必備 Point 2　**複合關係代名詞**是由關係代名詞 who、whom、which、whose 等字尾加上 -ever 構成，複合關係代名詞是「**先行詞 + 關係代名詞**」，因此其前不會有先行詞。

❶ Whoever is responsible for the error must correct it immediately.
對於這項錯誤應負責的任何人，都必須立即做出修正。

☞ Whoever = Anyone who（…的任何人），引導**名詞子句**作為句子的主詞。

❷ Whoever takes over this case, the deadline won't change.
無論是誰接手這案子，截止日期都不會改變。

☞ Whoever = No matter who（無論是誰…）引導**副詞子句**，此時複合關係代名詞 whoever 視為一**副詞連接詞**。

❸ Feel free to invite whomever you like to the party.
隨意邀請你喜歡的任何人來參加派對。

☞ Whomever = Anyone whom，引導**名詞子句**作為 invite 的受詞。

❹ Make sure whichever you choose aligns with your long-term goals.
務必確認你選擇的與你長期的目標一致。

☞ whichever = anything which，引導**名詞子句**。若改為副詞子句用法時，句子變成「Whichever you choose, make sure it aligns with your long-term goals. 無論你選擇哪個，務必確保它與你的長期目標一致。」

❺ Whoever's decision this is will greatly impact the project's future.
無論這是誰的決定，對這項計畫的未來都會產生重大影響。

☞ Whoever's = Anyone whose 引導**名詞子句**作為句子的主詞。

必備 Point 3　**複合關係副詞**是由 what、which、who、when、where、how 這 6 個疑問詞的字尾加上 -ever 構成，複合關係副詞是「**介系詞 + 先行詞 + 疑問詞**」引導副詞，因此其前也不會有先行詞。

❶ Whatever you do, I will always support your decisions.
無論你做什麼，我都會一直支持你的決定。

☞ Whatever = No matter what 無論什麼

❷ Whoever may challenge you, I will stand by your side.
無論是誰挑戰你，我都會站在你這邊。

☞ Whoever = No matter who 無論誰

❸ Whichever you choose, I will make sure everything is prepared.
無論你選擇哪一個，我都會確保一切準備就緒。

☞ Whichever = No matter which 無論哪一個

❹ You may contact our support team whenever you encounter issues with the software.
一旦您使用軟體遇到問題時，隨時都可以聯繫我們的支援團隊。

☞ whenever = at any time when= no matter when 無論任何時候

❺ Where(ver) there's a will, there's a will
有志者事竟成。

☞ wherever = at any place where= no matter where（無論在何處）。這句諺語以 where 來代替 wherever。

❻ You can customize the settings however you want to suit your preferences.
你可以隨自己喜好的方式自訂設定。

☞ however = in any way= no matter how 無論如何

必備 Point 4

關係形容詞主要有 which、what、whichever、whatever，引導的名詞子句或副詞子句不會有先行詞。

❶ You are free to take whichever course you feel best aligns with your personal interests.
你可以自由選擇任一個你認為最符合你個人興趣的課程。

☞ whichever = any... which / that... 任何的…

❷ Whatever decision you make, I will fully support you and stand by your side.
無論你做出什麼決定，我都會全力支持你並站在你這一邊。

☞ Whatever = No matter what... 無論什麼的…，引導一個副詞子句。

必備 Point 5

準關係代名詞主要是指 as、but、than 這三個，但必須有另一字詞與其搭配。必須注意的是，準關係代名詞嚴格來說，不能以一般關係代名詞（who / whom / which / that）來取代。

❶ I've never seen such a beautiful sunset as the one I witnessed on that island last summer.
無我從未見過像去年夏天在那座島上所目睹的那樣美麗的日落。

☞ 在「such...as...」句型中，as 也可以引導一個關係子句。準關係代名詞 as 搭配的是 such。本句的 as 是受格的關係代名詞。

❷ He showed the same dedication to his work as he always did, despite the challenges he faced.

儘管面臨挑戰，他仍展現出一如既往對工作的相同投入。

☞ 本句中與 as 搭配的是 the same。as 是受格的關係代名詞。

❸ This is as tough a decision as has ever been faced by any leader in history.

這是一個和歷史上任何領袖所面臨過的決定一樣艱難的決定。

☞ 本句中與 as 搭配的是 as。as 是主格的關係代名詞。

❹ There are no parents but love their children.

沒有不愛自己孩子的父母。

☞ 本句中與 but 不能以 who / that 取代。but 作為準關係代名詞時，前面主要子句必須是否定句。本句若關係代名詞要改成 that，可寫成雙重否定句的「There are no parents that don't love their children.」

❺ He shows more enthusiasm for his work than he ever did in his previous job.

他對工作的熱情比他在之前的工作中表現出來的要高得多。

☞ 先行詞有比較級形容詞修飾時，關係代名詞應用 than。

多益會怎麼考？

多益會考依句意選出適當的副詞子句連接詞的題目。

1. ---------- tries to change your mind, I won't let them influence your decision.

    (A) Who　　　(B) Whoever　　　(C) What　　　(D) Whatever

    翻譯 無論誰試圖改變你的想法，我都不會讓他們影響你的決定。

    解析 逗號後面是完整句，因此前面的「---------- tries to change your mind」這部分應為副詞子句，而選項中能夠引導副詞子句的只有複合關係代名詞 (B) Whoever 以及 (D) Whatever，從「試圖改變你的想法」的句意來看，動作的執行者應為「人」，故正確答案是 (B)。

多益會考依句意選出適當的關係代名詞的題目。

2. It's not so difficult a task ---------- can be completed with proper planning and effort.

    (A) which　　　(B) that　　　(C) as　　　(D) but

WEEK 06　關係詞與子句

> **翻譯** 這並不是一個那麼困難的任務，但可藉由適當的計劃和努力完成。
>
> **解析** 顯然空格要填入一個關係代名詞。雖然先行詞 task 是「事物」，但本題應留意到前面是個否定句，因此不能以一般的關係代名詞 that/which 來指稱，而是以準關係代名詞 but 來代替，故正確答案是 (D)。

▶ TOEIC 實戰演練

Part 5　請在以下四個選項中選出正確的答案

01 He is a very dedicated student, ---------- is a testament to his strong work ethic.

(A) who　　　(B) which　　　(C) that　　　(D) whoever

02 Both John and Sarah are excellent candidates for the position, either of ---------- is a great asset to the company.

(A) which　　　(B) who　　　(C) whom　　　(D) that

03 He is the only man ---------- has successfully completed the expedition under such extreme conditions.

(A) who　　　(B) that　　　(C) as　　　(D) whom

04 The team has reviewed the proposals, the content of which ---------- highly detailed and comprehensive.

(A) is　　　(B) has　　　(C) are　　　(D) being

05 They visited the museum, ---------- collection of ancient artifacts is renowned worldwide.

(A) that　　　(B) which　　　(C) where　　　(D) whose

06 He bought a fancy sports car, the color ---------- matches his suit perfectly.

(A) which　　　(B) that　　　(C) of which　　　(D) whose

07 The meeting was postponed to Friday --------- the entire team would be available to attend.

(A) that (B) when (C) which (D) where

08 I admire --------- he handles difficult situations with such calm and precision.

(A) how (B) what (C) whom (D) why

09 That'll be the --------- when he finally admits he was wrong.

(A) way (B) day (C) place (D) reason

10 The documents should be put --------- they are easily accessible for everyone.

(A) when (B) how (C) where (D) why

11 He always comes across as arrogant, --------- is an attitude I really feel hinders his ability to work well with others.

(A) which (B) whose (C) such (D) that

12 --------- friendly as he seems, I still find it hard to trust him completely.

(A) Whatever (B) However (C) How (D) As

13 You can succeed --------- you go, as long as you remain determined and focused.

(A) whatever (B) whoever (C) however (D) wherever

14 More guests --------- were originally invited showed up at the party.

(A) who (B) that (C) than (D) as

15 Offer your support to --------- you believe needs it most.

(A) whatever (B) whomever (C) whatever (D) as

WEEK 07 假設語氣

▶ 穩固基礎

假設語氣主要分為四種：與**現在事實**相反、與**過去事實**相反、對**未來狀況**的假設（或推測），以及**純條件**假設法。假設句的考點主要在於「**條件句**」與「**主要子句**」動詞時態的對應關係。此外，「**沒有 if 的假設語氣**」也是熱門考點。

必備 Point 1

與現在事實相反的假設：If + S + **動詞過去式／were**..., S + **would** (**could**, **might**, **should**) + **原形動詞** ...。例如：

❶ If she were here, she would know exactly what to do.
如果她在這裡，她會知道該怎麼做。

　☞ 這句可等於：As she was not here, she didn't know exactly what to do. 因為她不在這裡，所以她不知道確切來說要做什麼。

❷ If he told the truth, we could resolve this quickly.
如果他說實話，我們可以很快解決這件事。

必備 Point 2

與過去事實相反的假設：If + S + **had p.p.**..., S + **would** (**could**, **might**, **should**) + **have p.p.**...。例如：

❶ If she had taken the advice, the outcome might have been different.
如果她採納了那個建議，結果可能會不一樣。

❷ If you had been in my shoes, you could have understood my decision.
如果你處在我的位置，你可能就會理解我的決定。

必備 Point 3

對未來狀況的假設：If + S + **should + 原形動詞** ..., 主詞 + **助動詞** + **原形動詞** ...。例如：

❶ If our teacher should cancel the class tomorrow, we may have extra time to prepare.
如果明天我們老師取消這堂課，我們可能有額外的時間來準備。

❷ The meeting will be postponed if you should fall ill and be unable to attend.
如果你生病無法出席，會議將會延期。

☞ if 子句可放在主要子句前面或後面皆可，而主要子句使用**現在式助動詞**或**過去式助動詞**皆可，但前者意味可能性較高，後者則可能性較低。

必備 Point 4

純條件的假設：If + 主詞 + **現在式動詞** ..., 主詞 + **助動詞** + **原形動詞** ...。
例如：

❶ If he comes tomorrow, I will discuss the details of the proposal with him.
如果他明天來，我會和他討論提案的細節。

☞ if 條件子句沒有未來式，即使有未來的時間副詞。只有主要子句能用未來式。

❷ If she makes an apology for her mistake, she must ensure it is sincere and take responsibility for her actions.
如果她為她的錯誤道歉，她必須確保這是誠懇的，並對她的行為負責。

必備 Point 5

若 if 條件句動詞有 were、had + p.p.（過去完成式）、should（表「**萬一**」）時，可**省略掉 if** 並將上述詞類移至句首或主詞前。例如：

❶ Had you done it earlier, you would have avoided all the unnecessary stress.
如果你早點做這件事，你本可以避免所有不必要的壓力。

☞ 這是個與過去事實相反的假設句，可還原為「If you had done it earlier, ...」。

❷ Were she willing to take the opportunity now, you might achieve the success you've been hoping for.
如果你現在把握這個機會，你可能會達成你一直期望的成功。

☞ 這是個與現在事實相反的假設句，可還原為「If she were willing to, ...」。

❸ Should the manager approve the budget, I could initiate the new project as planned.
如果經理批准預算，我就可以依計劃啟動新項新計畫。

☞ 這是個表示未來狀況的假設句，可還原為「If the manager should approve the budget, ...」。

必備 Point 6

有些句子雖然沒有 if 條件句，但**句意上帶有假設語氣**（例如**對於過去事件的推測**）此時句子動詞時態應用「**助動詞 + have +p.p.**」的形式。例如：

❶ He talks in a confident way; he must have prepared thoroughly for the presentation.
   他的談話很有自信；他一定是為這次簡報做了充分的準備。
   ☞ 這是對過去事物進行推測的用法。

❷ I can't believe such a cautious man could have made a decision without considering all the risks.
   我不敢相信這樣一個謹慎的人會在沒有考慮所有風險的情況下做出決定。

多益會怎麼考？

多益會考在假設語氣句型中，選出正確的動詞時態。

1. If the global temperature ---------- to rise by just a few more degrees, many coastal cities would be afflicted with severe flooding and displacement of populations.

   (A) is　　　(B) was　　　(C) were　　　(D) will be

   翻譯 如果全球氣溫再上升幾度，許多沿海城市將遭受嚴重的洪水和人口遷徙之苦。

   解析 空格要填入 If 條件句的 be 動詞形式，所以我們直接看主要子句的動詞時態。從「would be afflicted」可知，這是個「與現在事實相反」的假設，所以 be 動詞不論人稱皆為 were，故正確答案是 (C)。

2. ---------- he clutch the opportunity with determination, I could guide you towards achieving remarkable success.

   (A) If　　　(B) Had　　　(C) Should　　　(D) Would

   翻譯 如果你緊緊抓住這個機會，我可以引導你取得大成功。

   解析 空格看似應填入一個副詞子句連接詞，但關鍵在 he 後面的 clutch 是原形動詞（不是第三人稱單數，也不是過去式），所以 (A) If 可直接刪除。本題考點是「省略 if」的假設句，在條件句中，因為主詞 he 後面是原形動詞，所以只有 should 可選，正確答案是 (C)。

▶ 關鍵概念

假設語氣更深入的考點還有「時態不一致」的假設、「違反真理」的假設、「But for...（若非…）」句型、與願望有關的「wish 與 if only」、「It is (high) time that...（該是…的時候了）」句型、「as if / as though 假設語氣」…等也必須多加注意。

必備 Point 1

時態不一致的假設常出現在考題中。例如，if 子句的時態是「過去完成式」（與過去事實相反），而**主要子句有表示「現在」、「今天」等時間副詞**時，動詞應為「過去式助動詞 + 原形動詞」。例如：

❶ If I had been more diligent in my studies, I could be pursuing my dream career now.
如果我當初在學業上更勤奮，我現在就能追求我的夢想職業了。

❷ If I had apologized earlier, she would still be speaking to me today.
如果當初我早點道歉，她今天還會和我說話。

必備 Point 2

違反真理的假設句：If + S + were to + 原形動詞 ..., S + 過去式助動詞 + 原形動詞。例如：

❶ I would marry you if the sun were to rise in the west.
如果太陽從西方升起，我就嫁給你。

❷ If I were to jump into the wayback machine, I would revisit key moments in history to witness how they truly unfolded.
如果我能進入時光機，我會重溫歷史上的關鍵時刻，親眼見證它們是如何真正發生的。

☞ wayback machine 是「時光機」的意思。

必備 Point 3

「**若非／要不是…**」的假設句，僅用於「**與現在／過去事實相反**」兩種假設語氣：

❶ **與現在事實相反**：If it were not for + N. / that + 子句 ..., S + 過去式助動詞 + 原形動詞。例如：

① If it were not for (= Were it not for = But for) his honesty, I wouldn't like him.

要不是他人老實，我才不會喜歡他。

☞「But for + 名詞」是個副詞片語，可等於「Without + 名詞」

② If it were not that (= Were it not that) he is an honest man, I wouldn't like him.
要不是他是個老實人，我才不會喜歡他。

☞ 注意：此時 that 子句動詞要用現在式。

❷ **與過去事實相反**：將前述 If 條件句的 were not 改成 had not been 即可。例如：

① If it had not been for (= Had it not been for = But for) the money he lent me, I wouldn't have been able to start my own business.
當初要不是他借給我的錢，我就無法開創自己的事業了。

☞ 若改成「But for / Without + 名詞」時，就只能從主要子句的時態去判斷與現在或過去事實相反了！

② If it had not been that (= Had it not been that) he lent me the money, I wouldn't have been able to start my own business.
當初要不是他借我錢，我無法開創自己的事業了。

☞ 注意：此時 that 子句動詞要用過去式。

必備 Point 4

表達「**願望**」的「**wish that...**（希望…，祝福…）」以及「**If only...**（但願…，要是…就好了）」的假設語氣都只有**與現在事實相反**和**與過去事實相反**兩種假設語氣。另外，這裡的 wish 也可以用 would rather 取代，而連接詞 that 亦可省略。

❶ I wish (= would rather) I were more confident in public speaking.
我希望自己在公開演講時更有自信。

❷ I wish (= would rather) that our team had won the championship last year.
我真希望我們的團隊去年贏得了冠軍。

❸ If only I were more confident in public speaking.
要是我能在公開演講時更有自信就好了。

☞ 此句雖然只有連接詞 If 引導的子句，看似沒有主要子句，可別以為這是個錯誤的句子！

> **補充**
>
> 與 wish 意思完全相同的 hope，後接 that 子句時，使用的是一般動詞時態，即表現在狀況用現在式，表未來狀況用未來式…等。例如：
>
> ① I **hope** (that) I **am** / **can be** more confident in public speaking.
>
> ② I **hope** (that) they **have finished** their jobs.

必備 Point 5

表達「**是…的時候了**」的「**It's (about / high) time that…**」的假設語氣，只有**與現在事實相反**的假設語氣，也就是 that 子句動詞要用過去式。例如：

It is time that we dissuaded our children from spending too much time on video games. 　現在是時候我們勸阻孩子們花太多時間在電玩上了。

必備 Point 6

表達「**彷彿／好像是…**」的「**as if / as though…**」假設語氣，引導的副詞子句中，動詞與一般 if 條件句一樣，可以用**現在式**、**過去式**、**過去完成式**。例如：

❶ It looks as if the company's recent strategic shift is finally yielding the expected results.
看起來公司的近期策略轉變似乎終於產生了預期的效果。

❷ She opened and closed her lips as if she had wanted to say something.
她張了張嘴，彷彿當時想說些什麼。

多益會怎麼考？

多益會考在假設語氣句型中選擇正確動詞類型的題目。

1. If she had finished her homework earlier, I ---------- her to the party today.

   (A) will invite 　　　　　　　　(B) would invite
   (C) would have invited　　　　(D) will be inviting

   翻譯 如果她早點完成作業，我今天就會邀請她參加派對。

   解析 空格要填入假設語氣中，主要子句正確的動詞時態。從 If 條件句來看是與過去事實相反的假設，但主要子句中有個關鍵的時間副詞 today，因此應用「過去式助動詞 + 原形動詞」，故正確答案是 (B)。

多益會考在假設語氣句型中，選擇副詞連接詞的題目。

2. ---------- it not been that it rained, I would have gone for a walk in the park.

(A) If　　　　　(B) Were　　　　　(C) Had　　　　　(D) Should

翻譯　如果不是下雨，我就會去公園散步。

解析　空格看似應填入一個副詞子句連接詞，但關鍵在後面的過去分詞 been。這是個省略 if 的假設語氣題型，如果選 If 的話，條件句沒有動詞，所以 (A) 可先刪除。接著注意到主要子句時態是「助動詞 + have + p.p.」，顯然這是與過去事實相反的假設，故正確答案是 (C)。

▶ TOEIC 實戰演練

Part 5　請在以下四個選項中選出正確的答案

01　If he ---------- more responsible, I would trust him with important tasks.

(A) is　　　　　(B) was　　　　　(C) had been　　　　　(D) were

02　If he had sent the report on time, I ---------- the project earlier.

(A) will finish　　　　　　　　　(B) might finish
(C) would have finished　　　　(D) will have finished

03　I will help you if you ---------- need any assistance during the event.

(A) should　　　　(B) would　　　　(C) will　　　　(D) might

04　---------- your teacher more patient, I might be more motivated to participate in class.

(A) Had　　　　(B) Were　　　　(C) If　　　　(D) Should

05　She didn't pick up my calls; she must ---------- too busy at the time.

(A) be　　　　(B) have　　　　(C) had been　　　　(D) have been

06　We would join the trip if you ---------- us earlier.

(A) invite　　　　(B) invited　　　　(C) have invited　　　　(D) had invited

07 --------- you change your mind, I could help you with the arrangements.

(A) Were (B) Should (C) Had (D) Have

08 The lights were still on in her office late at night; she must --------- behind to finish her work.

(A) stay (B) have stayed (C) be staying (D) be stayed

09 If you had told me about the meeting earlier, I would --------- better prepared now.

(A) be (B) have been (C) have had (D) have had been

10 --------- my timely warning, she wouldn't have avoided the accident.

(A) As for (B) Because of (C) With (D) Without

11 --------- the train not been delayed, I would have arrived on time for the meeting.

(A) Were (B) Had (C) Has (D) Should

12 My father wished I --------- a career in medicine, but I chose a different path.

(A) will pursue (B) pursued (C) have pursued (D) had pursued

13 --------- I had taken the opportunity when it was presented.

(A) Only if (B) If only (C) However (D) Would

14 It's about time you --------- taking responsibility for your actions instead of blaming others.

(A) start (B) started (C) will start (D) should start

15 The man spoke with such confidence as if he --------- an expert on the subject.

(A) is (B) was (C) were (D) had been

WEEK 08 特殊句型

▶ 穩固基礎

無論何種類型的英語測驗，**比較句型**、**倒裝句型**、**附加問句**都是考題中的重要來源。「比較句型」涉及形容詞與副詞的**原級**、**比較級**、**最高級**的變化；「倒裝句型」是將句子的某個部分**移至句首**，作為**強調**的作用；「附加問句」不太會直接出現在 TOEIC 考題中，但單句、對話、電子郵件等文章都會頻繁出現，也是必學的文法單元中之一，其重點在於敘述句與附加問句之間**主詞與動詞的連動關係**。以下進一步說明。

必備 Point 1

原級比較：as + adj. / adv. + as。例如：

❶ The job wasn't as glamorous as it seemed at first.
這份工作並不像最初看起來那樣光鮮亮麗。

❷ The company expanded its global reach as significantly as its commitment to innovation.
這家公司擴展全球影響力的程度與其對創新的承諾一樣強大。

必備 Point 2

一般比較：比較級 adj. / adv. + than。例如：

❶ Outsourcing the production proved to be cheaper than building an in-house facility.
這外包生產證明比建立內部設施更便宜得多。

☞ 原則上 1~2 個音節的形容詞，直接在字尾加 -er 形成比較級。

❷ She is more diligent than any of her colleagues when it comes to meeting deadlines.
在趕期限方面，她比任何同事都更加勤奮。

☞ 3 個音節以上的形容詞，在前面加 more 形成比較級。

❸ The moon shone less luminously than usual, casting only a faint glow over the landscape.
月亮比平常暗淡，僅在地景上投下一絲微光。

☞ 要表達否定的語意時，可以將 more 改成 less。

必備 Point 3

形容詞／副詞最高級：the + 最高級 adj. / adv. + of / among...。不過，最高級副詞通常不必再加定冠詞 the。例如：

❶ He is the boldest visionary of the three candidates, unafraid to challenge conventional thinking.
他是這三位候選人當中最大膽的遠見者，無懼於挑戰傳統思維。

☞ 最高級形成的比較對象一定是**三者以上**。

❷ She will be the most resourceful leader of the three executives chosen for the task.
在被選中負責這項任務的三位高管中，她將是最有資源的領導者。

❸ Mr. Chang responded to the critique most politely among the 5 candidates, showing remarkable professionalism.
張先生在五位候選人中最為禮貌地回應批評，展現了卓越的專業精神。

☞ 最高級副詞前不用加 the。

補充

原級形容詞變成**比較級、最高級**形容詞時，不是字尾加 -er、-est 就是前面加 more / less / most / least，可以稱為「規則變化」，但有些形容詞／副詞的比較級級最高級形式會完全變成另外一個字（不規則變化），例如：many → more → the most；little → less → the least；good → better → the best；bad → worse → the worst；well → better → best。另外，有些事必須重複字尾的，像是 hot → hotter → hottest。

必備 Point 4

TOEIC 考試中常出現的**倒裝句型**有「否定詞倒裝」、「Only 倒裝」、「So / Such 倒裝」三種：

❶ Never are unauthorized personnel allowed to access the confidential files. (=Unauthorized personnel are never allowed to...)
絕不允許未經授權的人員取得機密文件。

☞ 否定詞 never 移置句首時，be 動詞 are 要放在主詞前面。

❷ Only recently did the company realize the full potential of its emerging market strategy. (= The company only recently realized...)
只有到最近，這家公司才意識到其新興市場策略的全部潛力。

☞ 副詞 only 移置句首時，應依原動詞時態**補上助動詞**，放在主詞前面，而原本的動詞過去式應**改為原形動詞**。

❸ So influential is she that her opinions shape industry trends across the globe. (= She is so influential that...)
她的影響力如此之大，因此她的觀點塑造了全球產業趨勢。

☞ 在 so... that... 句型中，將 so 移置句首時，句子應倒裝。

❹ Such charisma did he exude that audiences were captivated by his every word. (= He exuded such charisma that...)
他的魅力如此強大，以至於觀眾被他每一句話所吸引。

☞ 在 such... that... 句型中，將 such 移置句首時，句子應倒裝。

> **補充**
>
> **so 開頭**的倒裝句也常見於「附和句」中，此時稱為「肯定附和句」，其句型為「..., and so + is / 助動詞 + 主詞」，注意前後動詞必須對等。例如：
>
> ① The project was meticulously planned, and so was its execution.
> 這項專案經過精心規劃，執行也是如此。
>
> ☞ 此句等於：The project was meticulously planned, and its execution was, too.
>
> ② Mrs. Lin can cook gourmet meals, and so can her husband.
> 林女士能烹製美味佳餚，她的丈夫也能。
>
> 如果是「否定附和句」，則附和句以 neither 開頭：
>
> ③ He won't compromise on his principles, and neither will his wife.
> 他不會在原則上妥協，他的妻子也不會。
>
> ☞ 此句等於：He won't compromise on his principles, and his wife won't, either.

必備 Point 5

肯定的直述句，後面接**否定**的**附加問句**，反之亦然。而直述句動詞是 be 動詞時，附加問句也得用 be 動詞；直述句動詞是 一般動詞時，附加問句用助動詞 do / does / did；直述句動詞包含助動詞時，附加問句也得用助動詞。最後，注意**前後動詞時態必須一致**。例如：

❶ He is always timid, isn't he?
他總是很孬，不是嗎？

❷ The mediator kept neutral all the way, didn't he?
調解人始終保持中立，是吧？

☞ 附加問句的主詞必須用代名詞。

❸ He can scarcely contain his excitement, can he?
　他幾乎無法抑制自己的興奮，對吧？

　☞ 注意 scarcely 是否定詞，形成否定的直述句，因此附加問句應為肯定。

> **補充**
>
> 關於**祈使句的附加問句**，因為主詞其實就是 you，所以後面的附加問句可以用「will / won't / would / could you?」；另外，**Let's... 開頭的祈使句**，因為是帶有邀請、建議的語氣，後面的附加問句用「..., shall we?」。若主詞是**不定代名詞的「人」**，像是 everyone / someone / everybody / somebody，附加問句的主詞一律用 they 表示。例如：
>
> ❶ Turn on the lamp, could you?
> 　把燈打開，好嗎？
>
> ❷ Let's go swimming this afternoon, shall we?
> 　我們下午一起去游泳，好嗎？
>
> ❸ Somebody has called you, haven't they?
> 　有人打過電話給你了，對吧？

多益會怎麼考？

多益會考在比較級、最高級的句型中填入正確字詞的題目。

1. Jessica is ---------- experienced in project management than any of her colleagues.

   (A) much　　(B) more　　(C) most　　(D) best

   翻譯 Jessica 在專案管理方面比她任何一位同事都更有經驗。

   解析 注意句子後面有 than，就應直接聯想到比較級的用法，所以正確答案是 (B)。

多益會考在倒裝句中填入正確字詞的題目。

2. The company faced significant challenges during the economic downturn, and so ---------- many of its competitors.

   (A) are　　(B) were　　(C) do　　(D) did

   翻譯 該公司在經濟衰退期間面臨了重大的挑戰，許多競爭對手也同樣如此。

   解析 看到空格前面的「..., and so」可知，本題考的是「附和句」，而且是「肯定附和句」，因此在 so 開頭的第二個子句必須倒裝，因為前面用的是過去式，附和句中的動詞應以過去式助動詞 did 表示，因此正確答案是 (D)。

▶ 關鍵概念

本單元將繼續探討與前述三大特殊句型相關的考點，包括「修飾比較級的副詞」、「本身已有比較級／最高級意味的形容詞」、「同範圍／不同範圍比較」、「地方副詞倒裝句」、「as 取代 though 的倒裝句」以及「『S + V + that 子句』的附加問句」。

必備 Point 1　有規則必有例外，這也是考生們必須有的文法概念！副詞雖然可以修飾形容詞，但可以**修飾比較級形容詞的副詞**，卻很有限。常見的有 much、far、a lot、a great deal、even、still、倍數詞等。請見以下例句：

❶ His actions were (still, ~~very~~) more inspiring than his words.
　他的行動比他的言辭更具有激勵作用。

❷ This solution is (~~quite~~, a lot) simpler than the previous one.
　這個解決方案比之前的簡單得多。

❸ The ancient tree in the park is (~~two~~, twice) older than any other in the area.
　公園裡這棵古樹的樹齡是這地區其他樹木的兩倍以上。

必備 Point 2　**沒有比較級**的形容詞：有一些字尾 -ior 的形容詞，不可用於 more / less... than... 的句型中，通常與**介系詞 to** 連用。請見以下例句：

❶ Her performance was clearly (superior to, ~~more superior than~~) that of her peers.
　她的表現明顯比她的同儕更優秀。

❷ He is (~~more junior than~~, junior to) me by three years in this company.
　在這家公司裡，他比我資歷淺三年。

必備 Point 3　**沒有最高級**的形容詞：有一些形容詞本身就有**極致**或**最高級**的意味，不能用於比較句型中，像是 top、perfect、superb、excellent、supreme... 等。請見以下例句：

❶ She is among the (top, ~~toppest~~) candidates in the selection process.
　她是選拔過程中最優秀的候選人之一。

76

❷ He handled the unexpected situation more (efficiently, ~~excellently~~) than John (X).
他處理這突如其來的情況比 John 更出色。

必備 Point 4

同範圍／不同範圍比較句構：

❶ This restaurant is better than any other option among the ones in this neighborhood.
這家餐廳比這個街區中的任何其他選擇都要好。

☞ 這是同範圍（among the ones in this neighborhood）內的比較，這裡的 any other option = all (the) other options = all (the) others。注意 any other 後面接**單數名詞**，all (the) other 後面接**複數名詞**。

❷ New York is probably busier than any city in Europe.
紐約可能比歐洲的任何一個城市都更繁忙。

☞ 這是不同範圍事物（紐約不在歐洲範圍內）的比較，這裡的 any city = all (the) cities = all。注意 any 後面接**單數名詞**，all (the) 後面接**複數名詞**。

必備 Point 5

地方副詞倒裝句構：地方副詞置於句首時，要用「地方副詞（片語）+ 不及物動詞 + 主詞（一般名詞）」的句型。

❶ In the doorway stood a figure cloaked in shadows, waiting silently.
門口站著一個身披陰影的身影，靜靜地等待著。

☞ 此句可還原為「A figure cloaked in shadows stood in the doorway, waiting silently.」。

❷ In the old chest is locked a secret that no one has discovered.
在那個老箱子裡鎖著一個無人發現的秘密。

☞ 此句可還原為「A secret that no one has discovered is locked in the old chest.」。

若**主詞為代名詞**時，句型為「地方副詞（片語）+ 主詞（代名詞）+ 不及物動詞」：

❸ In front of the fireplace they sat. *坐在壁爐前的是他們。*

☞ 此句可還原為「They sat in front of the fireplace.」。

❹ There you go again! *你又來了！*

☞ there 或 here 置於句首，主詞是代名詞 you 時，動詞要擺在主詞後面。

必備 Point 6

as 取代 though 的倒裝句構：在 though 引導的副詞子句中，可將 **be 動詞後面的形容詞或名詞**移至句首，或者如果有**副詞**的話，也可以移至句首，而 though 可以用 as 取代，但不可用 although 取代。

❶ Talented as / though he is, I still find his attitude hard to tolerate.
儘管他很有才華，但我仍然難以忍受他的態度。
☞ 此句可還原為「Though / Although he is talented, I still find his attitude hard to tolerate.」。

❷ A brilliant leader as / though she will be, I still worry about her lack of experience.
儘管她將會成為一位出色的領導者，但我仍然擔心她缺乏經驗。
☞ 此句可還原為「Though / Although she will be a brilliant leader, I still worry…」。

❸ Quickly as / though John responded, I still felt the situation could have been handled better.
儘管約翰回應得很快，但我仍覺得情況本可以處理得更好。
☞ 此句可還原為「Though / Although s John responded quickly, I still felt…」。

必備 Point 7

「代名詞主詞 + V（表達意見或觀點）+ that 子句」的附加問句：若前面敘述句主詞是第一人稱單數的 I，則附加問句的主詞應跟隨 that 子句的主詞；若前面敘述句主詞不是第一人稱單數的 I，則附加問句的主詞應跟隨主要子句主詞 I。

❶ I guess that you've already heard the news, (haven't you, ~~don't I~~)?
我猜你已經聽到這個消息了，對吧？

❷ They thought that the plan would work, didn't they?
他們以為這個計劃會奏效，不是嗎？

多益會怎麼考？

多益會考在修飾比較級的副詞位置填入正確字詞的題目。

1. Isn't this solution ---------- better than the last one?

(A) more　　　(B) very　　　(C) quite　　　(D) even

翻譯 這個解決方案不是比上次的還要更好嗎？

解析 注意空格後面的形容詞是比較級形容詞 better，能夠修飾比較級的只有 even，所以正確答案是 (D)。

多益會考與形容詞搭配的介系詞題目。

2. Do you believe this approach is inferior --------- the previous one?

(A) to　　　　(B) than　　　　(C) from　　　　(D) with

翻譯 你相信這辦法比前一次的還要糟糕嗎？

解析 空格前面的形容詞 inferior（較差的）本身就是個比較級形容詞，與介系詞 to 搭配是固定用語，因此正確答案是 (A)。

▶ TOEIC 實戰演練

Part 5　請在以下四個選項中選出正確的答案

01 He reacted --------- calmly than expected, which made everyone worry about his ability to handle pressure.

(A) much　　　(B) little　　　(C) less　　　(D) more

02 This solution is the most effective --------- the options we've considered.

(A) from　　　(B) of　　　(C) than　　　(D) as

03 Since the promotion, he has been working harder than he ---------.

(A) does　　　(B) did　　　(C) is　　　(D) was

04 The city is much older than --------- I last visited, with historic buildings showing signs of age.

(A) that　　　(B) where　　　(C) when　　　(D) X

05 Never did I --------- to find such tranquility in the heart of the bustling city.

(A) expect　　(B) expected　　(C) is expecting　　(D) will expect

06 --------- by receiving approval are senior members allowed to access the confidential files stored in the archive.

(A) Such　　　(B) So　　　(C) Even　　　(D) Only

07 So dedicated --------- that he often works late into the night without complaint.
(A) he is (B) is he (C) he does (D) does he

08 She values honesty above all, and so --------- everyone on her team.
(A) does (B) is (C) did (D) will

09 The project isn't progressing as planned, and --------- is the budget under control.
(A) so (B) such (C) either (D) neither

10 His decision to leave might hardly be seen as a mistake, might---------?
(A) he (B) him (C) it (D) itself

11 The final performance was --------- more captivating than any of the rehearsals.
(A) highly (B) always (C) pretty (D) still

12 The mountain peak covered in snow, with a clear blue sky above, created the --------- landscape for a postcard.
(A) perfect (B) more perfect (C) most perfect (D) perfectest

13 This diamond is more expensive than any other --------- in the entire collection.
(A) a gem (B) gem (C) gems (D) X

14 In the final assessment --------- a summary of each team's achievements.
(A) included (B) was including (C) was included (D) inclusive

15 Intelligent --------- he is, I still find it hard to trust his decisions completely.
(A) although (B) whether (C) however (D) as

WEEK 09

選出正確句子的題目

▶ 出題模式

必備 Point 1

選出正確句子是多益 Part 6 的題型之一，有點類似學測的「篇章結構」題型。考生必須根據空格的前後句、上下文甚至整篇文章的意旨，在四個「句子選項」中找出一個與前後句**語意連貫、符合文意**的句子。在 Part 6 中的四篇文章中各有 1 題這樣的題型。此題型給你 1 分鐘的時間，其餘 3 個選項加起來也是 1 分鐘，所以通常 Part 6 的 1 個題組要在 2 分鐘內解決掉（總共 8 分鐘解決這個 Part）。

必備 Point 2

空格出現在文章開頭、中間位置或是最後一句。若是在文章開頭，通常是表達這段文章的主旨或目的；若是在文章中，則必須考慮這個句子放進去之後，與其前後文的連接關係；若是在文章最後一句，很可能是內容的總結、強調、附加或衍生說明。每一題會有四個選項，每個選項都是一個**完整句子或子句**。請見以下範例（正確答案以顏色標示）：

文章開頭

> --------- It reinforces desirable actions and encourages continued effort. However, effective praise is specific and genuine, highlighting exactly what the child did well. This approach reinforces self-esteem and motivation, shaping their behavior positively. Moreover, consistency in praise cultivates a supportive environment where children feel valued and encouraged to exhibit good behavior consistently.

Q. (A) Exploring diverse hobbies fosters creativity and expands one's horizons.
(B) Praising people sometimes leads to defensiveness and resentment.
(C) Blaming children too often undermines their confidence and sense of security.
(D) Praising a child's positive behavior is pivotal in fostering their development.

文章中間

> Praising a child's positive behavior is pivotal in fostering their development. --------- However, effective praise is specific and genuine, highlighting exactly what the child did well. This approach reinforces self-esteem and motivation, shaping their behavior positively. Moreover, consistency in praise cultivates a supportive environment where children feel valued and encouraged to exhibit good behavior consistently.

Q. (A) Undeniably, pointing fingers at children is at times necessary.
(B) Praising a child sometimes leads to defensiveness and resentment.
(C) It reinforces desirable actions and encourages continued effort.
(D) It cultivates a wide range of personal interests as well.

文章結尾

> Praising a child's positive behavior is pivotal in fostering their development. It reinforces desirable actions and encourages continued effort. However, effective praise is specific and genuine, highlighting exactly what the child did well. This approach reinforces self-esteem and motivation, shaping their behavior positively. Moreover, consistency in praise cultivates a supportive environment where ---------.

Q. (A) their efforts may not be acknowledged or appreciated
(B) children feel valued and encouraged to exhibit good behavior consistently
(C) they probably feel discouraged in pursuing their goals
(D) their various passions help them cultivate more skills

▶ 解題步驟

解題 Step 1 — 先不看選項，只看空格前後句子，推測空格可能出現的內容。

了解要填入的句子與其前後文的連接關係，非常重要。如果從空格前後部分無法推測可能的內容，再往下多看一些內容。例如：

> Praising a child's positive behavior is pivotal in fostering their development. --------- However, effective praise should be specific and genuine, highlighting exactly what the child did well. This approach not only reinforces their self-esteem and motivation but also shapes their behavior positively. Moreover, consistency in praise cultivates a supportive environment where children feel valued and encouraged to exhibit good behavior consistently.

(A) Undeniably, pointing fingers at children is at times necessary.
(B) Praising a child sometimes leads to their defensiveness and resentment.
(C) It reinforces desirable actions and encourages continued effort.
(D) This can cultivate a wide range of personal interests as well.

☞ 空格前面是「Praising a child's positive behavior is pivotal in fostering their development.（稱讚孩子的正面行為對於促進他們的成長非常重要。）」後面是「However, effective praise is specific and genuine（不過，有效的稱讚應是具體且真誠的）」。因此我們可以斷定，第一句和空格這句，一定都與「稱讚孩子的好處」有關，後面才可以接 However, ... 這句轉折語。

解題 Step 2　閱讀選項，刪除選項中與空格前後不連貫的句子。所謂「前後不連貫」，也許是倒果為因、也許是背離文章要旨、邏輯錯誤…等。另外，選項中也許會有某字詞可對應文章中某字詞，但這不一定是可以優先考慮的選項，因為這是考題常見的陷阱。以下是四個選項的中譯：

(A) 無可否認，有時候責罵孩子是必要的。
(B) 稱讚孩子有時會讓孩子產生防禦心及心生不悅。
(C) 此舉強化了他們良好的行為，並鼓勵他們繼續努力。
(D) 這也可以培養他們各種個人興趣。

☞ 選項 (A) 的「無可否認，有時候責罵孩子是必要的。」與「稱讚孩子」的主題不符，所以可直接刪除；選項 (B) 的「稱讚孩子有時會讓孩子產生防禦心及心生不悅。」雖然提到稱讚孩子，但卻與本段文章「稱讚孩子的好處」意旨不符，當然也錯誤。選項 (C) 的「此舉強化了他們良好的行為，並鼓勵他們繼續努力。」算是對於前一句的補充說明；選項 (D) 提到可以培養個人興趣，但這跟「稱讚孩子」搭不上關係。所以看起來，選項 (C) 與前後句較為連貫。

解題 Step 3 ：**將選擇的答案填入空格，檢查是否能與前後／上下文通順連結。**
若選項中有代名詞、指示代名詞或連接性副詞等，應確認是否與前後句吻合。

☞ 選定正確答案為 (C) It reinforces desirable actions and encourages continued effort. 之後，可進一步確認指示代名詞 It 指的是不是「Praising a child's positive behavior」這件事：「稱讚孩子的正面行為」強化了他們良好的行為，並鼓勵他們繼續努力。若有時間的話，可以整體檢視一下整個段落：

中譯

> 稱讚孩子的正面行為對於促進他們的成長非常重要。稱讚孩子的正面行為強化了他們良好的行為，並鼓勵他們繼續努力。不過，有效的稱讚應是具體且真誠的，此舉可明確突顯孩子做得好的地方。這方式不僅增強孩子的自尊和動力，也塑造出他們正面的行為。此外，持續不斷地給予稱讚，這在培養一個支持性的環境中非常重要，在這環境中孩子會感受到被重視，並且持續展現良好的行為。

補充

常見重要的連接性副詞

區分	連接性副詞
相反	however, on the contrary, on the other hand, in contrast, nevertheless(= nonetheless), but, yet, even so
順序	first/second/third, next, then, afterwards, previously, finally, at present
因果關係	therefore, thus, as a result, consequently
結論，摘要	in short, in summary, in conclusion
比較	likewise, similarly
此外，更多說明	in addition, additionally, besides, also, furthermore, moreover
舉例	for example, for instance

多益會怎麼考？

多益會考以刪去法移除錯誤選項的題目：將選出的句子，與空格前的句子及空格後的句子連接看是否通順。

Dear Mr. William,
Next month, our current CEO and founder, Ken Gates, will be retiring. Replacing him will be Jane Roberts, who has been with our company for over 15 years and has served as Chief Operating Officer for the past five years. Jane brings a wealth of experience and a proven track record of leadership, and we are confident that she will continue to drive our company's success. ---------- We appreciate your continued support and look forward to this new chapter in our company's journey.

(A) It's a pity that she is about to be transferred to an overseas company.
(B) We sincerely wish her a wonderful retirement.
(C) We believe you will be more than capable of handling this new position.
(D) Ken will remain available to assist during the transition period to ensure a smooth handover.

翻譯 親愛的威廉先生：
下個月，我們的現任 CEO 兼創辦人 Ken Gates 將會退休。他的接任者將是 Jane Roberts，她在我們公司已服務超過 15 年，並且在過去五年擔任首席營運長。Jane 擁有豐富的經驗和卓越的領導記錄，我們相信她將繼續推動公司取得成功。----------我們感謝您一如既往的支持，並期待公司新的發展篇章。
(A) 只是可惜她就要調派至海外公司了。
(B) 我們誠摯祝福她即將擁有美好的退休生活。
(C) 相信您一定能夠勝任這個新的職位。
(D) Ken 會在過渡期間提供協助，以確保順利交接。

解析 空格前面提到擁有豐富的經驗和卓越的領導記錄，且相信她將繼續推動公司取得成功（Jane brings a wealth of experience... she will continue to drive our company's success.），後面這句則是對於受文者（公司的一位員工）的感謝與期待，並對公司未來抱以樂觀的期許。選項 (A) 說 Jane 要調派至海外公司，以及選項 (B) 的祝福她即將擁有美好的退休生活，顯然皆與「即將接任 CEO 的 Jane」這段敘述相矛盾；同樣，即將接任新職位（CEO）的是 Jane，而非這封信的受文者（you），所以選項 (C) 也明顯錯誤。那麼正確答案當然就是 (D) 了。

多益會考以指示代名詞為破題關鍵的題目：空格句後面若有 this、that、these、those、it、them 等，從選項句子中找出其指稱對象的句子。

---------- They include stricter deadlines and enhanced performance evaluations. The adjustments aim to boost productivity and ensure a higher standard of work across all departments.

(A) All employees should comply with this regulation.
(B) All other employees are expected to adhere to the new policy changes.
(C) The performance evaluation system is now in place.
(D) The quality of the office environment is very important.

翻譯 --------- 它們包括更嚴格的截止日期和更先進的績效評估。這些調整旨在提高生產力，並確保各部門的工作品質達到更高標準。
(A) 所有員工都應遵守這項規定。
(B) 所有其他員工預計都將遵守這些新的政策變更。
(C) 這項績效評估系統已就緒。
(D) 辦公室環境好壞與否相當重要。

解析 空格後面是代名詞 They 開頭，這是本題的關鍵點！接著要思考的是，They 到底指什麼？後面句子告訴我們「這些調整旨在提高生產力…（The adjustments aim to boost productivity...）」，所以與「這些調整」相關！且 They 不會是指單數的「this regulation」或「The performance evaluation system」，所以當然是指複數的「the new policy changes」（changes 對應後面的 adjustments），故正確答案是 (B)。至於 (D) 的敘述完全不相關，是當然的錯誤選項。

多益會考以連接性副詞作為線索的題目：空格句後面若有連接性副詞，應據此選出有對應或連接關係的句子。

The hotel service exceeded expectations with its prompt and courteous staff. ---------- Additionally, many online reviews said that its rooms were impeccably clean and well-stocked with amenities, creating a comfortable stay.

(A) Every guest felt welcomed and cared for.
(B) Some facilities are currently under repair.
(C) It is expected to celebrate its first anniversary next Sunday.
(D) Only a few guests have complained that there's not enough parking space.

翻譯 這間飯店的服務超出了預期，員工動作迅速且有禮。--------- 此外，許多網路評論指出，其客房一塵不染，且設備齊全，營造出舒適的入住體驗。
(A) 每位賓客都有賓至如歸的感覺。
(B) 目前一些設施還在修繕中。
(C) 它預計下週日慶祝其開幕一週年。
(D) 只是有少數賓客抱怨停車場太小。

解析 空格前句子的意思是「這間飯店的服務超出了預期，員工動作迅速且有禮」，後面句子則是以 Additionally（此外）開頭，繼續表示「許多網路評論指出，其客房間一塵不染，且…」。可想而知，空格這句一定與良好的飯店服務有關，且與其後面的「客房一塵不染，設備齊全…」構成這家飯店優勢或正面的敘述，所以正確答案是 (A)。

86

▶ TOEIC 實戰演練

Part 6 請在以下四個選項中選出正確的答案

Questions 1-4 refer to the following advertisement.

Explore Infinite Possibilities: Exclusive Magazine Subscription Offer! —1— a world of knowledge and inspiration with our exclusive magazine subscription offer! Dive into captivating articles on diverse topics —2— travel, fashion, health, and technology. Whether you're a trendsetter or a wellness enthusiast, our curated content is tailored just for you. Stay ahead with the latest trends, expert advice, and stunning visuals —3— straight to your doorstep every month. Subscribe now and embark on a journey of discovery and enrichment. Join our community of readers who trust us to deliver quality insights and entertainment. Don't miss out – —4—!

01 (A) Unlock
    (B) To unlock
    (C) Unlocking
    (D) Unlocked

02 (A) so that
    (B) but for
    (C) such as
    (D) at least

03 (A) delivering
    (B) delivered
    (C) to deliver
    (D) delivery

04 (A) our exclusive magazine will soon be launched
    (B) Enjoy this car magazine to your heart's content
    (C) we only accept credit card subscriptions
    (D) subscribe today and start exploring your passions

Questions 5-8 refer to the following letter.

To all staff members,

 We are going to introduce a new performance evaluation process next quarter. This —1— is designed to provide more comprehensive feedback and identify strengths and areas for improvement. We will conduct workshops to familiarize you —2— the new criteria and evaluation methods. —3— Let's work together to create a more transparent and supportive environment, enhancing our —4— growth and success. Thank you for your commitment and enthusiasm.

05 (A) category
  (B) disposal
  (C) heavyweight
  (D) initiative

06 (A) to
  (B) with
  (C) for
  (D) from

07 (A) The assessment of academic performance should include students' overall development.
  (B) The company will formulate a salary incentive plan based on employees' performance.
  (C) Your active involvement is crucial for the success of this transition.
  (D) A reasonable performance incentive system helps improve the overall performance of the team.

08 (A) individual
  (B) respective
  (C) miraculous
  (D) collective

Questions 9-12 refer to the following memo.

To: All Team Members
From: Project Management Office
Date: August 8, 2024
Subject: Project Deadline Update

Please —9— aware that the deadline for the Bergeron project has been moved up to September 1, 2024, due to client requirements. All teams are expected to adjust their schedules —10—, and prioritize any outstanding tasks. We understand this change may create additional pressure, but your cooperation is essential to —11— our client's expectations. —12— Please reach out with any concerns or resource needs.

Best regards,
Project Management Office

09 (A) make
(B) know
(C) do
(D) be

10 (A) technically
(B) accordingly
(C) respectively
(D) unknowingly

11 (A) meet
(B) beat
(C) gather
(D) connect

12 (A) Don't be discouraged by the delay in the project schedule.
(B) Please stick to your original work plan and keep up the good work.
(C) We are confident you can always deliver high-quality results.
(D) I hope you will be optimistic about the loss of clients.

WEEK 10 信件／電子郵件的題目

▶ 出題模式

必備 Point 1

信件與電子郵件是多益 Part 7 的必出的文章類型之一，最常考的內容大多與**公司營運或業務**、公司同事或不同公司**員工之間相關工作事項**、**場所設施或設備**、對於公司服務**表達不滿／道歉／稱讚／感謝**，或針對**服務**的問答、**通知**求職者獲得錄用、通知面試時間…等內容有關。

必備 Point 2

最常出現的問題類型：**尋找主題／目的**的問題、**附帶**問題、**5W1H 疑問詞**問題、**Not/True** 問題、**推論**問題、**放入句子**問題及**同義字詞**問題。例如：

❶ 詢問主旨／目的。例如：

① What is the purpose of the letter/email?

② Why was the email sent?

③ Why was the letter written?

❷ 有何附帶之物。例如：

① What is enclosed/included with this email?

② What was sent with this letter?

❸ 5W1H 疑問詞開頭的問題。可能詢問提議、請求、何時、何處、何人、用什麼方法…等**細節事項**。例如：

① What is Mr. Smith asked to do?

② Where did Ms. Anderson visit her grandparents in March?

③ Why has Ms. Hefner asked Mr. Voorhies to sign a document?

④ How can visitors register for a class?

⑤ Who most likely is Mr. Smith?

⑥ For whom is the email most likely intended?

❹ Not/True 問題。這類題型即所謂「**何者正確**」與「**何者為非**」，通常選項中的句子會比長，且往往必須讀完每一個選項，再一一到郵件中找尋線索。解題也會比較費時，是比較令人頭痛的題目。

題目可能問各選項內容對於電子郵件／信件中提到的人事物或其他特定對象的敘述是否正確或錯誤。通常題目句中會有 true、stated、mentioned、indicated 或 suggested 等字眼，而如果是 indicated 的題目，篇章內容中會有比較明確的答案線索，如果是 suggested 的題目，篇章內容中指會間接指出答案線索。例如：

① What is NOT stated in this letter?

② What is indicated about Mr. Smith?

③ What is suggested about Ms. Roberts?

④ Based on the email, what is true about...?

❺ **推論問題**。針對信件內容中提到的人、公司、特定事項等，詢問可以推論得知的事情，答案線索可能出現在信件中任何部分。例如：

① What is one action Mr. Smith is NOT thought to take?

② What brand did Mr. Smith most likely receive?

③ Which instructor is teaching a new course?

❻ **放入句子問題**。這類題目是在文章以外加入一個句子，要求考生藉由上下文脈絡來推導出該句應置於文章中的何處。由於標號的填空處分散於整篇文章之中，若未看過整篇文章便難以作答，因此解題也較為費時。通常題目會這麼問：

In which of the positions marked [1], [2], [3], and [4] does the following sentence best belong?

"............................."

❼ **同義字詞的題型**。從信件中特定單字，找出 4 個選項中意思最接近的詞彙。這個題型會用「The word "..." in paragraph X, line X, is closest in meaning to」的句型來問。

多益會怎麼考？

多益會考答案線索就在電子郵件主旨上的問題：

To:	Mr. Smith
From:	Jane Doe
Date:	August 12, 2024
Subject:	Upcoming Business Seminar Invitation

Dear Mr. Smith,
....
(中略)
Please let us know if you can attend. We look forward to your participation.

Question. **What was Mr. Smith invited to do?**
(A) Host a seminar
(B) Provide practical guidance
(C) Attend an activity
(D) Offer financial advisory services

翻譯

收件人：史密斯先生
寄件人：珍‧多伊
日期：2024 年 8 月 12 日
主旨：即將舉行的商業研討會邀請函

史密斯先生 您好：
....
（中略）

請告知我們您是否能夠參加。我們期待您的參與。

問題：**史密斯先生被邀請做什麼？**
(A) 主持一場研討會
(B) 提供實用的指導
(C) 參加一場活動
(D) 提供財務諮詢服務

解析 電子郵件常見的題型之一就是「請求（或邀請）」。題目詢問「Mr. Smith 被邀請做什麼」，Jane Doe 是這封信的寄件人，而 Mr. Smith 是這封信的收件人，因此應於信件內容中找尋與「邀請去做某事」相關的內容。從信件主旨（subject）「Upcoming Business Seminar Invitation」即可看出，「邀請」的事項就是去參加一場即將舉行的商業研討會，而且從本篇章最後的「Please let us know if you can attend. We look forward to your participation.」也可以看出，正確答案應為 (C)。

多益會考針對電子郵件（或信件）中提到的人、公司或其他特定對象，對照四個選項的敘述，選出何者正確或錯誤的題目：

I am writing to inform you that our company is hosting a business seminar on September 15, 2024. The seminar will focus on the latest trends in digital marketing and strategies to enhance business growth.

We have invited industry experts to share their insights and offer practical advice on how to implement these strategies in your business. The event will also provide networking opportunities with professionals from various industries.

The seminar will be held at the Grand Hotel Conference Center from 9:00 AM to 4:00 PM. We believe this will be an excellent opportunity for you and your team to gain valuable knowledge and make meaningful connections.

Question. **What is indicated about the invitation?**

(A) The seminar is designed to introduce a new product line.

(B) Invited experts will be asked to lead workshops on financial planning.

(C) It will also offer chances to communicate with professionals across different industries.

(D) Attendees are anticipated to present their own business strategies during the event.

翻譯 我寫這封信是為了通知您，我們公司將於 2024 年 9 月 15 日舉辦一場商業研討會。這次研討會將聚焦於數位行銷的最新趨勢以及提升業務增長的策略。我們邀請了業界專家來分享他們的見解，並提供實用的建議，幫助您將這些策略應用於您的業務中。這次活動還將提供與各行業專業人士交流的機會。

研討會將於上午 9:00 至下午 4:00 在大飯店會議中心舉行。我們相信，這將是您和您的團隊獲得寶貴知識並建立重要聯繫的絕佳機會。

問題：**關於這份邀請函，有指出了什麼？**
(A) 這場研討會旨在介紹一個新的產品線。
(B) 受邀的專家將被要求主持有關財務規劃的工作坊。
(C) 它還將提供與各行業專業人士交流的機會。
(D) 參加者預計會在活動中展示他們自己的商業策略。

解析 (A) 的敘述是錯誤的，因為 Email 中提到的研討會是聚焦於數位行銷的最新趨勢和提升業務增長的策略（The seminar will focus on the latest trends in digital marketing and strategies to enhance business growth.），而非介紹新的產品線。(B) 的敘述是錯誤的，因為 Email 中提到的專家是來分享見解並提供實用的建議（share their insights and offer practical advice on how to implement these strategies）。選項 (C) 是正確的，因為研討會的確會提供與來自不同產業的專業人士進行交流的機會（networking opportunities），這是 email 中明確提到的重點之一。(D) 的敘述是錯誤的，因為參加者只是受邀參與，並期待能夠獲得一些商業利益，並沒有要求他們在活動中展示商業策略。

▶ 實用策略

必備 Point 1

「電子郵件／信件」的「**詢問主旨／目的**」的題目，比起其他類型短文通常比較容易掌握，因為可以直接在上方「Subject: ...」找到線索。如果信件內容沒有提供這部分，那麼就注意**本文開頭第一句**（通常是 I am writing to...）。接著，注意替換表達方式。例如：（本文）I am writing to introduce our new professor of art history, Dr. Rosalind Furness, to you all. →（選項）To introduce a new staff member

必備 Point 2

詢問「**有何附帶之物**」的題目通常會有 enclosed、included 或是 sent with... 等字眼，可以在內容中找尋關鍵字詞即可輕易找到答案線索。例如：（本文）Enclosed you will find a document of anticipated expenses, which... →（選項）A price estimate

必備 Point 3

對於 **5W1H 疑問詞開頭**的問題，應先確認疑問詞再找出關鍵語句。例如「What will happen after August 2?」的疑問詞是 What，關鍵語句則是 August 2。在以下範例中，請注意文本與題目中，底線與套色部分的關係：

> ... All staff members are encouraged to contribute by placing their donated gifts in the designated containers located in each department. ...
>
> Question. Where can staff members leave their donations?
> (A) At the human resource department
> (B) At the charity's office
> (C) In labeled containers
> (D) On Ms. Malloy's desk

必備 Point 4

「**Not/True 問題**」要從 4 個選項中，選擇符合或不符合文本內容的答案，必須**先確認題目的關鍵詞或語句**。例如，以「What is NOT indicated about the new staff members?」這問題句來說，關鍵語句就是「the new staff members」。在以下範例中，請注意信件內容與題目中，底線與套色部分的關係：

The company has recently hired several new employees across various departments, including marketing, sales, and customer support. The new employees bring diverse skills and professional experiences that align well with the company's growth strategies. Each new hire has undergone an extensive orientation program designed to ensure they understand both the company's core values and operational procedures. In addition to enhancing productivity, the new team members are expected to improve cross-departmental cooperation. As they settle into their roles, they will also receive ongoing training tailored to their specific job functions. The company is optimistic that these new hires will contribute significantly to upcoming projects and help strengthen customer relationships.

Question. What is NOT indicated about the new staff members?
(A) The new staff members have completed an onboarding session.
(B) They are expected to improve collaboration between departments.
(C) They will need to receive specific training for their job functions.
(D) They were hired for the same department.

請注意，即使題目選項與信件內容敘述一致，通常不會寫得一模一樣讓考生一下就對上，因此**替換表達**（paraphrasing）的訓練就很重要了！例如這裡的「completed an onboarding session → undergone an extensive orientation program」。

必備 Point 5

「**推論問題**」的題型：因為題目要你「推論」，想必選項的敘述內容不會直接、明顯地寫在信件中。這類問題通常包含如 most likely、suggested、implied、probably 等字眼。在以下範例中，請注意信件內容與題目中，底線與套色部分的關係：

Destination Traveler, the premier publication in travel and tourism, has unveiled its yearly list of the world's finest luxury hotels. The rankings are determined by customer feedback, input from tour agents, and reviews from critics.

Who was NOT involved in determining ratings?
(A) Lodging visitors   (B) Travel organizers
(C) Amenity evaluators   (D) Booking agents

必備 Point 6

針對「**放入句子問題**」的題型」，先掌握信件內容架構，接著抓到這個句子的關鍵字詞，最後找出其最適當的擺放位置。請見以下範例：

> Thank you for your email. — [1] — You have requested time off from February 13-17 to attend a family wedding out of town. — [2] — However, please keep in mind that your supervisor, Michael Conners, also needs to approve this request. — [3] — I will inform you as soon as I receive his confirmation regarding your leave. — [4] — If anything changes in the meantime, please inform me immediately so that I can stay updated on the situation. Feel free to reach out if you have any questions or concerns.
>
> In which of the positions marked [1], [2], [3], and [4] does the following sentence best belong?
> "This is acceptable to the administration, as you still have 7 vacation days available."
> (A) [1]　　(B) [2]　　(C) [3]　　(D) [4]

句子裡的關鍵字詞應是：「acceptable to the administration」以及 .「vacation days available」然後試著去尋找信件中和此關鍵字詞有關的內容所在處：「...requested time off from February 13-17...」 以及「...your supervisor, Michael Conners, also needs to approve this request」，最後試著在對應的空格位置 [2] 填入句子，檢查是否語意通順連貫。

必備 Point 7

「**同義字詞**」題型：首先，從題目所指示的第幾段、第幾行找出 The word 後面引號中的字彙。接著閱讀包含這個單字的句子，掌握單字在文章脈絡中的意義。最後，選出最符合單字在文中意義的答案。

多益會怎麼考？

多益單篇文章的電子郵件（或信件）中，常考「放入句子」的題目：

> I am writing to inform you that our company is hosting a business seminar on September 15, 2024. The seminar will focus on the latest trends in digital marketing and strategies to enhance business growth. ----[1]----

We have invited industry experts to share their insights and offer practical advice on how to implement these strategies in your business. ----[2]---- The event will also provide networking opportunities with professionals from various industries.

The seminar will be held at the Grand Hotel Conference Center from 9:00 AM to 4:00 PM. ----[3]---- We believe this will be an excellent opportunity for you and your team to gain valuable knowledge and make meaningful connections. ----[4]----

Please let us know if you can attend. We look forward to your participation.

Question. In which of the positions marked [1], [2], [3], and [4] does the following sentence best belong?
"During the seminar, attendees will have the chance to participate in interactive sessions and panel discussions."
(A) [1]
(B) [2]
(C) [3]
(D) [4]

翻譯 我寫這封信是為了通知您，我們公司將於 2024 年 9 月 15 日舉辦一場商業研討會。這次研討會將聚焦於數位行銷的最新趨勢以及提升業務增長的策略。

我們邀請了業界專家來分享他們的見解，並提供實用的建議，幫助您將這些策略應用於您的業務中。這次活動還將提供與各行業專業人士交流的機會。

研討會將於上午 9:00 至下午 4:00 在大飯店會議中心舉行。我們相信，這將是您和您的團隊獲得寶貴知識並建立重要聯繫的絕佳機會。

請告知我們您是否能夠參加。我們期待您的參與。

問題：以下句子最適合放在哪個位置 [1]、[2]、[3] 和 [4] ？
「在研討會期間，與會者將有機會加入互動交流及小組討論。」

解析 這句話與「研討會將於上午 9:00 至下午 4:00 在大飯店會議中心舉行。（The seminar will be held at the Grand Hotel Conference Center from 9:00 AM to 4:00 PM.）」相連接，自然地介紹了研討會的具體安排。這裡提到的「互動交流及小組討論」是研討會的具體活動，符合在時間和地點之後介紹活動內容的邏輯。而接下來的句子：「我們相信，這將是您和您的團隊獲得寶貴知識並建立重要聯繫的絕佳機會。（We believe this will be an excellent opportunity for you and your team to gain valuable knowledge and make meaningful connections.）」進一步強調了參與這些互動環節的價值，因此這句話放在 [3] 位置能夠順暢、合理地銜接前後內容。

▶ TOEIC 實戰演練

Part 7　請在以下四個選項中選出正確的答案

Questions 1-2 refer to the following e-mail.

To:	Lars Andersson <landersson@ghjfinance.com>
FROM:	Oliver Grayson <ograyson@ghjfinance.com>
SUBJECT:	Hardware enhancements
DATE:	Sept. 13

Dear Mr. Andersson,
I understand that company policy dictates upgrading all computers every five years. This might sound reasonable a decade ago, but actually advancements in computer speeds these days have slowed significantly. Our current software is performing well, so upgrading the hardware doesn't seem essential at this point.

I've heard that you'll be making a decision on this matter the day after tomorrow, so I hope this email reaches you in time. If there's still room in the budget, purchasing some new office chairs might be a good idea. Office Oasis is having a sale from September 17 to 23, providing a great chance to get a good deal.

Oliver Grayson

01　What is the purpose of the e-mail?

　　(A) To remind someone of an update
　　(B) To advise against making a purchase
　　(C) To notify someone of a policy change
　　(D) To ask for more information

02　When is Mr. Andersson expected to make a decision?

　　(A) On September 13
　　(B) On September 14
　　(C) On September 15
　　(D) On September 17

Questions 3-5 refer to the following letter.

Harrison & Co.
123 Pioneer Avenue
Nampa, Idaho 83686

July 10
Ethan Harper
23 Maple Street
Linden, Idaho 74562

Dear Mr. Harper,

    Congratulations! I am delighted to let you know that Harrison & Co. would like to offer you the role of Senior Operations Manager for the state of Idaho. Beginning July 24, you will oversee the coordination of activities at our processing facilities throughout the state. The current SOM, Sam Reynolds, will provide you with the necessary training.

    Enclosed, you will find a copy of your contract. Please review the details and sign the documents if you decide to accept the position. Return the signed contracts to Casey Evans in our HR department. Once Ms. Evans receives the contract, she will assist you with the arrangements for your relocation to Nampa.

    Finally, I would like to extend an invitation to you and your wife, Andrea Harper, to attend our annual executives' reception at the Firenze Hotel on the evening of Friday, July 21. Please let me know if you will be able to join us.

    I look forward to your response.

Sincerely,
Jacob Sullivan
CEO
Harrison & Co.

03 What is the purpose of the letter?

(A) To ask friends over for a meal
(B) To extend a job offer
(C) To arrange a meeting
(D) To plan a series of events

04 What is Mr. Harper asked to do?

(A) Review an operations guide
(B) Participate in a training workshop
(C) Submit documents to the HR department
(D) Deliver a speech at an event

05 Who will help Mr. Harper with relocating arrangements?

(A) Jacob Sullivan
(B) Sam Reynolds
(C) Andrea Harper
(D) Casey Evans

Questions 6-9 refer to the following email.

To:	Technical Support <techsupport@intellnet.com>
From:	Emily Johnson <emily.johnson@mailman.com>
Date:	August 18
Subject:	Technical Malfunction

To whom it may concern,

I am writing in regard to a technical malfunction I have experienced with Affinity Designer. — [1] — The issue began on August 15, 2024, at approximately 10:00 AM and has significantly disrupted my workflow. Despite multiple attempts to troubleshoot, including restarting the software, clearing the cache, and reinstalling it, the problem persists. — [2] — This malfunction has rendered the reporting and data export functions unusable, which is particularly concerning as it directly affects my ability to meet an upcoming project deadline. — [3] —

I kindly request your urgent assistance in resolving this matter. Please advise on the next steps or provide any necessary support to rectify the issue. If further information is needed, I am happy to provide it. — [4] — I look forward to your swift resolution.

Best regards,
Emily Johnson

06 What was the purpose of the email?

   (A) To request an update on software
   (B) To inquire about some new features
   (C) To complain about software
   (D) To seek assistance with setting up software

07 Which solution has Ms. Johnson not tried?

   (A) Reconnecting to the Internet
   (B) Restarting the software
   (C) Performing a reinstallation
   (D) Emptying the cache

08 The word "rectify" in paragraph 2, line 12, is closest in meaning to

   (A) amplify
   (B) solve
   (C) adjust
   (D) simplify

09 In which of the positions marked [1], [2], [3], and [4] does the following sentence best belong?
   "I even checked for software updates, but there were none available to handle the issue."

   (A) [1]
   (B) [2]
   (C) [3]
   (D) [4]

WEEK 11 訊息對話的題目

▶ 出題模式

必備 Point 1

在 TOEIC 的 PART 7 中，**訊息對話**通常會佔兩個題組。第 1 個對話題組會出 2 道題，通常是 2 名對話者；第 2 個對話題組會出 4 道題，參與對話者會有 3~4 人。透過手機或電腦通訊軟體彼此溝通、討論工作或業務上的問題，因為是對話的性質，原則上較容易理解，故**應先掌握對話的主旨**，以及**參與對話者之間的關係**。

必備 Point 2

最常出現的問題類型：兩個題組各有 1 題是**掌握意圖**的問題，其餘可能是**尋找主題**、**5W1H** 問題、**Not/True** 問題或者**推論**問題。例如：

❶ **掌握意圖**：詢問對話中某人說的話所指為何。通常你會看到題目這麼問：
At + 幾點幾分, what does + 某人 + mean when he/she writes, "..."?

❷ **尋找主題**的問題：可能詢問整個對話的主旨或對話參與者參與討論的目的。例如：
① Why did Mr. Smith contact Ms. Cooper?
② What is the topic of the text message chain?

❸ **5W1H 疑問詞的問題**：可能詢問對話者的要求事項或其他細節的問題。例如：
① When will the technician come to complete a repair?
② What happened on September 6?
③ Why is production delayed?
④ Who most likely is Mr. Smith?

❹ **Not/True 問題**：詢問各選項的敘述，對照對話中提到的人事物之敘述，何者正確或錯誤。例如：
① What is NOT mentioned about the seminar?
② What is indicated about Mr. Roberts?

❺ **推論問題**：針對參與對話的人，或提及的活動或相關內容，詢問可以「間接得知」事情。這類題型會比其他題型難度高一些，因為答題線索往往不會直接出現在對話的內容中。題目中通常會有 suggested、implied、inferred、most likely、probably…等字眼。例如：

① For whom is the invitation most likely intended?

② What will Mr. Smith probably do next?

③ What can be inferred about Mr. Smith?

多益會怎麼考？

多益會考對話中某人說的一段話是什麼意思的問題：

James Parker　　　　　　　　　　　　　　　　　2:29 P.M.
We're set to start shipping the computers to outlets at the beginning of next month. Do you think we can meet that deadline?

Emma Davis　　　　　　　　　　　　　　　　　2:31 P.M.
It's out of the question, considering the current situation.

Question. At 2:31 P.M., what does Ms. Cohen mean when she writes, "It's out of the question"?
(A) She believes the production volume of a certain product is sufficient.
(B) She doesn't think that a product set to launch soon will sell well.
(C) She doesn't believe that a certain department has enough staff to complete the task on time.
(D) She thinks it's possible for the computers to ship on the scheduled date.

翻譯　詹姆斯・帕克　　　　　　　　　　　　　　　　下午 2:29
我們計劃在下個月初開始將電腦出貨到各銷售點。你認為我們能趕上這個期限嗎？
　　　艾瑪・戴維斯　　　　　　　　　　　　　　　　下午 2:31
以目前的情況來看，這是不可能的。

問題：在下午 2:31 時，柯恩女士表示「這是不可能的」，她的意思是什麼？
(A) 她認為某產品的產量嚴重不足。
(B) 她不認為近日要上市的某產品會賣得很好。
(C) 她不認為某部門有足夠的人力可以按時完成任務。
(D) 她認為電腦可能在計劃中的日期出貨。

解析 題目問的是柯恩女士所言的意圖，應確認提及問題的引用語句 (It's out of the question) 前後文意。前一句中 James Parker 提到「下個月初開始將電腦出貨到各銷售點。你認為我們能趕上這個期限嗎？」然後 Davis 回答了「It's out of the question（這是不可能的）」，顯然她不認為電腦會按照計劃中的日期出貨，而人力不足可能是個原因，故正確答案是 (C) She doesn't believe that a certain department has enough staff to complete the task on time.。

多益考題會詢問訊息對話中特定人物的職業或工作地點：

Sophia Bennett　　　　　　　　　　　　　　　　　　　　　　[2:01 P.M.]
As you all probably heard in the Monday announcement, the board has decided to open the Erik Masterson art exhibit next month. This will be a significant event for us.

Michael Grant　　　　　　　　　　　　　　　　　　　　　　[2:04 P.M.]
I've completed the custom invitation designs for all attendees from our previous exhibit. However, there's something we need to discuss...

Question. What type of establishment is Ms. Bennett most likely employed in?
(A) An art gallery
(B) A nearby university
(C) A marketing and advertising agency
(D) A company specializing in printing

翻譯 蘇菲亞‧班奈特　　　　　　　　　　　　　　　　　　　　　　[下午 2:01]
如大家在週一的公告中所聽到的，董事會已決定艾瑞克‧馬斯特森的藝術展於下個月開幕。這將會是我們的一項重要活動。

麥可‧葛蘭特　　　　　　　　　　　　　　　　　　　　　　[下午 2:04]
我已為所有參加過我們上一場展覽的來賓，設計了客製化邀請卡。不過，有些事情我們還需要討論……

問題：班奈特女士最有可能在哪種類型的機構工作？
(A) 藝術畫廊　　　　(B) 當地大學　　　　(C) 行銷與廣告公司　　　　(D) 專業印刷公司

解析 這是針對問題核心語句 (Ms. Bennett ~ work for) 的推論問題。Ms. Bennett 提到，董事會已決定艾瑞克‧馬斯特森的藝術展於下個月開幕 (the board has decided to open the Erik Masterson art exhibit)，她並且告訴大家這將會是他們公司一項重要活動，接著 Michael Grant 說，他已為所有參加過前一場展覽的來賓，設計了客製化邀請卡 (the custom invitation designs for all attendees from...)，因此可推論 Sophia Bennett 在舉辦美術展覽的畫廊工作，所以正確答案是 (A)。

▶ 實用策略

必備 Point 1

「文字訊息／線上對談」的「**掌握意圖**」題型，是針對發言者在某個時間點說出的某一句話或一句話的某個部分，其代表的真正的意義，自然不會讓你可以直接從字面去理解，必須回到對話中，找到該句的位置，了解說話者是在什麼樣的脈絡之下說出這句話。此外，通常該句話或字詞都是日常口語中常聽到的，可能是慣用語，故應趁此機會學起來。例如：

❶ **Absolutely!**（那是當然！）→ 相當於 Sure!、Certainly!、Of course! 此用語是用來回應需求或要求，所以必須知道前面的訊息提出何種要求。

❷ **Hold on.**（稍等一下。）→ 相當於 Wait a moment/minute. 此用語是用來回應需求或要求，所以必須知道前面的訊息提出何種要求。

❸ **Couldn't be better.**（那真是再好也不過了；真是太棒了）→ 這句話必須確認前文提到了什麼好康的東西。

❹ **You can say that again!**（你說對了！／我同意你的說法！）→ 相當於 Agreed!，此用語是用來表達認同，所以應確認前文提到什麼爭議或爭論的問題。

❺ **You can leave me out.**（你可以不用把我算進去！）→ 相當於 Don't count me in! 或 Count me out!，此用語是用來表示自己不想參加某項活動，或不願意涉入某事件，所以應確認前文提到什麼活動徵求參與意願。

必備 Point 2

看懂前後文脈絡是解鎖「掌握意圖」題型的關鍵！重點不在於你能否理解「指定語句」本身，而是你能否體會說了該語句的人「**心裡在想什麼**」，因此**這類題型的解題線索在指定語句的**上下文語境。例如，在以下對話中，(A)、(B)、(C)、(D) 哪一句代表 Mr. Hunt 說出「We won't make it without their support.」的意圖？

Michael Lawson   10:50 A.M.
The deadline for placing orders for inventory for the upcoming season is coming soon.
David Hunt   10:55 A.M.
I know. Have you contacted the sales department? We won't make it without their support.

> Michael Lawson　　　　　　　　　　　　　　　　11:00 A.M.
> That's right. I'm making a call to Jason right now.
>
> (A) They need to support the sales department.
> (B) They need some collaborative effort.
> (C) There's no problem for them to meet the deadline.
> (D) The effort to reduce inventory is not necessary for the time being.

從這句話的上下文派絡來看，對話內容與訂貨有關。他們需要業務部的支援才能在截止日期前完成出貨，所以答案是 (B)。

必備 Point 3　對話訊息的題目要「**一口氣讀完，掌握完整內容**」：通常對話的篇章文字量相對較少，要理解其內容不會太困難與費時，因此跟其他閱讀題型不同的是，訊息對話要**從頭閱讀整篇**，不論是針對「掌握意圖」或是上述提及的其他類型題目。如果中途看到了題目要考的發言者那句話，<u>不必馬上去看四個選項的內容</u>，而是應繼續讀到最後，先<u>掌握對話主旨與重要內容是最重要的</u>。

必備 Point 4　常見「**詢問意圖以外的題型**」包括「詢問職業或行業」、「題目中有 indicated、mentioned 或 suggested」、「詢問談話結束後會發生何事」、「某人接下來會去做的事」、「關於某人某事的特定細節」…等，其解題技巧如下：

❶ **詢問職業或行業**，例如「What type of business does Ms. William probably work for?」。可將**對話中出現的設備或服務**當作解題線索。例如在對話中提到客房、房卡、前台等內容，即可推測參與該段對話的人是在飯店裡工作。

❷ **題目中有 indicated、mentioned 或 suggested**，例如「What is suggested about Ms. William?」、「What is (NOT) mentioned about the job fair?」…等。首先，判斷題目所詢問的人物是**對話參與者，或只是對話參與者提及的人物**。若是參與者，應以其發言內容為依據，尋找解題線索，否則，就得以整體對話內容來判斷。

❸ **詢問談話結束後會發生何事**，例如「What might (be going to) happen next?」、「What does Ms. William say she will do?」、「What will Ms. William most likely do next?」…等。針對談話結束後會發生的事，或對話參與者在結束對話後打算去做的事，

大多會以 I will~ 這類表示未來時態的句子當作解題線索，不過要注意的是，此題型的**線索不一定會出現在對話快結束的位置**。

❹ **關於某人某事的特定細節**。這類題型可能以 5W1H 疑問詞開頭的問句來問，例如「Why does Ms. William need assistance？」、「What is Ms. William asked to do?」、「Who will be a representative to the career fair?」…等。這類題型應針對題目中的「**關鍵語句**」，尋找與其有關的對話內容去找線索。

多益會怎麼考？

多益訊息對話的題組中，常考關於某人事物的特定細節題目：

James Cooper [9:13 A.M.]
There was some complaint about our Help Center page. But don't worry. We finally had it fixed last night.

Sonia Patel [9:14 A.M.]
That's indeed good news, but there's actually another problem concerning the product details page. Some customers mentioned that some pictures of our new arrivals aren't displaying.

Riya Mitchell [9:16 A.M.]
Thanks for letting me know. I'll reach out to the technical team to have this looked into right away. It might be a server issue, but I'll make sure they prioritize it.

Question. What problem with the website needs to be solved?
(A) Displaying the customer support menu
(B) Accessing the return policy information
(C) Viewing customer reviews
(D) Loading images of certain products

翻譯 James Cooper [9:13 A.M.]
我們網站的「幫助中心」頁面有收到一些投訴。不過別擔心，我們終於在昨晚修好了。

Sonia Patel [9:14 A.M.]
這確實是好消息，但其實還有另一個問題與「產品詳情」頁面有關。一些顧客反映我們部分新品的圖片無法顯示。

Riya Mitchell [9:16 A.M.]
謝謝你的告知。我會立即聯繫技術團隊來檢查這個問題。這可能是伺服器的問題，不過我會確保他們優先處理。

> 問題：有什麼關於網站的問題需要解決？
> (A) 顯示顧客支援選單
> (B) 查詢退貨政策資訊
> (C) 查看顧客評價
> (D) 載入特定商品的圖片
>
> **解析** 本題是問有什麼（what）關於網站的問題需要解決的細節問題，故應針對問題的核心語句（problem... needs to be solved）相關的內容去找線索。Sonia Patel 在「Some customers mentioned that some pictures of our new arrivals aren't displaying.」中提到，一些顧客反映我們部分新品的圖片無法顯示，故正確答案是 (D) Loading images of certain products。

▶ TOEIC 實戰演練

| Part 7 | 請在以下四個選項中選出正確的答案

Questions 1-2 refer to the following text message chain.

Alex Turner [1:31 p.m.]
Taylor, are you available now? The GM just requested an ad hoc meeting with the R&D team in about an hour.

Taylor Chen [1:33 p.m.]
Yes, I am, but my team is currently working at our main office downtown. They won't be back until at least 4:00.

Alex Turner [1:35 p.m.]
Do you think you could manage it on your own? I believe it will go smoothly even without your team members there.

Taylor Chen [1:36 p.m.]
I think that'll work out fine. Is there anything I need to prepare?

Alex Turner [1:40 p.m.]
They want to ask questions about our new product release, so bring your market survey, budget projections, and other documents prepared by you and your team. The meeting will be held in Meeting Room 5B.

Taylor Chen [1:41 p.m.]
I'll make sure to attend.

01 At 1:36 p.m., what does Mr. Chen mean when he writes, "I think that should work out fine"?

(A) He is satisfied with the product launch.
(B) He believes his team members will be back in time.
(C) He thinks the meeting will go well without his participation.
(D) He is confident he can manage a discussion alone.

02 What materials does Alex request Taylor bring to the meeting?

(A) Videos of the company's history
(B) Documents related to company values
(C) Some official business files
(D) Customer feedback and testimonials on previous products

Questions 3-6 refer to the following online chat discussion.

Liam Carson [11:07 A.M.]
Leah Moreno from Verdurex has just made a call to complain that the self-served drink machine and warming plates she had ordered is still pending delivery because they were scheduled to arrive yesterday.

Sophie Bennett [11:08 A.M.]
I was out of the office yesterday due to a business trip, so I have no idea what the matter is with that order.

Raj Mehta [11:09 A.M.]
Over the past week, our tracking software has encountered a bug, causing some orders to appear as having shipped from the warehouse while actually they hadn't even been processed. The issue has now been fixed. I think future orders will run smoothly.

Isabella Cruz [11:11 A.M.]
Should Ms. Moreno's equipment be still out of stock, this may result in further delays.

Raj Mehta [11:12 A.M.]
What amazing luck! A sizable shipment from TPL Manufacturing arrived, and I unpacked it first thing today.

Liam Carson [11:13 A.M.]
Sounds good. I'll contact Ms. Moreno right away to inform her that her order is en route, as she needs the items for a party she's hosting soon.

Sophie Bennett [11:15 A.M.]
Wait a minute. Should we check with the warehouse manager first to confirm if there's enough stock?

Isabella Cruz [11:16 A.M.]
Yes, I'll go over there now. Liam, if everything's okay, I'll let you know, and then you can call Ms. Moreno.

03 Why hasn't Ms. Moreno received her order yet?

(A) There was a problem with the software.
(B) Her payment was insufficient.
(C) A warehouse employee was absent.
(D) Some merchandise was damaged during shipment.

04 What is most likely one of Verdurex's items in business?

(A) Manufacturing and sale of software
(B) Rental of plates and utensils
(C) Delivery services
(D) Food and beverage provision

05 At 11:12 A.M., what does Mr. Mehta mean when he writes, "What amazing luck!"?

(A) Some errors have been handled.
(B) They won't need to work overtime.
(C) A new supply source is available.
(D) The warehouse still holds some forgotten inventory.

06 What will Ms. Cruz probably do next?

(A) Ask the warehouse employees to work overtime
(B) Make a call to Ms. Moreno
(C) Confirm if there's enough stock for Ms. Moreno
(D) Go to TPL Manufacturing to check the goods on arrival

WEEK 12 表格＆單據的題目

必備 Point 1

表格／單據 通常包括**行程表**（schedule）、**請款單**（receipt / request form）、**傳單**（flyer）、**票券**（ticket / voucher / coupon）、**發票**（invoice / cash receipt）等各種形式的文本。此類文本大多與其他類型文章一起出現在雙篇或三篇文章的題組中（Week16-18 將進一步介紹），但也有少部分單獨出現在 Part 7 的單篇文本考題中。

必備 Point 2

常考問題類型：**尋找主題**、**5W1H** 問題、**Not/True** 問題及**推論**問題。例如：

❶ **尋找主題／目的**：可能詢問表單中提到的活動主旨，或者製作個人行程表的目的。例如：

① What is the purpose of the event?

② What is the coupon for?

③ What is advertised in the flyer?

❷ **5W1H 疑問詞的問題**：可能詢問之後的行程計畫、做某項安排的理由或其他細節。例如：

① What will take place on June 15?

② When does Ocean Mist Reserve close on Sundays?

③ What information is NOT included in this coupon?

④ How did Mr. Smith pay his bill?

⑤ Who will be the keynote speaker at 2:30 P.M.?

❸ **Not/True 問題**：詢問各選項的敘述，對照文本中提到人事物之敘述，何者正確或錯誤。例如：

① What is mentioned about the Business Exchange?

② What is NOT stated about Mr. Smith in the request form?

③ What does the restaurant NOT request feedback on?

❹ **推論問題**。針對表格或單據的閱讀對象，或其中提及特定人事物的細節，可以推論得知什麼事情。例如：

① <u>For whom</u> is the flyer <u>intended</u>?

② What is <u>suggested</u> about the hotel?

③ What type of product is <u>most likely</u> the AdaptSound Pro X9?

多益會怎麼考？

多益會考一張票券中所不包含的資訊問題：

Ocean Breeze Park

Ticket for Adults (16 and above)：$40

Operating Hours:
Mondays to Fridays: 8:00 A.M. ~ 6:00 P.M.
Weekends and public holidays: 8:00 A.M. ~ 7:00 P.M.
Parking: $3 per hour (applies to weekdays, weekends and holidays)
Date: September 12, 2024
※Each ticket provides a $5 credit toward any in-park purchases for food and drinks, valid on the day of admission only.

Question. What is NOT specified on the ticket?
(A) The admission fee
(B) The date the ticket expires
(C) Parking area detail
(D) The age bracket for holding this ticket

翻譯 海風公園

成人票（16歲及以上）：$40
開放時間：
週一至週五：上午8:00 ～ 下午6:00
週六、週日及國定假日：上午8:00 ～ 下午7:00
停車費：每小時$3（平日、週末及假日皆適用）
日期：2024年9月12日
※ 每張門票可於當日入園時抵扣園內餐飲消費$5。

問題：這張票上未指明的是什麼？
(A) 入場費
(B) 券的有效期限
(C) 停車區域細節
(D) 持本張票者的年齡

解析 這是在短文中尋找門票的相關資訊後，與各選項對照的 Not/True 問題。選項 (A) 的部分可以從「Ticket for Adults (16 and above) : $40」得知，這張門票價格為 40 美元，所以是有提到的；(B) 的部分可以從「Date: September 12, 2024」以及「valid on the day of admission only」得知，所以是有提到的。(C) 是沒提到的內容，關於停車的部分只提到每小時 3 美元。故 (C) Parking area detail 是正確答案。(D) 的部分可以從「Ticket for Adults (16 and above)」得知，所以是有提到的。

多益會以 5W1H 疑問詞為開頭詢問票券內容提及的事項：

Operating Hours

Mondays to Fridays: 8:00 A.M. ~ 6:00 P.M.
Weekends and public holidays: 8:00 A.M. ~ 7:00 P.M.
Parking: $3 per hour (applies to weekdays, weekends and holidays)
Date: September 12, 2024

Question. When does the amusement park close on Sundays?
(A) At 5:00 P.M.
(B) At 6:00 P.M.
(C) At 7:00 P.M.
(D) At 8:00 P.M.

翻譯 開放時間

週一至週五：上午8:00 ~ 下午6:00
週六、週日及國定假日：上午8:00 ~ 晚上7:00
停車費：每小時$3（平日及週末假日皆適用）
日期：2024年9月12日

問題：遊樂園週日幾點關閉？
(A) 在下午5點
(B) 在下午6點
(C) 在晚上7點
(D) 在晚上8點

解析 這是在問遊樂園星期日什麼時候 (when) 關閉的 5W1H 問題。在此票券內容中，與問題核心語句「amusement park close on Sundays」相關的「Weekends and public holidays: 8:00 A.M. ~ 7:00 P.M.」提到，遊客週末可在公園待到晚上7點，故答案是 (C) At 7:00 P.M.。

▶ 實用策略

必備 Point 1

「**尋找主題／目的**」的問題，通常可以在這些表格、單據或票券等的**開頭或前面幾句**找到，所以要特別注意一開頭的資訊。例如：

① **優待券**（coupon）

> **2 for the Price of 1!**
>
> Enjoy the rich taste of premium latte – Double the delight, perfect for you and a friend to share!
>
> ....
>
> Question. What is the coupon for?
> (A) A complimentary iced/hot coffee (B) A free reusable coffee cup
> (C) A half-priced coffee   (D) A discounted latte upgrade

從標題的「2 for the Price of 1!」可知，這是個「**買一送一**」的廣告，而標的物即是「premium latte」（**精品拿鐵咖啡**），換句話說，就是可以獲得 1 杯**免費的**（complimentary）咖啡，所以 (A) 是正解。雖然 (B) 有 free，但還是得看清楚它指的是什麼（→ coffee cup），作答時切忌看到影子就開槍！

② **邀請函**（invitation）

> **Kingston Books Collective in Collaboration with Merrick House Publishing Invites You with Pleasure to: An Evening with Lena Caldwell**
>
> July 15, 6:30 p.m.
> At Kingston Books, 572 Oakwood Lane, Fairview
>
> We are excited to welcome all Kingston Book Club members to this exclusive gathering! Join us as Lena Caldwell unveils her most recent literary creation!
>
> ……..
>
> Question. What is the purpose of the event?
> (A) To host a book signing
> (B) To celebrate the anniversary of a bookstore
> (C) To introduce a newest publication
> (D) To discuss a classical literary work

從最上方粗體字內容，對照四個選項的敘述，尚無法看出這張邀請函的目的，因此我們要繼續看下方的文字。從最後面的「as Lena Caldwell unveils her most recent literary creation」可知，這場盛會的目的是要介紹給大家一本最新出爐的文學作品，也就是「a newest publication」，所以答案是 (C)。

必備 Point 2

「**5W1H 疑問詞**」的問題，除了確認疑問詞（what/when/where/who...）本身之外，**找出題目的「關鍵語句」**是最重要的，接著要尋找與關鍵語句**相同或經過改寫的部分**，並在上下文中查找**與答案相關的線索**。例如：

清單（list）

> *Globe Discovery Magazine's Annual Hotel Selection*
>
> The esteemed travel and tourism publication, *Globe Discovery*, has announced its yearly ranking of the finest luxury hotels in the world. Evaluations are drawn from reviews by guests, travel agents, and some experts. Among more than 1,000 hotels worldwide, the following list shows three top-notch spots...
> ......
> Question. Who was NOT part of the rating decision?
> (A) Hotel customers
> (B) Tour operators
> (C) Service reviewers
> (D) Hotel staff

這是在問給予評比者不包括「誰（who）的 5W1H 問題，從「Evaluations are drawn from reviews by guests, travel agents, and some experts.」這句話可知，給予評比的人有飯店住客、旅行業者以及專家，所以 (D) 的「飯店員工」是不包括在內的。其中 (C) 的 Service reviewers（飯店服務評論者）其實就是指 experts。

※ 通常內容中有「A, B, C and D」這種對等、並列式資訊的，常常出現在考題中！

必備 Point 3

「**NOT/true**」的問題中，通常會有 true、indicated、stated、mentioned…等字眼。如果是針對整個文本來問，例如「What is stated in this invitation?」這種題目沒有關鍵語句的情況，那就直接看四個選項的關鍵語句。接著

在表格／單據的內容中找尋「**表達用語經過改寫**」的線索。例如：

優待券（coupon）

> ……..
> Enjoy the rich taste of premium latte – Double the delight, perfect for you and a friend to share!
> ……..
> This offer is not valid with any other discounts or coupons.
> *** Valid until July 31
>
> Question. What is mentioned about using this coupon?
> (A) Only groups are eligible for this offer.
> (B) This coupon becomes effective after July 31.
> (C) One coupon is permitted per person.
> (D) It can't be combined with additional offers.

這是針對票券上的內容與各選項相對照的 Not/True 問題。從最後提到的「This offer is not valid with any other discounts or coupons.」可知，這項優惠不得與其他折扣項目或優惠券同時使用，所以 (D) 是正確答案。

必備 Point 4

「**推論**」問題就是要**找出沒有直接提到的線索**。題目中常常有 inferred、suggested、implied…等字眼。表格／表單／清單等文本，很少針對整篇內容來考**推論型的細節問題**，通常針對其中一個「點」來看。例如：

> **Welcome Supermarket Digital Order Form**
>
> Name: Nathaniel Harris
> Address: 1827 South Maple Drive, Scottsdale, AZ 85251
> Customer account number: 689587
> Reward points earned: 2,300
> Order date: December 12
>
> | Product | Unit Price | Number of Unit |
> |---|---|---|
> | Organic Bananas | 0.69 | 2 |
> | Whole Wheat Bread | 2.99 | 1 |
> | Chicken Breast | $5.99 | 2 |

> Question. What can be inferred about Mr. Harris?
> (A) He will receive his order on December 12.
> (B) He will need to pay more than $17 in total.
> (C) He chooses to pay his bill by credit card.
> (D) He has made purchases from Welcome Supermarket before.

從表格上的「Name: Nathaniel Harris」可知，下這張訂單的人就是 Mr. Harris，接著「Reward points earned」告訴我們，他已經獲得的回饋點數（Reward points earned）是 2300，由此可推論他之前曾經在這家超市買過東西，故答案是 (D)。

多益會怎麼考？

多益會針對行程表中的行程安排，考 5W1H 疑問詞的問題：

> **Riverbend Community Business Alliance (RCBA)**
> **Startup Funding Application Seminar**
> **Thursday, January 15**
> **9:30 a.m. – 5:30 p.m.**
> **Riverbend Center**
>
> Agenda of Activities
>
> | 9:30-9:45 A.M. | Opening Remarks and Welcome by Cara Sullivan, RCBA president, Owner of Custom Coffee Roastery |
> |---|---|
> | 9:45-10:30 A.M. | "Exploring Grant Options and Funding Strategies," presented by Dr. Ben Sutherland, Lecturer of Innovation and Leadership, Western Institute of Technology, followed by a 10-min break. |
> | ... ... | ... ... |
>
> Question. What comes next after Dr. Sutherland's talk?
> (A) Pre-recorded video session
> (B) Discussion about state-run projects
> (C) One-hour meal service
> (D) Short recess

> **翻 譯**

> **弗本德社區商業聯盟 (RCBA)**
> **創業資金申請研討會**
> **1月15日（星期四）**
> **上午9:30 至 下午5:30**
> **里弗本德中心**
>
> 活動議程
>
> | 上午 9:30 - 9:45 | 開幕致詞與歡迎辭 ——卡拉·蘇利文，RCBA 會長，暨「訂製咖啡烘焙店」老闆 |
> |---|---|
> | 9:45-10:30 A.M. | 「探索補助選項與資金策略」——由班·薩瑟蘭博士主講，「西方科技學院」的「創新與領導學」講師。接著休息 10 分鐘。 |
> | … … … … | … … … … |
>
> 問題：薩瑟蘭博士的演講結束後，緊接著的是什麼活動？
> (A) 預錄影片放映
> (B) 關於政府項目的討論
> (C) 一小時的用餐服務
> (D) 短暫休息

> **解 析** 題目問的是 Dr. Sutherland 演說結束後，緊接著的是什麼（what）活動，故應針對問題的核心語句（comes next after Dr. Sutherland's talk）相關的內容去找線索，從「…presented by Dr. Ben Sutherland…, followed by a 10-min break」的內容可知，正確答案是 (D)。recess 就是 break 的意思。

▶ TOEIC 實戰演練

| Part 7 | 請在以下四個選項中選出正確的答案

Questions 1-2 refer to the following schedule.

Production: *Through Shadows and Light*
Produced by: Starlight Haven Productions
Directed by: Marcus Bellamy

MARCUS BELLAMY'S SCHEDULE

April 11 to 22

Mon.	Tue.	Wed.	Thu.	Fri.
11 9:00 a.m. Location scouting with the production team		13 11:00 a.m. Review and approve set design concepts	14 1:30 p.m. Meet with casting director to discuss new talent	15 2:00 p.m. Script read-through with leading cast
18 10:00 a.m. Consult with composer on the film's main theme	19 10:00 a.m. Read through lines with the starring cast again		21 11:00 a.m. Attend editing session to review rough cuts	22 1:30 p.m. Check camera equipment and set up for day's shoot

01 Which task was not planned for Ms. Bellamy?

(A) Brainstorming main theme concepts with the composer
(B) Evaluating new talent prospects with the casting director
(C) Exploring potential filming sites with production crew
(D) Reviewing storyboards for key action scenes

02 What time will the second script reading take place?

(A) At 9:00 a.m.
(B) At 10:00 a.m.
(C) At 1:30 p.m.
(D) At 2:00 p.m.

Questions 3-5 refer to the following survey form.

Maplewood Retreat Lodge
Guest Experience Feedback

Your opinion matters to us! Please take a moment to complete this survey and share your thoughts, which will help us improve the quality of our services. Mark all answers with a "√".

DATE(S) OF STAY: June 18-19   NAME: Glenn Parker
PHONE: (606) 778-9348   E-MAIL: glenn@freemail.com

	Absolutely	Mostly	Not Really
1. On the whole, my experience at Maplewood Retreat Lodge was...			
a memorable and enjoyable getaway with beautiful surroundings.	√		
offered more than expected for the cost.		√	
2. At the front desk, I was...			
welcomed with a warm smile and prompt service.	√		
provided with clear and helpful information about the amenities.	√		
3. As I walked into my room, it felt like...			
a calm and soothing place to relax after a long day.	√		
a thoughtfully designed room that met all my needs.	√		
the temperature was comfortable	√		
4. I found the facilities at Maplewood Retreat Lodge to be...			
spacious and thoughtfully designed for guest comfort.	√		
well-organized and user-friendly.	√		
5. From check-in to check-out, the staff at Maplewood Retreat Lodge were...			
friendly and attentive to all my needs.		√	
efficient in handling requests and providing information.			√
knowledgeable and quick to address questions or concerns.		√	
6. Feel free to share any other thoughts or suggestions here:			

My stay at Maplewood Retreat Lodge was generally enjoyable. The room was absolutely lovely—spacious, well-lit, and comfortable. The bed was perfect for a good night's sleep, and the view from my window was stunning. However, I did encounter a few challenges during my stay. I was hoping to extend my stay by one more night shortly after I entered the room. When I made a call to the front desk, the staff seemed a bit uncertain about whether it could be arranged. They said they would check, but I didn't hear back until I was almost scheduled to check out, and by then, they asked me if I could accept a quad room on the second night, which exceeded my budget. In the end, I only had to book a room somewhere else.

03 What is NOT included in this feedback questionnaire?

(A) The responsiveness of employees
(B) The comfort and amenities provided in the room
(C) The reliability and speed of the Wi-Fi connection
(D) The availability and condition of facilities

04 What is suggested about Mr. Parker?

(A) He found the room amenities to be challenging.
(B) He experienced a delay in response to a request.
(C) He didn't have enough money to pay for a longer stay in the same room.
(D) He had wanted to leave earlier than his scheduled check-out.

05 What did Mr. Parker want to do after entering his room?

(A) Order a room service
(B) Exercise at the hotel gym
(C) Extend his stay
(D) Make a phone call to his boss

WEEK 13 新聞＆報導的題目

▶ 出題模式

必備 Point 1

新聞／報導（article / report）的篇幅會長一點且難度稍高，通常與商業界、各種產業動向、社會議題、環境問題或健康相關研究結果等文章有關，用字用詞的難度通常比其他類型的文本較高，且在雙篇與三篇題組中出現的頻率也極高。

必備 Point 2

常考問題類型：**尋找主題／目的**、**5W1H** 問題、**Not/True** 問題、**推論**問題及**放入句子**的問題。例如：

❶ **尋找主題／目的**：可能詢問報導的目的或主要關於什麼。例如：
① What is the article mainly about?
② What is the purpose of the article?
③ What is the main topic of the article?

❷ **5W1H 疑問詞的問題**：可能詢問報導中提到的人物、天氣、時間…等其他的細節。例如：
① Who is responsible for managing the project's budget?
② What caused the delay in the product launch?
③ When is the deadline for submitting the proposal?
④ Where will the company relocate its headquarters?
⑤ How did the team resolve the issue with the software?

❸ **Not/True 問題**：可能詢問報導中提到的人物、事件發生原因、時間或順序、計畫或預期活動、數據或數量…等，和選項的敘述是否一致。例如：
① What is suggested about the new marketing strategy?
② Which of the following is NOT true about the expansion project?
③ What can be inferred about Ms. Chen's role in the project?

④ What is NOT mentioned as a challenge faced by the company?

❹ **推論問題**。主要針對報導中提到的人事物，或其相關的特定事項，甚至報導者的態度或立場、事件的潛在影響或後續發展，詢問可以推論得知的事情。例如：

① What can be inferred about the company's future plans?

② Where would this type of report most likely be found?

③ What can be assumed about the target audience of this article?

❺ **放入句子問題**。這類題目除了會出現在信件類的文章，通常在「報導」（article / report / information）中也會有一題。題目要求考生藉由上下文脈絡來推導出該句應置於報導中的哪個位置。由於標號的填空處分散於整篇文章之中，若未看過整篇便難以作答，因此解題也較為費時。同樣地，題目會這麼問：

In which of the positions marked [1], [2], [3], and [4] does the following sentence best belong?
"............................."

多益會怎麼考？

多益會考關於一篇報導主旨或目的問題：

TechCorp Acquires FinStart to Expand Fintech Services

By Alicia Grant
San Francisco, CA, November 10

TechCorp, a Silicon Valley technology giant, confirmed today that it has acquired FinStart, a promising fintech startup specializing in mobile payment solutions for small businesses. The acquisition, valued at $50 million, aims to strengthen TechCorp's presence in the rapidly growing fintech market. According to a TechCorp spokesperson, this strategic move will enable the company to incorporate FinStart's innovative payment technology into its existing suite of financial services.

"We see enormous potential in integrating FinStart's technology to enhance our product offerings," said CEO Mark Redding. ......

Question. What is the main purpose of this article?
(A) To highlight a company's success in raising funds for expansion
(B) To announce the purchase of a company by a leading tech corporation
(C) To provide an in-depth analysis of the fintech market's growth trends
(D) To explain the global challenges in the mobile payments industry

翻譯 TechCorp 收購 FinStart 擴展金融科技服務
撰稿人：艾莉西亞·格蘭特
加州舊金山，11月10日

矽谷科技巨頭 TechCorp 今日證實成功收購金融科技新創公司 FinStart。FinStart 主要業務是為小型企業提供行動支付解決方案，其充滿發展潛力。本次收購案金額是 5,000 萬美元，其目的是強化 TechCorp 在迅速成長的金融科技市場中的地位。TechCorp 發言人表示，這一策略性舉措將使公司能夠將 FinStart 的創新支付技術整合到其現有的金融服務產品中。

TechCorp 執行長馬克‧雷丁表示，「我們看到整合 FinStart 技術來提升產品的巨大潛力」……

問題：這篇報導的主要目的為何？
(A) 強調一家公司在籌資擴展方面的成功
(B) 宣布一家科技巨擘收購另一家公司
(C) 提供金融科技市場成長趨勢的深入分析
(D) 說明行動支付產業的全球挑戰

解析 「TechCorp, a Silicon Valley technology giant, confirmed today that it has acquired FinStart, ...small businesses.」這部分提到，矽谷科技巨頭 TechCorp 今日證實成功收購金融科技新創公司 FinStart。FinStart 主要業務是為小型企業提供行動支付解決方案，其充滿發展潛力。故正確答案是 (B) To announce the purchase of a company by a leading tech corporation。

多益會以 5W1H 疑問詞為開頭詢問報導內容提及的事項：

The acquisition will bring together TechCorp's data centers, servers, network systems, data security architecture, and other critical IT assets with FinStart's agile and customer-focused approach to fintech solutions. Industry analysts predict that this partnership could lead to a suite of new features designed to streamline mobile payments, increase accessibility for small businesses, and potentially set new standards for security in digital transactions.

> Question. What is NOT a strength TechCorp owns?
> (A) Strong and stable framework
> (B) Comprehensive resources
> (C) Advanced transaction methods
> (D) A variety of financial solutions

翻譯 此次收購將結合 TechCorp的數據中心、伺服器、網絡系統、數據安全架構,以及其他關鍵的IT資產,並融入 FinStart 敏捷且以客戶為導向的金融科技解決方案。業界分析師預測,這項合作可能帶來一系列新功能,以簡化行動支付流程、提高小型企業的可及性,並有望為數位交易安全樹立新標準。

問題:下列何者不是 TechCorp 的優勢?
(A) 堅固且穩定的架構　　　　　(B) 全面的資源
(C) 先進的交易方法　　　　　　(D) 多樣的金融解決方案

解析 這是在報導中找尋與問題核心語句(a strength TechCorp owns)相關的內容並與各選項相對照的 Not/True 問題。從「... bring together TechCorp's data centers, servers... with FinStart's agile and customer-focused mobile payments...」的內容可知,數據中心、伺服器、網絡系統、數據安全架構,以及其他關鍵的IT資產都是 TechCorp 的優勢,選項中只有「Advanced transaction methods」屬於「FinStart's agile and customer-focused mobile payments」,故答案是 (C) Advanced transaction methods。

▶ 實用策略

「報導」的文章內容多樣且繁雜,通常在解題上較為費時且吃力。因此,應**先解決其他題組,再來處理「報導」類的文章**。另外,這類題組中,很多題目都與**專有名詞**有關。如果是有 3 個問題以上的題組,應先將句子裡的「**大寫開頭**」的字圈出來。最後,注意「引用句」的部分,因為很多答題線索都在裡面。

必備 Point 1 新聞或報導的「**尋找主題/目的**」問題,就是在詢問**新聞的焦點**為何,通常可以在會**在第一段(1~2 句)**找到線索,所以要特別注意一開頭的資訊。例如:

> **TechCorp Acquires FinStart to Expand Fintech Services**
>
> By Alicia Grant
> San Francisco, CA, November 10
> TechCorp, a Silicon Valley technology giant, confirmed today that it has acquired FinStart, a promising fintech startup specializing in mobile payment solutions for small businesses. The acquisition, valued at ……..

如果題目詢問「這篇報導的主要目的為何？」那麼一開頭的「TechCorp, a Silicon Valley technology giant, confirmed today that it has acquired...」就是解題線索。另外。再次強調，通常選項中的用字不會完全與文本內容的一樣，比如這裡報導中的 acquire（收購），選項中可能用 purchase 或 buy out（買斷，買下）。

必備 Point 2

在「**5W1H 疑問詞**」的問題中，除了辨識疑問詞（what/when/where/who...）之外，找出題目的「核心語句」相當重要。接著要在報導的文本中搜尋與核心語句有關或經過改寫的部分，並在上下文中尋找與答案相關的提示。例如：

> **Inovasi University to Develop Skill Training Center**
>
> ...
> Liang Zemin, governor of Langka State, said, "We welcome this decision by the Bayan government and Inovasi University and expect the new academic complex to create thousands of new jobs and strengthen educational opportunities in the region."
> ...
> Question. What does Mr. Zemin anticipate will happen?
> (A) The state is expected to welcome more international visitors.
> (B) A major transportation route will be under construction.
> (C) More school buildings will be constructed with funding from the government.
> (D) More employment opportunities will become available for local residents.

這是在問 Zemin 先生預期會有什麼「what」事情發生的 5W1H 問題，從「Liang Zemin... expect the new academic complex to create thousands of new jobs and strengthen educational opportunities in the region.」這句話可知，預

期新的學術綜合大樓將創造數千個新的工作機會，並加強該地區的教育機會，其中 (D) 的 More employment opportunities will become available 其實就是指 create thousands of new jobs。

必備 Point 3

「**NOT/true**」的問題，通常題目中會有 true、indicated、stated、mentioned、implied…等字眼。題目可能針對人物、公司、活動表演…等詢問「有指出／提到什麼」的問題。接著在新聞／報導的內容中找尋「**所指雷同但用語經過改寫**」的線索。例如：

> Maplewood — On a brisk morning, I visited Maple Bistro, a newly opened restaurant on Oak Avenue. At first glance, it seemed like another typical eatery in the bustling Maplewood area. However, stepping inside, I quickly noticed the difference. "I wanted to bring a taste of the world to our town," shared owner David Lin. ...
> ...
> David, previously the head chef at Golden Spoon Café, dedicated months to looking for where his dream restaurant would be. "When I saw the empty space where the bookstore used to be, I knew it was the perfect spot," he said. He spent considerable time on renovations to create a cozy, elegant space for diners.
> ...
>
> Question. What is indicated about Mr. Lin?
> (A) He spent much time selecting a location that he felt would be ideal for his restaurant.
> (B) He wanted to open a restaurant in a location with a large kitchen.
> (C) He was hesitant to leave his job at Golden Spoon Café.
> (D) He opened his restaurant without making any changes to the space.

Mr. Lin 就是 David Lin，是 Maplewood 這地方一家新餐廳的老闆。從「dedicated months to looking for...」的內容可推知，他花了不少時間挑選他要開的餐廳位置，所以 (A) 是正確答案。

必備 Point 4

「**推論**」問題就是要**找出沒有直接提到的線索**。題目中常常有 inferred、suggested、implied…等字眼。例如：

> ……
> While Maple Bistro is slightly more expensive than nearby restaurants, it serves a diverse array of thoughtfully made cuisine. With David's culinary expertise and commitment to service, Maple Bistro is set to become a beloved spot on Oak Avenue. It's open from 9 A.M. to 9 P.M. daily, except Mondays. ……
>
> Question. What is implied about Maple Bistro?
> (A) It plans to expand to multiple locations soon.
> (B) It aims to attract customers looking for quality over low prices.
> (C) It primarily offers affordable, quick meals for busy customers.
> (D) It is the only restaurant in the area that serves international cuisine.

從「...slightly more expensive than nearby restaurants, it offers a rich variety of well-prepared dishes.」的敘述可知，這家餐廳的**價格較高**，但同時**提供優質多樣的菜色**，這暗示該餐廳**以高品質吸引顧客，而非靠低價競爭**，因此 (B) 是正確答案。而 (C) 的「提供平價快速的餐點給忙碌的顧客」顯然與此經營理念背道而馳。而 (A) 的「計畫快速拓展多家分店」以及 (D) 的「當地唯一提供國際料理的餐廳」皆是沒有提到的內容。

必備 Point 5

「**放入句子**」問題中，如果有**指示代名詞**（或**指示形容詞**）it、that、these…等），代表其前句裡有其指稱的對象！例如：

❶ 要放入的句子是「This breakthrough has gained worldwide attention.」，那麼就可以把它擺像是在像是「The scientist made a groundbreaking discovery in renewable energy.」這樣的句子後面。

❷ 要放入的句子是「These are easy to implement in daily routines.」，那麼就可以把它擺在像是「The instructor shared some useful tips on improving productivity.」這樣的句子後面。

要放入的句子如果有**連接性副詞**（however、therefore、instead… 等），就去找和這個句子有相互關係的句子，並確認前後句的連接是否通順自然。例如：

❸ 要放入的句子是「Instead, they will use the time to improve its features based on user feedback.」，那麼就可以把它擺在像是「The team decided against launching the product this quarter.」這樣的句子後面。因為 Instead 代表前後句意思相反，這裡第二句說明「不在本季度推出產品」，而是「利用目前的時間」做某事的替代方案。

❹ 要放入的句子是「As a result, overall productivity has increased by 20%.」，那麼就可以把它擺在像是「The company implemented a new employee training program last quarter.」這樣的句子後面。也就是說，到文章中去尋找「生產力增加20%」的原因 →「執行新的員工訓練計劃」。

多益會怎麼考？

多益會針對報導文章中提到的人事物，考「何者為是／非」的問題：

> **Eco-Friendly Auto Showcase Set for May 21**
>
> May 10, 2024, New York City
> Reported by Jane Michaels
> The International Car Exhibition will take place on May 21 at the Grand Convention Center, highlighting cutting-edge automotive innovations. Organized by Alex Turner, president of the Automotive Enthusiasts Association, the event focuses on eco-friendly vehicles. A portion of ticket sales will support the Green Roads Initiative, a project aimed at sustainable transportation development.
>
> Question. What is NOT true about Mr. Turner?
> (A) He has been the president of the Automotive Enthusiasts Association.
> (B) He is a promoter of eco-friendly vehicle development.
> (C) He is involved in the organization of the car exhibition.
> (D) He initiated the Green Roads Initiative project.

翻譯 環保汽車展覽定於 5 月 21 日舉行
2024 年 5 月 10 日，紐約市
記者：Jane Michaels
國際汽車展將於 5 月 21 日在大會中心舉行，屆時將展示最先進的汽車創新技術。本次活動由汽車愛好者協會會長亞歷克斯·特納（Alex Turner）籌辦，重點推廣環保汽車。部分門票收入將捐助「綠色道路倡議」活動，該計劃旨在促進可永續性的交通發展。

問題：以下關於特納先生的敘述，哪一項不正確？
(A) 他是「車愛好者協會」長。 　　(B) 他是環保汽車發展的推廣者。
(C) 他參與了本次汽車展的組織工作。 (D) 他發起了「綠色道路倡議」計劃。

解析「何者為非」的題型通常必須四個選項逐一對照內文。(A) 的部分可以從「Alex Turner, president of the Automotive Enthusiasts Association」確認是有提到的；(B) 和 (C) 的部分可以從標題「Eco-Friendly Auto Showcase Set for May 21」以及「... Organized by Alex Turner」確認都是有提到的；只有 (D) 的部分是文中未提及的，因此答案就是 (D)。

▶ TOEIC 實戰演練

Part 7 請在以下四個選項中選出正確的答案

Questions 1-3 refer to the following article.

The Riverside Art Space: Portraits of Our Community

The Riverside Art Space is hosting a unique art exhibition this September. Instead of showcasing works by famous artists, the exhibition features paintings created by residents of the local community.

Twenty local participants, aged from sixteen to eighty-four, were invited to create portraits that celebrate the people of Riverside. Visitors can enjoy a wide range of paintings, from depictions of the town's cheerful baker and the lively children at the community playground to portraits of the Riverside Fire Chief and a beloved pet dog. One painting even portrays the art space itself.

Sophia Lark, curator of the Riverside Art Space, shared her enthusiasm for the activity: "Being part of a small, close-knit community allows us to highlight the extraordinary talent of ordinary people." Reflecting on her previous role in the bustling city of Arkwell, she added, "This is something I couldn't have done at the Metropolitan Art Center. It's a different kind of connection."

Portraits of Our Community will be on display until September 30, with admission priced at just $5.00.

---

01 Which section of a newspaper is most suitable for this article?

(A) Lifestyle
(B) Travel
(C) Education
(D) Local news

02 What subject will NOT be included in the portraits?

(A) Children
(B) Pets
(C) Famous landmarks
(D) Local professionals

03 What is implied about Sophia Lark?

(A) She has worked in a large city before.
(B) She is a talented painter herself.
(C) She grew up in Riverside.
(D) She prefers working in urban art spaces.

Questions 4-7 refer to the following article.

Audiflow Opens Doors for Musinex Plus to Launch

By Clara Venn, music correspondent

Music giant Audiflow, which manages the rights for over 65 record labels, has finalized a global licensing agreement with streaming platform Musinex. This deal lays the foundation for the launch of Musinex Plus, a premium music subscription service. — [1] — Musinex already licenses content from multiple top record labels, but it previously lacked access to Audiflow's extensive library of contemporary tracks.

The partnership with Audiflow will dramatically expand the range of music Musinex can offer, bringing the highly anticipated Musinex Plus closer to launch. This paid service has been in the works for three years. — [2] — "We're thrilled about the opportunity to make our artists' music accessible on Musinex's platforms, both online and on mobile," said Audiflow CEO Daniel Morvin. "Although we value our collaborations with Musinex's competitors, none match Musinex's global presence." — [3] —

Musinex boasts over 200 million active users, while its closest competitor, StreamVibe, has just 25 million. However, much of Musinex's traffic stems from users watching free video content rather than streaming music. — [4] — In contrast, more than 52 percent of StreamVibe's users pay for a monthly subscription to enjoy its extensive music library. Whether Musinex Plus can persuade its users to do the same remains to be seen.

04 What is true about Musinex Plus?

(A) It has already launched but is available only in select regions.
(B) It focuses exclusively on classic music tracks.
(C) It has not yet been made available to the public.
(D) It will offer discounts to its first subscribers.

05 According to the article, what competitive advantage does Musinex have?

(A) It includes a video-streaming feature.
(B) It has a significantly larger user base than its competitors.
(C) It charges lower subscription fees than other services.
(D) It offers a unique offline listening mode.

06 What does the article mention about StreamVibe?

(A) Nearly half of its users pay for a subscription.
(B) It has recently signed a deal with Audiflow.
(C) It primarily attracts users interested in video streaming.
(D) Its mobile app is one of the most downloaded globally.

07 In which of the positions marked [1], [2], [3], and [4] does the following sentence best belong?

"Once it is launched, users will be able to access an expanded catalog of music and videos, available in a premium digital format."

(A) [1]
(B) [2]
(C) [3]
(D) [4]

WEEK 14 廣告 & 通知的題目

▶ 出題模式

必備 Point 1

廣告／通知（advertisement / notice）都是針對公眾或特定眾人發佈的文章而「公告（announcement）」、「備忘錄（memo）」、「資訊（information）、「網頁（web page）、」等，也可能屬於此類文本。這類題型不僅會出現在單篇題組，在多篇題組中也很常見。廣告的題組可能與**產品**、**服務**、**活動**、**房地產**廣告等有關。如果是**求才廣告**，要關注的是負責什麼樣的工作、應徵資格、應徵方式。在通知或布告欄的題組中，要關注的是它的主題、要求事項、進行方式等。

必備 Point 2

常考問題類型：**尋找主題／目的**、**5W1H** 問題、**Not/True** 問題及**推論**問題。例如：

❶ **尋找主題／目的**：可能詢問報導的目的或主要關於什麼。例如：

① What (position) is being advertised?

② What is the purpose of the notice / memo?

③ What is the announcement aimed at?

❷ **5W1H 疑問詞的問題**：可能詢問廣告中購買者可以得到的優惠、可以得到或者申請什麼的資格，或者廣告中的其他細節內容。通知的題組可能詢問內容是要給誰看的、某人被要求去做什麼、某人如何申請或辦理、誰在籌備活動…等。例如：

① What type of merchandise does the company sell?

② What is required of applicants?

③ When is the Banff Travel Bureau closed?

④ Where is the complimentary publication available for pickup?

⑤ How can a copy of the free booklet be obtained?

⑥ Who is organizing the event?

⑦ For whom is the notice intended?

❸ **Not/True 問題**：通常詢問關於廣告業主、廣告宣傳產品或服務的敘述是否正確。同樣地，題目通常會有 indicated、mentioned、stated、(NOT) true…等字眼。例如：

① What is indicated about the company's return policy?

② Which of the following is NOT highlighted as a feature of the advertised service?

③ What can be inferred during the discount period for the promotion?

④ What is NOT mentioned as a benefit of using the product?

⑤ What is stated as the reason for the change in schedule?

⑥ Which of the following is NOT included in the list of prohibited items?

❹ **推論問題**：主要針對廣告或通知中提到的人事物（應徵者資格、產品、服務…等），或其相關的特定事項，詢問可以推論得知的事情。通常題目中會有 inferred、implied、suggested……等字眼。例如：

① What can be inferred about the target demographic of this advertisement（廣告的目標族群）?

② What can be assumed about the recipients of this notice?

③ What is suggested about the fitness equipment line?

❺ **放入句子問題**：此題型偶爾出現在廣告／通知的題組中。題型模式請參考 Week 10、Week 13 中相關敘述即可。

❻ **同義字問題**：此題型也會出現在廣告／通知的題組中。要求從 4 個選項中選出**意義最接近的字詞**，通常會用「The word "........" is closest in meaning to 的句型來詢問。」

多益會怎麼考？

多益考題會詢問一篇廣告要給誰看的問題：

KEEP AN EYE ON EVERYTHING

Ensure the safety of your home and business with Eagle Eye Surveillance Systems. We specialize in advanced security solutions such as high-definition surveillance cameras, motion-activated recording, night-vision technology, and remote-access systems. Eagle

Eye also offers a comprehensive range of services, including professional installation and ongoing support, to safeguard your property, assets, and loved ones. Our team of experienced consultants is ready to visit your location, assess your needs, and provide a tailored solution with a detailed cost estimate. Let us handle your security, so you can focus on what matters most.

Don't compromise on security. Visit our showroom at 789 Pine Street, downtown Hamilton. Or, call us today to schedule a free consultation at 1-800-298-733.

EAGLE EYE SURVEILLANCE SYSTEMS

Question. For whom is the advertisement intended?
(A) Tourists searching for travel insurance
(B) Business owners concerned about protecting their premises
(C) Homeowners seeking personal health monitoring devices
(D) Event organizers needing sound and lighting equipment

翻譯 全面掌握一切動態

使用「鷹眼」監視系統，確保您的居家及公司安全。我們致力於提供先進的安全解決方案，包括高清監視器、動態觸發錄影、夜視技術以及遠端存取系統。「鷹眼」還提供全面性的服務，包括專業安裝及不間斷的支援，以保障您的財產、資產及家人的安全。我們經驗豐富的顧問團隊可前往您的地點評估需求，並提供量身定制的解決方案與詳細報價。將安全交給我們處理，讓您專注於更重要的事情。

別在安全問題上做出任何妥協！歡迎蒞臨我們位於漢密爾頓市中心 Pine 街 789 號的展示廳，或立即致電 1-800-298-733 預約免費諮詢。

鷹眼監視系統

問題：這篇廣告是要給誰看的？
(A) 尋找旅遊保險的觀光客
(B) 關心公司場所安全的業主
(C) 尋找個人健康監控裝置的房主
(D) 需要燈光和音響設備的活動主辦方

解析 一開始提到 Eagle Eye 監視系統的目的是「確保居家或公司場所的安全（Ensure the safety of your home or business）」，並提及其提供的專業安全解決方案如高解析度監視器、夜視技術和遠端存取系統（high-definition surveillance cameras, motion-activated recording, night-vision technology, and remote-access systems），這些功能非常符合商業場所對於保護資產和監控活動的需求，故正確答案是 (B) Business owners concerned about protecting their premises。

多益會以 5W1H 疑問詞詢問公告中要求或建議事項的題目：

> Our revised weekday hours are 11 a.m. to 4 p.m., Monday to Friday. Weekend hours remain unchanged, with operations on Saturdays from 10 a.m. to 9 p.m. and Sundays from 12 p.m. to 5 p.m. During this period, the East Wing parking lot will be temporarily closed, so <u>we suggest visiting shoppers</u> park their vehicles at the parking lot adjacent to the South Wing on Riverdale Road.
>
> Thank you for your cooperation and support. For further updates and information about our services and promotions, please visit our website at www.havenplaza.com.
>
> <u>Question.</u> What are patrons advised to do?
> (A) Visit during extended evening hours
> (B) Use another parking lot
> (C) Shop online for better deals
> (D) Attend a community safety workshop

翻譯 我們調整後的平日營業時間為週一至週五上午 11 點至下午 4 點。週末營業時間維持不變，週六為上午 10 點至晚上 9 點，週日為中午 12 點至下午 5 點。在此期間，東翼停車場將暫時關閉，因此我們建議來訪的顧客將車輛停放在南翼旁邊、Riverdale 路的停車場。

感謝您的配合與支持。如需更多最新資訊以及我們服務與促銷活動的詳細內容，請造訪我們的網站：www.havenplaza.com。

問題：顧客被建議做什麼？
(A) 在延長的夜間營業時間來訪
(B) 使用另一個停車場
(C) 上網購物以獲得更優惠的價格
(D) 參加社區安全講座

解析 題目中的 patrons 就是指內文中的 shoppers。題目問顧客被告誡要做什麼（what），從「we suggest visiting shoppers park their vehicles at the parking lot adjacent to the south wing on Riverdale Road」可知，建議來訪的顧客將車輛停放在南翼旁邊、Riverdale 路的停車場，故答案是 (B) Use another parking lot。

▶ 實用策略

求職 / 求才廣告的內容編排通常是固定的：**工作職稱 → 求職者資格 → 公司簡介**與**員工福利 → 額外的有利條件**。「通知」的內容編排，一般來說順序為**主題 → 計畫 → 要求事項 → 進行方式**」。

必備 Point 1

廣告或通知的「**尋找主題／目的**」問題，就是在詢問廣告的標的、通知事項為何。通常解題線索集中在**廣告的大小標題**中、通知的**開頭前兩句**。例如：

> **Seeking Two Marketing Associates at San Francisco office**
>
> Henderson & Co. Ltd is a rapidly growing digital marketing agency specializing in brand development for startups and small businesses. We are looking to recruit creative and driven individuals to join our Marketing Associate program. A degree in marketing, communications, or business is preferred, and applicants must have strong proficiency in social media management tools and data analysis platforms...
>
> Question. What is being advertised?
> (A) Job openings for graphic designers in a marketing company
> (B) Positions for marketing professionals in a growing digital agency
> (C) Internship opportunities for students in marketing management
> (D) Freelance roles for social media influencers

標題已經告訴我們要找的職缺是「Marketing Associates」，且提到「A degree in...」，顯然 (C)、(D) 都是錯的。另外，可別看到 (A) 的 marketing company 就以為答案是它了，graphic designers 並非應徵的職位，故答案是有「Positions for marketing professionals」的 (B)。

必備 Point 2

在「**5W1H 疑問詞**」的問題中，除了辨識疑問詞（what/when/where/who...）之外，找出題目的「核心語句」相當重要。接著要在廣告／通知中搜尋與核心語句有關的部分，並在上下文中尋找與答案相關的提示。以下是一篇飯店公告的部分內容：

> Various dining options are available, all of which include complimentary drinks and desserts. They are as follows:
> **Basic Meal** — choice of one main dish with a side salad and a drink: $12
> **Standard Meal** — choice of one main dish, two sides, a dessert, and a drink: $18
> **Deluxe Meal** — choice of two main dishes, two sides, a dessert, a drink, and a complimentary appetizer: $25
>
> Question. What is only available in a Deluxe Meal?
> (A) A side salad
> (B) A complimentary appetizer
> (C) A dessert
> (D) A drink

(A) → A side salad 包含於 Basic Meal（choice of one main dish with a side salad and a drink）中，因此並非只有 Deluxe Meal 提供。(B) → A complimentary appetizer 只有 Deluxe Meal 提供，因此是正確答案。(C) 與 (D) → 短文中提到所有餐點都包括 desserts 以及 drink，因此皆非 Deluxe Meal 獨有

必備 Point 3

對於「**Not/True**」的問題，務必先確認問題的解答是否必須在**整個篇章**中尋找，或者是可以在**特定區域**找到的細節問題。如果篇章長度較短，無論題型屬於何種，都較容易解題；但若篇章較長且解題線索在不特定位置，那就**先解答其他問題**，藉此了解內容後有助於解答最後的棘手問題。請見以下一場音樂會（concert）通知的一部分：

> Join us tonight for an unforgettable musical experience! The Angel Trio will perform tonight, bringing their signature harmonies to Life Arts Center at 8:00 PM. Relax and enjoy the performance while indulging in complimentary snack and beverages. Doors open at 7:30 PM, and seating is on a first-come, first-served basis. This is a perfect way to unwind and celebrate the joy of music. Don't miss it!
>
> Question. What is indicated about the concert?
> (A) Tickets must be purchased in advance.
> (B) The event will take place outdoors.
> (C) Only classical music will be performed.
> (D) Refreshments will be provided.

從「... enjoy the performance while indulging in complimentary snack and beverages」的關鍵線索可知，音樂會現場提供免費的點心和飲料，所以 (D) 是正確答案。請注意 Refreshments → complimentary snack and beverages 的替換用語。

必備 Point 4

細節「**推論**」問題，在「廣告」與「通知」類型的文本中是必考的。考生們不一定要讀完整篇內容才能解答，重點還是先擺在題目提供的「**關鍵語句**」，然後找出文本中相關的**替換表達**（paraphrasing）。另外，請特別注意文本中出現的**數字**（例如**序數**）、**例外情況**、**最高級等**字眼。請見以下一篇年度促銷活動廣告的一部分：

> **Annual Sale is Here – Exciting Offers Await!**
>
> Get ready for unbeatable deals at our exclusive sale event! During the sale, stores will be open from 10:00 a.m. to 10:00 p.m., with extended hours during the special event that gives you plenty of time to shop for your favorite items. Enjoy discounts of up to 50% on selected products, including fashion, electronics, and home essentials. You can purchase at both our City Center and Riverdale Mall, ensuring convenience no matter where you are. Stock is limited, so don't wait—visit us today and take advantage of these incredible savings!
>
> Question. What can be inferred about the company?
> (A) All of its products are discounted by 50%.
> (B) All its stores close by 10:00 p.m. on regular days.
> (C) It has more than one location.
> (D) The sale is only available online.

廣告中有提到和「the company」相關的敘述是「You can purchase at both our City Center and Riverdale Mall」，由此可知，促銷活動的地點在該公司的 City Center 和 Riverdale Mall 都有，廣告這裡的 both 就是個「數字」類型的字眼，因此可推論該公司不只一個營業據點，正確答案為 (C)。

必備 Point 5

如果看到「**放入句子**」問題，請先處理題組中的其他問題，最後再解決此問題。接著以 3 條線索來解題：

WEEK 14 廣告&通知的題目

❶ 以「插入句」中的指示詞為線索。例如：
要放入的句子是「With this award, the company has reached a significant milestone in its history.」，那麼就可以把它擺在「This year, the company received the prestigious Innovation Award.」這個句子後面。因為有「this award」，其前一句一定會提到某個獎項。

❷ 以「插入句」中的連接性副詞為線索。例如：
要放入的句子是「Meanwhile, the customer service team is working on resolving other urgent issues.」，那麼就可以把它擺在「The technical team is focused on addressing the recent software glitches.」這個句子後面。因為有 meanwhile 表示同時發生的另一件事情，與前一句形成同時發生的對照，因此應放在該句後。

❸ 以「插入句」本身的關鍵內容作為線索。例如：
要放入的句子是「As a team leader, he aims to foster a more collaborative work environment.」，那麼就可以把它擺在「Mr. Stevens was recently promoted to the role of department manager.」這個句子後面。因為「插入句」中的 team leader 與前一句的「部門經理」相呼應，所以應注意**前後兩句的相關聯字彙**，就很容易可以確認答案。

多益會怎麼考？

多益會針對通知中提到的人事物，考細節型的「推論」問題：

NOTICE: Temporary Service Suspension
Posted on November 19

At Riverbank Trust, we are committed to providing reliable and secure services to our valued customers. To maintain this standard, periodic updates to our systems are essential. We must temporarily **suspend mobile banking services** to complete critical upgrades.

Service Interruption Details:
Service Affected: Mobile banking application
Start Time: 11:00 PM, November 25
End Time: 6:00 AM, November 26

We sincerely apologize for any inconvenience this may cause. For urgent account transactions during this period, please contact our 24-hour customer service staff. ...

Question. What is a recommended **alternative during the service interruption**?
(A) Visiting the bank's headquarters during the business hours
(B) Using a different mobile banking application
(C) Dialing a hotline for assistance
(D) Waiting until the service resumes

翻譯 公告：臨時服務暫停
張貼日期：11月19日

為了向我們寶貴的客戶提供可靠且安全的服務，河岸信託銀行始終致力於提升服務品質。為了維持此標準，我們需定期進行系統更新。我們將暫時停用行動銀行服務以完成關鍵升級。

服務中斷詳情：
受影響的服務：行動銀行應用程式
開始時間：11月25日 晚上11:00
結束時間：11月26日 早上6:00

我們對此期間可能給您帶來的不便深感抱歉。如需在此期間處理緊急帳戶交易，請聯繫我們的24小時客服人員。

問題：問題：在服務中斷期間，有什麼建議的替代方案？
(A) 在營業時間內前往銀行總部
(B) 使用不同的行動銀行應用程式
(C) 撥打客服熱線尋求協助
(D) 等待服務恢復

解析 題目關鍵與句是「alternative during the service interruption」，問的是「服務中斷期間，有什麼建議的替代方案」。從「For urgent account transactions during this period, please...」這部分可推知，「撥打客服專線」是替代方案，所以答案是 (C)。

▶ TOEIC 實戰演練

Part 7 請在以下四個選項中選出正確的答案

Questions 1-2 refer to the following advertisement.

COMPUTER COURSES AT SUNRISE SCHOOL

Are you looking to enhance your digital skills? Do you want to learn how to use essential computer tools effectively? If so, join us in Room 202 at

Sunrise School on Thursdays at 7 p.m. from January 10 to February 28. Emily Wong, an experienced IT educator, will guide participants in mastering basic computer operations, document editing, and creating impactful presentations using widely-used software programs. The fee is $25 per session.

To register, please visit www.sunriseschool.edu/courses/computers. A detailed course outline will be available soon.

For more information about our wide range of classes, including art workshops and foreign language programs, visit www.sunriseschool.edu/courses.

01 Why was the advertisement written?

(A) To promote a summer camp program
(B) To encourage participation in a school's computer courses
(C) To showcase a new software application
(D) To provide information about a library's resources

02 What will Emily Wong teach?

(A) Creating effective presentations
(B) Editing technical manuals
(C) Repairing hardware components
(D) Practicing foreign language skills

Questions 3-5 refer to the following notice.

Pulse Fitness Center: Member Guidelines

At Pulse Fitness Center, we are committed to creating a welcoming and safe environment for all our members. To maintain this standard, we would like to inform you of the following policies regarding the use of our facilities. — [1] —.

Lockers are available in our changing rooms for storing your belongings during workouts. However, please refrain from storing highly valuable items in the lockers, as Pulse Fitness Center cannot be held responsible for lost or stolen property. — [2] —. For added security, you may deposit valuables at the front desk, where they will be stored securely. — [3] —.

If you misplace any items during your visit, please approach the front desk immediately. Our staff will assist you in checking the lost-and-found section and taking necessary steps to locate your belongings.

— [4] —. Thank you for your understanding and support. Should you have any further questions or require assistance, feel free to reach out to our friendly staff members.

    The Management

---

03   What is the purpose of the notice?

    (A) To describe the center's membership benefits
    (B) To explain policies about personal items and valuables
    (C) To announce updates on the center's opening hours
    (D) To provide instructions for using exercise equipment

---

04   According to the notice, what should members do to secure their valuable items?

    (A) Place them in the lockers provided in the changing rooms
    (B) Keep them with themselves at all times during workouts
    (C) Deposit them at the front desk for safekeeping
    (D) Place them in the rented lockers provided by the fitness center

---

05   In which of the positions marked [1], [2], [3], and [4] does the following sentence best belong?

    "Please note that locker use is on a first-come, first-served basis."

    (A) [1]
    (B) [2]
    (C) [3]
    (D) [4]

WEEK 15 備忘錄 & 說明的題目

▶ 出題模式

必備 Point 1

備忘錄（memo）有點像電子郵件的編排方式，通常用來傳達公司內部政策或設施相關、工作通知、公司舉辦活動等。**說明**（information）是提供資訊的文本，其涵蓋範圍很廣，可能是產品、飯店設施或各種活動的使用說明，也可能以**網頁**（web page）的形式呈現。

必備 Point 2

常考問題類型：尋找主題／目的、5W1H 問題、Not/True 問題及推論問題。例如：

❶ 尋找主題／目的：可能詢問備忘錄／說明的目的或主要關於什麼。例如：

① Why was the memo written?

② What is mainly disclosed in the memo?

③ What is the information about?

④ What is the purpose of the information?

❷ 5W1H 疑問詞的問題：「備忘錄」可能詢問特定任務、工作截止日、未來行程或計劃、誰是此項任務的負責人或聯絡人，或其他相關細節事項…等；「說明」可能詢問受眾是誰、流程或規則的細節、遵守的事項、如何申請、所需條件為何，或者提到的特定例外情況…等。例如：

① What steps should staff take after receiving this memo?

② Who is the memo addressed to?

③ When is the Banff Travel Bureau closed?

④ Where can employees find additional details?

⑤ When is the deadline mentioned in the information?

⑥ Who is responsible for implementing the changes outlined in the information?

⑦ For which department is this information most relevant?

❸ Not/True 問題：通常詢問關於備忘錄的發文者、傳達的訊息或所涉及的政策與指示是否正確；而「說明」通常詢問關於文本提供的資訊、操作步驟、

流程或條款的敘述是否正確。題目通常會有 indicated、mentioned、stated、(NOT) true…等字眼。例如：

① What is indicated about the deadline?

② Which of the following is NOT listed as an action required by employees?

③ What is mentioned as a reason for the policy update?

④ What is stated as the primary goal of the information provided?

⑤ Which of the following is NOT included in the memo as a department's responsibility?

❹ 推論問題：主要針對備忘錄中提到的事項（如指示、規定、負責人或後續行動計劃等），或說明文章中提供的資訊（如程序、條款、建議或背景原因等），或與此相關的具體內容，詢問可以推論得知的資訊。通常題目中會有 inferred、implied、suggested 等字眼。例如：

① What can be inferred about intended audience of the memo?

② What can be considered a matter of urgency for the company?

③ What is suggested about the guidelines?

多益會怎麼考？

多益考題會詢問備忘錄要給誰看的問題：

To: All Department Staff
Subject: Updated Responsibilities for Q1 Campaigns

Dear Team,
Starting next month, all team members are expected to collaborate closely with the Design and Sales departments to ensure a successful launch of **our Q1 marketing campaigns**. Specific tasks include reviewing promotional materials, analyzing target audience feedback, and providing weekly progress updates during team meetings. Please ensure all tasks are completed by the specified deadlines. For further clarification, contact the department head by email.

Thank you,
Management

Question: Who is the memo addressed to?
(A) Marketing department staff
(B) The employees of the sales department
(C) Design department personnel
(D) Entire company staff

翻譯 收件人：全體部門員工
主旨：第一季度活動責任更新

親愛的團隊成員：
從下個月開始，所有團隊成員需與設計部門和業務部門密切合作，確保我們第一季度行銷活動的順利推出。具體任務包括審核宣傳材料、分析目標受眾的回饋，以及在團隊會議中提供每週進度更新。請確保所有任務在指定的截止日期前完成。如需進一步了解，請以電子郵件聯繫部門主管。

感謝您！
管理部

問題：這備忘錄是寫給誰看的？
(A) 行銷部門員工
(B) 業務部門員工
(C) 設計部門員工
(D) 全公司員工

解析 題目問備忘錄的受眾為何人，首先當然是先從一開始的「To: ...」來看，不過通常題目的設計很少會讓考生這麼輕鬆找到答案，所以這裡從「To: All Department Staff」完全無法確定是「哪個部門」，所以得繼續往下找線索。從「to ensure a successful launch of our Q1 marketing campaigns」可知，這是給行銷部門的員工看的，故正確答案是 (A)。

多益會考何種產品「使用說明」的細節推論問題：

SAFETY INSTRUCTIONS

This machine is designed for safe and efficient use when operated properly. However, improper use or lack of maintenance can result in injury or damage. For your protection, follow the steps below:

Placement: Ensure it is placed on a flat, stable surface in a well-ventilated area. Keep it away from walls or objects to allow free movement.

Usage: Wear proper footwear and avoid loose clothing to prevent entanglement. Always use the safety key and start at a low speed before gradually increasing the pace.

Inspection: ...

Maintenance: ...

Question. Where would the instruction most likely appear?
(A) On a food product package
(B) In a treadmill user manual
(C) In a guide for gym exercises
(D) On a poster in a fitness store

翻譯 安全使用指南

本機器在正確操作下的設計是安全且效果不錯的。然而，不當使用或鮮少進行維護的話，可能導致受傷或損壞。為了您的安全，請遵循以下步驟：

置放：務必將機器放置在平坦穩固的表面上，且位於通風良好的區域。將機器與牆壁或其他物體保持適當距離，以確保使用時有足夠的活動空間。

使用：穿著合適的運動鞋，避免穿著寬鬆的衣物以防捲入機器。務必使用安全鑰匙，並以低速啟動後逐漸提高速度。

檢查：...

維護：...

問題：以上指南最有可能出現在哪裡？
(A) 食品包裝上
(B) 跑步機使用手冊中
(C) 健身運動指南中
(D) 健身器材商店的海報上

解析 此類題型的答題線索可能在文本中的任何位置。一開始提到是一部機器（machine）的安全使用說明，所以 (A) 可直接剔除。接著從 Placement（擺放位置）和 Usage（使用方式）的「placed on a flat, stable surface」、「Wear proper footwear」、「use the safety key」、「start at a low speed」等可推知，這是一部跑步機的使用說明，故答案是 (B)。

▶ 實用策略

備忘錄或說明的內容編排通常具條理性和結構化。因此表現在各類題型上，比較有跡可循。其中常有條列式的具體訊息、指示或細節，通常也是答題線索的來源。另外，特別留意與「期限」、「聯絡方式」有關的敘述。

必備 Point 1

備忘錄或說明的「**尋找主題／目的**」問題，就是在詢問這篇「備忘錄」要傳達的主要訊息或這篇說明的核心目標。通常解題線索集中在備忘錄的主題（subject）行或開頭段落，以及「說明」內容中的第一段文字。例如：

MEMORANDUM
To: All R&D Engineers
From: Michael Chen, Department Manager
Subject: Project Update Submissions
Date: November 15

I understand that your workloads are often heavy, and I greatly value the dedication you bring to your projects. However, it is essential that you adhere to the schedule for submitting project updates promptly. Please note that all progress reports must be completed and submitted by the end of each week, detailing...

Question. Why was the memo written?
(A) To remind workers of handing in their tasks punctually
(B) To announce changes in project deadlines
(C) To request feedback on progress reports
(D) To commend engineers for their dedication to work

對於「尋找主旨」的題型，需注意並仔細地確認備忘錄的前面部分，第二句的「it is essential that you adhere to the schedule for submitting project updates promptly」提到，請大家務必按時遵守提交專案更新的內容，故答案是 (A)。

必備 Point 2

在「**5W1H 疑問詞**」的問題中，除了辨識疑問詞（what/when/where/who...）之外，找出題目的「核心語句」相當重要。接著要在備忘錄／資訊中搜尋與核心語句有關的部分，並在上下文中尋找與答案相關的提示。以下是一篇游泳池管理站發布的資訊部分內容：

> **SUNSET SWIMMING POOL**
>
> The team at Sunset Swimming Pool aims to ensure all visitors have a safe and enjoyable experience. To help us maintain a pleasant environment, we kindly ask that visitors observe the following guidelines:
> 　（中略）
> … For information about swimming lessons or water aerobics classes, please inquire at the front desk.
>
> Question. How can visitors register for a swimming lesson?
> (A) By contacting the main office of the pool management
> (B) By approaching a staff member at the service counter
> (C) By visiting a lifeguard around the swimming pool
> (D) By registering directly through the coaches

題目的核心語句是「visitors register for a swimming lesson」，從「For information about swimming lessons or water aerobics classes, please inquire at the front desk」的敘述可知，如需了解游泳課程或水中有氧運動課程的相關資訊，請至服務櫃檯洽詢，因此答案為 (B)。

必備 Point 3

「**Not/True**」的問題，同樣必須針對題目的關鍵語句，確認問的是整個篇章所有內容，或者是關於特定人事物的細節事項。通常備忘錄和資訊的篇章較長，可以先處理其他問題，同時亦可大略先了解一些內容。例如，以下度假中心主管發文給所有員工的備忘錄：

> To:　　　All staff
> From:　　Edward Chen, Resort General Manager
> Subject: Exclusive Group Stay
> Date:　　November 15
> 　（中略）
> The agreement specifies that all meals will be provided at no additional cost to them. Additionally, guests will enjoy complimentary access to the resort's pool, fitness center, and wellness lounge. However, charges will apply for any room service orders or international phone calls they make.

題目可能這麼問：What is NOT mentioned about the service for the guests? 接著請從以下四個選項找出正確答案：

(A) They will receive complimentary transportation to the resort.
(B) They don't have to pay for the use of recreational facilities.
(C) No extra fees will be required for any of the guests' meals.
(D) They will be billed for making overseas calls.

從「The agreement specifies that...」這段內容可知，所有餐點免費提供給賓客。此外，他們還可以免費使用度假村的游泳池、健身中心和健康休息室。然而，若使用客房服務或撥打國際電話，則需另行收費。但並未提到免費接送服務，因此答案是 (A)。

必備 Point 4

針對細節「**推論**」問題，請先確認題目的關鍵語句，如果是沒有關鍵語句，例如「What can be inferred from the memo/information?」這種無法縮小線索範圍的題目，就放到最後再處理。以下是一篇行政助理發文給所有員工的備忘錄。題目可能問：關於 Sunlit Publishing 這家出版社，暗示著什麼？

To: All Editorial Team
From: Anna Liang
Subject: Guest Speaker Event
Date: November 23

Hello everyone,
I'm excited to inform you about a special speaking event taking place at our Sunlit Publishing headquarters on Friday, December 15. Renowned author David Harper, best known for his book Crafting Stories That Captivate, will be joining us to share his insights on storytelling and narrative techniques. Mr. Harper has collaborated with several prestigious publishing houses, including Global Ink and Narrative Press, making his expertise highly relevant to our work.
（中略）

Anna Liang
Assistant to the President

Question. What is suggested about Sunlit Publishing?
(A) David Harper is the editor-in-chief for the publisher.
(B) It specializes in strategic marketing techniques
(C) It hosts a speaking event every year.
(D) It has at least one branch elsewhere.

從「I'm excited to inform you about a special speaking event taking place at our Sunlit Publishing headquarters...」的敘述可知，Sunlit Publishing 的總公司舉辦一場講座，這暗示著它在別的地方還有分公司或分據點，因此答案為 (D)。

多益會怎麼考？

多益會針對網頁資訊篇章中提到的人事物，考「NOT true」問題：

---

http://www.orchardhotel.com/services

| HOME | ABOUT | SERVICES | CONTACT | ROOMS |

Orchard Hotel offers a variety of premium services for guests:

ROOM SERVICE: Enjoy in-room dining with our 24-hour room service. A $10 service fee applies for orders below $50, while orders exceeding this amount are delivered free of charge. This service is available to all hotel guests during their stay.

EVENT CATERING: Orchard Hotel provides professional catering services for conferences, celebrations, and private gatherings. We can accommodate groups of up to 500 guests and will help you customize a menu to suit your event. Tableware, glassware, and linens can be included without any additional fee. For inquiries, contact our catering specialist, Linda Wong, at lwong@orchardhotel.com.

Question. What is NOT true about the hotel's catering service?
(A) Its conference facilities can accommodate up to 100 participants.
(B) It offers catering services for both large and small-scale events.
(C) Room service is free for all hotel guests, regardless of the order amount.
(D) Event catering inquiries can be directed to Linda Wong.

翻譯 http://www.orchardhotel.com/services
首頁 | 關於我們 | 服務項目 | 聯絡方式 | 房間

Orchard 飯店提供多樣化的高級服務，滿足客人的需求：

客房服務： 享受我們全天候 24 小時的客房餐飲服務。若訂單金額低於 50 美元，需支付 10 美元的服務費；訂單金額超過此數額則免服務費。本服務適用於所有入住期間的飯店客人。

WEEK 15 備忘錄 & 說明的題目

活動餐飲：Orchard Hotel 提供專業的餐飲服務，適用於會議、慶祝活動及私人聚會。我們最多可接待 500 人的團體，並協助您量身訂製活動菜單。同時提供餐具、玻璃杯及桌布，不再額外收費。如需諮詢，請聯絡我們的餐飲專員 Linda Wong，電子郵件地址為 lwong@orchardhotel.com。

問題：以下哪一項關於飯店的餐飲服務敘述是不正確的？
(A) 其會議設施可容納最多 100 名參加者。
(B) 提供適用於大小型活動的餐飲服務。
(C) 客房服務給予所有飯店住客均免費，不論訂單金額大小。
(D) 活動餐飲服務的相關諮詢可聯絡 Linda Wong。

解析 本題線索可縮小範圍至 EVENT CATERING 這一段。(A) 的敘述可對照「We can accommodate groups of up to 500 guests...」這部分，所以是錯誤的敘述；(B) 的敘述可對照「help you customize a menu to suit your event」這部分，所以是正確的敘述；(C) 的敘述可對照「Tableware, glassware, and linens can be included without any additional fee」這部分，所以是正確的敘述；(D) 的敘述可對照「For inquiries, contact our catering specialist, Linda Wong」這部分，所以是正確的敘述。故本題答案應選 (A)。

▶ TOEIC 實戰演練

Part 7 請在以下四個選項中選出正確的答案

Questions 1-2 refer to the following memo.

GREEN MEADOWS RESIDENTIAL COMMUNITY

Date: November 25
To: All Residents
From: Emily Wong, Community Manager
Subject: Temporary Water Supply Interruption

Dear Residents,

  We would like to inform you that there will be a temporary interruption to the water supply in our community on Monday, November 27, from 9:00 AM to 4:00 PM, due to essential maintenance work on the main water line. During this time, we kindly ask all residents to plan ahead and store enough water for your needs.

Please note:

   Restroom and kitchen water supply will be unavailable during the maintenance period.

   Drinking water stations will be set up at the community clubhouse for your convenience.

   We appreciate your understanding and cooperation during this temporary disruption. Should you have any questions or concerns, please contact the management office at 555-123-4567.

Thank you,

Emily Wong

Community Manager

01 What is the purpose of the memo?

(A) To inform residents of a planned water outage
(B) To announce new community guidelines
(C) To notify residents of an emergency repair
(D) To explain changes to water billing

02 What did Ms. Wong recently do?

(A) Announced the opening of a new clubhouse
(B) Arranged alternative drinking water provisions
(C) Installed additional water storage tanks
(D) Extended the water outage duration

Questions 3-6 refer to the following information.

Global Adventures Travel Cancellation Policies

   Planning a vacation with Global Adventures Travel requires detailed arrangements for both our agency and our clients. We understand that unexpected changes can arise and have developed the following cancellation policies to accommodate our customers while covering the costs incurred by our operations.

   To cancel your booking, you may email us at cancellations@globaladventures.com or mail a written request to our office at 200 Explorer Avenue, Los Angeles, CA 90015. Alternatively, cancellations can be made by calling our hotline at 1-888-555-9090. Please provide a contact phone number in your request. All rescheduling requests are subject to approval on a case-by-case basis. Refund details for cancellations are outlined below.

Days prior to departure	Refund amount
10 days or less	No refund
11 to 20 days	30% refund of the package price
21 to 40 days	60% refund of the package price
41 days or more	Full refund of the package price

For any questions or assistance, please contact our customer service team at the toll-free number listed above.

03 What is the purpose of the information?

(A) To encourage early reservations
(B) To provide a guideline for cancellations and refunds
(C) To explain service fees for package adjustments
(D) To outline special offers for rescheduled trips

04 The word "arise" in paragraph 1, line 3, is closest in meaning to _____.

(A) rise
(B) occur
(C) vary
(D) elevate

05 Which of the following is NOT mentioned in the information?

(A) Refund percentages depend on cancellation timing.
(B) Customers must provide a contact number in their request.
(C) Cancellations can only be submitted via email.
(D) A full refund is given if canceled 41 days in advance.

06 What is necessary for a cancellation request?

(A) The reservation code
(B) A valid reason for cancellation
(C) Contact details for follow-up
(D) A signature from the customer

WEEK 16 雙篇文章題組

▶ 出題模式

必備 Point 1

信件／電子郵件／通知／公告是 TOEIC 雙篇文章題組出題比例較高的文本，通常出 2 個題組，各 5 小題，出現在第 176-185 題。每一個題組有 4 題是**可以根據題目句的關鍵字詞或語句，直接從其中一篇找到答案**，只有 1 題是必須**綜合兩篇的線索才能解題**（又稱為「連結問題」）。「雙篇文章」難度較高的是「**文章 + 文章**」（例如「article 報導 + letter 信件」、「advertisement 廣告 + email 電郵」…），而最常配在一起的就是「**信件 + 信件**」。此外，雙篇文章的連結問題在 GEPT 或 TOEFL 等閱讀測驗考試中，也必然會出現，因此學習此類題型的解題技巧是不可或缺的！

必備 Point 2

可鎖定單篇解題線索的題型：雙篇題組可能出現先前提及的「5W1H 疑問詞」問題、「NOT/true」問題、推論問題、同義字詞…等，但不會考「插入句子」的問題。以 TOEIC 而言，由於必須在 75 分鐘內，做完 100 題閱讀測驗題目，其實是一個「實力」及「速度」的考驗，在答題上自然也必須掌握一些技巧，而不是傻傻地讀完每一篇才開始作答。接著，大略掃過兩篇文章的類型，然後閱讀下面的題目，確認這一題可以直接從哪一篇找答案，如此才能縮短答題時間。例如：

❶ According to the notice, what was the problem with...?

☞ 如果一篇是 email，一篇是 notice，那麼就直接在 notice 的內容中找答案。

❷ Why did Mr. Zepeda write an e-mail?

☞ 如果雙篇文章是兩篇 email，那麼就直接在寄件者（From: ...）是 Mr. Zepeda 的那封 email 的內容中找答案。

❸ For whom is the advertisement intended?

☞ 如果雙篇文章是一篇 letter，一篇 advertisement，那麼就直接在 advertisement 的內容中找答案。

❹ In the email (sent to...) / notice / advertisement, the word "....." in paragraph X, line X, is closest in meaning to...

☞ 直接從指定的文本中找答案。

155

必備 Point 3

以題目關鍵字詞或關鍵語句來鎖定搜尋範圍的題型：這類題型又稱之為「**特定細節**」題型。如果題目句未點出要你在哪一篇中找答案，通常就會針對特定的人事物來提問，這也是為什麼要先大略掃過兩篇文本的內容。例如：

❶ Why was Mr. Winters not satisfied with the light fittings?

☞ 題目問 Mr. Winters 為何不滿意燈具／燈飾，所以要找到相關內容的位置。比方說，提到「燈具的品質沒有先前允諾的那麼好（The quality of the light fittings is not as high as it was promised.）」的那篇，可能就是答案的關鍵線索。

❷ What is suggested about Ms. Swanson?

☞ 如前提及，這既是「Not/true」也是「推論」問題，必須先讀過四個選項，並針對關鍵字詞「Ms. Swanson」到其中一篇中找線索。比方說，其中一篇提到「I spoke briefly with our public relations director, Millie Swanson, and she has determined that...」，而選項中可能有「She works as a public relations director.」，那麼這就是正確答案了。雖然這類題型比較棘手且費時，但立即鎖定兩篇中的其中一篇找答案是很重要的。

必備 Point 4

必須對照兩個文本才能解答的題型：這類題型又稱之為「**連結問題**」題型。首先，抓住題目句的關鍵字，判斷要先看哪一個文本。接著，根據題目句的關鍵字找出第一個線索，然後在另一篇文本中找出第二個線索。最後，綜合兩個線索，選出正確答案。請見以下範例。

多益會怎麼考？

雙篇文章的題組一定會出 1 題「連結問題」。例如，以下的 email 與 notice 題組：

Dear Sir/Madam,
As a frequent visitor to the Greenfield Library, I would like to offer a suggestion. It seems that the periodicals section lacks sufficient publications geared towards younger audiences. Many people in my age group would appreciate seeing a wider selection of magazines focused on film, music, and current trends. I hope you will consider expanding the selection to include more of these topics in the future.

Best regards,
Alex Harper

GREENFIELD PUBLIC LIBRARY

Your suggestions help us improve our facility and better serve the public. We are pleased to now offer the following titles of magazines for your reading pleasure in our periodicals section:

- Golden Years Gazette: A monthly magazine for the active senior citizen
- Movie Buff Weekly: A weekly publication for young movie lovers
- Paws & Pastimes: A quarterly magazine for pet owners
- Culinary Creations: A bi-monthly magazine for cooking enthusiasts

If you have recommendations for the titles you would like to see in the library, send us a message at service@ greenfieldlibrary.com.

01 What publication in the library does Mr. Harper probably love most?

(A) Golden Years Gazette
(B) Movie Buff Weekly
(C) Paws & Pastimes
(D) Culinary Creations

02 How often is Paws & Pastimes published?

(A) Every month
(B) Once a week
(C) Four times a year
(D) Twice a month

翻譯 先生／女士 您好：

我是格林菲爾德圖書館的常客，在此想提出一項建議。我發現期刊區缺少針對年輕讀者的刊物。我這個年齡層的許多人都很希望看到更多關於電影、音樂以及時尚類的雜誌。我希望您能考慮在未來增加更多這些題材的出版刊物。

謹啟
亞歷克斯·哈珀

格林菲爾德公共圖書館
您的建議有助於我們改進設施品質並為公眾提供更好的服務。我們很高興現在可以提供您以下期刊區的閱讀雜誌：

- 《黃金歲月報》：為活躍的老年人設計的月刊
- 《電影迷週刊》：給年輕電影愛好者的週刊
- 《毛孩與樂趣》：為寵物主人提供的季刊
- 《美食創意》：為烹飪愛好者提供的雙月刊

如果您對本圖書館有任何建議收藏的刊物，請發送郵件至 service@greenfieldlibrary.com。

> **解析** 01 題目問 Mr. Harper 在這家圖書館可能最愛的刊物為何。因為提到 Mr. Harper 這個關鍵字詞的，只有在第一篇的 email，而提到圖書館的刊物只有在第二篇的 notice，顯然本題是**必須對照兩篇文本的「連結問題」**。從第一篇的「It seems that the periodicals section lacks sufficient publications geared towards younger audiences. Many people in my age group would appreciate...」可知，Mr. Harper 屬於年輕世代的讀者，愛好的是電影、音樂 ... 等。接著我們在第二篇 notice 中發現「Movie Buff Weekly: A weekly publication for young movie lovers」，因此可推斷 Mr. Harper 應該會喜愛圖書館內的「Movie Buff Weekly」，所以答案是 (B)。
>
> 02 題目問《毛孩與樂趣》多久出刊一次（How often...），這個問題只要針對第二篇相關內容找線索即可。從「Paws & Pastimes: A quarterly magazine...」中的 quarterly（每季的）可知，答案是 (C)。

▶ 實用策略

必備 Point 1　以**雙信件的題組**而言，如果可以從寄件人或收件人發現解題線索，就可直接到那一篇信件去找答案。另外，雙信件的題組常考**特定人物相關問題**或**其之間的關係**。例如：

❶ （第一封 email/letter）　　　　　（第二封 email/letter）
From: Ms. Lin　　　　　　　　　From: Mr. Chang
To: Mr. Chang　　　　　　　　　To: Ms. Lin
Subject: York Symphony Night　　Subject: Re: York Symphony Night

---

（題目句）What did Mr. Chang advise Ms. Lin should do?

☞ 題目問 Mr. Chang 建議 Ms. Lin 去做什麼，所以通常直接在第二封 email 找線索的機會比較大些，因為寄件人是 Mr. Chang。

（題目句）What is Mr. Chang asked to do?

☞ 若題目問某人被要求做什麼事，通常可以直接在收件人為某人的那一封 email 找線索。所以這裡可以從第一封 email 找線索。

❷ （第一封 email/letter）　... I may need your assistance...

（第二封 email/letter）　... Please dial my extension 113...

（題目句）What is indicated about Mr. Chang and Ms. Lin?

☞ 選項中可能提到「兩人關係」的敘述，那麼從分機號碼（extension）（公司同事間才會有的）來判斷，兩人應是 colleagues 的關係，而非員工與客戶，或其他關係。

❸（第一封 email/letter） ... I won't be able to attend the annual conference on June 5, but I think either you or Ms. Huang will handle it...

（第二封 email/letter） ... I'll have something scheduled that day, but Ms. Huang is available to...

（題目句）Who will attend the meeting on June 5?

☞ 這是「關於特定人物」的問題。在這個例子中，題目敘述的事情（attend the meeting）在第一封出現，但仍無法得知「誰」將去參加。因此就得繼續進入第二封尋找解題線索。

必備 Point 2

以「**一般文章 + 表格**」的題組而言，像是「email 電子郵件 + invoice 發票」、「notice / announcement 通知／公告 + form 表格」…等，通常較不費時且難度較低，看懂條列式的表格內容也不會是大問題。如果表格內容中有提供額外資訊（像是「*...」、「NOTE: ...」…等），通常會是考題中的解題線索。另外，在有行程表（schedule / agenda）的問題中，通常會有行程安排上的變更內容，且是必考，在連結問題中出現的機率很高。例如：

❶（第一篇 article）

... At the festival, there will also be an auction, giving guests a chance to bid on all the wines served during the event...

（第二篇 list）

Food and Wine List

Location	Food	Wines
Section One	Cranberry-Infused Spinach Salad	Golden Mist Pinot Gris (White Wine)
Section Two	Mozzarella Olive Focaccia	Crimson Crest Pinot Noir (Red Wine)
Section Three	Brown Sugar Mustard-Glazed Salmon	Silver Blossom Moscato (Sparkling Wine)

（題目句）What is suggested about the auction?
(A) It will establish the opening bids for the food items on offer.
(B) The bidding items have been contributed by SRA members.
(C) Participants will be given a box of chocolate truffles.
(D) Red wine will be up for bidding.

☞ 這是「關於特定事物」的「何者正確」問題（→ 比較好解決，因為只要找到 1 個選項符合內文敘述，那麼答案就是它了。）同時也是個連結問題。第一步：有提到 auction（拍賣會）這個關鍵字的是第一篇的報導（article），可得到的資訊是：前來參加的賓客皆可參與酒類產品的競標。第二步：在選項中找關於競標的正確敘述，如果選項中的敘述無法從兩篇文本任何一個地方找到（也就是無中生有的敘述），那就直接判定是錯誤選項。

注意：表格中食物與酒的名字完全不重要，只是試圖造成你視覺上的干擾。

多益會怎麼考？

在「商品廣告＋訂購單」的題組中，可能考「優惠資格」的連結問題：

Fashion Heaven Outlet
Elevate your wardrobe with ease by shopping at Fashion Heaven Outlet! We offer a unique shopping experience...
（中略）
This month, we're thrilled to bring you exclusive offers. First, place an order before December 15 and receive a 10% discount voucher for your next purchase. Additionally, all orders over $200 qualify for free shipping. As a bonus, new customers who purchase any 3-piece outfit set will receive a complimentary accessory to complete the look.

Fashion Heaven Outlet Online Order Form
Name: Madison Carter
Address: 1852 East Lakeside Drive, Orlando, FL 32803
Customer account number: 072631
Points accumulated: 1,450
Order date: December 13

Product Number	Product Name	Price
J732	Casual summer dress, medium	$45
M416	Men's slim-fit chinos, size 32	$35
T894	Unisex cotton hoodie, large	$28
A587	Leather belt, black, one size	$18
F362	Classic white sneakers, size 8	$55

Total: $181

Question. What special offer is Madison Carter eligible for?
(A) A free shipping for this order
(B) A complimentary accessory with her purchase
(C) A voucher for 10% off her next purchase
(D) A discount applied directly to this order

翻譯

時尚天堂名品特賣中心
輕鬆提升您的衣櫥品味，就在時尚天堂名品特賣中心！我們提供與眾不同的購物體驗…
（中略）
本月，我們為您帶來多項獨家優惠。首先，凡在 12 月 15 日前下單的顧客，可獲得 下一次購物 10% 折扣優惠券。此外，所有滿 $200 的訂單均享免運費。最後，對於首購顧客，凡購買任何 3 件套裝系列，還可獲得免費配件，完美搭配您的造型。

時尚天堂名品特賣中心 線上訂購單
姓名：瑪迪森·卡特
地址：美國佛羅里達州奧蘭多市東湖畔大道1852號，郵遞區號32803
顧客帳戶號碼：072631
累積點數：1,450
訂購日期：12 月 13 日

商品編號	商品名稱	價格
J732	夏日休閒洋裝，中碼	$45
M416	男士修身休閒褲，32 號	$35
T894	男女通用棉質連帽衫，大碼	$28
A587	黑色皮帶，單一尺寸	$18
F362	經典白色運動鞋，8 號	$55

總計：$181

問題：瑪迪森·卡特有資格享受什麼特別優惠？
(A) 本次訂單享受免運費
(B) 購物時可獲得免費配件
(C) 下一次購物可享 10% 折扣券
(D) 本次訂單直接享有折扣

解析 當題目問某人可享有什麼優惠時，首先去找「訂購單」中購買內容，然後再與「廣告」的優惠條件作配對。從訂購單的「Total: $181」以及廣告的「all orders over $200 qualify for free shipping」可知，(A) 錯誤；從訂購單的「Points accumulated」以及廣告的「new customers who... will receive a complimentary accessory」可知，(B) 錯誤；從訂購單的「Order date: December 13」以及廣告的「place an order before December 15 and receive a 10% discount voucher for your next purchase」可知，(C) 正確；(D) 是「無中生有」的敘述，顯然錯誤。

▶ TOEIC 實戰演練

Part 7 請在以下四個選項中選出正確的答案

Questions 1-5 refer to the following brochure and e-mail.

The Holland Heritage Manor is an excellent venue for family gatherings. For more than a century, this historic site has welcomed visitors, with over fifty million people exploring its house and gardens. From August to October this year, the Holland Heritage Manor will host a series of intriguing events. Visitors can enjoy a special flower garden exhibit, take a guided tour of the house and its antique furnishings, and participate in traditional Dutch craft workshops like ceramics and loom weaving.

In September, even more events are on the schedule, including a weekly Wednesday concert series called "Harmonies of Holland in the Park." After each concert, attendees will have the opportunity of playing traditional instruments provided by the musicians.

From August to October, The Manor will be open from 11:00 A.M. to 6:00 P.M. on weekdays, 11:00 A.M. to 7:00 P.M. on Saturdays, Sundays and other national holidays. For more details, visit www.holland_heritage_manor.co.nl. Please be aware that although the Wednesday concerts are free, tickets are necessary for the music classes and can be purchased on-site.

To: Clara van der Meers <clarameers@hotmail.co.nl>
From: Juliette Renaud <jr@gmail.com>
Subject: Thank You!
Date: Sept. 15

Dear Clara,

How have you been? I wanted to thank you for sending me the brochure about the Holland Heritage Manor. I took my boyfriend there this Monday, the Labor Day, and we had a lot of fun. I think you and your family must have enjoyed it when you went there, right?

I particularly enjoyed using traditional instruments supplied by the musicians. They were very helpful, and both of us learned a lot. Besides, Willem thoroughly enjoyed strolling through the flower display. He was so pleased that we ended up staying until the house closed!

There's so much to do at the great Manor that we're thinking about going back next month. How about you and your husband join us? Let me know as soon as possible, and thanks again for recommending such a great place.

See you soon,
Juliette

---

01 What is the brochure intended for?

(A) To introduce a newly-established attraction
(B) To advertise a scenic spot
(C) To publicize a great house for sale
(D) To provide traditional craft workshops

02 What is implied about the music classes?

(A) Tickets can be purchased on the website.
(B) Admission is allowed only with tickets.
(C) They are held once a week.
(D) Attendees can meet some pop singers there.

03 According to the e-mail, what did Juliette do at the Holland Heritage Manor?

(A) She took a guided tour.
(B) She enjoyed the flower garden.
(C) She tried out some classical musical instruments.
(D) She went walking in the forest.

04 What is indicated about Clara?

(A) She works at the Holland Heritage Manor.
(B) She has a boyfriend called Willem.
(C) She has been to Holland Heritage Manor before.
(D) She planned to visit Holland Heritage Manor again sooner or later.

05 When did Juliette most likely leave the Holland Heritage Manor?

(A) 11:00 A.M.
(B) 6:00 P.M.
(C) 7:00 P.M.
(D) 8:00 P.M.

Questions 6-10 refer to the following announcement and form.

Greenwood Academy is excited to host its second annual Greenwood Charity Bazaar next month. The event will take place from 11 A.M. to 7:30 P.M. on Wednesday, September 9, in the school's central auditorium. Visitors can browse a wide array of used goods and enjoy performances by the school's singing club and a dance troupe from Harrison College. As in previous years, the market aims to raise funds for assistance for displaced families.

At the end of the day, there will be a drawing for 5 latest Apple smartphones. Whoever purchases a ticket to the market will be automatically entered into the raffle. Tickets can be purchased for $6 at the entrance of the school.

In addition, various food stalls from vendors across the country will be available on-site. Food tickets can be bought at the entrance of the school. If you're interested in setting up a food stall, please contact Ms. Elena Rodriguez at 666-0606 or email her at elena@greenwood.edu.

The organizers are also seeking volunteers to assist with the event. If you're willing to help, please fill out the online application form at www.greenwood.com/marketvol or go to the administrative office to pick up a form and return it by August 30. Volunteers will be allowed to enter the market free of charge.

Volunteer Enrollment Application

2nd Annual Greenwood Charity Bazaar

---

1. Complete the fields below and submit the form to Greenwood Academy by Friday, August 30.
2. Once we process your form, you will receive a name tag that should be worn at the charity bazaar.

Date:	August 24
Name:	Sophia Bennett
Address:	4825 Maple Lane, Oakville L8K 1N4
E-mail:	sophia.bennett@gmail.com
Phone:	(540) 313-4858

What are you willing to assist in?

Food service	
Sales booths	
Ticket sales	
Cleanup	√

06 What is indicated about the Greenwood Charity Bazaar?

(A) It will last more than 10 hours on September 9.
(B) It will feature dancing performances by the school's dancing club.
(C) It aims to raise funds for local animal shelters this year.
(D) It was first held last year.

07 What are volunteers asked to do?

(A) Buy tickets at the school's main office
(B) Hand in an application form
(C) Talk with the school's principal
(D) Make donations for displaced families

08 Who will possibly win a smartphone?

(A) All the students of Greenwood Academy
(B) Ticket-holding visitors
(C) Performers from Harrison College
(D) Approved volunteers

09 What does Ms. Bennett probably want to do?

(A) Attends Greenwood Academy
(B) Raise funds for displaced families
(C) Participate in the event for free
(D) Help to sell foods in the event

10 What will Ms. Bennett most likely do on September 9?

(A) Arrange sales stands for attendees from abroad
(B) Tidy up the auditorium after the event
(C) Handle ticket sales for those attending the event
(D) Staff the booths where different types of food will be offered

WEEK 17 三篇文章題組（1）

▶ 出題模式

三篇文章的題組唯獨出現在 TOEIC 閱讀測驗中。主要測試考生在職場環境中處理多源訊息的能力。通常會出 3 個題組，每一個題組會有 5 小題選擇題，共 15 題，出現在第 186-200 題。

必備 Point 1

信件／電子郵件是 TOEIC 三篇文章題組中出現比例最高的文本，最常搭配**網頁**（web page）、**報導**（article）的文本一起出現在題組中，其次是**廣告**（advertisement）、**評論**（review, comment）、**通知**（notice）、**公告**（announcement）等，也可能搭配一則**圖表**類型的文本，例如**單據**（bill）、**發票**（invoice）、**行程表**（schedule）、**優惠券**（voucher）…等。不過，三篇文章題組中的一般文章（email, letter, web page, article...）相較於雙篇文章題組中的會更短一些，因此解題所要花的時間不一定會比雙篇題組還長，且解題技巧也和前面提到過的雙篇題組差不多。

必備 Point 2

可鎖定單篇解題線索的題型：三篇文本的每一個題組通常有 **3 題**這樣的題型，考生必須掃過三篇文本的大致內容，並針對題目要問的特定人事物來確認答案線索在哪一篇。這些題目可能詢問「整體內容」、「特定細節」、「同義字詞」…等問題。同樣地，大略掃過每一篇文本的開頭一兩句，或每一段開頭一兩句，確認這一題可以直接從哪一篇找答案，如此才能縮短答題時間。例如：

❶ 詢問整體內容：

① Why did Mr. Smith send the e-mail to Ms. Johnson?

② What is the purpose of the memo?

③ What is the advertisement about?

❷ 詢問特定細節：

① What is Ms. Uedy advised to do on Feb. 21?

② Who is the contact for the annual conference?

③ Which product was Mr. Smith most satisfied with?

❸ 同義字詞問題：

In the article, the word "unattended" in paragraph 3, line 2, is closest in meaning to

---

必備 Point 3 **以題目關鍵字詞或語句來鎖定答題線索**：這裡針對上述「**詢問特定細節**」進一步說明。當題目句沒有明顯指出要你在哪一篇中找答案，這時候就得**在題目句中找出關鍵訊息**。例如，當第 1 篇是 advertisement，第 2 篇是 email，第 3 篇是 invoice 時，有題目這麼問：

❶ How can customers obtain a discount?
　☞ 廣告內容都會有產品說明、折扣優惠等內容，因此可直接在 advertisement 那篇找答案。

❷ What is mentioned about Mr. Smith?
　☞ 「關於某人」的事，不會出現在廣告中，所以可以在 invoice 和 email 當中找線索。

必備 Point 4 **必須對照 2~3 個文本才能解答的題型**：即所謂「**連結問題**」，通常針對其中兩篇的相關內容來出題，只有少數題型是必須綜合三篇內容（必須找到三個線索）才能解題的。同樣地，要先抓住題目句的**關鍵字詞或語句**，判斷要先看哪一個文本。接著，找出相關的第一個線索，然後判斷第二個線索會出現在其他兩個文本的哪一篇。最後，綜合兩個線索，選出正確答案。通常連結問題本身有以下特點：

❶ 一般來說，題目順序與解答的排序會是一致的，所以在解題時，按照題號順序即可。也就是說，解題線索也是按照 文本 1-2-3 的順序，跳躍式的線索布局是比較少見的。

❷ 表格的內容在題目句中出現，或者選項皆為表格中的資訊 — 又稱為「數字型考題」，基本上一定是連結問題。

❸ 題目句帶有 probably、most likely... 等字眼的「推論」題型，有很高的機率是「連結」問題。例如：

① How long did Mr. Thompson probably work for Pinnacle Publishing?

② Who will most likely become the new CEO of the company?

❹ 詢問有關特定人物的事，也就是「何者正確」或「何者為非」的題型，就必須讀完四個選項。例如：

① What is indicated/implied about Ms. Miller?

② What is suggested about Mr. Smith?

③ What is (NOT) true about Professor Huang?

多益會怎麼考？

三篇文章常考「廣告＋表格＋信件」的題組：

(Advertisement)

Northstar Publishing Group is recognized for creating some of the most widely-read periodicals in both North America and the United States. Our publications are known for the high-quality journalism and in-depth analysis. Additionally, we have received numerous awards for excellence in editorial content and design ...

Now, we are offering an exclusive opportunity for our valued readers! Subscribe today and enjoy up to 20% off your first-year subscription. Simply visit our website and enter the promo code READ20 at checkout to unlock this special offer. Don't miss this chance...

(Invoice)

Northstar Publishing Group
Subscriber: Jameson Carter

Periodical	Details	Number of Issues	Price
Current Highlights	Inaugural Issue	1	$20.0
Culinary Mastery	August Issue	1	$25.0

(Email)

I'm writing to inform you about a problem with the invoice. It appears that the total amount billed does not match the sum of the individual items listed. Specifically, the invoice incorrectly reflects a charge of $50.00. Please review the details and revise the invoice accordingly ...

Question.
01 How can subscribers get a discount?
(A) Send an email to the editorial team
(B) Call customer service to request it
(C) Shop online and use a discount key during checkout
(D) Visit a local bookstore and show a promo code

02 How much did Mr. Carter overcharged?
(A) $5　　(B) $10　　(C) $20　　(D) $25

翻譯

（廣告）
北極星出版集團因創作出北美和美國最受歡迎的期刊之一而廣受讚譽。我們的出版物以高品質新聞報導和深入的分析聞名。此外，我們在編輯內容和設計方面也屢獲殊榮…
現在，我們為尊貴的讀者提供一個獨家機會！立即訂閱，享受首年訂閱最高八折優惠。只要上我們的官網，在結帳時輸入促銷代碼 READ20，即可解鎖此優惠。不要錯過這個機會…

（發票）
北極星出版集團
訂閱者：詹姆森·卡特

期刊名稱	細目	期數	價格
《時事精選》	創刊號	1	$20.0
《美食大師》	八月號	1	$25.0

（電子郵件）
我寫這封信是為了告知您關於發票的問題。看起來總計金額與列出的各項目價格加總後的金額不符。具體而言，發票上顯示的總計費用為 $50.00，但這似乎有誤。請您檢查發票明細並進行相應的修正…

問題：
01 訂閱者如何獲得折扣？
(A) 發送電子郵件給編輯團隊　　(B) 致電客戶服務部門請求折扣
(C) 上網購物並在結帳時使用折扣碼　　(D) 前往當地書店並出示促銷代碼

02 卡特先生多被收取了多少金額？
(A) $5　(B) $10　(C) $20　(D) $25

解析 01 題目問訂閱者如何獲得折扣（How... get a discount）。這樣的問題通常可以直接在廣告內容中找到線索。從「Simply visit our website and enter the promo code READ20」可得知，只要上網購買，並在結帳時輸入一個促銷代碼即可獲得折扣，所以答案是 (C)。

02 題目問卡特先生（訂閱者）被多收的金額，這類提出抱怨或問題的線索，要先看訂購者在電子郵件中怎麼說。其中提到「the invoice incorrectly reflects a charge of $50.00」，接著我們再對照發票中的兩項訂購金額合計是 $45，所以是被多收了 $5，答案是 (A)。

▶ TOEIC 實戰演練

Part 7　請在以下四個選項中選出正確的答案

Questions 1-5 refer to the following notice, memo and e-mail.

Elevator Maintenance Notice

The elevator in the Willow Tower is set, on a regular basis, for maintenance on Monday, June 15. The elevator servicemen will start at 10:30 A.M. and the inspection will last about 1.5 hours, provided everything goes as planned. Should any issues arise, the work crew will work until they are resolved.

The elevator, therefore, will be out of service while the crewmen are on duty, and everyone can take the stairwells located on the east side of the building. Thank you for your patience and we look forward to your understanding that city regulations require annual elevator inspections, which are essential for ensuring the safety and reliability of the equipment for all building occupants.

If you have any questions or feedback, don't hesitate to reach out to the management office. You can contact us at 987-5454 and please request Alex Thompson when you call.

To: All Staff, Apex Solutions
From: Jamie Taylor
Subject: Elevator Maintenance
Date: June 12

Please note that elevator maintenance will occur in the building next

Monday morning, starting at 10:30 AM and expected to end at noon. Since our office is on the top floor of Willow Tower, I recommend avoiding any trips downstairs during that time unless you're willing to use the staircase.

If you have any clients coming in during that time, consider rescheduling your meetings

or finding an alternative location to meet them. If you'll be ordering delivery, please make sure to inform them in advance to have the food delivered after 12:00. I'm sure they'll understand once you explain the situation.

To: Mia Thompson <miat@ apexsolutions.com>
From: Liam Carter < liamcarter@fasttrackshipping.com>
Subject: Arrival Notice
Date: June 15

I attempted to deliver your package to your office today (June 15) at 1:30 PM, and found that the elevator was not available due to maintenance. Besides, I couldn't find a security guard to sign for it. One of the maintenance workers told me that they might need about another hour to finish the work. Since your package weighs approximately 25 kilograms, I was unable to carry it up to the ninth floor.

I also tried to reach you at your cellphone number (0987-123456), but failed to get through. Now, I plan to return with the package on the morning of Friday, June 19. If you need it sooner, please contact the Fast Track Shipping office at 808-5432 to rearrange a pickup before Friday.

Best,
Liam Carter
Fast Track Shipping

---

01 According to the notice, what is indicated about the Willow Tower?

(A) The maintenance work is expected to be done within 2 hours.
(B) It is a mixed-use building that combines residential and commercial spaces.
(C) It had some renovation work done last year.
(D) There are two elevators in the entire building.

02 Why did Mr. Taylor write the memo?

(A) To make public an upcoming activity
(B) To reschedule a meeting
(C) To alert staff about a possible issue
(D) To grant his employees a day off

03 In the memo, the word "trips" in paragraph 1, line 3, is closest in meaning to ----------.

(A) rides
(B) sights
(C) worries
(D) walks

04 What is implied about the elevator servicemen?

(A) While working on the elevator, they identified some additional issues.
(B) They plan to tackle some unexpected problems this weekend.
(C) The elevator maintenance took them 1.5 hours.
(D) They are permanent staff members of Apex Solutions.

05 What is NOT true about Apex Solutions?

(A) Its employees were advised to avoid using the elevator on June 15.
(B) It is located in a 10-story building.
(C) Fast Track Shipping is one of its regular suppliers.
(D) Both Mia Thompson and Jamie Taylor are its employees.

Questions 6-10 refer to the following web page, e-mail and schedule.

| HOME | Latest Updates | Travel Booking | Carry-On & Checked Bags | Customer Service |

Skyway Airlines is committed to enhancing our services consistently for our clients. Recently, we have renovated the relaxation areas at three major airports. These facilities are specifically available for all members of the Skyway Airlines Miles Program.

From July 1 onwards, we will launch direct flights connecting Riverdale City and Crestwood for the debut service. Travelers who use this new route before September 1 will benefit from a 20% deduction.

To stay informed about the latest updates from Skyway Airlines, including our broadening international flight offerings next year, subscribe to our monthly newsletter here.

To: Olivia Martinez <o.martinez@crestviewcapital.com>
From: James Carter <carterj@entrepreneurnetwork.com>
Date: July 21
Subject: Forthcoming Business Seminars

Dear Ms. Martinez,

I've arranged a direct flight for you from Crestwood to Riverdale City on August 15, with a return two days later. The flight is with Skyway Airlines, and I'll let you know the full itinerary with you soon.

I also wanted to inform you that there has been some unexpected roof damage at the venue. Consequently, seminars that were set for the Sapphire Room will now take place in the Platinum Room, and those planned for the Silver Room will be held in the Main Hall. Please disregard the schedule I sent you on July 5.

I know you prefer not to use a rental car. So since the organizer does not offer an airport shuttle service, My assistant will drive over to fetch you. He'll meet you at the arrivals hall with a sign.

I appreciate your agreeing to take part in the Business Network's seminar series.

Sincerely,
James Carter

\	Spring Seminar Series – Business Network We understand the value of everyone's time, so each lecture will begin exactly as scheduled. Please make sure to plan accordingly.		
Time	**Keynote Speaker**	**Corporation**	**Seminar Location**
1:30 p.m.	Samantha Pierce	Pinnacle Ventures	Sapphire Room
2:30 p.m.	Jameson Brooks	Summit Financial	Platinum Room
	Intermission		
3:00 p.m.	Olivia Martinez	Crestview Capital	Sapphire Room
4:00 p.m.	Derek Callahan	Vertex Solutions	Silver Room
5:00 p.m.	Frank Torres	Sterling Group	Main Hall

Distributed July 5

06 What is NOT true about Skyway Airlines?

(A) It has renovated the passenger areas at all its major airports.
(B) It will soon initiate non-stop flights between Riverdale City and Crestwood.
(C) It currently operates both domestic and overseas flights.
(D) It offers a loyalty program to passengers.

07 What is suggested about Ms. Martinez?

(A) She is scheduled to return on August 16.
(B) She'll need to connect to a flight to Riverdale City.
(C) She lives in Riverdale City.
(D) Her flight offers a price reduction.

08 How will Ms. Martinez get to the conference facility?

(A) By taking a shuttle bus
(B) By taking a booked taxi
(C) By taking a ride with Mr. Carter's coworker
(D) By getting a lift from one of her best friends

09 In the email, the word "fetch" in paragraph 3, line 2, is closest in meaning to

(A) collect
(B) expect
(C) grasp
(D) capture

10 Where will Ms. Pierce deliver a speech?

(A) In the Sapphire Room
(B) In the Main Hall
(C) In the Platinum Room
(D) In the Silver Room

WEEK 18 三篇文章題組 (2)

▶ 實用策略

快速掃描 3 篇文本的類型與大致內容，大略掌握 3 篇之間的關係，是處理 3 篇文章題組的第一步。接下來**閱讀並標記**每一個文本的**標題**、**開頭幾句**及**結尾**，抓取**核心訊息**。由於**電子郵件**在三篇題組中頻繁出現，要注意的是**日期**、**時間**、**姓名**、**地點**等重要資訊。此外，掌握**圖表**上的基本元素就能掌握住重點。再次提醒：請優先處理簡單問題，特別是「**可鎖定單篇解題線索的題型**」，逐步構建對整體文章的理解。以下介紹 TOEIC 三篇文章題組中，最頻繁出現的組合及「**連結問題**」解題策略。

必備 Point 1

電子郵件／信件 + 相關文章 + 表格的題組：電子郵件或信件搭配廣告、通知…等相關文章，再加上一則表格的題組中，首先要注意**寄件人或收件人的相關資訊**。例如：

（第一篇 email/letter）

> To: Maria Lin <m.lin@ecoimpact.org>
> From: Lucas Grant <l.grant@ecoimpact.org>
> ...
> Dear Maria,
> I've reviewed the reports you prepared on renewable energy adoption and carbon offset strategies. Frankly, it's hard to determine which one would be better suited for publication. ... Whichever report they choose not to publish could be submitted for the upcoming conference in Copenhagen.
> ...

（第二篇 notice）

> **Global Renewable Energy and Sustainability Conference**
> December 10 | Copenhagen, Denmark
> Organized by the International Council for Environmental Progress in partnership with EcoImpact Research, this conference brings

together leading experts, policymakers, and academics to discuss…
…

（第三篇 schedule）

Global Renewable Energy and Sustainability Conference
EVENT ITINERARY
1:00 - 2:00 p.m. Presentation: Innovations in Renewable Energy, with Lucas Grant
2:30 - 4:00 p.m. Presentation: Carbon Offset Strategies, with Maria Lin
4:30 - 6:00 p.m. Networking Event at Copenhagen Green Center
…

（題目可能這樣問） What is true about Ms. Lin?

（可能的答案選項） Her report on renewable energy adoption was chosen for publication.

☞ Ms. Lin 就是 email 的收件人，也就是 Maria Lin。電子郵件中提到，她提出兩份報告：renewable energy adoption 以及 carbon offset strategies。未被選中出版的報告，將允許在哥本哈根的發表會上發表。在發表會的行程表中，可以看到「2:30 - 4:00 p.m. Presentation: Carbon Offset Strategies, with Maria Lin」，也就是說被選中出版的是 renewable energy adoption 這份報告。

必備 Point 2

表格＋相關文章的題組：第一篇可能是請款單／發票（invoice）、收據（receipt）、報名表（registration form）…等。第二、三篇是與該表格相關的信件。例如：

（第一篇 registration form）

EDUTRAIN
Advanced Training Center for Professionals
NAME:
COMPANY:
TEL:
…

[1]**Advanced Presentation Skills**, with *Clara Martinez*	Master the art of delivering impactful and professional presentations
Time Management for Professionals, with *Eric Dawson*	Boost your productivity by learning effective time management techniques.
...	

(第二篇 email)

To: Jamie Foster
From: Olivia Carter
Subject: Edutrain

Hi Jamie,
I just finished attending the course, and I must say, it was an incredibly valuable experience. [1]It taught essential strategies for creating memorable and highly effective skills in briefing with confidence and clarity...
Although we first agreed on just one course, I'm considering adding another on enhancing productivity [2]if I can successfully negotiate a reduced cost for a pair of courses.
...

(第三篇 email)

To: Olivia Carter
From: EDUTRAIN customer service
Subject: Training Sessions

Dear Ms. Carter,
In line with our agreement, a one-day training session is set to be held at your workplace on Wednesday, August 12. [2]"Time Management for Professionals" will be held in the morning and "Sales Management Mastery" in the afternoon...
...

❶（題目可能這樣問）Whose class did Mr. Carter attend?

（答案選項）Clara Martinez

☞ 題目問 Mr. Carter 去參加誰的課程，那麼就從他寄的 email 中找第一個線索。其中有提到他去參加的課程感到很滿意，因為該課程教的是創建令人難忘且高效的簡報技巧，幫助自己自信和清晰表達。那麼教導簡報技巧的是哪一位老師呢？答案當然就在第一篇的報名表上。注意這裡相關的替換表達：presentation → briefing。

❷（題目可能這樣問）What is suggested about Mr. Carter?

（可能的答案選項）He successfully negotiated a reasonable cost.

☞ 關於 Mr. Carter 的事，當然跟一張空白的報名表沒有任何關係。所以要在兩篇電郵中找線索。在他寫的 email 那篇中看到「如果他能夠成功地協商出**雙課程的減免價格（a reduced cost for a pair of courses）**」。接著在機構發給他的電郵中提到，根據彼此的約定，「專業人員時間管理術」以及「精通銷售管理」舉行的時間與地點，因此我們可推知他確實獲得了減免的優惠價格。

必備 Point 3

報導 + 相關文章的題組：活動、企業動向、新產品相關報導，搭配討論此消息的信件或電子郵件等。此外，郵件中的**日期**、提到的**例外狀況**或**變故**等，通常會是解題線索。例如：

（第一篇 article）

TechSphere to Open Third Store in San Francisco
By Kevin Grant

TechSphere, a renowned electronics retail chain, has announced plans to open its third store in San Francisco...
... Unlike the [2]flagship downtown store in New York, which houses a coffee lounge, [1]a streamlined shopping experience with self-checkout kiosks and express pick-up services for online orders.
...

（第二篇 letter）

May 10
Kevin Grant
Tech Today News

Unit 234, Parker Building, 789 Oak Avenue
Los Angeles, CA 90210

Dear Mr. Grant,
… ¹our new location would include self-checkout kiosks. While this is a feature we are considering, it is not confirmed at this time.
We kindly request that corrections be made in your next publication to ensure clarity for your readers.
…

（第三篇 email）

TO: Claire Roberts
FROM: Kevin Grant
SUBJECT: Apologies for inaccuracies
²DATE: May 12

Dear Ms. Roberts,
I sincerely apologize for the inaccuracies in the article. I misunderstood details during ²my conversation with a team member at TechSphere's flagship location last month.
…

❶ （題目可能這樣問）What is NOT true about TechSphere's new store?

（可能的答案選項）Its Customers can use a self-pay machine to check out now.

☞ 關於 TechSphere 的新分店，最詳細的資訊當然在第一篇的 article 中，可以直接從「The new branch will feature…」這一段找線索，其中提到「self-checkout kiosks」，不過在 letter 當中提到這項設施目前是未定案，所以「**目前顧客可以使用自助付款機結帳**」的敘述是不正確的。

❷ （題目可能這樣問）What is suggested about Mr. Grant?

（可能的答案選項）He went to New York in April.

☞ Mr. Grant 就是報社的採訪記者，在他寫的致歉 email 中提到，他上個月在 TechSphere 總旗艦店與一位該店員工交談時，誤解了一些訊息，而 email 上面的日期是 5 月 12 日。接著從第一篇的 article 可知，總旗艦店位於紐約，所以總結兩篇的線索可以推知「**他四月份時去過紐約**」的敘述是正確的。

> **必備 Point 4**

廣告＋相關文章的題組：新店開張、周年慶活動的宣傳、新產品廣告⋯，搭配新產品體驗意見表，以及相關電子郵件⋯等。例如：

（第一篇 advertisement）

Majestic Heights Hotel: Celebrating 5 Years of Excellence!

...
Book a deluxe room for just $300 per night and receive complimentary breakfast for two at our award-winning Summit Bistro. Guests will also enjoy a 20% discount on spa services and free access to our rooftop infinity pool and wellness center. ...
...

（第二篇 email）

TO:	Evelyn Hughes <evhughes@wanderlustmail.com>
FROM:	Gabriel Turner <gturner@wanderlustmail.com>
SUBJECT:	Re: Anniversary getaway idea
DATE:	November 5

Evelyn,

I checked out the Majestic Heights Hotel anniversary offer you mentioned. It's a fantastic deal and seems like the perfect opportunity for a relaxing getaway.
...

（第三篇 review）

Majestic Heights Hotel
Your feedback matters to us⋯

Please share your experience of staying at Majestic Heights Hotel! Your comments help us...

1. How did you hear about Majestic Heights Hotel?
   ...
2. Would you recommend Majestic Heights Hotel to your friends?
   ...

3. What were the best aspects of your stay?
The spa was phenomenal, the rooftop infinity pool offered stunning views, and the live jazz performance by Evelyn Brooks was magical. The staff were...

...
NAME: Gabriel Turner
DATES OF STAY: November 18-20
E-MAIL: gturner@wanderlustmail.com

（題目可能這樣問） What did Mr. Turner most likely have to do?

（可能的答案選項） Pay extra to enjoy spa facilities

☞ 關於 Mr. Turner 最有可能必須做什麼的問題，我們從第三篇的 review 中可得知，對於「住宿期間最滿意的部分」的回答中有「**水療設施很棒**（The spa was phenomenal）」的評論，然後對照第一篇 advertisement 中提到「**住宿賓客享用水療設施可享八折的優惠**（Guests will also enjoy a 20% discount on spa services）」。因此可推斷 **Mr. Turner 額外支付了一些費用享用水療設施**。

必備 Point 5　**通知／公告＋相關文章**的題組：介紹活動的通知、公司新計畫的公告…，搭配活動報導、相關表單，再加上要求進行相關工作或未來計畫…等的電子郵件。請注意，通知、報導中提到的**日期**、**金額**或其他**數字**，通常會是解題線索。例如：

（第一篇 notice）

> **The Midland College of Engineering**
> **Innovative Engineering Design Competition**
>
> The Midland College of Engineering is excited to announce its first Innovative Engineering Design Competition. This contest is open to graduate students with...
>
> ...
>
> The top six finalists will be chosen, and the winners will be announced at an awards ceremony at the Grand Midland Hall on April 30. The first-place winner will receive a $25,000 prize to support the development of their idea.

(第二篇 article)

> The Midland College of Engineering Announces Competition Winner
>
> Midland, May 2 – Linda Zhao, a second-year graduate student in the mechanical engineering program at Eastern Pacific University, was named the first-place winner of the Innovative Engineering Design Competition hosted by The Midland College of Engineering last night....
>
> ...

(第三篇 email)

> To: Linda Zhao <lindazhao@epu.edu>
> From: Richard Huang <rhuang@brightmaterials.com>
> Subject: Job Offer from Bright Materials Inc.
> Date: May 15
>
> Dear Ms. Zhao,
> I hope this email finds you well. My name is...
>
> ...
>
> Please let me know if you would like to discuss this opportunity further. I am happy to schedule a call or an in-person meeting at your earliest convenience.
>
> ...

（題目可能這樣問） What is mentioned about the design competition?

（可能的答案選項） It concluded with an event held at the Grand Midland Hall on May 1.

☞ 關於設計競賽提及的事，在第一篇的通知中提到，6 位最後的角逐者（top six finalists）將於 4/30 在 Grand Midland Hall 這地方舉行的頒獎典禮宣布，不過最終的獲勝者是誰尚不得而知，因此我們得繼續在第二篇的報導中找尋線索。從 5/2 發布的新聞報導可知，「昨晚」宣布了第一名獲獎者，因此可推知**這場競賽的最終行程於 5/1 全部結束**。

▶ TOEIC 實戰演練

Part 7　請在以下四個選項中選出正確的答案

Questions 1-5 refer to the following article, letter and e-mail.

TechSphere to Open Third Store in San Francisco

By Kevin Grant

　　TechSphere, a renowned electronics retail chain, has announced plans to open its third store in San Francisco. According to Claire Roberts, TechSphere's marketing director, the new store will be located in the Sunset District and is expected to cater to tech enthusiasts and everyday consumers alike. "The demand for our products and services in San Francisco has been overwhelming. This new store will help us serve our customers better while bringing the latest in consumer electronics to the neighborhood," said Roberts.

　　The new branch will feature an expansive showroom displaying the latest gadgets, including smartphones, laptops, and smart home devices. A dedicated service center will offer device repairs, consultations, and upgrades. Unlike the flagship downtown store in New York, which houses a coffee lounge, this location will focus on creating a streamlined shopping experience with self-checkout kiosks and express pick-up services for online orders.

　　TechSphere plans to inaugurate the new store in mid-November. For updates or inquiries, visit www.techsphere.com.

April 10

Kevin Grant

Tech Today News

Unit 234, Parker Building, 789 Oak Avenue

Los Angeles, CA 90210

Dear Mr. Grant,

Thank you for featuring TechSphere's upcoming store launch in your recent article. We're grateful for the coverage. However, we noticed a couple of inaccuracies that we'd like to address:

The article mentioned the opening date as mid-November. While we are targeting that timeframe, the exact date has not yet been finalized.

It was stated that our new location would include self-checkout kiosks. While this is a feature we are considering, it is not confirmed at this time.

We kindly request that corrections be made in your next publication to ensure clarity for your readers.

Best regards,
Claire Roberts
Marketing Director, TechSphere
claire.roberts@techsphere.com

TO: Claire Roberts claire.roberts@techsphere.com
FROM: Kevin Grant k.grant@techtodaynews.com
SUBJECT: Apologies for inaccuracies
Attachment: Draft
DATE: April 14

Dear Ms. Roberts,

I sincerely apologize for the inaccuracies in the article. I misunderstood details during my conversation with a team member at TechSphere's downtown location last month. I have discussed this with my editor, and we will publish a correction in our next issue. Please find a draft of the corrected piece attached for your review.

Additionally, I would love to stay informed about the exact opening date, as we may wish to feature a follow-up piece or conduct a live store review.

Thank you for bringing this to my attention, and I apologize once again for any inconvenience caused.

Warm regards,
Kevin Grant

Question.

01 According to the article, why is TechSphere opening a new store?

(A) To expand its operations beyond San Francisco
(B) To introduce a new product line
(C) To meet increasing customer demand
(D) To compete with other retailers in the area

02 What is indicated about TechSphere's new store?

(A) It will have an exclusive coffee lounge.
(B) It will have self-checkout kiosks in mid-November.
(C) It will host regular technology workshops.
(D) It may open later than in mid-November.

03 What does Ms. Roberts state about the article?

(A) It mentioned some good features that are actually in place.
(B) It incorrectly described the store's location.
(C) Some details need to be corrected in the future.
(D) It omitted details about the store's service center.

04 What is suggested about Mr. Grant?

(A) He has been to New York in March.
(B) He actually visited TechSphere's downtown location in April.
(C) He plans to attend the store's opening ceremony.
(D) He misquoted an executive in his article.

05 In the letter, the word "finalized" in paragraph 2, line 2, is closest in meaning to ----------.

(A) located
(B) settled
(C) completed
(D) confirmed

Questions 6-10 refer to the following advertisement, email and review.

Majestic Heights Hotel: Celebrating 5 Years of Excellence!

Join us in celebrating the 5th anniversary of Majestic Heights Hotel, located in the heart of Aspen, Colorado. From November 15th to November 30th, guests can enjoy exclusive anniversary offers that combine luxury and affordability.

Book a deluxe room for just $300 per night and receive complimentary breakfast for two at our award-winning Summit Bistro. Guests will also enjoy a 20% discount on spa services and free access to our rooftop infinity pool and wellness center. As part of the festivities, we're hosting live jazz nights on Fridays and Saturdays featuring renowned artists like Evelyn Brooks.

Don't miss this chance to experience exceptional service, breathtaking views, and unforgettable moments. For reservations or more details, visit www.majesticheights.com or call (970) 555-0163.

TO: Evelyn Hughes <evhughes@wanderlustmail.com>
FROM: Gabriel Turner <gturner@wanderlustmail.com>
SUBJECT: Re: Anniversary getaway idea
DATE: November 5

Evelyn,

I checked out the Majestic Heights Hotel anniversary offer you mentioned. It's a fantastic deal and seems like the perfect opportunity for a relaxing getaway. The deluxe room rate of $300 per night includes breakfast for two, and the 20% discount on spa services is a great bonus. Plus, the live jazz nights with Evelyn Brooks sound like an amazing experience.

I'm planning to book a two-night stay from November 18th to 20th. This should be a wonderful way to celebrate the hotel's 5th anniversary while enjoying some downtime. Let me know if you're interested in joining—we could coordinate and make the most of this special offer!

Gabriel

Majestic Heights Hotel

Your feedback matters to us…

Please share your experience of staying at Majestic Heights Hotel! Your comments help us improve our services and ensure every guest enjoys a remarkable stay. Rest assured, your information will remain confidential.

1. How did you hear about Majestic Heights Hotel?
   It was recommended to me by a travel blog.
2. Would you recommend Majestic Heights Hotel to your friends?
   Yes, especially to couples looking for a romantic getaway.
3. What were the best aspects of your stay?
   The spa was phenomenal, the rooftop infinity pool offered stunning views, and the live show on Saturday night was magical. The staff were courteous and attentive.
4. How could your stay have been better?
   The room service was a bit slow during peak hours, and the complimentary shuttle to downtown Aspen could have run more frequently.
5. Would you like to receive regular e-mail updates from Majestic Heights Hotel?
   YES ☑ NO ☐

After completing this review card, please put it into the suggestion box that is located next to the front desk. Thanks for your cooperation.

NAME: Gabriel Turner

DATES OF STAY: November 18-20

E-MAIL: gturner@wanderlustmail.com

Question.

06 What does Mr. Turner mention about the hotel during his stay?

(A) The room service could have been faster.
(B) The live jazz performance was canceled.
(C) The rooftop pool was not well-maintained.
(D) The staff seemed unprepared for the event.

07 What is mentioned about the deluxe room package?

(A) It includes tickets to local attractions.
(B) It provides complimentary dinner for two.
(C) It features a special spa deal.
(D) It is available until mid-November only.

08 What is the purpose of the e-mail?

(A) To suggest booking a group event at the hotel
(B) To propose a coordinated anniversary trip
(C) To request further discounts on spa services
(D) To inquire about additional hotel amenities

09 What is indicated about the review?

(A) It should be submitted online only.
(B) It gives guests a lucky draw opportunity.
(C) It can be handed to the staff at the front desk in person.
(D) It is supposed to be inserted into a box.

10 What did Mr. Turner most likely do during his stay?

(A) Hitch a ride in a friend's car to downtown Aspen
(B) Order room service at midnight
(C) Write a review for a travel blog
(D) Pay extra to enjoy spa facilities

TOEIC 實戰演練　解答／解析／翻譯

▶ Week 01

01 (D)　02 (D)　03 (B)　04 (A)　05 (D)　06 (B)　07 (C)　08 (C)
09 (A)　10 (A)　11 (B)　12 (D)　13 (B)　14 (D)　15 (C)

01.
翻譯 這名經驗豐富的登山客抵達了這座高山的頂端。

解析 本題考的是「名詞才能當主詞」。句中主詞不完整，所以空格是**主詞的位置**，可以當動詞（reached）動作主體的 (D) climber（登山者）是正確答案。

02.
翻譯 New-Tech 提供的軟體升級功能可消除安全風險並提升電腦的效能。

解析 本題考「名詞才能當主詞」+「主詞與動詞一致性」。這個句子的動詞是複數的 remove and improve，而主詞是「The software ------- that New-Tech offers」，所以要填入一個複數的名詞作為主詞，故正確答案是 (D)。

03.
翻譯 這位 CEO 在一連串的財務醜聞後可能會被公司革職。

解析 本題考「助動詞 + 原形動詞」+「正確語態的判斷」。依句意應為被動式，且空格前面有助動詞 may，所以應選原形動詞的 be ousted，故正確答案是 (B)。

04.
翻譯 警方制伏了這名嫌疑犯，以防止他造成進一步的傷害。

解析 本題考「動詞的位置」+「正確語態的判斷」。空格應填入句子的動詞，動名詞的 (B)、不定詞的 (C) 都不能放在動詞的位置，且依句意，「警方制伏嫌疑犯」為主動的行為，所以正確答案是 (A)。

05.
翻譯 提議的合併案預計將獲得監管機構的批准。

解析 本題考「受詞的位置」+「正確型態的受詞」。可以當受詞的當然是具有名詞功能的字詞，動詞 (A) 可直接刪除，雖然動名詞 (B) 及不定詞 (C) 也可以當名詞作為動詞的受詞，但「獲得批准」正確說法是 receive approval，所以正確答案是 (D)。

06.
翻譯 關於新預算提案的討論將於下週一舉行。

解析 本題考「主詞的位置」。可以當主詞的是名詞，所以正確答案是 (B)。

07.
翻譯 由於忙碌的行程，他們往往很難安排定期的家庭晚餐，這可能讓他們無法共度高品質的時光。

解析 本題考「代名詞當受詞」。選項中可以當受格的代名是 (C) 與 (D)，但 themselves

191

是反身代名詞，必須與主詞所指一致，而關係子句的主詞是「晚餐（dinners）」，所以 (D) 錯誤，故正確答案是 (C)。

08.

翻譯 許多青少年發現自己沉溺於社交媒體，因為社交媒體總是隨手可觸及且內容吸引人。

解析 本題考「受詞補語」的位置。受詞是 themselves，指的是「青少年自己」，而某人「沉溺於…」的說法是「人 + be addicted to...」，所以正確答案是 (C)。

09.

翻譯 最近的研究顯示，定期運動可以顯著改善心血管健康。

解析 本題考「動詞」的位置。動名詞或現在分詞的 (B)、不定詞的 (C)、名詞的 (D) 都不能當動詞，所以正確答案是 (A)。

10.

翻譯 委員會在這項新政策上達成共識後，決定從下個月開始實施。

解析 本題考「分詞構句」的用法。因為句子的主詞（the committee）、動詞（decided）都已經有了，顯然「-------- consensus on the new policy」這部分是修飾語，而因為「委員會達成共識」的語意，應選表主動的 Achieving，故正確答案是 (A)。

11.

翻譯 張先生主張增加業務團隊規模，而王女士則建議改善客戶服務。

解析 本題考「副詞連接詞」的用法。副詞連接詞可引導一個副詞子句的修飾語。因為空格前後皆為完整句子，所以要有一個連接詞連接兩個子句，故正確答案是 (B)。關係代名詞的 (D) which 雖然也可以連接句子，但語意不符。

12.

翻譯 這項計畫的啟動因未知的技術性問題而受到延遲了。

解析 本題考「選出語意正確的介系詞」。空格後面是個名詞，所以不能用連接詞連接，(A)、(B) 不必考量。語意是「由於技術性問題而受到延遲」，故正確答案是 (D)。

13.

翻譯 雖然代表們對這項提案有不同意見，但主席強調在繼續進行之前有必要先達成共識。

解析 本題考「選出符合句意的主詞」。空格要填入的是 Although 這個副詞子句的主詞，所以名詞的 (A)、(B) 是可能的選項。句意是「代表們對這項提案有不同意見」，所以正確答案是 (B)。(A) representation 是指代理（的狀態或權限）。

14.

翻譯 這項新的政策倡議被認為是達成環境永續目標的重要一步。

解析 本題考「動詞位置」及「選擇正確語態」。空格要填入的是句子的動詞，所以不定詞的 (C) 直接剔除。deem 的意思是「將…視為」，相當於 consider 的用法（deem/consider A B → 將 A 視為 B），而句意是「…被視為…的重要一步」，應用被動式」，所以正確答案是 (D)。

15.

翻譯 被毒蛇咬傷的登山客正接受緊急的診治。

解析 本題考「過去分詞表被動」。句子的主詞是「The hiker -------- by a venomous snake」，動詞是 is receiving，所以空格不能再填入一個動詞，且空格後面有 by，應填入表被動的 bitten，以符合「被毒蛇咬傷的登山客」的句意。所以正確答案是 (C)。

▶ Week 02

01 (D)　02 (C)　03 (C)　04 (B)　05 (A)　06 (B)　07 (C)　08 (D)
09 (A)　10 (B)　11 (A)　12 (D)　13 (A)　14 (C)　15 (C)

01.
翻譯 這間舒適的咖啡廳有著溫暖的氛圍，背景中播放的輕柔原聲旋律更增添了其魅力。

解析 本題考的是「符合句意的形容詞」。句子大意是「被輕柔的原聲旋律增添了溫暖的氛圍」，所以 (D) acoustic 是正確答案。

02.
翻譯 在進行任何重大投資之前，諮詢財務專家是明智的。

解析 本題考「易混淆形容詞判別」。選項都是形容詞，要找出一個符合句意的，而句子大意是「諮詢財務專家是明智的」，所以 (C) advisable 是正確答案。(D) advisory 是「顧問的，諮詢的」的意思。

03.
翻譯 這款產品的品質在耐用性和設計上都超過其競爭對手。

解析 本題考「單數指示代名詞的運用」。用來代替前面提到過的事物，單數用 that，複數用 those。句意是「這項產品的品質」超越「競爭對手產品的品質」，前後皆為單數，故正確答案是 (C)。

04.
翻譯 如果我們想要獲得更大的成功，就必須挑戰自我。

解析 本題考「填入符合句意的反身代名詞」。主詞是 We，而動詞的受詞指向主詞本身，所以 we 的反身代名詞 (B) ourselves 是正確答案。

05.
翻譯 如果你有任何必要文件，請於本週末前提交。

解析 本題考「不定代名詞的選擇」。從後面受格的 them 來看，它指向「-------- of the required documents」這整個名詞詞組，所以 (B)、(D) 直接刪除了。句意是「如果你有**任何必要文件**」，可以用 any required documents 和 any of the required documents，所以 (A) 是正確答案。(C) others 必須有個出現過的名詞作為對照，所以錯誤。

06.
翻譯 新的行銷策略對重視永續發展的年輕消費者具有吸引力。

解析 本題考「be appealing to...」這個慣用語用法，表示「對…有吸引力」，為固定用法。所以正確答案是 (B)。

07.
翻譯 這項專案最終比原定計劃晚了兩個月完成。

解析 本題考「一段時間 + later than...」這個慣用語用法，且空格後面有 than，(A)、(B) 完全不用考慮。選 (D) 的話會造成前面「The project was finally completed two months」這句話不合邏輯。

08.
翻譯 長途跋涉之後，我累得幾乎睜不開眼睛。

解析 本題考「填入符合句意的副詞」。句子大意是「累得幾乎睜不開眼睛」，(D) barely 有「幾乎不」的意思，故為正確答案。

09.
翻譯 我謹代表整個團隊感謝大家的努力和奉獻。

解析 本題考「填入正確的名詞，以形成符合句意的介系詞」。句子大意是「代表整個團隊感謝⋯」，on behalf of... 是介系詞，表示「代表⋯」。其餘 on account of 表示「因為⋯」、on top of 表示「加在⋯之上」、on condition of 表示「以⋯作為條件」。答案為 (A)。

10.
翻譯 這些登山客發現自己受制於突如其來的暴風雨。

解析 本題考「符合語意的（片語）介系詞」。句子大意是「發現自己任由暴風雨的擺布⋯」，at the mercy of... 是介系詞，表示「受制於⋯，任由⋯擺布」。其餘 in the event of 表示「在⋯情況下」、in accordance with 表示「依照⋯」、with respect to 表示「與⋯有關」。答案為 (B)。

11.
翻譯 學習風險管理對於確保任何組織的長期成功相當重要。

解析 本題考「名詞＋名詞＝複合名詞」。首先請注意，空格後面是名詞的話，還是得理解句意，不一定填入的是形容詞。句子大意是「學習風險管理⋯」risk management 來表示「風險管理」。如果是 risky management，意思就會變成「有風險的管理」→ 這樣的管理方式是有風險的，顯然不合句意。答案為 (A)。

12.
翻譯 這項專案面臨多次挫敗，然而，團隊仍然齊心並致力於實現成功。

解析 本題考「符合上前後句意的連接副詞」。由於前後兩句意思是相反（**專案面臨多次挫敗　仍致力於實現成**功），第二句有轉折意思，所以要用 (D) Nevertheless。

13.
翻譯 有些學生在傳統教室環境中成長茁壯，但另一些學生則更喜歡線上學習，因為它具有靈活性。

解析 本題考「表非特定範圍的『Some...; others...』」句型。看到前一句句首的 Some... 在看看四個選項，應該就知道要考的是「**有些⋯，其他則⋯**」的句型。(B)、(D) 皆為單數，所以錯誤。the others 表「特定範圍」的「其他人」，在此不符句意，所以答案是 (A) others。

14.
翻譯 尋求知識的人總是能夠找到機會。

解析 本題考不定代名詞「those who...」用法，表示「**⋯的人們**」。這裡的 those 也可以用 people 取代。答案為 (C)。

15.
翻譯 許多人在困難時期會在寫作和朗誦詩歌中找到慰藉。

解析 本題考「不可數名詞」用法。poetry 表示「**詩，詩集**」，為集合名詞、不可數，這裡的 poetry 可以用 poems 取代。答案為 (C)。

▶ Week 03

01 (A)　02 (B)　03 (C)　04 (D)　05 (B)　06 (A)　07 (B)　08 (D)
09 (C)　10 (B)　11 (A)　12 (D)　13 (C)　14 (B)　15 (D)

01.
翻譯 經驗豐富的護士知道如何安撫術後病人的不適感。

解析 本題考的是「填入及物動詞（後面需接受詞）」。空格要填入一個動詞，而後面有受詞，所以要填入一個及物動詞，選項中只有 (A) soothe（安撫）是及物動詞。

02.
翻譯 她的目光在那張舊照片上停留了一會兒，然後才把它收起來。

解析 本題考「填入不及物動詞（後面不直接接受詞）」。空格要填入一個動詞，而後面接介系詞，所以不能放及物動詞，所以答案是 (B) lingered（逗留，徘徊）。

03.
翻譯 董事會任命他為新專案團隊的經理。

解析 本題考「不完全及物動詞」用法。空格要填入一個動詞，且後面有兩個受詞：him 與 manager of...，所以要填入的是表「指派…（某人為某職稱）」的 (C) appointed。

04.
翻譯 經過長途旅行後，她看起來疲憊不堪，但對於能回到家感到鬆了一口氣。

解析 本題考「不完全不及物動詞」用法。空格要填入一個動詞，且後面是形容詞（tired 和 relieved），所以要填入 (D) appeared（顯得…，看起來…）這個不完全不及物動詞（亦稱連綴動詞），以符合「看起來疲憊不堪」的句意。

05.
翻譯 經過幾次嘗試，他們終於找出了如何解決這個複雜方程式的方法。

解析 本題考「填入適當的動詞片語」。句子大意是「找出…的解決方法」，所以答案是 (B) figured out。(A)、(C)、(D) 意思分別是「對…感到驚艷」、「（使）安定下來」、「涉及」。

06.
翻譯 用餐後，請把帳單遞給我，讓我可以結帳。

解析 本題考「授予動詞」用法，空格後面有間接受詞（me）以及直接受詞（the bill），且句意是「把帳單交給我」，所以答案是 (A) hand。

07.
翻譯 當延誤的情況越來越嚴重時，她一開始時對於專案的憂慮證實是真的。

解析 本題考「填入（不完全不及物動詞後面的）主詞補語」。「證實為真」是 prove true，動詞 prove 的用法類似 be 動詞，後面接形容詞作為主詞補語。答案為 (B)。

08.
翻譯 儘管進行了多次更新，軟體的技術問題仍然持續了幾個月。

解析 本題考「易混淆動詞」。句子大意是「…問題持續了幾個月」，所以 (D) persisted 是正確答案。(A)、(B)、(C) 意思分別是「幫助」、「組成，構成」、「堅稱」。

09.

翻譯 公司每週一召開會議討論新策略。

解析 本題考「一個句子只能有一個動詞」。空格前已經有本句的動詞 holds，因此 (A)、(D) 皆不可選；雖然 (B) 可能是個分詞，但不符語意，故答案是不定詞 (C) to discuss。

10.

翻譯 在收到這驚人的消息後，他仔細考慮了最佳行動方案，同時亦仔細評估了潛在的風險。

解析 本題考「對等連接詞前後動詞的一致性」。主要子句後面 and 接過去式動詞（weighed），所以應填入一個過去式動詞，答案是 (B) contemplated。

11.

翻譯 無人看管的小營火引發了一場毀滅性的野火，迅速蔓延了整個乾燥的森林。

解析 本題考「主詞與動詞時態一致性」。空格要填入的是 that 形容詞子句的動詞形式。主要子句動詞是過去式（kindled），所以子句的動詞也必須是過去式，答案是 (A) spread。

12.

翻譯 公司每年的研發支出達到數百萬美元。

解析 本題考「主詞與動詞單複數一致性」。句子的主詞是「The company's annual expenditures on research and development」，核心字彙是 expenditures，所以動詞應用複數形，答案是 (D) amount。

13.

翻譯 當這項計畫終於完成時，我們將已經實現了迄今最具挑戰性的目標之一。

解析 本題考「填入未來完成式的動詞時態」。「When the project is finally completed」代表的是一個未來的時間點，所以句子的動詞必須是未來式或未來完成式，答案是 (C) will have achieved。

14.

翻譯 珍對於同事們不斷且不請自來的請求回饋，感到被騷擾。

解析 本題考「表被動的過去分詞」。題目中的 felt 是感官動詞，後面通常接形容詞作為主詞補語。句意是「（人）感到被騷擾」，故應選表被動的過去分詞 harassed，答案是 (B)。

15.

翻譯 這家創新設計的新餐廳，已連續三年被評選為本市最佳用餐體驗的餐廳。

解析 本題考「被動語態的正確時態」。從句尾表「for + 一段時間」的 for three consecutive years 來看，動詞時態應為「完成式」，且句意是表被動的「被評選為本市最佳…」，所以答案是 (D)。

196

▶ Week 04

01 (B)　02 (A)　03 (D)　04 (C)　05 (A)　06 (C)　07 (D)　08 (B)
09 (A)　10 (D)　11 (A)　12 (D)　13 (C)　14 (B)　15 (A)

01.
翻譯 她提交了一份履歷，強調自己在專案管理方面的豐富經驗以及領導跨部門團隊的能力。

解析 本題考的是「填入正確的動狀詞」。句意是「提交一份強調…的履歷」，原句應為「...a résumé that emphasizes her extensive experience...」，可簡化為「...a résumé emphasizing her extensive experience...」，所以答案是現在分詞 (B)。選不定詞 (C) 的話，意思會形成「為了強調…而提交一份履歷」這樣奇怪的語意。

02.
翻譯 這款新產品將於下個月起在授權的零售店獨家販售。

解析 本題考「形容詞位置」+「現在分詞與過去分詞的選擇」。空格要填入一個形容詞（也可能是名詞），所以 (C) 直接剔除。句意是「在獲得授權的零售店獨家販售」，所以表被動的 (A) authorized 是正確答案。如果是 authorization retailers，顯得語法不通且語義模糊，似乎在表達「「零售商本身是某種授權」」。不符合自然的英語用法。

03.
翻譯 在會議期間，他藉由分享一個近期旅行中的趣事來緩和氣氛。

解析 本題考「形容詞位置」+「現在分詞與過去分詞的選擇」。空格要填入一個形容詞（也可能是名詞），所以 (B) 直接剔除。句意是「分享一個有趣的故事來緩和氣氛」，所以表主動的 (D) amusing 是正確答案。如果是 amusement story，可能會被理解為「娛樂相關的故事」或「關於娛樂的故事」，但這不是自然的英文表達方式。

04.
翻譯 在機器出現故障跡象後，工程師被叫來檢查設備。

解析 本題考「不定詞用來表示目的」。句意是「工程師被召來檢查機械」，應用表目的的不定詞 (C) to inspect。如果選 (A) inspecting 意思變成「被召來」和「檢查」這兩個動作同時發生，不合邏輯與語意。

05.
翻譯 由於本身出色的領導能力，她證明自己是領導這項專案的最佳人選。

解析 本題考「不定詞作名詞的後位修飾語」。從四個選項來看，空格後面的名詞作為「領導」這個動作的受詞。此句要表達的是，候選人的目的是要「帶領這個專案計畫」，所以不定詞 (A) to lead 是正確答案。如果選 (C) leading 意思變成「成為正在領導這個專案的候選人」，不合邏輯與語意。

06.
翻譯 我們需要收集更多數據，以便我們做出關於後續步驟的明智決策。

解析 本題考「不定詞的主被動態辨別」。in

order for us 是引導目的的片語，意為「為了讓我們」，接著要用一個「主動的」不定詞來表達行動的目的，所以答案是 (C) to make。

07.

翻譯 委員會的輕輕點頭使這項提案在無需進一步辯論的情況下獲得批准。

解析 本題考「不定詞作受詞補語 + 主被動態判別」。句意是「委員會的默許使提案在未經進一步討論的情況下被批准」，所以表被動的 (D) to be approved 是正確答案。

08.

翻譯 找老闆爭取加薪需要仔細準備，並清晰展示你的成就。

解析 本題考「動名詞片語作為句子主詞」。句子的動詞（requires）已經有了，所以空格不能再放動詞。主詞是「--------- your boss for a raise」，因此要填入表主動的 (B) Approaching。

09.

翻譯 新實習生預計在工作的最初幾週內要完成幾項繁瑣的任務。

解析 本題考「固定搭配不定詞的動詞」。空格前是 are expected 這個被動式的動詞，而表示「期望某人去做某事」是「expect sb. to do sth.」，故答案是不定詞 (A) to complete。

10.

翻譯 在如此短的時間內準備這麼多演講會導致更大的壓力與疲勞。

解析 本題考「動名詞當主詞，搭配單數動詞」。空格要填入句子的動詞，而句子的主詞是「Preparing for so many presentations in such a short time」，

這是個動名詞片語，視為第三人稱單數，搭配單數動詞，所以答案是 (D) results。

11.

翻譯 天氣炎熱難耐，且我辛苦地要找個陰涼處。

解析 本題考「可以當副詞的現在分詞」。空格要填入可以修飾其後形容詞 hot 的副詞，選項中只有 (A) scorching 可以當副詞用。

12.

翻譯 他們決定延後提交報告，直到收集到所有必要的數據為止。

解析 本題考「一定要接動名詞的動詞」。空格前面是 delay 這個動詞，其後須接動名詞作為受詞，答案是 (D) submitting。

13.

翻譯 她停下來欣賞美麗的日落，然後繼續在海灘上散步。

解析 本題考「stop to-V 與 stop Ving 的辨別」。句意是「停下來，然後欣賞日落」，所以要用「表目的」的不定詞 (C) to admire。如果選 (B) admiring 變成「停止欣賞日落」，這就不符句意了。

14.

翻譯 孩子們看到小丑時尖叫不已，且當他開始玩弄五顏六色的球時，空氣中瀰漫著他們的興奮心情。

解析 本題考「獨立分詞構句」。空格所在句子的前面只有逗號，沒有連接詞，所以不能再有動詞，(C)、(D) 皆可直接刪除。如果把 (A) 視為表被動的分詞構句，但因為後面有受詞（the air），所以錯誤，答案是表主動的 (B) filling。

15.

翻譯 會議結束後，我前往辦公室，並從會議室取回我的筆記型電腦。

解析 本題考「分詞構句：現在分詞與過去分詞的判別」。空格所在句子的前面是完整句子且沒有連接詞，後面有作為受詞的名詞（my laptop），所以表主動的 (A) retrieving 是正確答案。

▶ Week 05

01 (B)　02 (B)　03 (C)　04 (A)　05 (D)　06 (A)　07 (C)　08 (B)
09 (C)　10 (D)　11 (D)　12 (A)　13 (D)　14 (D)　15 (C)

01.

翻譯 我追求的不僅僅是成功，還有當下的滿足。

解析 本題考的是「相關連接詞：not... but...（不是…而是…）」。空格要填入一個連接 success 和 fulfillment 這兩個名詞的連接詞，前面有 not 所以與其搭配的是 but，為固定用法，答案是 (B)。

02.

翻譯 這是一個如此有說服力的論點，以致於觀眾都鴉雀無聲。

解析 本題考「相關連接詞：such... that...（如此…以致於…）」。空格前後都是完整句，要填入一個接詞。句子前半部有 such a...，因此與其搭配的是 that，為固定用法，答案是 (B)。

03.

翻譯 我寧願接受不確定性，也不願滿足於平庸。

解析 本題考「相關連接詞：would rather... than...」。空格要填入一個連接 embrace 和 settle 這兩個動詞的連接詞，前面有 would rather 所以與其搭配的是 than，為固定用法，答案是 (C)。

04.

翻譯 這項決策被延後至所有數據都能被徹底分析為止。

解析 本題考「表「時間」的連接詞 until」用法。句意是「決策被延後，直到…為止」，所以正確答案是 (A) until。

05.

翻譯 他的語氣充滿自信，彷彿他是這會議室裡的專家。

解析 本題考「表「彷彿」的連接詞 as though 用於假設語氣」。從空格後面 he were... 來看，要填入一個引導假設語氣的連接詞。選項中只有 (D) as though 可用於假設語氣。(C) only if 雖然也可以用來表達假設，但語意不符。

06.

翻譯 雖然我很感謝有這些回饋意見，但我永遠無法妥協我的核心價值觀。

解析 本題考「與 though/although 同義的 while」。句意是「雖然感謝提供回饋意見，但本身的價值觀不容妥協」，所以答案是 (A) while。

07.

翻譯 要麼我們適應變化的環境，要麼就面臨被時代淘汰的風險。

解析 本題考「相關連接詞：Either... or...」。空格要填入一個連接 we adapt to the changing environment 和 we risk becoming obsolete 這兩個子句的連接詞。後面有 or 所以與其搭配的是 Either，為固定用法，答案是 (C)。

08.

翻譯 不僅是參與者，組織者也重視過程中的透明度。

解析 本題考「not only A but (also) B 當主詞時的動詞單複數問題」。句子的主詞有兩個，且用「not only... but also...」這個相關連接詞連接，動詞單複數應跟著 but also 後面的主詞，所以答案是 (B) values。

09.

翻譯 領導者和團隊成員都提倡創新的解決方案。

解析 本題考「A as well as B 當主詞時的動詞單複數問題」。句子的主詞有兩個（The leader 和 the team members），且用「as well as」這個連接詞連接，動詞單複數應跟著 The leader，所以答案是 (C) advocates。

10.

翻譯 真可惜這樣的資質在這個行業中未受到應有的重視。

解析 本題考「that 子句在特定名詞後面當同位語」。有一些名詞的後面可以放「that 子句」作為補充說明，pity 就是其中之一。這裡的「It's a pity that...」為固定用法，表示「…是令人惋惜的事」，故答案是 (D)。

11.

翻譯 延遲的原因是因為這些利益相關者需要更多數據才能繼續進行。

解析 本題考「reason 與 because 子句的搭配」。because 引導的子句可以當主詞 reason 的補語，表示「…的理由是因為…」所以答案是 (D)。(C) since 雖然也有「因為」的意思，但沒有這種用法。

12.

翻譯 我想知道最近的變化是否真的能提升我們的生產力。

解析 本題考「if 引導名詞子句作動詞的受詞」。wonder if... 表示「想知道／好奇…是否…」，if 可用 whether 取代，所以答案是 (A)。

13.

翻譯 無論誰領導這項倡議活動，都得為其成敗負責。

解析 本題考「whoever 引導名詞子句作主詞」。句子的主詞是「------ leads the initiative」，動詞是 is，所以不具連接詞功能的 (A)、(B) 均不可選；因為 is 是第三人稱單數動詞，所以不能選 (C) Those who，所以答案是 (D) Whoever (= Anyone who)。

14.

翻譯 這項專案將依計劃進行，而前提是我們獲得必需的資金。

解析 本題考「表示「條件」的連接詞 provided that」。空格前是「專案將依計劃進行」，後面是「我們獲得必需的資金」，顯然前面是「成果」，後面這句是「條件」，所以表「條件是…」的 (D) provided (後接 that) 是正確答案。

15.

翻譯 只要有奉獻和努力，你就可以實現你為自己設定的任何目標。

解析 本題考「whatever 引導名詞子句當動詞的受詞」。不能連接句子的 (A) those 可率先剃除。依句意是「你就可以實現…的任何目標」，所以可作為關係形容詞的 (C) whatever 是正確答案。(B) what 雖然也可以當關係形容詞，但語意不符。

▶ Week 06

01 (B)　02 (C)　03 (B)　04 (A)　05 (D)　06 (C)　07 (B)　08 (A)
09 (B)　10 (C)　11 (A)　12 (B)　13 (D)　14 (C)　15 (B)

01.

翻譯 他是一個非常認真的學生，這證明了他強烈的工作倫理。

解析 本題考的是「關係代名詞 which 代替前面整句」。空格前有逗號，所以 (C) 可直接剃除。關係子句（----- is a testament...）顯然修飾的不會是「人」，所以 (A) 也錯誤，且 (D) whoever 也不能是 testament，所以答案是 (B) which，代替的是前面整句。

02.

翻譯 約翰和莎拉都是這個職位的優秀候選人，他們當中的任何一位都是公司的重要資產。

解析 本題考「前面有介系詞時，關係代名詞用受格」。依句意，這裡關係代名詞的先行詞是 candidates（而非 position），因為前面有 either of，所以要用受格的 (C) whom。

03.

翻譯 他是唯一在如此極端條件下成功完成探險的男人。

解析 本題考「先行詞前有「絕對性字眼」時，關係代名詞限用 that」。雖然先行詞是「人」，但其前有 only 這個形容詞，所以關係代名詞要用 that。答案為 (B)。

04.

翻譯 團隊審查了這些提案，其內容都非常詳盡且全面。

解析 本題考「關係子句動詞與先行詞一致」。關係子句的主詞是 the content of which，為單數，所以要搭配單數動詞，答案是 (A) is。(C) has 則不符文法規則。

05.

翻譯 他們參觀了那座博物館，其古代文物的收藏舉世聞名。

解析 本題考「關係代名詞的位置：選擇關係代名詞所有格」。空格後面是個完整句子，但關係子句主詞（collection of ancient artifacts）還缺少個限定詞，所以要填入關係代名詞所有格 (D) whose。

06.

翻譯 他買了一輛豪華跑車，車子的顏色和他的西裝完美匹配。

解析 本題考「關係代名詞所有格的變體」。選 (A) which、(B) that 兩個關係代名詞，

201

或是關係代名詞所有格 (D) whose 的話，都會變成 the color 是 a fancy sports car 的同為語，顯然文法錯誤。正確答案是 (C) of which。

07.

翻譯 會議被延後到星期五，屆時全體團隊都可以出席。

解析 本題考「關係副詞 when 引導形容詞子句」。空格後面是完整句，所以 (A) that 和 (C) which 皆錯誤。空格前面是 Friday 這個表時間點的名詞，所以要選 (B) when。

08.

翻譯 我欽佩他處理困難情況時的冷靜與精準。

解析 本題考「名詞子句連接詞的位置：關係副詞的選擇」。名詞子句動詞 handles 後面已經有受詞了，所以 (B) what 錯誤；(C) whom 不符文法結構；(D) where 則不合語意邏輯，故答案是 (A) how。

09.

翻譯 那一天就是他終於承認自己錯了的時候。

解析 本題考「選擇關係子句前的先行詞」。從四個選項來看，要填入的是「when he...」這個形容詞子句修飾的對象，所以答案是表時間點的 (B) day。

10.

翻譯 這些文件應該放在每個人都能輕鬆取得的地方。

解析 本題考「表『地方』的副詞子句連接詞 where」。從空格前面動詞 should be put 的語意來看，應選表「地方」的 (C) where。這裡的「where they are... everyone」可視為「地方副詞子句」，表示「…的地方」，其概念等同「地方副詞（片語）」

11.

翻譯 他總是表現得很傲慢，我真的覺得這種態度妨礙了他與他人良好合作的能力。

解析 本題考「關係詞的選擇：關係形容詞 which」。空格後面是個完整句子，但關係子句主詞 attitude 不能單獨存在（前面還要有個限定詞），所以要填入一個關係形容詞或關係代名詞所有格，(C) such、(D) that 可直接刪除。但若選 (B) whose 的話，前面找不到一個名詞作為先行詞，所以也是錯誤選項，故正確答案是 (A) which。這裡的 which attitude 就是指前面正句話。

12.

翻譯 無論他看起來多麼友善，我仍然覺得難以完全信任他。

解析 本題考「副詞子句連接詞的位置：複合關係副詞 however 用法」。空格後面是形容詞（friendly），所以 (A) 錯誤，而 (D) As、(C) How 皆不符「無論他在怎麼看起來友善」的語意。故正確答案是 (B) However (= No matter how)。

13.

翻譯 無論你去到哪裡，只要保持堅定與專注，你都能成功。

解析 本題考「副詞子句連接詞的位置：複合關係副詞 wherever 用法」。從空格後面的 you go 來看，自然要選表地方的 (D) wherever。

14.

翻譯 出席派對的賓客比原本邀請的還要多。

解析 本題考「關係代名詞的位置：選擇準關係代名詞」用法。先行詞 guests 前面有

比較級形容詞 more，所以要填入準關係代名詞 (C) than。

15.

翻譯 向你認為最需要幫助的人提供支持。

解析 本題考「名詞子句連接詞的位置：選擇複合關係代名詞」。從空格後面的「needs it most」可知，提供支持的對象是「人」，所以答案是 (B) whomever。

▶ Week 07

01 (D)　02 (C)　03 (A)　04 (B)　05 (D)　06 (B)　07 (B)　08 (B)
09 (D)　10 (D)　11 (B)　12 (D)　13 (B)　14 (B)　15 (D)

01.

翻譯 如果他更有責任感，我就會把重要的任務交給他。

解析 本題考的是「與現在事實相反的假設語氣」。條件句 be 動詞恆用 were」。空格要填入的是 If 條件句的 be 動詞，從主要子句動詞 would trust 可知，為與現在事實相反的假設，所以 be 動詞要填入 (D) were。

02.

翻譯 如果他準時送出報告，我就會更早完成這個專案。

解析 本題考「與過去事實相反的假設語氣：選擇主要子句正確的動詞型態」。if 條件的動詞是「had + p.p.」（had sent），所以主要子句動詞要用「would have + p.p.」，正確答案是 (C) would have finished。

03.

翻譯 萬一你在活動期間需要任何幫助，我會協助你。

解析 本題考「對未來狀況的假設：if 子句動詞用『should + V』」，所以答案是 (A) should。

04.

翻譯 如果你的老師更有耐心，我可能會更有動力參與課堂活動。

解析 本題考「省略 if 的假設：原條件句有 were」。依句意，「------ your teacher more patient,」是個條件子句，但若選 (C) If 則缺少動詞，所以錯誤，因此要從「條件句倒裝，省略 if」的文法觀點來解題。這是與現在事實相反的假設，所以應選 (B) were。

05.

翻譯 她沒有接我的電話；她當時一定是太忙了。

解析 本題考「對於過去事件的推測：must have + p.p.」。從第一句的動詞過去式（didn't pick up）來看，這是對於過去事件的猜測，故動詞要用 must have been。答案為 (D)。

06.

翻譯 如果你早點邀請我們，我們會參加這次旅行。

解析 本題考「與現在事實相反的假設語氣：選擇條件子句正確的動詞型態」。從主要子動詞 would join 來看，if 條件句動詞要用過去式 (B) invited。

203

07.

翻譯 如果你改變主意，我可以幫助你安排相關事宜。

解析 本題考「省略 if 的假設：原條件句有 should」。依句意，「------- you change your mind,」是個條件子句，且後面有原形動詞 change，所以應選助動詞 (B) Should。

08.

翻譯 深夜時她辦公室的燈還亮著，想必她是留下來完成工作了。

解析 本題考「對於過去事件的推測：must have + p.p.」。從第一句的動詞過去式（were）來看，這是對於過去事件的猜測，故動詞要用 must have stayed。答案為 (B)。

09.

翻譯 如果你早點告訴我會議的事，我現在就能準備得更充分。

解析 本題考「與過去事實相反的假設」。If 子句動詞是 had told，主要子句動詞型態應為「would have + p.p.」，所以答案是表時間點的 (D) have had been。

10.

翻譯 要不是我及時警告，她就無法避免那場意外。

解析 本題考「表『若非…就不會…』的假設語氣」。依「若非我及時警告，她早就…」的句意來看，空格應填入 (D) Without（沒有…的話，若非…）。

11.

翻譯 如果不是因為火車誤點，我本來可以準時趕上會議。

解析 本題考「省略 if 的假設句：與過去事實相反」。從主要子句動詞 would have arrived 來看，這是與過去事實相反的假設，且條件句省略 if，因此空格應填入 (B) Had。

12.

翻譯 我父親希望我能從事醫學相關的職業，但我選擇了不同的行業。

解析 本題考「wish 的假設句：與過去事實相反」。句中 wish 用過去式，是用假設語氣，因此子句內動詞應比照「與過去事實相反」的假設，故正確答案是 (D) had pursued。

13.

翻譯 如果當時我抓住了那次機會就好了。

解析 本題考「表『要是…就好了』的假設語氣：與過去事實相反」，所以答案是 (B) If only（但願…）。(A) Only if 和 (C) However 都只是個副詞子句連接詞，除對話內容之外，一般不能單獨存在；(D) Would (that)... 雖然也可用於「假設語氣」，但通常用來祝福別人。

14.

翻譯 你早該開始為自己的行為負責，而不是一昧地責怪別人。

解析 本題考「表『該是…的時候了』的假設語氣」。「It's time (that)...」只有「與現在事實相反的假設」用法，所以答案是過去式的 (B) started。

15.

翻譯 那個男人說話時充滿自信，好像他是這方面的專家一樣。

解析 本題考「表『彷彿／就好像…』的假設語氣：與現在事實相反」。從前面句子動詞過去式（spoke）可知，as if 子句內動詞應用過去完成式，所以答案是 (D) had been。

▶ Week 08

01 (C)　02 (B)　03 (B)　04 (C)　05 (A)　06 (D)　07 (B)　08 (A)
09 (D)　10 (C)　11 (D)　12 (A)　13 (B)　14 (C)　15 (D)

01.

翻譯 他的反應比預期中少了冷靜，這讓大家擔心他承受壓力的能力。

解析 本題考的是「依句意填入正確的副詞比較級」。從後面的句意「讓大家擔心他承受壓力的能力」來看，前面應該是「他的反應比預期更不冷靜」，所以答案是否定的 (C) less。

02.

翻譯 這個解決方案是我們考慮過的選項中最有效的。

解析 本題考「比較句型：形容詞最高級搭配的介系詞 of」。空格前句子是最高級形容詞（the most effective）用法，所以後面表達範圍的介系詞要用 (B) of。

03.

翻譯 自從升遷後，他比以前更加努力。

解析 本題考「比較句型：同一個人現在與過去的比較」，than 前面動詞用的是「現在完成進行式」，所以 than 後面要用過去式的 (B) did (= worked)。

04.

翻譯 這座城市比我上次造訪時老舊了許多，歷史建築顯現出歲月的痕跡。

解析 本題考「相同主詞比較時有 when 子句，可省略「相同主詞 + be 動詞」」。本句可還原為「The city is much older than the city was when I last visited...」，其中底線部分是可以省略的，所以應選 (C) when。

05.

翻譯 我從未料想到能在繁忙的城市中心找到這樣的寧靜。

解析 本題考「否定副詞的倒裝句型：助動詞後跟著原形動詞」。句首有否定副詞 Never，句子須倒裝，而助動詞 did 後面要接原形動詞，所以答案是 (A) expect。

06.

翻譯 只有資深成員被允許查閱存放在檔案庫中的機密文件。

解析 本題考「only 置於句首的倒裝句」。句意是「只允許資深成員…」，所以 (D) Only 是正確答案，其餘選項的副詞皆不符語意。另外，當動詞是 be 動詞時，only 置於句首不倒裝。

07.

翻譯 他如此投入工作，因此經常工作到深夜也毫無怨言。

解析 本題考「so 置於句首的，主詞與動詞必須倒裝句」。從句首的 So dedicated 來看，be 動詞與主詞（he）必須倒裝，所以答案是 (B) is he。

08.

翻譯 她重視誠實勝於一切，她的團隊成員也是如此。

解析 本題考「肯定附和句 so 的用法」。從前

面句子動詞 values 以及後面第三人稱單數主詞 everyone 來看，附和句的助動詞要用 (A) does。

09.

翻譯 此專案未按計劃進展，預算也未在控制中。

解析 本題考「否定附和句」。前面句子是否定（…isn't progressing…），因此附和句開頭應選否定的 (D) neither。

10.

翻譯 他要離開的決定或許不會被視為錯誤，是嗎？

解析 本題考「附加問句的主詞：選擇適當的代名詞」。前面句子主詞是「His decision to leave」，所以附加問句主詞應為 (C) it。

11.

翻譯 最終的這場表演比先前任何一次排演都還要精彩。

解析 本題考「可用來修飾比較級的副詞：still」。空格後面是比較級形容詞（more captivating），要填入一個可以修飾比較級的副詞，所以答案是 (D) still。

12.

翻譯 被白雪覆蓋的山峰在湛藍的天空襯托下，構成了一幅如明信片般完美的風景。

解析 本題考「填入適當的形容詞：沒有最高級的形容詞」。形容詞 perfect 沒有比較級與最高級的用法，所以答案是 (A)。

13.

翻譯 這顆鑽石比整個收藏中的任何其他寶石都要昂貴。

解析 本題考「同範圍的比較：than any other + 單數名詞」。這裡的「同範圍」是指「這整個收藏中」，所以答案是單數名詞的 (B) gem。

14.

翻譯 在最終評估中包含了每個團隊成果的總結。

解析 本題考「地方副詞置於句首的倒裝的」，所以答案是 (C) was included。

15.

翻譯 儘管他很聰明，但我仍然覺得難以完全信任他的決策。

解析 本題考「倒裝句型：as 取代 though」。句子大意是「儘管他很聰明，但我…」，副詞子句是個倒裝句，所以只能用 (D) as。(A) although 雖然符合句意，但不能用於此句型中，須改成 though 才行。

▶ **Week 09**

01 (A)　02 (C)　03 (B)　04 (D)　05 (D)　06 (B)　07 (C)　08 (D)
09 (D)　10 (B)　11 (A)　12 (C)

題目 1~4 請參考以下廣告內容。

翻譯 探索無限可能：獨家雜誌訂閱優惠！
想解鎖知識與靈感的世界，立即訂閱我們的獨家雜誌吧！深入探索諸如旅行、時尚、健康和科技等多樣話題的迷人文章。不論您是時尚先鋒還是健康愛好者，我們精選的內容都是為您量身打造的。每月最新趨勢、專家建議和精彩的視覺享受都直接送到您家門口。立即訂閱，開始探索知識與豐富人生的！加入我們的讀者社群，信任我們提供的優質見解和娛樂。千萬不要錯過 — 請立即訂閱，並開始發掘您的熱情！

解析
1. 這是個祈使句，因為空格所在句子後面都沒有動詞，所以答案是 (A) Unlock。

2. 空格後面是 4 個名詞的並列（非完整句），所以連接詞 (A) so that 直接剔除。句意是「…探索像是旅行、時尚、健康和科技等多樣話題…」，所以答案是 (C) such as。

3. 空格後面是修飾前面名詞（latest trends, expert advice, and stunning visuals → 表示訂閱雜誌的話可以看到的東西）的分詞片語，所以「遞送到家門口」這動作應為被動式，答案是 (B) delivered。

4. 這是個「選擇句子」的問題。空格前面是「千萬不要錯過」這句話，承接一整段介紹雜誌與訂閱好處的內容，所以最後這句會與進一步鼓勵訂閱有關，答案是 (D) subscribe today and start exploring your passions。以下是四個選項的中文翻譯：
   (A) 我們的獨家雜誌即將上市
   (B) 盡情享受這本汽車雜誌的精彩內容吧
   (C) 我們僅接受信用卡訂閱
   (D) 今天就訂閱，開啟探索您熱情的旅程吧

題目 5~8 請參考以下信件內容。

翻譯 致全體員工：

我們將在下個季度引入新的績效評估流程。這項創舉旨在提供更全面的反饋，並支持您的職業發展。我們將舉辦工作坊，讓大家熟悉這些新標準及評估方法。您的積極參與對於這次轉變的成功非常重要。讓我們共同努力，創造一個更加透明和支持性的環境，提升我們的集體成長和成功。感謝您的奉獻和熱情。

解析
5. 空格這個名詞指的就是前一句提到的「新的績效評估流程」，(A) 是「範疇」，(B) 是「丟棄」，(C) 是「大人物」，(D) 是「創舉」，所以 (D) initiative 是最符合句意的。

6. 「familiarize sb. with sth.」是「使某人熟悉某事物」的意思，搭配介系詞 with，為固定用法，所以答案是 (B)。

7. 這是個「選擇句子」的問題。空格前面句子是「讓大家熟悉新標準及評估方法」，後面是「大家共同努力創造一個…的環境」，顯然這句子應與如何共同努力有關，所以 (C) Your active involvement is crucial for the success of this transition. 是最能夠適當連接前後文的句子。以下是四個選項的中文翻譯：
   (A) 學業表現的評估應包括學生的整體發展。
   (B) 公司將根據員工的表現制定薪酬激勵計劃。
   (C) 您的積極參與對於此轉型的成功相當重要。
   (D) 合理的績效激勵制度有助於提升團隊的整體表現。

8. 前面提到「共同努力」，所以這句的提升成長和成功應是「集體的」，而非「個人的」，答案是 (D) collective。其餘 (A) 是「個人的」，(B) 是「各別的」，(C) 是「奇蹟的」。

題目 9~12 請參考以下備忘錄。

翻譯 受文者：全體團隊成員
發文者：專案管理處

日期：2024 年 8 月 8 日
主旨：專案截止日更新

由於客戶要求，Bergeron 專案的截止日期已提前至 2024 年 9 月 1 日，請知悉。所有團隊應對此調整工作計劃，並優先處理任何未完成的任務。我們理解這一變更可能會增加壓力，但您的配合對滿足客戶期望相當重要。我們有信心您一向都可以交出高品質的成果。如有任何疑慮或資源需求，請隨時聯繫我們。

謹啟
專案管理處

解析 9. aware 是個形容詞，應擺在 be 動詞後面，「be aware of + N. / that...」是「知悉…（某事）」的意思，所以答案是 (D)。

10. 前一句提到截止日期已提前，而空格所在句子意思是所有團隊應調整工作計劃，顯示前後句「相呼應」，所以 (B) accordingly（相應地）是最符合句意的。其餘 (A) 是「技術性地」，(C) 是「各別地」，(D) 是「不自覺地」。

11. 從句尾的名詞 expectations（期望）可知，動詞要選 (A) meet。「meet one's expectation(s)」是固定用語，表示「**達到／符合某人的期望**」。

12. 這是個「選擇句子」的問題。空格前面句子提到「您的配合對滿足客戶期望相當重要」，而後面句子鼓勵對方有任何疑慮或需求的話可隨時聯繫，因此這句話應與「**滿足客戶期望**」有關，故 (C) We are confident you can always deliver high-quality results. 是最能夠適當連接前後文的句子。以下是四個選項的中文翻譯：
(A) 別為這次專案進度落後感到喪志。
(B) 請維持您原本的工作計畫，繼續努力。
(C) 我們有信心您一直都可以交出高品質的成果。
(D) 希望大家樂觀看待客戶流失的問題。

▶ Week 010

01 (C)　02 (C)　03 (B)　04 (C)　05 (D)　06 (C)　07 (A)　08 (B)
09 (B)

題目 1~2 請參考以下電子郵件。

翻譯

收件人：	Lars Andersson <landersson@ghjfinance.com>
寄件人：	Oliver Grayson <ograyson@ghjfinance.com>
主旨：	硬體升級
DATE：	⁰²9 月 13 日

親愛的 Andersson 先生：
我明白公司有規定 ⁰¹每五年將所有電腦升級一次。雖然在十年前聽起來也許是合理的，但事實上這些年來電腦速度的提升已顯著趨緩。我們目前的軟體運行良好，因此 ⁰¹在這個時候升級硬體似乎沒那麼必要。
⁰² 我聽說您將在後天決定這件事，希望您能及時收到這封電郵。如果預算還有空間，買些新的辦公椅可能是不錯的主意。Office Oasis 將在 9 月 17 日至 9 月 23 日舉辦促銷活動，這是撿便宜的絕佳機會。
Oliver Grayson

01. 這封電子郵件的目的為何？
　(A) 提醒某人進行一項更新

(B) 建議不要進行購物
(C) 通知某人更改規定
(D) 索取更多資訊

02. Andersson 先生預計何時會做決定？
(A) 9 月 13 日
(B) 9 月 14 日
(C) 9 月 15 日
(D) 9 月 17 日

解析 01. 通常電子郵件的目的可以從「主旨（subject）」窺知一二，不過本題卻是個例外，因為重點在第一段的第一句和最後一句。其中提到，雖然過去每 5 年會進行一次軟體升級，但目前似乎沒有必要了，這表示此項公司政策有所變更，所以答案是 (C) To notify someone of a policy change。

02. 從題目關鍵語句（Mr. Andersson expected to make a decision）可知，線索在第二段第一句：我聽說您將在後天決定這件事，而從這封郵件的日期（9 月 13 日）來看，答案是 (C) On September 15。

題目 3~5 請參考以下信件內容。

翻譯

Harrison & Co.
愛達荷州南帕市
先驅大道 123 號 (83686)

7 月 10 日
Ethan Harper
愛達荷州林登市
楓樹街 23 號 (74562)

親愛的 Harper 先生：
恭喜！我很高興要告訴您，Harrison & Co. 想 [3] 提供您位於本州的高級運營經理職位。從 7 月 24 日開始，您將負責協調我們全州處理設施的各項活動。現任運營經理 Sam Reynolds 將會提供您必要的培訓。

本信附上給您的合約副本。請查看一下合約細節，並於決定接受此職位後在文件上簽字。[4] 請將簽好的合約寄回給我們人力資源部門的 Casey Evans。[5]Evans 女士收到合約之後，將協助您安排搬遷至南帕市的一切事宜。

最後，我想邀請您和您的妻子 Andrea Harper 參加我們在 7 月 21 日（星期五）晚上於佛羅倫斯飯店舉行的年度高管招待會。請告訴我們您們是否能夠參加。

期待您的回覆。

謹啟
執行長 Jacob Sullivan
Harrison & Co.

03. 這封信的目的為何？
(A) 邀請朋友來用餐
(B) 提供工作機會
(C) 安排會議
(D) 規劃一系列活動

04. Mr. Harper 被要求做什麼？
(A) 檢視操作指南
(B) 參加培訓研討會
(C) 提交文件給人力資源部門
(D) 在活動中發表演說

05. 誰將協助 Harper 先生處理搬遷事宜？
(A) Jacob Sullivan
(B) Sam Reynolds
(C) Andrea Harper
(D) Casey Evans

解析 03. 信件的目的，通常在信件一開頭就看得到：I am delighted to let you know that Harrison & Co. would like to offer you the role of Senior Operations Manager...，表示提供對方一份工作，所以答案是 (B) To extend a job offer。

04. 信件內容提到「Return the signed contracts to Casey Evans in our HR department」，表示請對方將簽好的合約寄回給人力資源部，所以答案是 (C) Submit documents to the HR department。

05. 信件內容提到「Once Ms. Evans receives the contract, she will assist you with the arrangements for your relocation to Nampa」，表示 Evans 女士收到合約之後將協助 Harper 先生安排搬遷，所以答案是 (D) Casey Evans。

題目 6~9 請參考以下電子郵件。

翻譯

收件人：技術支援部門
　　　　<techsupport@intellnet.com>
寄件人：Emily Johnson <emily.
　　　　johnson@mailman.com>
日期：8 月 18 日
主旨：技術性功能失常

敬啟者：
我寫這封信是 [1] 因為我在使用 Affinity Designer 時遇到了一個技術性故障問題。— [1] — 這個問題於 2024 年 8 月 15 日上午約 10 點開始，並已嚴重影響到我的工作流程。儘管我已多次嘗試進行故障排除，包括 [2] 重啟軟體、清除快取和重新安裝，但問題仍然存在。— [2] — 此次故障造成報告和數據匯出功能失效，這尤其令人擔憂，因為它直接影響到我能否在即將到來的專案截止日期前完成工作。— [3] —

我懇請您儘快協助解決此問題。請告知後續步驟或提供任何必要的支援來 [3] 修復此問題。如果需要進一步的資訊，我很樂意提供。— [4] — 我期待您能迅速解決此問題。

謹啟，
Emily Johnson

06. 這封電子郵件的目的是什麼？
(A) 請求軟體更新
(B) 詢問一些新功能
(C) 抱怨某軟體的問題
(D) 尋求設定軟體的協助

07. Johnson 女士尚未嘗試過哪種解決方案？
(A) 重新連接到網絡
(B) 重新啟動軟體
(C) 執行重新安裝
(D) 清空快取

08. 第 2 段第 12 行中的單字「rectify」意思最接近 ＿＿＿＿＿＿＿。
(A) 擴大
(B) 解決
(C) 調整
(D) 簡化

09. 以下這個最適合放在文中 [1], [2], [3], [4] 哪個位置？
「我甚至檢查了軟體更新，但沒有可用的更新來處理此問題。」
(A) [1]
(B) [2]
(C) [3]
(D) [4]

解析 06. 從一開始的「I am writing in regard to a technical malfunction I have experienced with Affinity Designer.」可知，寫這封 email 的目的是要告知或抱怨使用 Affinity Designer 這個軟體時遇到了技術上的故障問題，所以答案是 (C) To complain about software。

07. 從「Despite multiple attempts to troubleshoot, including restarting the software, clearing the cache, and reinstalling it, the problem persists.」可知，嘗試過的做法包括重啟軟體、清除快取和重新安裝，只有 (A) Reconnecting to the Internet 是沒有提到的。

08. 在「Please advise on the next steps or provide any necessary support to rectify the issue.」這句子中，rectify 是「**修復，解決**」的意思，最接近 (B) solve 的意思。

09. 這是「插入句子」的問題。題目提供的句子意思是「**我甚至檢視過軟體更新問題，但沒有可供之更新可以處理此問題。**」這表示它前面應該已提

到嘗試處理此問題的作為，因此放在「... including restarting the software, clearing the cache, and reinstalling it, the problem persists.」的後面是最適當的，所以答案是 (B) [2]。

▶ Week 11

01 (D)　02 (C)　03 (A)　04 (D)　05 (C)　06 (C)

題目 1~2 請參考以下訊息對話。

翻譯

| 亞歷克斯·特納　　　　　　［下午 1:31］ |
| 泰勒，你現在有空嗎？總經理剛剛臨時要求在大約一小時後與研發團隊開會。 |
| 泰勒·陳　　　　　　　　　［下午 1:33］ |
| 我有空，但我的團隊目前正在市中心的主要辦公室工作。他們至少要到 4 點才會回來。 |
| 亞歷克斯·特納　　　　　　［下午 1:35］ |
| [1] 你覺得可以自己應付嗎？我相信即使沒有你的團隊成員在場，會議也能順利進行。 |
| 泰勒·陳　　　　　　　　　［下午 1:36］ |
| [1] 我想應該沒問題。需要我準備什麼嗎？ |
| 亞歷克斯·特納　　　　　　［下午 1:40］ |
| 他們想問一些關於我們新產品發布的問題，所以 [2] 帶上你的市場調查、預算預測以及你和你的團隊準備的其他文件。會議將在 5B 會議室舉行。 |
| 泰勒·陳　　　　　　　　　［下午 1:41］ |
| 我一定會出席。 |

01. 在 1:36 p.m.，陳先生說「I think that should work out fine.」時，他的意思是什麼？
    (A) 他對產品發佈會感到滿意。
    (B) 他相信他的團隊成員會及時回來。
    (C) 他認為即使沒有他參加，會議也能順利進行。
    (D) 他有信心可以獨自應對討論會。

02. 亞歷克斯要求泰勒帶什麼資料參加會議？
    (A) 公司歷史的影片
    (B) 有關公司價值的文件
    (C) 一些正式的商務文件
    (D) 對於先前產品的顧客回饋意見和使用見證

解析 01. 在 Taylor Chen 於 1:36 p.m. 說「I think that should work out fine.」之前，Alex Turner 問他「Do you think you could manage it on your own?」這表示 Taylor Chen 有信心自己可以處理討論會的事，所以答案是 (D) He is confident he can manage a discussion alone.。

02. 本題關鍵語句是「materials... Alex request Taylor bring to the meeting」。Alex Turner 在下午 1:40 時說「...bring your market survey, budget projections, and other documents prepared by you and your team（市場調查、預算預測以及你和你的團隊準備的其他文件）...」，所以答案是 (C) Some official business files。

題目 3~6 請參考以下線上聊天內容。

翻譯

| 李安·卡森　　　　　　　　［上午 11:07］ |
| Verdurex 的 [3] 莉亞·莫雷諾剛打電話來抱怨，[4] 她訂購的自助飲料機和加熱盤仍等待出貨中，因為這些商品原定昨天應該要到貨。 |

211

| 蘇菲・班尼特 | [上午 11:08] |

我昨天出差不在辦公室，所以不清楚那個訂單發生了什麼問題。

| 拉傑・梅塔 | [上午 11:09] |

[3] 在過去一週以來，我們的追蹤軟體遇到了一些問題，導致一些訂單顯示已經從倉庫發貨，實際上這些訂單甚至都還沒處理的情況。這個問題現在已經修復了。我想未來的訂單會順利進行。

| 伊莎貝拉・克魯茲 | [上午 11:11] |

如果莫雷諾女士訂購的設備仍缺貨，這可能導致更嚴重的延遲。

| 拉傑・梅塔 | [上午 11:12] |

[5] 真是太幸運了！我今天早上第一件事就是拆開了一大批來自 TPL Manufacturing 的貨。

| 李安・卡森 | [上午 11:13] |

聽起來不錯。我會立刻聯繫莫雷諾女士，告訴她，她的訂單出貨中，因為她需要這些物品來舉辦即將到來的派對。

| 蘇菲・班尼特 | [上午 11:15] |

等等。[6] 我們是不是應該先跟倉庫經理確認一下新到的貨是否足夠呢？

| 伊莎貝拉・克魯茲 | [上午 11:16] |

[6] 是的，我現在就過去一趟。李安，如果一切足夠，我會告訴你，然後你再打電話給莫雷諾女士。

03. 為什麼莫雷諾女士還沒有收到她的訂單？
(A) 軟體出了問題。
(B) 她的付款不夠。
(C) 倉庫的員工不在。
(D) 某些商品在運輸過程中損壞。

04. 何者最有可能是 Verdurex 公司的營運項目之一？
(A) 軟體製造與販售
(B) 餐盤和餐具的租借
(C) 快遞服務
(D) 餐飲供應

05. 在上午 11:12，拉傑寫道「真是太幸運了」，他的意思是什麼？
(A) 一些錯誤已處理完畢。
(B) 他們不需要加班。
(C) 有了新的供貨來源。
(D) 倉庫裡還有一些被遺忘的存貨。

06. 克魯茲女士接下來可能會做什麼？
(A) 要求倉庫人員加班
(B) 打電話給莫雷諾女士
(C) 確認是否有足夠的庫存給莫雷諾女士
(D) 前往 TPL Manufacturing 檢查到貨的物品。

解析 03. 本題針對關鍵語句「...hasn't Ms. Moreno received her order」找尋線索。從「Leah Moreno... complain that... she had ordered is still pending delivery」可知，莫雷諾女士訂購的自助飲料機和加熱盤仍在等待出貨，而接下來 Raj Mehta 說「Over the past week, our tracking software has encountered a bug」，這表示該公司追蹤軟體遇到了一些問題，所以答案是 (A) There was a problem with the software.。

04. 本題是針對關鍵語句「one of Verdurex's items in business」的推論問題。從「the selfserved drink machine and warming plates she had ordered」可知，Verdurex 公司要購買自助飲料機和加熱盤，這些東西應該是餐飲供應業者的生財器具，所以答案是 (D) Food and beverage provision。

05. 本題是詢問**說話者意圖**的問題。Mr. Mehta 說了「真是太幸運了！（What an amazing luck!）」之後接著說「A sizable shipment from TPL Manufacturing arrived, and I unpacked it first thing today.」表示他今天早上第一件事就是拆開了一大批來自 TPL Manufacturing 的貨，意味著有了新的供貨來源，所以

212

以答案是 (C) A new supply source is available.。

06. 本題是針對關鍵語句「Ms. Cruz probably do next」詢問**接下來要做的事**之推論問題。首先，Sophie Bennett 在 11:15 A.M. 問說「Should we check with the warehouse manager first to confirm if there's enough stock?」，接著 Ms. Cruz 回答說「Yes, I'll go over there now. Liam, if everything's okay, I'll let you know, and then you can call Ms. Moreno.」，這表示她稍後將過去跟倉庫經理確認一下新到的貨是否足夠，所以答案是 (C) Confirm if there's enough stock for Ms. Morenon。

▶ Week 12

01 (D)　02 (B)　03 (C)　04 (B)　05 (C)

題目 1~2 請參照以下行程表。

翻譯　　　　　　片名：《穿越陰影與光明》
　　　　　　　　製作商：星光港製片公司
　　　　　　　　導演：馬可斯·貝拉米

馬可斯·貝拉米的行程表
4月11日至22日

週一	週二	週三	週四	週五
11 上午 9:00 ¹⁽ᶜ⁾ 與製作團隊進行外景探勘		13 上午 11:00 檢視並批准場景設計概念	14 1:30 p.m. ¹⁽ᴮ⁾ 與演員陣容負責人會面，討論新進演員	15 下午 2:00 與主要演員一起閱讀劇本
18 上午 10:00 ¹⁽ᴬ⁾ 與作曲家商討電影的主題曲	19 上午 10:00 再次與主演陣容逐句閱讀劇本		21 上午 11:00 參加剪輯會議，檢視粗剪片段	22 下午 1:30 檢視攝影器材並為當天拍攝進行設置

01. 哪一項任務不是為貝拉米女士安排的？
    (A) 與作曲家集思廣益討論主題概念
    (B) 與選角導演評估新進演員人選
    (C) 與製作團隊一起勘查潛在的拍攝地點
    (D) 檢視關鍵動作場景的分鏡腳本

02. 第二次閱讀劇本會在幾點時進行？
    (A) 在上午 9:00
    (B) 在上午 10:00
    (C) 在下午 1:30
    (D) 在下午 2:00

解析 01. 本題屬於「何者為非」的問題。選項 (A) 的敘述可以對照 18 號的「Consult with composer on the film's main theme」；選項 (B) 的敘述可以對照 14 號的「Meet with casting director to discuss new talent」；選項 (C) 的敘述可以對照 11 號的「Location scouting with the production team」，只有選項 (D) 是沒有提到的。

02. 本題關鍵字詞是 second script reading，正好對照 19 號 10:00 a.m. 的行程內容：Read through lines with the starring cast again，因此答

案是 (B)。

題目 3~5 請參照以下調查表。

翻譯

楓木渡假小屋
賓客體驗回饋表

您的意見對我們非常重要！請花一點時間完成此問卷，並分享您的想法，這將有助於提升我們的服務品質。請用「✔」標記所有答案。

住宿日期：6 月 18-19 日
姓名：格倫·帕克
電話：(606) 778-9348
電子郵件：glenn@freemail.com

	完全認同	尚認同	不認同
1. 整體來說，我在楓木渡假小屋的體驗是⋯			
一段難忘且愉快的旅程，且周邊環境非常美麗。	✔		
物超所值。		✔	
2. 在 ³⁽ᴬ⁾ 櫃檯服務處，我受到了⋯			
熱情的微笑和 ³⁽ᴬ⁾ 快速的服務。	✔		
清晰且有幫助的設施資訊介紹。	✔		
3. ³⁽ᴮ⁾ 當我走進房間時，感覺是⋯			
一個經過漫長一天後可以放鬆的平靜舒適之地。	✔		
一間經過細心設計且能滿足我所有需求的房間。	✔		
房間溫度非常舒適。	✔		
4. ³⁽ᴰ⁾ 我發現楓木渡假小屋的設施⋯			
寬敞且是針對客人舒適度精心設計的。	✔		
井然有序且易於使用。	✔		
5. 從入住到退房，楓木渡假小屋的員工都⋯			
友善且貼心，關心我的所有需求。	✔		
在處理要求和提供資訊時效率很高。			✔
知識豐富，能迅速解答問題或疑慮。	✔		

6. 請不吝於此分享其他想法或建議：

我在楓木渡假小屋的住宿整體來說是愉快的。房間非常漂亮——寬敞、光線充足且舒適。床鋪很適合安穩的夜眠，窗外的景色也令人驚艷。然而，住宿期間我遇到了一件困難的事。⁵ 我剛進房後不久，臨時想再多住一晚。於是我打電話到前台時，員工似乎不是很確定能否進行這項安排。他們表示會確認，但 ⁴ 我一直等到幾乎要退房時才收到回覆，並告知我是否可以接受第二晚入住一間四人房，然而它的價格超出我的預算。最後我只好在其他地方訂了一間房。

03. 以下哪一項不包含在這份意見調查中？
    (A) 員工的回應速度
    (B) 房間的舒適度與提供的設施
    (C) Wi-Fi 連線的可靠性和速度
    (D) 設施的可用性和狀況

04. 關於帕克先生，有何暗示？
    (A) 他認為房間設施不好用。
    (B) 他提出的需求在收到回覆時已太遲。
    (C) 他沒有足夠的預算在同一房間續住。
    (D) 他希望能比原定退房時間更早離開。

05. 帕克先生進入房間後想做什麼？
    (A) 點客房服務
    (B) 在飯店健身房運動
    (C) 延長住宿時間
    (D) 打電話給他的老闆

解析 03. 本題屬於「**何者為非**」的問題。選項 (A) 的敘述可以對照「2. At the front desk, I was... welcomed with a warm smile and prompt service. 」；選項 (B) 的敘述可以對照「3. As I walked into my room, it felt like...」以下的內容；選項 (C) 是沒有提到的內容，所以本題答案就是 (C)。選項 (D) 的敘述可以對照「4. I found the facilities at Maplewood Retreat Lodge to be...」以下的內容。

04. 本題屬於「**何者正確**」的，同時是關於某人的「**推論**」問題。在下方的補充說明中提到「I was hoping to extend my stay... They said they would check, but I didn't hear back until I was almost scheduled to check out...」這表示他提出想續住一晚的需求，在收到回覆時已太遲，所以答案是 (B) He experienced a delay in response to a request.。

05. 本題是針對題目關鍵句「Mr. Parker want to do after entering his room」詢問的 5W1H 問題。同樣在最下方那段話中，Mr. Parker 提到「I was hoping to extend my stay by one more night shortly after I entered the room.」所以答案是 (C) Extend his stay。

▶ Week 13

01 (D)　02 (C)　03 (A)　04 (C)　05 (B)　06 (A)　07 (B)

題目 1~3 請參考以下報導內容。

🔖 翻 譯

> 河濱藝術空間：我們社區的寫照
>
> 「河濱藝術空間」將於今年九月舉辦一場別具一格的藝術展覽。這次展覽並非展示著名藝術家的作品，而是 [1] 以當地社區住戶創作的畫作為主。
>
> 展覽邀請了二十位年齡介於十六至八十四歲的當地參與者，創作出展現河濱鎮人們風貌的樣像。參觀者可以欣賞到多元化的作品，包括描繪鎮上和藹可親的 [2(C)] 麵包師傅、[2(A)] 社區遊樂場裡活潑的孩童、河濱消防隊長的肖像，以及一隻 [2(B)] 備受喜愛的寵物狗。其中甚至有一幅畫描繪了這個藝術空間本身。
>
> 河濱藝術空間的策展人蘇菲亞·拉克（Sophia Lark）對此活動表達了她的熱情：「身處一個小型且緊密聯繫的社區，讓我們得以突顯普通人身上的非凡才華。」回憶起 [3] 她之前在繁忙的阿克威爾市（Arkwell）的工作經歷，她補充道：「這是我在大都會藝術中心無法做到的事，這是一種截然不同的連結方式。」
>
> 「我們社區的寫照」將展出至九月三十日，入場費僅為 5 美元。

01. 這篇報導最適合刊登在報紙上的哪個版面？
    (A) 生活專欄
    (B) 旅遊版
    (C) 教育專欄
    (D) 地方新聞

02. 以下何者不是這次展覽畫作的主題？
    (A) 孩童
    (B) 寵物
    (C) 著名地標
    (D) 當地專業人士

03. 關於蘇菲亞·拉克，有何暗示？
    (A) 她曾在大城市工作過。
    (B) 她本身是一位才華洋溢的畫家。
    (C) 她在河濱鎮長大。
    (D) 她更喜歡在都市的藝術空間工作。

解析 01. 本題是詢問「**報導出處**」的 5W1H 問題，通常讀完第一段應該可以知道答案。從「…the exhibition features paintings created by members of the local community」的敘述可知，報導以當地社區成員創作的畫作為主，所以答案為 (D) Local news。

02. 本題屬於「**何者為非**」的問題，除了掌握關鍵語句（subject… NOT … included in the portraits），**並列資訊**的部分通常會是答題線索。從「a wide range of paintings, from depictions of…」這部分的內容可知，(A)、(B)、(D) 都是有提到的（lively children、beloved pet dog、baker），只有 (C) Famous landmarks 沒有提及。

03. 本題屬於「**何者為是**」的**推論**問題。從關鍵字詞（Sophia Lark）來看，解題線索在第二段：Sophia Lark, curator of the Riverside Art Space, … Reflecting on her previous role in the bustling city of Arkwell, …，這表示她之前在繁忙的阿克威爾市（Arkwell）工作過，因此答案是 (A) She has worked in a large city before.。

題目 4~7 請參考以下報導內容。

翻譯

[4(A,C)]Audiflow 準備推出 Musinex Plus 音樂平台

撰稿人：音樂特派記者 Clara Venn

音樂巨頭 Audiflow 擁有超過 65 家唱片公司的版權管理，近期與串流平台 Musinex 簽訂了一項全球授權協議。此舉為 Musinex Plus ── 一項高級音樂訂閱服務──的推出奠定了基礎。─ [1] ─ Musinex 已經獲得多家頂級唱片公司的內容授權，而在此前一直無法獲取 Audiflow 大量的現代音樂曲庫。

與 Audiflow 的合作將 [4(B)]大幅拓展 Musinex 可提供的音樂範圍，使得備受期待的 Musinex Plus 離正式上線更進一步。[7]這項付費服務已籌備三年。─ [2] ─ Audiflow 的執行長 Daniel Morvin 表示：「我們很高興能讓我們旗下藝術家的音樂，透過 Musinex 的網路及行動平台觸及更多聽眾。」他補充說：「雖然我們重視與 Musinex 競爭對手的合作，但無一家能與 Musinex 的全球影響力相比。」─ [3] ─

[5]Musinex 擁有超過 2 億名活躍用戶，而其最接近的競爭對手 StreamVibe 僅有 2,500 萬用戶。不過，Musinex 的大部分流量來自用戶觀看免費影片，而非串流音樂。─ [4] ─ 相比之下，[6]StreamVibe 擁有超過 52% 的用戶每月付費訂閱，以欣賞其豐富的音樂曲庫。Musinex Plus 能否吸引用戶為其服務付費，尚待觀察。

04. 關於 Musinex Plus，下列敘述何者正確？
 (A) 它已經上線，但僅限於特定地區提供服務。
 (B) 它主要經營經典音樂曲目的播放。
 (C) 它尚未正式開放使用。
 (D) 它將為首批訂閱者提供折扣優惠。

05. 根據報導，Musinex 擁有什麼競爭優勢？
 (A) 它包含影片串流功能。
 (B) 它的用戶數量遠高於競爭對手。
 (C) 它的訂閱費用比其他服務更低。
 (D) 它提供獨特的離線聆聽模式。

06. 關於 StreamVibe，文章提到什麼？
 (A) 有近一半的用戶付費訂閱。
 (B) 它最近與 Audiflow 簽訂了一項協議。
 (C) 它主要吸引對視頻串流感興趣的用戶。
 (D) 它的行動應用程式是全球下載量最高的之一。

07. 以下句子最適合放在哪個位置？
「服務推出後，用戶將能夠存取更多的音樂和影片，且皆以高品質的數位格式來呈現。」
(A) [1]
(B) [2]
(C) [3]
(D) [4]

解析 04. 因為報導內容就是在講 Musinex Plus，所以必須選項逐一對照內容。(A) 是錯誤的，因為從標題「Audiflow Opens Doors for Musinex Plus to Launch」即可推斷，這個平台尚未正式推出；(B) 是錯誤的，因為從第二段的「...expand the range of music Musinex can offer...」可得知；(D) 是沒有提到的內容，所以正確答案是 (C)。

05. 本題關鍵語句是「competitive advantage... Musinex have」。從「Musinex boasts over 200 million active users, while its closest competitor, StreamVibe, has just 25 million.」可知，Musinex 擁有超過 2 億名活躍用戶，而其最接近的競爭對手 StreamVibe 僅有 2,500 萬用戶，因此答案是 (B) It has a significantly larger user base than its competitors.。

06. 本題屬於「**何者為是**」的問題。從關鍵字詞（StreamVibe）來看，解題線索在第三段：... more than 52 percent of StreamVibe's users...。表示 StreamVibe 擁有超過 52% 的付費用戶，所以答案是 (A)。

07. 本題是「**放入句子**」的問題。題目提供的這句表示，一旦服務推出後，使用者能夠享有的高品質音樂與影片，可見其前句子應該與正式推出前的情況有關，因此應擺在「This paid service has been in the works for three years.」這句話的後面，正確答案為 (B) [2]。

▶ Week 14

01 (B)　02 (A)　03 (B)　04 (C)　05 (B)

題目 1~2 請參考以下報導內容。

翻譯

問題 1-2 請參考以下廣告。

「日出學苑」電腦課程

您是否希望提升數位技能？[1] 想學習有效地運用基本電腦工具嗎？如果是的話，歡迎加入我們的課程，時間是 1 月 10 日至 2 月 28 日，每週四晚上 7 點，地點是在「日出學苑」202 教室。[2] 資深資訊科技教育家 Emily Wong 將帶領學員們學習掌握基礎電腦操作、文件編輯，以及用常見的軟體來打造震撼人心的簡報。課程費用為每堂 25 美元。

請至 www.sunriseschool.edu/courses/computers 註冊，詳細課程大綱將於近期公布。

如需了解更多課程資訊（包括藝術工作坊及外語課程），請連上 www.sunriseschool.edu/courses 的網址參考看看。

01. 為何撰寫了這篇廣告？
(A) 推廣夏令營活動
(B) 鼓勵參加學校的電腦課程
(C) 展示一款新的軟體應用
(D) 提供圖書館資源的相關資訊

217

02. Emily Wong 將教導什麼？
(A) 製作有效的簡報
(B) 編輯技術手冊
(C) 修理硬體元件
(D) 練習外語技能

解析 01. 本題為**詢問主旨**的問題，而廣告的主旨通常可以先從廣告標題（COMPUTER COURSES AT SUNRISE SCHOOL）著手。如果還不太確定，可以從第一段的內容的「Do you want to learn how to use essential computer tools effectively?」確認，目的是鼓勵參加學校電腦課程，所以答案是 (B)。

02. 這是針對題目關鍵字詞（Emily Wong）的 5W1H 問題，其中提到「Emily Wong, an experienced IT educator, ... and creating impactful presentations using widely-used software programs.」，所以答案是 (A) Creating effective presentations。

問題 3-5 請參考以下公告內容。

翻譯

Pulse 健身中心：會員指南

我們在 Pulse 健身中心致力於為所有會員打造一個友好且安全的環境。為了維持此標準，³ 我們要通知您一些使用設施的相關規定。— [1] —。

³ 更衣室內提供置物櫃以便您在運動時存放個人物品。然而，請勿將貴重物品存放於置物櫃內，因為 Pulse 健身中心無法為遺失或被盜的物品負責。— [2] —。⁴ 為了增加安全性，您可以將貴重物品存放於前台，我們將提供妥善保管。— [3] —。

如果您來此遺失了物品，請立即聯繫前台。我們工作人員將協助您查看失物招領處，並採取必要措施幫助尋找您的物品。

— [4] —。感謝您的理解與支持。如有其他疑問或需要協助，請隨時聯繫我們友善的工作人員。

管理團隊

3. 這則公告的目的為何？
(A) 說明健身中心的會員福利
(B) 說明有關個人物品及貴重物品的規定
(C) 宣布健身中心新的營業時間
(D) 提供使用健身器材的指南

4. 根據公告內容，會員應如何妥善保管貴重物品？
(A) 將其存放於更衣室內提供的置物櫃
(B) 運動期間隨身攜帶
(C) 將其存放於前台以確保安全
(D) 放在健身中心提供的租用保險櫃內

5. 以下句子最適合放在 [1]、[2]、[3] 或 [4] 中的哪個位置？
「請注意，置物櫃的使用採先到先得原則。」
(A) [1]
(B) [2]
(C) [3]
(D) [4]

解析 03. 本題為**詢問主旨**的問題。從第一段結尾的「we would like to inform you of the following policies regarding the use of our facilities」以及第二段開頭的「Lockers are available in our changing rooms for storing your belongings during workouts.」可知，這則公告旨在說明有關個人物品及貴重物品的規定，所以答案是 (B) To explain policies about personal items and valuables。

04. 這是針對題目關鍵語句（should members do to secure their valuable items）的 5W1H 問題，其中提到「For added security, you may deposit valuables at the front desk, where they will be stored securely.」，所以答案是 (C) Deposit them at the front desk for safekeeping。

05. 本題是「**放入句子**」的問題。題目提供的語句表示「請注意，置物櫃的使用採先到先得原則。」可見其前句子應該與置物櫃的使用有關，因此應擺在「However, please refrain from storing highly valuable items in the lockers, as Pulse Fitness Center cannot be held responsible for lost or stolen property.」這句話的後面，正確答案為 (B) [2]。

▶ Week 15

01 (A)　02 (B)　03 (B)　04 (B)　05 (C)　06 (C)

題目 1~2 請參考以下報導內容。

翻譯

綠草原住宅社區

日期：11 月 25 日
收件人：全體住戶
發件人：社區經理 Emily Wong
[1] 主旨：臨時停水通知

親愛的住戶們：

我們在此通知您，因進行主要水管的必要維修工作，本社區將於 11 月 27 日（星期一）上午 9:00 至下午 4:00 暫停供水。在此期間，請各位住戶提前做好準備，儲存足夠的水以供使用。

請注意以下事項：
維修期間，廁所和廚房將無法供水。
[2] 為方便大家，社區會館將設置臨時飲用水站。

對於此次臨時不便，我們深表歉意，並感謝您的理解與配合。如有任何疑問或需協助，請聯繫管理辦公室，電話：555-123-4567。

謝謝！
Emily Wong
社區經理

01. 備忘錄的目的是什麼？
    (A) 通知住戶計劃中的停水事宜
    (B) 宣布新的社區規範
    (C) 通知住戶緊急維修事宜
    (D) 解釋水費變動

02. Emily Wong 最近做了什麼？
    (A) 宣布新會館的開幕
    (B) 安排臨時飲用水供應
    (C) 安裝額外的蓄水設備
    (D) 延長停水時間

解析 01. 本題為**詢問主旨或目的**的問題。以備忘錄來說，應先查看「Subject: ...」的部分。從「Subject: Temporary Water Supply Interruption」可知，這份備忘錄的目的是**停水通知**，所以答案是 (A) To inform residents of a planned water outage。

02. 本題為針對關鍵字詞「Emily Wong」詢問的 5W1H 問題。Emily Wong 是社區管委會的經理、這篇備忘錄的發文者。其中提到「Drinking water stations will be set up at the community clubhouse for your convenience.」，所以答案是 (B) Arranged alternative drinking water provisions。

問題 3-6，請參考以下資訊。

翻譯

[3] 環球冒險旅行社之取消規定

環球冒險旅行社所規劃的假期，需要我們公司和客戶雙方進行詳細的安排。我們理解生活中可能會 [4] 有意想不到的變化，因此制定以下取

消制度，在照顧客戶需求的同時，也能平衡我們的營運成本。

如需取消預訂，您可以發送電子郵件至 **cancellations@globaladventures.com** 或寄送書面申請至我們的辦事處地址：加州洛杉磯探險者大道 200 號，郵編 90015。另可撥打我們的專線 **1-888-555-9090** 進行取消事宜。^{5(B)/6} 請於申請時提供聯絡電話。所有重新安排的申請將根據個別情況核可。^{5(A)} 取消退款的具體條款如下：

10 天或以下	不退款
11 至 20 天	退款團費 30%
21 至 40 天	退款團費 60%
^{5(D)}41 天或以上	團費全額退款

如需任何協助或有任何疑問，請聯繫我們的客服團隊，撥打上述免付費電話號碼。

03. 這篇資訊的目的是什麼？
 (A) 鼓勵提早預訂
 (B) 提供取消和退款的指南
 (C) 說明調整團費的服務費用
 (D) 列出重新安排行程的特別優惠

04. 第一段第三行中的單字「arise」最接近以下的 _____。
 (A) 上升
 (B) 發生
 (C) 變動
 (D) 提升

05. 以下哪一項敘述是這篇資訊中是未提及的？
 (A) 退款金額比例取決於行前取消的時間長短。
 (B) 客戶需在申請中提供聯絡電話號碼。
 (C) 取消僅能透過電子郵件提交。
 (D) 提前 41 天取消可獲得全額退款。

06. 申請取消時必須提供什麼？
 (A) 預訂代碼
 (B) 取消的正當理由
 (C) 後續聯絡方式
 (D) 客戶的簽名

解析 03. 本題為**詢問主旨或目的**的問題。從標題的「Global Adventures Travel Cancellation Policies」可知，這篇資訊類似一種通知或公告，內容肯定是關於旅行社行程預訂的取消規範，所以答案是 (B) To provide a guideline for cancellations and refunds。

04. 本題為**同義字詞**的問題。arise 這個動詞所在的句子是「We understand that unexpected changes can arise and have developed the following cancellation policies...」，依句意它有「發生」的意思，所以答案是 (B) occur。

05. 本題為針對整個文本內容詢問的**何者為非**問題，故須逐一選項對照內容。從「Refund details for cancellations are outlined below.」底下的表格可知，退款金額比例取決於行前取消的時間長短，所以 (A) 是正確的敘述；從「Please provide a contact phone number in your request.」可知，申請時要求提供聯絡電話，所以 (B) 是正確的敘述；從「To cancel your booking, you may email us... or mail a written request to... Alternatively, cancellations can be made by calling our hotline...」的敘述可知，有多種聯繫方式，所以 (C) 是錯誤的敘述；從表格中「41 days or more ｜ Full refund of the package price」可知，(D) 是正確的敘述。

06. 本題為針對題目關鍵語句（necessary for a cancellation request）詢問的 **5W1H** 問題。從「Please provide a contact phone number in your request.」的敘述可知，申請時提供聯絡電話是必要的，所以答案是 (C) Contact details for follow-up。

Week 16

01 (B)　02 (B)　03 (C)　04 (C)　05 (C)　06 (D)　07 (B)　08 (B)
09 (C)　10 (B)

題目 1~5 請參考以下宣傳手冊與電子郵件。

翻 譯

「荷蘭遺產莊園」是一個非常適合家庭聚會的場所。這個歷史悠久的景點已經接待了超過一個世紀的來賓，超過五千萬人曾探索過它的住宅和花園。[01] 今年八月至十月，「荷蘭遺產莊園」將舉辦一系列引人入勝的活動。遊客可以欣賞到特別的花卉花園展覽、參加導覽行程、參觀莊園內的古董家具，並參與傳統的荷蘭手工藝工作坊，如陶瓷製作和織布。

在九月份，還有更多的活動安排，其中包括每週三的音樂會系列，名為「公園的荷蘭和聲音樂」。每場音樂會結束後，參加者將有機會玩玩音樂家提供的傳統樂器。

在這三個月期間，本園開放時間為：平日上午 11:00 到下午 6:00，[05] 週六日及其他國定假日則從上午 11:00 到下午 7:00。如需更多詳細資訊，請上 www.holland_heritage_manor.co.nl 網站。請注意，雖然週三的音樂會是免費的，但 [02] 音樂課程需要購票，票券可以在現場購買。

[04] 收件人：Clara van der Meers <clarameers@hotmail.co.nl>
[03] 寄件人：Juliette Renaud <jr@gmail.com>
主旨：謝謝！
日期：9 月 15 日

親愛的 Clara，
近來可好？我想感謝你寄給我有關「荷蘭遺產莊園」的宣傳冊。[05] 我這個星期一，也就是勞動節，帶著我的男朋友去了那裡，我們玩得非常開心。[04] 我想你和你的家人去那裡的時候肯定也玩得很開心吧？

[03] 我特別喜歡把玩音樂家提供的傳統樂器。他們非常熱心，我們倆都學到了很多。此外，Willem 也非常喜歡在花卉展覽中漫步，他非常滿意，所以 [05] 我們待到莊園關門才離開！

那個美妙的莊園有太多的活動，我們正在考慮下個月再去一次。你和你先生要不要一起來？請儘快告訴我，再次感謝你推薦了這麼棒的地方。

期待見到你，
Juliette

01. 宣傳冊的目的為何？
　　(A) 介紹新設立的景點
　　(B) 宣傳一個觀光景點
　　(C) 宣傳一棟待售豪宅
　　(D) 提供傳統工藝工作坊

02. 關於音樂課程，暗示了什麼？
　　(A) 票券可以上網購買。
　　(B) 只有持票才能進入。
　　(C) 每週舉行一次。
　　(D) 參加者可以在那裡遇到一些流行樂歌手。

03. 根據電子郵件內容，Juliette 在「荷蘭遺產莊園」做了什麼？
　　(A) 她參加了導覽行程。
　　(B) 她欣賞了花卉花園。
　　(C) 她試玩了一些傳統樂器。
　　(D) 她在森林中散步。

04. 關於 Clara，以下哪項敘述是正確的？
　　(A) 她在「荷蘭遺產莊園」工作。
　　(B) 她有一位名叫 Willem 的男朋友。
　　(C) 她之前曾經去過「荷蘭遺產莊

園」。
(D) 她計劃不久後再次拜訪荷蘭傳承莊園。

05. Juliette 最有可能何時離開「荷蘭遺產莊園」？
(A) 上午 11:00
(B) 下午 6:00
(C) 晚上 7:00
(D) 晚上 8:00

解析 01 這是針對第一個文本的 brochure 詢問的**主旨／目的**問題。手冊沒有標題，所以直接從第一段找線索。從「From August to October this year, the Holland Heritage Manor will host a series of intriguing events. Visitors can enjoy...」可知，荷蘭遺產莊園在宣傳為期三個月的特別活動，歡迎遊客前來觀光，所以答案是 (B) To advertise a scenic spot。

02 這是針對 music classes 詢問的**推論問題**。提到「音樂課程」的部分是在宣傳冊最後的「tickets are necessary for the music classes and can be purchased on-site」，所以答案是 (B) Admission is allowed only with tickets。

03 這是針對電子郵件這篇，以及「Juliette do at the Holland Heritage Manor」這個關鍵語句詢問的 **5W1H 問題**。從寄件者是 Juliette Renaud 以及第二段的「I particularly enjoyed using traditional instruments supplied by the musicians.」可知，她特別喜歡把玩音樂家提供的傳統樂器，這表示她在「荷蘭遺產莊園」試玩了一些傳統樂器，所以答案是 (C)。

04 這是針對題目關鍵字詞 Clara 詢問的「**何者為真**」問題。因為關於某人的事，不會出現在 brochure 那篇，所以直接在 email 找線索。Juliette 在第一段最後對 Clara 說「I think you and your family must have enjoyed it when you went there, right?」由此可見，Clara 之前曾經去過「荷蘭遺產莊園」，所以答案是 (C)。

05 這是針對 Juliette 最有可能**何時**（when）離開「荷蘭遺產莊園」的**連結問題**。首先，在電子郵件中，Juliette 表示她這個星期一，也就是勞動節，帶著她男友去了荷蘭遺產莊園（I took my boyfriend there this Monday, the Labor Day），而且他們待到莊園關門才離開（we ended up staying until the house closed）。接著我們要在 brochure 中確認當天莊園關門的時間。從第三段「11:00 A.M. to 7:00 P.M. on Saturdays, Sundays and other national holidays」可知，Juliette 和她男友離開的時間應該是 7:00 P.M.，因為 Labor Day 也是一個 national holiday。所以答案是 (C)。

問題 6-10 請參考以下的公告與表格。

翻譯

⁶Greenwood Academy 很高興宣布將於下個月舉辦第二屆年度 Greenwood 慈善市集。此次活動將於 9 月 9 日星期三，上午 11 點至晚上 7:30 在學校的中央禮堂舉行。來賓可以逛逛各式各樣的二手商品，並欣賞學校合唱團的表演以及來自 Harrison 大學的舞蹈團演出。與往年一樣，市集的目的是為了募集資金以協助流離失所的家庭。

活動結束時將會舉行抽獎活動，⁸獎品是 5 支最新款的 Apple 智慧型手機。凡是購買市集門票入場者將自動參加抽獎。每張門票售價 6 元，可在學校入口處購買。

此外，現場將設有來自全國各地攤商設置的美食攤位。如果您有興趣設立攤位，請聯繫 Elena Rodriguez 女士，電話 666-0606 或發送電子郵件至 elena@greenwood.edu。

⁷主辦單位還在尋找志工來協助活動。如

果您願意幫忙，請上網填寫申請表，網址為 www.greenwood.com/marketvol，或前往總務處索取表格並於 8 月 30 日前提交。⁹ 志工將可免費進入市集。

志工登記申請表

第二屆年度 Greenwood 慈善市集

----

1. 請填寫以下空格處，並於 8 月 30 日（星期五）前將表格提交至 Greenwood Academy。
2. 當我們處理完您的表格後，您將收到一個名牌，需在慈善市集上佩戴。

日期：8 月 24 日．
⁹ 姓名：Sophia Bennett.
地址：橡樹鎮楓樹巷 4825 號，L8K 1N4.
電子郵件：sophia.bennett@gmail.com.
電話：(540) 313-4858.

您願意協助哪些工作？
食品服務　_____
銷售攤位　_____
票務銷售　_____
¹⁰ 清潔工作　_____　✔

---

06. 關於 Greenwood 慈善市集，有指出什麼？
    (A) 它在 9 月 9 日的活動時間將超過 10 個小時。
    (B) 它將由學校的舞蹈社團提供舞蹈表演。
    (C) 今年的目的是為當地動物收容所募集資金。
    (D) 它是去年首次舉辦的。

07. 志工們被要求去做什麼？
    (A) 在學校的辦公總部購買門票。
    (B) 提交申請表。
    (C) 與學校校長洽談。
    (D) 為流離失所的家庭捐款。

08. 誰可能會贏得智慧型手機？
    (A) 所有 Greenwood Academy 的學生。
    (B) 持有門票的來賓。
    (C) 來自 Harrison College 的表演者。
    (D) 獲准參加的志工。

09. Bennett 女士可能想做什麼？
    (A) 就讀 Greenwood Academy。
    (B) 為流離失所的家庭募集資金。
    (C) 免費參加活動。
    (D) 協助在活動中銷售食品。

10. Bennett 女士最有可能在 9 月 9 日做什麼？
    (A) 為來自國外的參加者安排銷售攤位。
    (B) 活動結束後整理禮堂。
    (C) 處理參加者的票務銷售。
    (D) 在提供不同類型食物的攤位工作。

解析 06 關於「Greenwood 慈善市集」的事，直接看第一個文本的 announcement 即可。一開始提到「Greenwood Academy is excited to host its second annual Greenwood Charity Bazaar next month.」這表示今年是第二屆，那麼去年就是首屆舉辦，所以答案是 (D) It was first held last year.。

07 這是針對關鍵語句「volunteers asked to do」提問的 5W1H 問題。直接看第一個文本的 announcement 即可。從「The organizers are also seeking volunteers... please fill out the online application form at...」的敘述可知，主辦單位要求志工上網填寫申請表，所以答案是 (B) Hand in an application form。

08 這是針對關鍵語句「win a smartphone」提問的 5W1H 問題。關於「誰能夠贏得獎品的問題，直接看第一個文本的 announcement 即可。從「...there will be a drawing for 5 latest Apple smartphone. Whoever purchases a ticket to the market will be automatically entered into the raffle」的敘述可知，凡購買市集門票入場者可參加最新款的 Apple 智

慧型手機的抽獎，所以答案是 (B) Ticket-holding visitors。

09 題目問「Ms. Bennett 可能想做什麼」，但這個名字不可能出現在 announcement 中。所以先從第二個文本（form）找線索。從「Name: Sophia Bennett」可得知，Ms. Bennett 想申請當志工，但四個選項中找不到這樣的敘述，因此可斷定這是個連結問題，必須繼續在第一個文本中找線索。從「Volunteers will be allowed to enter the market free of charge.」的敘述可知，志工可免費進入市集，因此我們可推論 Ms. Bennett 也許是想免費參加這場活動，所以答案是 (C) Participate in the event for free。

10 本題有兩個關鍵語句：September 9 以及 Ms. Bennett most likely do，所以也算是個連結問題。首先，從第一個文本的 announcement 中可知，Greenwood 慈善市集在 9 月 9 日舉行，而從第二個文本可知，Ms. Bennett 申請加入志工且她選擇的工作是：Cleanup。所以，其實題目真正要問的就是「以下何者是 Cleanup 的工作？」故正確答案是 (B) Tidy up the auditorium after the event。

▶ Week 17

01 (C)　02 (C)　03 (D)　04 (A)　05 (B)　06 (A)　07 (D)　08 (C)
09 (A)　10 (C)

題目 1~5 請參考以下通知、備忘錄與電子郵件。

翻譯

電梯維修通知

威洛大廈的電梯將於 [5(A)] 6 月 15 日（星期一）進行定期維修。[4] 維修人員將於上午 10:30 開始，預計維修時間約 1.5 小時，若一切順利進行。如若遇到任何問題，維修團隊將繼續作業直至問題解決。

因此，維修期間電梯將無法使用，大家可以使用位於大樓東側的樓梯。感謝您的耐心，也期待您可以理解：[1] 根據市政規定，電梯必須每年檢查一次，這對於確保所有使用者的安全與設備的可靠性相當重要。

如有任何問題或建議，請隨時聯繫管理處。您可以撥打 987-5454，[5(D)] 來電時請找 Alex Thompson。

收文者：Apex Solutions 全體員工
發文者：Jamie Taylor
主旨：電梯維修
日期：6 月 12 日

請注意，下週一早上將進行電梯維修，維修時間從上午 10:30 開始，預計中午就能結束。由於 [5(B)] 我們的辦公室在威洛大廈的頂樓，[3] 建議在此期間避免下樓，除非您願意走樓梯。

[2] 如果這段時間有客戶來訪，請考慮重新安排會面或找其他地點與他們會面。如果要叫外送，請務必事先告知，請他們 12:00 過後再將餐點送達。我相信只要您解釋情況，他們會理解的。

5(D)收件人：Mia Thompson <miat@apexsolutions.com>
寄件人：Liam Carter <liamcarter@tigerfasttrackshipping.com>
主旨：到貨通知
日期：6 月 15 日

我今天（6 月 15 日）4 下午 1:30 時試圖將您的包裹送到您的辦公室，但因為電梯維修中，且找不到管理員可以代為簽收。一位維修人員告訴我，他們可能還需要一個小時左右才能完工。5(B) 因為您的貨重約 25 公斤，我無法將其搬到九樓。

我也試圖撥打您的手機號碼（0987-123456）聯繫您，但未能接通。現在，我計劃在 6 月 19 日（星期五）早上帶著包裹再次前來。如果您需要包裹更早送達，請聯繫「快捷遞送」辦公室，電話是 808-5432，可以週五之前送達。

謹啟，
Liam Carter
5(C)快捷遞送

01. 根據這則通知，關於威洛大廈，有指出什麼？
    (A) 它的電梯維修工作預計 2 小時內完成。
    (B) 這是一棟住宅商辦大樓。
    (C) 去年有進行過修繕作業。
    (D) 整棟大樓有兩部電梯。

02. 泰勒先生為什麼寫這份備忘錄？
    (A) 公布即將舉行的活動
    (B) 重新安排會議
    (C) 提醒員工們注意可能出現的問題
    (D) 給員工放一天假

03. 在備忘錄中，第 1 段第 3 行的「trips」一字最接近的意思是什麼？
    (A) 乘坐
    (B) 觀光
    (C) 跌倒
    (D) 步行

04. 關於電梯維修人員，有何暗示？
    (A) 在維修電梯時，他們另外發現了一些問題。
    (B) 他們計劃在這個週末處理一些意外問題。
    (C) 電梯維修花了他們 1.5 小時。
    (D) 他們是 Apex Solutions 的正式員工。

05. 關於 Apex Solutions 這家公司，以下哪一項是不正確的？
    (A) 員工被告知 6 月 15 日當天避免使用電梯。
    (B) 它位於一棟 10 層樓的建築物中。
    (C) 「快捷遞送」為其固定供應商之一。
    (D) Mia Thompson 和 Jamie Taylor 都是該公司的員工。

解析 01. 從「According to the notice」可知，只要針對第一個文本找答案即可。從「city regulations require annual elevator inspections」可知，電梯必須每年檢查一次，這表示這棟樓去年也進行過修繕作業，所以答案是 (C) It had some renovation work done last year.。

02. 題目問為什麼「Mr. Taylor write the memo」，所以只要針對第二個文本找答案即可。從「If you have any clients coming in during that time, consider rescheduling your meetings or finding an alternative location to meet them」可知，其目的是提醒員工們注意可能會遇到的問題，所以答案是 (C) To alert staff about a possible issue。

03. 本題為**同義字詞**問題。trips 這個字位於備忘錄中的「I recommend avoiding any **trips** downstairs during that time unless you're willing to use the staircase.」意思是「我建議在此期間避免下樓，除非您願意走樓梯」，所以最接近意思的是 (D) walks。

04. 本題為與「elevator servicemen」有

關的連結問題，所以要先看電子郵件裡怎麼說：...at 1:30 PM... One of the maintenance workers told me that they might need about another hour to finish the work.。這表示在下午 1:30 時快遞人員從一位維修人員口中得知，還需要 1 個小時左右才能完工。接著我們再對照一開始的 notice 中所寫的：The elevator servicemen will start at 10:30 A.M. and the inspection will last about 1.5 hours。這表示原預計應於中午 12:00 結束的電梯維修工程，到下午 1:30 尚未完成，這暗示維修人員在工作時，另外發現了一些問題，所以答案是 (A) While working on the elevator, they identified some additional issues.。

05. 本題為與「Apex Solutions」有關的「何者為非」問題，且是個連結問題，必須逐一選項對照。(A) 可以從 notice 一開始的「The elevator in the Willow Tower is set, on a regular basis, for maintenance on Monday, June 15.」以及 第二篇的 memo 告知所有 Apex Solutions 員工這件事得知，是正確的敘述；(B) 可以從 email 的「I was unable to carry it up to the ninth floor」以及 memo 的「our office is on the top floor of Willow Tower」確認，是錯誤的敘述，故答案為 (B) It is located in a 10-story building.。(C) 可以從 email 的「... please contact the Fast Track Shipping office at 808-5432 to rearrange a pickup before Friday」得知，是正確的敘述；(D) 可以從 email 的「To: Mia Thompson <miat@apexsolutions.com>」以及 memo 的「From: Jamie Taylor」得知，是正確的敘述。

問題 6-10 請參考以下網站、電子郵件與行程表。

翻譯

| 主頁 | 最新消息 | 預約旅遊行程 | 隨身 & 托運行李 | 客服 |

「天際航空」一直努力為顧客提升服務品質。^{6(A)} 最近，我們在國內 3 個主要機場的旅客休息區進行了設備的升級，這些設施特別 ^{6(D)} 開放給所有「天際航空里程專案」會員使用。

^{6(B)} 從 7 月 1 日起，我們將推出河谷市與克雷斯特伍德之間的直航服務。[7] 於 9 月 1 日前使用這條新航線的旅客可享受 20% 的折扣。

要獲取天際航空的最新消息，包括 ^{6(C)} 明年擴展的國際航班資訊，請在這裡訂閱我們的月刊通訊。

收件人：Olivia Martinez <o.martinez@crestviewcapital.com>
寄件人：James Carter <carterj@entrepreneurnetwork.com>
日期：7 月 21 日
主旨：即將舉辦的商業研討會

馬丁尼茲女士 您好：

[7] 我已為您安排了一班從 Crestwood 直飛 Riverdale 市的班機，出發日期是 8 月 15 日，兩天後返程。這是「天際航空」公司的班機，我會很快告知您完整的行程。

我還得通知您，會場的屋頂出現了一些意外的損壞。因此，[10] 原定於藍寶石廳舉行的研討會將改至白金廳舉行，而原本計劃在白銀廳的活動將移至主廳。請忽略我在 7 月 5 日發給您的行程表。

我知道您比較不喜歡租車。由於主辦單位未提供機場接送服務，[8/9] 我的助理將開車過去接您。他會在入境大廳等您，並會舉著一個標示牌。

非常感謝您同意參加這次的商業交流研討會系列。

謹啟，
詹姆士 · 卡特

春季研討會系列 – 商業網絡

我們了解每個人的時間寶貴,因此每場講座將準時開始。請務必做好相應的安排。

時間	主講人	公司	座談會地點
1:30 p.m.	10 薩曼莎·皮爾斯	頂峰創投	10 藍寶石廳
2:30 p.m.	詹姆森·布魯克斯	尖峰金融	白金廳
中場休息			
3:00 p.m.	奧利維亞·馬丁尼茲	峰景資本	藍寶石廳
4:00 p.m.	德瑞克·卡拉漢	頂點解決方案	白銀廳
5:00 p.m.	弗蘭克·托雷斯	銀星集團	主廳

於七月五日分發佈

06. 關於天際航空公司,哪一項是不正確的?
(A) 它已為其所有機場的旅客休息區進行修繕。
(B) 它即將啟用來往河谷市與克雷斯特伍德的直飛航班。
(C) 它目前國內與國際航班都有營運。
(D) 它提供旅客忠誠計劃。

07. 關於馬丁尼茲女士,有暗示了什麼?
(A) 她預定在 8 月 16 日返回。
(B) 她需要轉機前往河谷市。
(C) 她住在河谷城。
(D) 她的班機有提供優惠價格。

08. 馬丁尼茲女士將如何前往會議場所?
(A) 搭乘接駁巴士
(B) 搭乘預訂的計程車
(C) 搭乘卡特先生同事的便車
(D) 由她的一位好朋友搭載

09. 在電子郵件中,第三段第二行的單字 fetch 意思最接近 _____。
(A) 接走
(B) 期待
(C) 抓取
(D) 捕獲

10. 皮爾斯女士將在哪裡發表演講?
(A) 在藍寶石廳
(B) 在主廳
(C) 在白金廳
(D) 在銀廳

解析 06 本題是針對關鍵字詞 Skyway Airlines 詢問的「**何者為非**」問題。從第一個文本的 web page 中「Recently, we have renovated the relaxation areas at three major airports.」可知,Skyway Airlines 在國內 3 個主要機場的旅客休息區進行了設備的升級,但這並不意味「在國內所有機場」,所以 (A) 不正確;從「From July 1 onwards, we will launch direct flights connecting Riverdale City and Crestwood for the debut service.」可知,(B) 是正確的敘述;從「including our broadening international flight offerings next year」可知,(C) 是正確的敘述;從「available for all members of the Skyway Airlines Miles Program」可知,(D) 是正確的敘述。

07 本題是針對關鍵字詞 Ms. Martinez 詢問的「**何者正確**」,也是個連結問題。我們要先從寄人為 Ms. Martinez 的電子郵件來看,一開始提到「I've arranged a direct flight for you from Crestwood to Riverdale City on August 15, with a return two days later」,表示 Ms. Martinez 的同事 James Carter 為她安排了一班從 Crestwood 直飛 Riverdale 市的班機,出發日期是 8 月 15 日,兩天後返程。接著在 web page 中提到「Travelers who use this new route before September 1 will benefit from a 20% deduction.」,因此她搭乘的班機有提供優惠價格,答案是 (D)。

227

08 本題是針對題目關鍵語句「Ms. Martinez get to the conference facility」詢問「如何前往會議場所」的 5W1H 問題。在電子郵件中提到「My assistant will drive over to fetch you. He'll meet you at the arrivals hall with a sign.」，所以答案是 (C) By taking a ride with Mr. Carter's coworker。

09 本題是**同義字詞**問題。fetch 的所在句子是「My assistant will drive over to **fetch** you.」意思是「我的助理將開車過去**接**您」，所以答案是 (A) collect。collect 一般來說，其受詞是「事物」的話，有「**收集，領取**」的意思；若其受詞為「人」時，就是「**接走**」的意思。

10 本題是針對關鍵語句 Ms. Pierce deliver a speech 詢問「在哪裡（where）發表演說」的 5WH 問題，也是個連結問題。雖然從第三個文本 schedule 中的「Samantha Pierce｜Pinnacle Ventures｜Sapphire Room」可以明顯得知，她在藍寶石廳發表演說，不過，考生要有對題目的敏感度：通常多益考題的設計，不會這麼輕易讓你找到答案！在電子郵件中提到「I also wanted to inform you that there has been some unexpected roof damage at the venue. Consequently, seminars that were set for the Sapphire Room will now take place in the Platinum Room, ...」所以答案是 (C) In the Platinum Room。

▶ Week 18

01 (C)　02 (D)　03 (C)　04 (A)　05 (D)　06 (A)　07 (C)　08 (A)
09 (D)　10 (D)

題目 1~5 請參考以下報導、信件和電子郵件。

翻 譯

TechSphere 即將在舊金山開設第三家店面

撰文：Kevin Grant

TechSphere，一家知名的電子產品零售連鎖店，宣布計畫在舊金山開設第三家店面。根據 TechSphere 的行銷總監 Claire Roberts 表示，新店將位於日落區，預計將為科技愛好者及一般消費者提供服務。Roberts 表示：「[1] 我們的產品和服務在舊金山的需求量十分驚人。這家新店將幫助我們提供顧客更好的服務，同時將最新的消費電子產品帶入這個社區。」

新分店將擁有寬敞的展示廳，展示最新的科技產品，包括智慧手機、筆記型電腦和智慧家居設備。一個專門的服務中心將提供設備維修、諮詢和升級服務。[2(A)] 不像 [4] 位於紐約市中心的旗艦店設有咖啡休息區，這個地點將重點打造流暢的購物體驗，[2(B)] 配備自助結帳機和線上訂單的快速取貨服務。

[2(D)] TechSphere 計畫在 11 月中旬為新分店舉行開幕儀式。如需最新消息或查詢，請上 www.techsphere.com 的網站。

2024 年 4 月 10 日
Kevin Grant
《今日科技要聞》
加州洛杉磯橡樹大道 789 號 Parker 大樓 234 單元

親愛的 Grant 先生：

感謝您近期專門報導了 TechSphere 即將開設新分店的消息，我們非常感激您的報導。然而，[3]我們發現報導中有幾處錯誤，我們希望進行更正：

[2(D)] 報導提到開幕日期為 11 月中旬。雖然我們的目標是這個時間點，但確切的日期尚未 [5] 定案。

[2(B)] 文中提到我們的新地點將設有自助結帳機台。雖然這是我們正在考慮的功能，但目前尚未確認。

我們懇請您在下次發布的報導中進行更正，以便為讀者提供準確的訊息。

謹啟，
Claire Roberts
TechSphere 行銷總監
claire.roberts@techsphere.com

收件人：Claire Roberts claire.roberts@techsphere.com
寄件人：Kevin Grant
k.grant@techtodaynews.com
主旨：為發布錯誤訊息致歉
附件：修正版草稿
日期：2024 年 4 月 14 日

親愛的 Roberts 女士：

我對文章中的不錯誤訊息深感抱歉。[4]我在上個月與 TechSphere 市中心店的一名團隊成員交談時，對一些細節產生了誤解。我已經與我的編輯討論過，我們會在下一期雜誌中發表更正訊息。附件中包含了更正後的文章草稿，請您過目。

此外，我希望能即時取得確切開幕日期的消息，因為我們可能會想要撰寫後續報導或進行現場的店鋪評論。

感謝您指出這些問題，再次為給您帶來的不便致歉。

謹啟，
Kevin Grant

---

01. 根據報導，TechSphere 為什麼要開設新店？
    (A) 為了將業務擴展到舊金山以外地區
    (B) 為了推出全新的產品線
    (C) 為了應對日益增加的顧客需求
    (D) 為了與其他地區的零售商競爭

02. 關於 TechSphere 的新店，以下哪一項是正確的？
    (A) 它將設有專屬的咖啡休息區。
    (B) 它將於十一月中旬設置自助結帳機。
    (C) 它將定期舉辦科技工作坊。
    (D) 它可能會在 11 月中旬之後開張。

03. 關於這篇報導，Roberts 女士表示了什麼？
    (A) 它提到了一些實際上已經落實的優點。
    (B) 它錯誤地描述了店鋪的地點。
    (C) 有些細節需要在未來進行更正。
    (D) 它遺漏了關於店家服務中心的細節。

04. 關於 Grant 先生，有何暗示？
    (A) 他在三月份時去過紐約。
    (B) 他實際上在四月份造訪了 TechSphere 的市中心店。
    (C) 他計畫參加店鋪的開幕儀式。
    (D) 他在文章中錯引了一位主管的話。

05. 在信件中，「finalized」一詞（第 2 段第 2 行）的意思最接近哪一個選項？
    (A) 定位
    (B) 確定
    (C) 完成
    (D) 確認

解析 01 在第一個文本（article）中，從「The demand for our products and services in San Francisco has been overwhelming.」可知，TechSphere 在舊金山開設第三家店面是因為其產品和服務在舊金山的需求量十

分驚人，所以答案是 (C) To meet increasing customer demand。

02 這是針對關鍵字詞 TechSphere 詢問與其相關敘述的**連結問題**。(A) 的敘述可以從第一個文本（article）的「Unlike the flagship downtown store in New York」得知，是錯誤的；(B) 的敘述可以從第二個文本（letter）的「It was stated that our new location would include self-checkout kiosks. While this is a feature we are considering, it is not confirmed at this time.」得知，是錯誤的；(C) 是沒有提到的敘述，所以錯誤；(D) 的敘述可以從第二個文本（letter）的「The article mentioned the opening date as mid-November. While we are targeting that timeframe, the exact date has not yet been finalized.」得知，是正確的。

03 題目詢問 Roberts 女士對於報導的看法，所以直接就她寫給 Grant 先生的 letter 內容找答案即可。其中提到「we noticed a couple of inaccuracies that...」，所以答案是 (C) Some details need to be corrected in the future.。

04 這是針對關鍵字詞 Mr. Grant 詢問與其相關敘述的**連結問題**。(A) 的敘述可以從第三個文本（email）的「I misunderstood details during my conversation with a team member at TechSphere's downtown location last month.」得知，她上個月去了 TechSphere 的旗艦店，以及第一個文本的「Unlike the flagship downtown store in New York...」得知，旗艦店位於紐約，因此綜合兩個線索可以確認，(A) 是正確的。

05 finalized 這個字所在的句子是「While we are targeting that timeframe, the exact date has not yet been finalized.」，這表示，雖然那是該分店開張的目標時間點，但確切的日期尚未**定案**。」所以答案是 (D) confirmed。

問題 6-10 請參考以下廣告、電子郵件及評論。

瑰麗高地飯店：慶祝風光 5 週年！

歡迎加入我們，共同慶祝位於科羅拉多州阿斯本市中心的瑰麗高地飯店五週年！從 11 月 15 日到 11 月 30 日，賓客可享受結合奢華與實惠的專屬周年慶優惠。

預訂每晚僅需 300 美元的豪華客房，即可於我們屢獲殊榮的 Summit Bistro 獲得雙人免費早餐。此外，賓客還可享受 20% 的 Spa 服務折扣以及免費使用我們的屋頂無邊際泳池與健身中心。作為慶祝活動的一部分，[6] 每週五與週六將舉辦現場爵士音樂之夜，邀請知名藝術家 Evelyn Brooks 現場演出。

不要錯過體驗卓越的服務、欣賞壯麗景色並創造難忘回憶的機會。欲預訂或了解更多詳情，請造訪：www.majesticheights.com 或致電 (970) 555-0163。

收件人：Evelyn Hughes <evhughes@wanderlustmail.com>
寄件人：Gabriel Turner <gturner@wanderlustmail.com>
主旨：回覆：週年慶假期計畫
日期：11 月 5 日

Evelyn，

我查看了你提到的 Majestic Heights Hotel 的周年慶優惠。這是一個超值的優惠，也似乎是個完美的放鬆機會。[7] 豪華客房每晚 300 美元，還包括雙人早餐，加上 [10]Spa 服務的 20% 折扣，非常划算。而且，Evelyn Brooks 的現場爵士之夜聽起來十分令人期待。

我計劃預訂 11 月 18 日到 20 日的兩晚住宿。這應該是慶祝酒店五週年並放鬆一下的美好方式。[8] 如果你有興趣一起去，告訴我，我們可以協調行程，充分利用這個

特別的優惠！

Gabriel

瑰麗高地飯店

您的意見對我們非常重要……

請分享您在 Majestic Heights Hotel 的住宿體驗！您的回饋意見將幫助我們改善服務，確保每位賓客都能享受卓越的住宿體驗。請放心，您的資訊將被保密。

1. 您是如何知道 Majestic Heights Hotel 的？
   我從旅遊部落格得知的。

2. 您會推薦瑰麗高地飯店給朋友嗎？
   會，特別是尋找浪漫假期的情侶。

3. 您認為住宿期間最棒的部分是什麼？
   ¹⁰水療體驗非常棒，屋頂無邊際泳池的景色令人驚豔，且 ⁶週六晚上的現場表演十分精彩，工作人員也非常有禮且體貼。

4. 如何讓您的住宿體驗更好？
   高峰時段的客房服務速度可以更快一些，且免費接駁車到阿斯本市區的班次可以更頻繁一些。

您想收到 Majestic Heights Hotel 的定期電子郵件更新嗎？是 ☑ 否 ☐

填寫完這張意見卡之後，⁹請將其放進位於前面櫃檯的建議箱內。感謝您的合作。

姓名：Gabriel Turner
入住日期：11 月 18-20 日
電子郵件：gturner@wanderlustmail.com

06. Gabriel Turner 對於在飯店住宿方面提到什麼？
    (A) 爵士表演非常棒。
    (B) 現場爵士表演被取消了。
    (C) 屋頂泳池沒有被好好維護。
    (D) 工作人員對活動準備不足。

07. 關於豪華客房，有提到什麼？

(A) 包含當地景點的門票。
(B) 提供免費雙人晚餐。
(C) 含有特別的水療池優惠。
(D) 僅限 11 月中旬前可預訂。

08. 電子郵件的目的是什麼？
    (A) 建議在這家飯店團訂
    (B) 提出一個周年慶旅行計畫
    (C) 詢問水療服務是否有更多折扣
    (D) 諮詢飯店的其他設施

09. 關於這張意見卡（評論），有指出什麼？
    (A) 它只能以線上方式提交。
    (B) 它給予賓客一個抽獎的機會。
    (C) 它可以親自交到前台工作人員。
    (D) 它應被放入一個箱子裡面。

10. Turner 先生在住宿期間最可能做了什麼？
    (A) 搭朋友便車去 Aspen 市區
    (B) 在午夜時叫客房服務
    (C) 為旅遊部落格撰寫了一篇評論
    (D) 額外付費享用水療設施

解析 06 題目詢問關於 Gabriel Turner 的住宿體驗**何者正確**。(A) 的敘述必須綜合第三個文本（review）的「the live show on Saturday night was magical」以及第一個文本（advertisement）的「we're hosting live jazz nights on Fridays and Saturdays」兩個線索，可確認是正確的，所以答案是 (A)，(B) 當然錯誤；(C)、(D) 都是沒有提及的內容。

07 本題是針對關鍵字詞「deluxe room package」詢問與其相關的「**何者正確**」問題。電子郵件中提到「The deluxe room rate of $300 per night includes breakfast for two, and the 20% discount on spa services is a great bonus.」所以 (C) It features a special spa deal. 是正確的敘述。(A) 是沒有提到的內容；(B) 應將 dinner 改成 breakfast 才正確；從「I'm planning to book a two-night stay

from November 18th to 20th.」的內容可知，(D) 是錯誤的敘述。

08 從電子郵件的主旨（Re: Anniversary getaway idea）尚無法看出寫這封郵件的目的為何，因此要在郵件內容中找尋。從第二段的「Let me know if you're interested in joining...」可得知，答案是 (A) To suggest booking a group event at the hotel。

09 題目針對 review 這篇的所有內容，詢問**何者正確**。從「After completing this review card, please put it into the suggestion box that is located next to the front desk.」可以得知，填寫完這張意見卡之後，將其放進位於前面櫃檯的建議箱內，所以 (D) 是正確的，而 (A)、(C) 顯然錯誤；(B) 是沒有提到的內容。

10 題目是針對「Mr. Turner most likely do during his stay」這個關鍵語句提問的 5W1H 問題，所以當然要從他寫的意見卡尋找線索。(A) 可以從「the complimentary shuttle to downtown Aspen could have run more frequently」得知，是錯誤的；(B) 可以從「The room service was a bit slow during peak hours」得知，是錯誤的；(C) 的敘述顯然錯誤；(D) 的敘述可以從第三篇 review 的「The spa was phenomenal」，加上第二篇的 email 中「the 20% discount on spa services」得知，他額外付費享用水療設施，所以是正確的敘述。

Week 01

穩固基礎與關鍵概念　w01_1.mp3

☐ disciplinary	adj. 紀律的，懲戒的	☐ cemetery	n. 墓地，公墓
☐ vary	v. 變化，不同	☐ reflection	n. 反射，反思
☐ significantly	adv. 顯著地，大幅度地	☐ remembrance	n. 紀念，回憶
☐ disclose	v. 揭露，公開	☐ pass away	phr. 去世，離世
☐ classified	adj. 機密的，分類的	☐ census	n. 人口普查，統計調查
☐ unauthorized	adj. 未經授權的，非法的	☐ insight	n. 眼光，洞察力
☐ absent-minded	adj. 心不在焉的，健忘的	☐ demographic	adj. 人口統計，人口特徵
☐ lead... to...	phr. 導致…結果，引導…到…	☐ dynamics	n. 動態，力學
		☐ certified	adj. 認證的，有資格的
☐ questioning	n. 詢問，質疑	☐ familiarize oneself with	phr. 使自己熟悉，了解
☐ elicit	v. 引出，誘導出		
☐ relieve	v. 減輕，緩解	☐ interface	n. 介面，界面
☐ retrieve	v. 取回，檢索	☐ accelerate	v. 加速，促進
☐ carousel	n. 旋轉木馬，行李輸送帶	☐ allocate	v. 分配，撥出
☐ bachelor	n. 單身男子，學士	☐ streamline	v. 簡化，使效率化
☐ immerse	v. 浸泡，沉浸	☐ postpone	v. 延期，推遲
☐ immerse oneself in	phr. 投入於，沉迷於	☐ unforeseen	adj. 意料之外的，突發的
		☐ beyond one's control	phr. 超出控制範圍，無法掌控
☐ rollout	n. 首次發佈		
☐ preparation	n. 準備，配製	☐ fiddle with	phr. 擺弄，亂動
☐ catastrophe	n. 災難，不幸事件	☐ anxiety	n. 焦慮，緊張
☐ aim to-V	phr. 目標是做…，計劃做…	☐ entrance	n. 入口，進入
		☐ alien	n. 外星人，陌生人
☐ infrastructure	n. 基礎設施，公共建設	☐ abduct	v. 綁架，誘拐
☐ analyze	v. 分析，解析	☐ call off	phr. 取消，叫停
☐ analysis	n. 分析，解析	☐ principal	n. 校長；adj. 主要的
☐ analyzer	n. 分析器，測試儀	☐ commend	v. 稱讚，表揚
☐ analytical	adj. 分析的，善於分析的		

☐ emigrate	v. 移居國外，移民	☐ timeline	n. 時間軸，時間表，歷史脈絡
☐ distract	v. 使分心，分散注意力	☐ nuance	n. 細微差異，微妙之處
☐ striking resemblance	n. 驚人的相似，極為相像	☐ navigate	v. 導航，引導，指引
☐ (be) mistaken for	phr. 被誤認為，被錯認為	☐ protocol	n. 協議，規範，禮儀
☐ consistently	adv. 持續地，一貫地	☐ hazardous	adj. 危險的，有害的
☐ be key to + N. / Ving	phr. 是……的關鍵，對……至關重要	☐ board of directors	n. 董事會，理事會
☐ documentary	n. 紀錄片，文獻片	☐ evident	adj. 明顯的，顯而易見的
☐ marine life	n. 海洋生物，海洋生態	☐ experimentation	n. 實驗，試驗
☐ implement	v. 實施，執行	☐ stop by	phr. 順路停留，短暫拜訪
☐ sweeping	adj. 全面的，大規模的	☐ register for	phr. 報名參加，登記註冊
☐ reform	n. 改革，革新	☐ workshop	n. 研討會，工作坊
☐ address	v. 解決	☐ keynote speaker	n. 特邀講者
☐ systemic	adj. 系統性的，全局性的	☐ insightful	adj. 有見地的，富有洞察力的
☐ inequality	n. 不平等，不公平	☐ deteriorate	v. 惡化，退化
☐ positive review	n. 正面評價，好評	☐ unexpectedly	adv. 意外地，出乎意料地
☐ industry expert	n. 行業專家，業界權威	☐ ground	v. 使停飛，禁足
☐ degradation	n. 退化，降解，惡化	☐ indefinitely	adv. 無限期地，無期限地
☐ aftermath	n. 餘波，後果，影響	☐ stall	v. 停滯，熄火，拖延
☐ unchecked	adj. 不受控的	☐ repeatedly	adv. 反覆地，再三地
☐ expansion	n. 擴展，擴張，發展	☐ steadfast	adj. 堅定的，不動搖的
☐ mastery	n. 精通，掌握，熟練	☐ diplomatic	adj. 外交的，圓滑的，策略的
☐ intricate	adj. 錯綜複雜的，精細的	☐ socioeconomic	adj. 社會經濟的
☐ algorithm	n. 演算法，計算程序	☐ profound	adj. 深刻的，深遠的，深奧的
☐ potential	n. 潛力，可能性	☐ migration	n. 遷移，移居，移動
☐ correlation	n. 相關性，關聯，相互關係	☐ revelation	n. 啟示，揭露，發現
☐ heritage	n. 遺產，傳統，文化資產	☐ trial	n. 試驗，審判，嘗試
☐ preservation	n. 保存，保護，維護		

☐ adhere to	phr. 遵守，堅持，依附於	☐ validate	v. 驗證，確認，證實
☐ procedural	adj. 程序上的，步驟性的	☐ validation	n. 驗證，確認，批准
☐ validity	n. 有效性，正當性		

TOEIC 實戰演練　w01_2.mp3

☐ summit	n. 高峰，頂點，峰會	☐ representative	n. 代表，代理人；adj. 代表性的
☐ enhancement	n. 提升，增強，改善	☐ represent	v. 代表，象徵，表現
☐ oust	v. 驅逐，罷免	☐ initiative	n. 倡議，主動性，積極行動
☐ scandal	n. 醜聞，醜事，恥辱		
☐ restrain	v. 抑制，制止，約束	☐ sustainability	n. 永續性，可持續性
☐ suspect	v. 懷疑；n. 嫌疑人	☐ venomous	adj. 有毒的，惡毒的
☐ merger	n. 合併，併購		
☐ regulatory authorities	n. 監管機構，主管機關		
☐ (be) addicted to	phr. 沉迷於，對⋯上癮		
☐ availability	n. 可用性，可獲得性，供應情況		
☐ engaging	adj. 迷人的，有吸引力的，吸引注意的		
☐ cardiovascular	adj. 心血管的		
☐ consensus	n. 共識		
☐ advocate	n. 倡導者，支持者；v. 主張		
☐ differing	adj. 不同的，不一致的		
☐ representation	n. 代表，象徵，表現		

Week 02

穩固基礎與關鍵概念 w02_1.mp3

☐ indigeous	adj. 原住民的	☐ implement	v. 實施
☐ artillery	n. 大砲	☐ beside the point	phr. 偏離正題，不相關
☐ defend against	phr. 抵禦	☐ speak up	v. 大聲說出
☐ hostile	adj. 敵意的	☐ a solution to + N./Ving	phr. 解決…的方法
☐ courier	n. 快遞，信使	☐ in the event of	phr. 在…情況下，如果…
☐ leave sb. speechless	phr. 讓某人無言以對	☐ evacuation	n. 撤離，疏散
☐ fabric	n. 布料，纖維	☐ on earth	phr. 到底
☐ batch	n. 一批	☐ compensation	n. 補償
☐ (be) capable of	phr. 能夠…的	☐ in person	phr. 親自
☐ express concerns about	phr. 表達對…的擔憂	☐ efficiency	n. 效率
☐ hurricane	n. 颶風	☐ advisable	adj. 明智的
☐ devastating	adj. 毀滅性的	☐ advisory	adj. 建議性的，諮詢的
☐ coastal	adj. 沿海的	☐ beneficial	adj. 有益的
☐ dubious	adj. 抱持懷疑態度的	☐ beneficent	adj. 仁慈的
☐ effectiveness	n. 效能	☐ comparable	adj. 可比較的
☐ invigorating	adj. 令人振奮的	☐ comparative	adj. 比較的
☐ crisp	adj. 清爽的	☐ considerate	adj. 體貼的
☐ be short of	phr. 缺少…	☐ considerable	adj. 相當大的
☐ spectacular	adj. 壯觀的	☐ economic	adj. 經濟的
☐ unpredictable	adj. 不可預測的	☐ economical	adj. 節約的
☐ flourish	v. 茁壯，繁榮	☐ responsive	adj. 有反應的
☐ immensely	adv. 極其，非常	☐ successive (to...)	adj. 連續的，後繼的
☐ above expectation	phr. 超出預期	☐ professional n.	n. 專業人士
☐ sustainable	adj. 永續的	☐ cost-effective	adj. 具成本效益的
☐ consistently	adv. 恆常地，持續地	☐ align with	v. 與…一致
		☐ sustainability	n. 可持續性，永續性

TOEIC 實戰演練　w02_2.mp3

☐ cozy	adj. 溫馨的	☐ on condition of	phr. 在⋯條件下
☐ ambiance	n. 氛圍	☐ at the mercy of	phr. 任由⋯擺布
☐ melody	n. 旋律	☐ in accordance with	phr. 依照⋯
☐ acoustic	adj. 原聲的	☐ with respect to	phr. 關於⋯
☐ tangible	adj. 有形的	☐ risk management	n. 風險管理
☐ disgusting	adj. 令人厭惡的	☐ setback	n. 挫折
☐ appalling	adj. 令人震驚的	☐ focused	adj. 專注的
☐ consult	v. 諮詢	☐ (be) committed to	phr. 致力於⋯
☐ surpass	v. 超越	☐ thrive	v. 茁壯成長，繁榮
☐ durability	n. 耐久性	☐ setting	n. 場景，環境
☐ marketing strategy	n. 行銷策略	☐ flexibility	n. 靈活性
☐ appealing	adj. 吸引人的	☐ solace	n. 慰藉
☐ exhausted	adj. 筋疲力盡的	☐ find solace in	phr. 在⋯中找到慰藉
☐ on behalf of	phr. 代表⋯	☐ recite	v. 背誦
☐ on account of	phr. 由於⋯		
☐ on top of	phr. 除⋯之外		

Week 03

穩固基礎與關鍵概念　w03_1.mp3

☐ fulfilling	adj. 令人滿足的	☐ intently	adv. 專注地
☐ trial	n. 審判	☐ thoughtful	adj. 體貼的，為人著想的
☐ crucial	adj. 重要的	☐ find sb. guilty of	phr. 判定某人有⋯罪
☐ suspect	n. 疑犯	☐ charge	n. 指控
☐ innocent	adj. 無辜的，無罪的	☐ embezzlement	n. 侵占
☐ prove sb. guilty	phr. 證明某人有罪	☐ appraise	v. 評估

☐ demonstrate	v. 展示		☐ meticulously	adv. 一絲不苟地
☐ algorithm	n. 演算法		☐ approach	v. 接近
☐ optimize	v. 優化		☐ go out	phr. 熄滅
☐ retrieval	n. 檢索		☐ emergency supplies	n. 應急物資
☐ environmental engineering	n. 環境工程		☐ liberalize	v. 使自由，解放
☐ groundbreaking	adj. 突破性的		☐ straight	adv. 連續地
☐ initiative	n. 倡議（活動）		☐ aggravate	v. 加劇
☐ strategic	adj. 戰略的		☐ dissatisfaction	n. 不滿
☐ framework	n. 框架		☐ extradite	v. 引渡
☐ address	v. 解決		☐ home country	n. 祖國
☐ regarding	phr. 關於		☐ permeate	v. 滲透
☐ pending	adj. 未決的		☐ rumor	n. 謠言
☐ thought-provoking	adj. 發人深省的		☐ squash	v. 鎮壓
☐ captivated	adj. 著迷的		☐ official	adj. 官方的，正式的

TOEIC 實戰演練　w03_2.mp3

☐ soothe	v. 安撫		☐ appoint	v. 任命，指派
☐ prevail	v. 盛行		☐ abolish	v. 廢除
☐ thrive	v. 茁壯成長，繁榮		☐ broaden	v. 擴大
☐ vanish	v. 消失		☐ disregard	v. 忽視
☐ gaze	n. 凝視		☐ correlate	v. 有關聯
☐ undermine	v. 削弱，破壞		☐ marvel	v. 驚嘆
☐ linger	v. 徘徊		☐ figure out	v. 弄清楚，想出
☐ endanger	v. 危及		☐ settle down	v. 安定下來
☐ board of directors	n. 董事會		☐ be involved in	phr. 參與，涉及
			☐ pile up	phr. 堆積
☐ abandon	v. 拋棄，放棄		☐ consist	v. 由…組成
☐ allege	v. 聲稱		☐ insist	v. 堅持

☐ persist	v. 持續		☐ amount to	phr. 總計為…
☐ contemplate	v. 深思		☐ to date	phr. 迄今
☐ unattended	adj. 無人看管的		☐ harass	v. 騷擾
☐ kindle	v. 點燃		☐ unsolicited	adj. 未經請求的
☐ devastating	adj. 毀滅性的		☐ consecutive	adj. 連續的
☐ expenditure	n. 支出			

Week 04

穩固基礎與關鍵概念　w04_1.mp3

☐ abduct	v. 綁架		☐ blinding	adv. 刺眼地，相當地
☐ defy	v. 藐視，反抗		☐ enroll in	phr. 註冊加入
☐ precedent	n. 先例		☐ programming	n. 程式設計
☐ disregard	v. 忽視，不理會		☐ bulletin board	n. 公佈欄
☐ obligate	v. 使有義務		☐ sculpture	n. 雕塑
☐ adhere to	phr. 遵守		☐ unveil	v. 揭幕，揭開
☐ protocol	n. 協議		☐ ahead of schedule	phr. 提前
☐ go astray	phr. 迷失方向		☐ thoroughly	adv. 徹底地
☐ dismantle	v. 拆解		☐ devote... to Ving	phr. 將…投入在…
☐ in place	phr. 就定位		☐ blend	v. 混合
☐ inhibit... from...	phr. 阻止…做…		☐ texture	n. 質地，材質
☐ promising	adj. 有前途的		☐ vibrant	adj. 充滿活力的
☐ assess	v. 評估		☐ flavor	n. 風味
☐ extended	adj. 延長的		☐ craft	n. 工藝
☐ freezing	adv. 極冷地，相當地		☐ take on	phr. 承受，接受
☐ scorching	adv. 酷熱地，相當地		☐ capture	v. 捕捉
☐ tiring	adv. 令人疲憊地，相當地		☐ brushstroke	n. 筆觸
☐ astonishing	adv. 令人驚訝地，相當地			

☐ horizon	n. 地平線	☐ a bouquet of flowers	n. 一束花
☐ transform	v. 改變	☐ rearview mirror	n. 後照鏡
☐ canvas	n. 畫布		
☐ pour down	phr. 傾盆而下		

TOEIC 實戰演練　w04_2.mp3

☐ authorized	adj. 授權的	☐ intern	n. 實習生
☐ authorization	n. 授權	☐ tedious	adj. 繁瑣的
☐ lighten	v. 減輕	☐ presentation	n. 報告
☐ machinery	n. 機械	☐ fatigue	n. 疲勞
☐ informed	adj. 有見識的，見多識廣的	☐ shriek	v. 尖叫
☐ approach	v. 找…（某人）商量（或連繫）	☐ juggle	v. 耍（球，盤等），耍弄
		☐ retrieve	v. 取回

Week 05

穩固基礎與關鍵概念　w05_1.mp3

☐ beg for one's forgiveness	phr. 懇求某人的原諒	☐ diplomat	n. 外交官
☐ benefit from	phr. 受益於…	☐ implement	v. 實施，執行
☐ engaging	aj. 引人入勝的	☐ productivity	n. 生產力
☐ attentive	adj. 專注的	☐ significantly	adv. 顯著地，大大地
☐ session	n. 會議	☐ alternative	n. 替代方案
☐ mutual respect	n. 相互尊重	☐ unrealistic	adj. 不切實際的
☐ collaboration	n. 合作	☐ dictate	v. 支配，命令
☐ thrive	v. 蓬勃發展	☐ thoroughness	n. 徹底
☐ navigate	v. 操控，掌握	☐ critical thinking	n. 思辨能力
☐ experienced	adj. 有經驗的	☐ immense	adj. 巨大的

☐ under... pressure	phr. 在…的壓力之下	☐ ethical	adj. 倫理的
☐ speak volumes about	phr. 充分展現…	☐ stance	n. 立場
☐ character	n. 性格，個性	☐ adapt to	phr. 適應
☐ intricate	adj. 錯綜複雜的	☐ stakeholder	n. 利益相關者
☐ innovation	n. 創新	☐ proceed with	phr. 繼續進行…
☐ resignation	n. 辭職	☐ attorney	n.（私人）律師
☐ align with	phr. 與…一致		

TOEIC 實戰演練　w05_2.mp3

☐ fulfillment	n. 實現，滿足	☐ compromise	v. 妥協
☐ compelling	adj. 有說服力的	☐ core value	n. 核心價值
☐ leave sb. in silence	phr. 使…（某人）鴉雀無聲	☐ obsolete	adj. 過時的
☐ uncertainty	n. 不確定性	☐ transparency	n. 透明度
☐ settle for	phr. 勉強接受	☐ advocate for	phr. 提倡
☐ mediocrity	n. 平庸	☐ dedication	n. 奉獻

Week 06

穩固基礎與關鍵概念　w06_1.mp3

☐ excel in	phr. 擅長…	☐ date back…	phr. 回溯自…（多久以前）
☐ respective	adj. 各自的	☐ chef	n. 主廚
☐ diligent	adj. 勤奮的	☐ be renowned for	phr. 以…而聞名
☐ internship	n. 實習	☐ fusion	n. 融合
☐ revolutionize	v. 徹底改革	☐ prestigious	adj. 有聲望的
☐ house	v. 容納，把…儲藏在房內	☐ groundbreaking	adj. 開創性的
☐ a collection of…	phr. …藏物	☐ unwavering	adj. 堅定不移的
☐ artifact	n. 文物		

☐ determination	n. 決心	☐ customize	v. 客製化
☐ composure	n. 冷靜	☐ witness	v. 親眼見到

TOEIC 實戰演練　w06_2.mp3

☐ dedicated	adj. 努力用功的，奉獻心力的	☐ precision	n. 精密，精確
☐ testament	n. 見證	☐ accessible	adj. 可取得的
☐ ethical	n. 道德的	☐ come across	phr. 表現出
☐ (an) asset to + N.	phr. …的資產	☐ arrogant	adj. 傲慢的
☐ expedition	n. 探險	☐ hinder	v. 阻礙
☐ under... condition	phr. 在…條件下		

Week 07

穩固基礎與關鍵概念　w07_1.mp3

☐ make an apology	phr. 道歉	☐ wayback machine	n. 時光機
☐ sincere	adj. 真誠的	☐ unfold	v. 展開，顯露，呈現
☐ take responsibility for	phr. 對…負起責任	☐ dissuade... from...	phr. 勸阻…（某人去做某事）
☐ initiate	v. 發起	☐ strategic	adj. 策略性的
☐ cautious	adj. 謹慎的	☐ shift	n. 轉變
☐ be afflicted with	phr. 承受…之苦	☐ yield	v. 產生，產出
☐ displacement	n. 遷移，遷徙		

TOEIC 實戰演練　w07_2.mp3

☐ trust sb. with sth.	phr. 交付給某人…（工作、任務等）	☐ stay behind	phr. 留下
		☐ timely	adj. 及時的
☐ motivated	adj. 有動力的		
☐ arrangement	n. 安排		

Week 08

穩固基礎與關鍵概念 w08_1.mp3

☐ glamorous	adj. 迷人的		☐ charisma	n. 魅力
☐ immensely	adv. 極大地		☐ exude	v. 散發
☐ commitment	n. 承諾		☐ captivate	v. 吸引
☐ innovation	n. 創新		☐ meticulously	adv. 謹慎地，細緻地
☐ outsource	v. 將…（工作、任務等）外包		☐ execution	n. 執行
☐ when it comes to (Ving)	phr. 說到…，就…而言		☐ gourmet	adj. 美食家
☐ luminous	adj. 發光的		☐ compromise	v. 妥協
☐ faint	adj. 微弱的		☐ timid	adj. 膽小的
☐ glow	n. 光輝		☐ mediator	n. 調解人
☐ bold	adj. 大膽的		☐ neutral	adj. 中立的
☐ visionary	n. 有遠見的人		☐ contain	v. 壓抑，抑制
☐ conventional	adj. 傳統的		☐ downturn	n. 衰退
☐ resourceful	adj. 足智多謀的，最有資源的		☐ (be) superior to	phr. 優於…
☐ executive	n. 主管		☐ (be) junior to	phr. 比…資淺
☐ critique	n. 評論		☐ superb	adj. 極好的
☐ professoinalism	n. 專業精神		☐ supreme	adj. 至高無上的
☐ unauthorized	adj. 未經授權的		☐ (be) cloaked in	phr. 披著…的；籠罩在…
☐ confidential	adj. 機密的		☐ chest	n. （有蓋子的）箱子
☐ emerging	adj. 新興的		☐ fireplace	n. 壁爐
☐ influential	adj. 有影響力的		☐ tolerate	v. 容忍
☐ across the globe	phr. 在全世界		☐ brilliant	adj. 出色的，閃耀的
			☐ (be) inferior to	phr. 比…低劣的

TOEIC 實戰演練　w08_2.mp3

☐ signs of age	n. 歲月的痕跡	☐ rehearsal	n. 排練，排演
☐ tranquility	n. 寧靜	☐ assessment	n. 評估，評鑑
☐ bustling	adj. 繁華的，熱鬧的	☐ work late into the night	phr. 熬夜工作
☐ archive	n. 檔案		
☐ captivating	adj. 迷人的		

Week 09

出題模式與解題步驟　w09_1.mp3

☐ reinforce	v. 強化	☐ point fingers at	phr. 指責（某人）
☐ genuine	adj. 真誠的，真正的	☐ transition	n. 過渡（時期）
☐ self-esteem	n. 自尊	☐ evaluation	n. 評估，評價
☐ motivation	n. 動力	☐ adjustment	n. 調整
☐ consistency	n. 一致性	☐ boost	v. 提升
☐ cultivate	v. 培養	☐ productivity	n. 生產力
☐ supportive	adj. 支持的	☐ adhere to	phr. 遵守
☐ consistently	adv. 一貫地	☐ prompt	adj. 動作敏捷的
☐ diverse	adj. 多元的	☐ courteous	adj. 有禮貌的
☐ foster	v. 培養，促進	☐ impeccably	adv. 無可挑剔地
☐ horizon	n. 地平線	☐ well-stocked	adj. 存貨充足的
☐ defensiveness	n. 防禦心理	☐ amenity	n. 便利設施
☐ resentment	n. 怨恨	☐ cared-for	adj. 受到照顧的，被在意的
☐ undermine	v. 破壞，削弱		
☐ pivotal	adj. 關鍵的		

TOEIC 實戰演練　w09_2.mp3

☐ infinite	adj. 無限的
☐ subscription	n. 訂閱
☐ dive into	phr. 深入探索
☐ captivating	adj. 迷人的
☐ trendsetter	n. 時尚先鋒
☐ wellness	n. 健康
☐ curated	adj. 精心策劃的
☐ tailor	v. 量身定製
☐ stay ahead with	phr. 領先於…
☐ stunning	adj. 驚豔的
☐ visual	n. 視野，視覺
☐ embark on	phr. 著手開始，啟程
☐ enrichment	n. 充實
☐ to one's heart's content	phr. 盡情地

☐ category	n. 類別，範疇
☐ disposal	n. 處置，丟棄
☐ heavyweight	n. 重量級人物
☐ initiative	n. 倡議
☐ familiarize	v. 使熟悉
☐ formulate	v. 制定
☐ incentive	n. 激勵
☐ involvement	n. 參與
☐ collective	adj. 集體的
☐ accordingly	adv. 相應地
☐ prioritize	v. 將…視為第一優先，優先考慮
☐ stick to	phr. 堅持
☐ optimistic	adj. 樂觀的

Week 10

出題模式與實用策略　w10_1.mp3

☐ seminar	n. 研討會
☐ insight	n. 見解
☐ implement	v. 實施
☐ networking	n. 人脈建立
☐ professional	n. 專業人士
☐ attendee	n. 參加者
☐ enclosed	dj. 隨附的
☐ anticipated	adj. 預期的
☐ estimate	n. 估計

☐ designated	adj. 指定的
☐ container	n. 容器
☐ labeled	adj. 標示的
☐ hire	n. 受雇者（= employee）
☐ orientation	n. （對新進者的）培訓
☐ core value	n. 核心價值
☐ settle into one's role	phr. 逐漸適應自己的角色

☐ (be) tailored to	phr. 為…量身訂作，專為…設計	☐ supervisor	n. 主管，監督
		☐ leave	n. 不在，請假
☐ strengthen	v. 加強，強化	☐ in the meantime	phr. 與此同時
☐ critic	n. 批評家，評論家	☐ stay updated on	phr. 隨時掌握…的最新資訊
☐ lodging	n. 住宿，住所		
☐ evaluator	n. 評鑑者	☐ panel discussion	n. 小組討論會
☐ request time off	phr. 請假		

TOEIC 實戰演練　w10_2.mp3

☐ enhancement	n. 提升，增強，改善	☐ troubleshoot	v. 故障排除
☐ dictate	v. 規定，指定，命令	☐ cache	n. 快取
☐ room	n. 允許的空間	☐ persist	v. 持續，堅持
☐ oversee	v. 監督	☐ render	v. 使得
☐ relocation	n. 搬遷	☐ unusable	adj. 無法使用的
☐ malfunction	n. 故障，功能不彰	☐ rectify	v. 修正
☐ disrupt	v. 中斷	☐ swift	adj. 迅速的
☐ workflow	n. 工作流程		

Week 11

出題模式與實用策略　w11_1.mp3

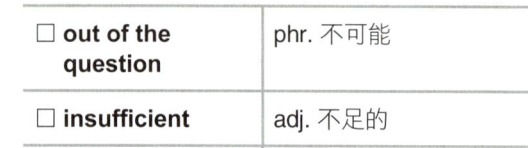

☐ out of the question	phr. 不可能	☐ for the time being	phr. 暫時
☐ insufficient	adj. 不足的	☐ look into	phr. 深入檢查（或研究）
☐ inventory	n. 庫存	☐ prioritize	v. 將…視為第一優先，優先考慮

TOEIC 實戰演練　w11_2.mp3

☐ ad hoc	adj. 特別的	☐ (be) pending delivery	phr. 尚未出貨
☐ product release / launch	n. 產品發表	☐ out of stock	phr. 沒有存貨
☐ projection	n. 預測，推估	☐ sizable	adj. 相當大的，大小相當的
☐ testimonial	n.（顧客的使用）見證	☐ en route	adj. 正在路上
☐ self-served	adj. 自助的		
☐ warming plate	n. 保溫盤		

Week 12

出題模式與實用策略　w12_1.mp3

☐ admission	n. 入場	☐ luxury	adj. 奢華的
☐ specify	v. 指定，指出	☐ evaluation	n. 評估
☐ expire	v. 逾期，（期限）終止	☐ top-notch	adj. 頂尖的
☐ age bracket	n. 年齡層	☐ premium	adj. 高級的
☐ amusement park	n. 遊樂園	☐ (be) eligible for	phr. 有⋯資格的
☐ premium	adj. 高級的	☐ (be) combined with	phr. 結合⋯的
☐ complimentary	adj. 免費的	☐ reward point	n. 回饋點數
☐ reusable	adj. 可重複使用的	☐ unit price	n. 單價
☐ discounted	adj. 折扣的	☐ alliance	n. 聯盟
☐ upgrade	n. 升級	☐ startup	n. 初創事業
☐ collective	adj. 集體的，共同的	☐ agenda	n. 議程
☐ collaboration	n. 合作	☐ opening remarks	n. 開場白
☐ unveil	v. 揭開，揭示	☐ roastery	n. 咖啡烘焙店
☐ classical	adj. 古典的	☐ institute of technology	n. 工學院
☐ selection	n. 精選	☐ state-run	adj. 國營的
☐ esteemed	adj. 受人尊敬的	☐ recess	n. 休息時間

TOEIC 實戰演練　w12_2.mp3

☐ scout	v. 搜索，物色	☐ getaway	n. 短暫休假
☐ set design	n. 場景設計	☐ amenity	n. 設施
☐ script read-through	n. 劇本通讀	☐ soothing	adj. 舒緩的
☐ composer	n. 作曲家	☐ spacious	adj. 寬敞的
☐ rough cut	n. 粗略剪片	☐ (be) attentive to	phr. 關注於…
☐ talent prospect	n. 有潛力的人選	☐ (be) quick to-V	phr. 在…（做某事方面）動作迅速
☐ production crew	n. 製作團隊	☐ address	v. 解決
☐ storyboard	n. 劇本中關鍵動作場景的分鏡圖	☐ well-lit	adj. 燈光美的
☐ retreat	n. 逃離日常生活的場所	☐ stunning	adj. 極漂亮的，絕色的
☐ lodge	n. 簡單而舒適的住宿設施	☐ hear back	phr. 得到回覆消息
☐ memorable	adj. 難忘的	☐ quad room	n. 四人房

Week 13

出題模式與實用策略　w13_1.mp3

☐ acquire	v. 獲得，收購	☐ in-depth	adj. 深入的，有深度的
☐ technology giant	n. 科技巨頭	☐ product offerings	n. 產品選項，產品種類
☐ mobile payment	n. 行動支付	☐ analysis	n. 分析
☐ solution	n. 解決方案	☐ analyst	n. 分析師
☐ acquisition	n. 收購	☐ architecture	n. 結構，構造，建築學
☐ (be) valued at...	phr. 價值是…	☐ strength	n. 強項，優勢
☐ presence	n. 市占	☐ agile	adj. 敏捷的
☐ strategic	adj. 策略的	☐ streamline	v. 使有效率，使簡化
☐ incorporate... into...	phr. 將…整併入…	☐ accessibility	n. 無障礙性／可達性
☐ suite	n. 套組，系列	☐ transaction	n. 交易

☐ governor	n. 州長,省長		☐ a diverse array of	phr. 多樣的
☐ complex	n. 複雜的		☐ cuisine	n. 菜餚
☐ brisk	adj. 輕快的／興旺的		☐ expertise	n. 專業知識
☐ at first glance	phr. 乍看之下		☐ affordable	adj. 負擔得起的,平價的
☐ eatery	n. 小餐館		☐ showcase	n. 展示
☐ bustling	adj. 熱鬧的		☐ cutting-edge	adj. 尖端的
☐ dedicate... to...	phr. 將…奉獻於…		☐ automotive	adj. 汽車的
☐ renovation	n. 翻新		☐ sustainable	adj. 可持續的,永續的
☐ cozy	adj. 舒適的			
☐ make a change to	phr. 對…進行更改			

TOEIC 實戰演練　w13_2.mp3

☐ portrait	n. 肖像		☐ (music) track	n.（一首）歌曲
☐ depiction	n. 描述,描繪		☐ partnership	n. 合夥（關係）
☐ curator	n. 館長,策展人		☐ dramatically	adv. 戲劇性地,劇烈地
☐ close-knit	adj. 關係緊密的		☐ in the works	phr. 正在籌畫中
☐ reflect on	phr. 反思,反省		☐ accessible	adj. 可得的,可接近的
☐ metropolitan	adj. 大都會的		☐ boast	v. 誇耀,誇張地說
☐ on display	phr. 展示中,展出		☐ traffic	n.（網路）流量
☐ record label	n. 唱片公司,唱片品牌		☐ stem from	phr. 來自…
☐ licensing	adj. 授權		☐ select	adj. 挑選出來的,精選的
☐ streaming platform	n. 串流平台		☐ competitive advantage	n. 競爭優勢
☐ lay the foundation for	phr. 為…奠定基礎		☐ video-streaming	adj. 影片串流
☐ subscription	n. 訂購,訂閱		☐ offline	adj. 離線的
☐ music library	n. 音樂收藏庫		☐ user base	n. 用戶數,用戶群體,用戶規模
☐ contemporary	adj. 當代的			

Week 14

出題模式與實用策略　w14_1.mp3

☐ surveillance	n. 監視，監控	☐ main dish	n. 主菜，主餐
☐ specialize in	phr. 專攻，專精於	☐ side salad	n. 附加的小份沙拉
☐ high-definition	adj. 高清的，高解析度的	☐ side	n. 配菜
☐ motion-activated	adj. 動作觸發的，感應啟動的	☐ appetizer	n. 開胃菜
☐ remote-access	adj. 遠端存取的，遠程處理的	☐ deluxe	adj. 豪華（級）的
		☐ trio	n. 三個（或三人）一組；三重唱
☐ comprehensive	adj. 全面的，綜合的	☐ signature	adj. 具有代表性的，標誌性的
☐ ongoing	adj. 持續的，進行中的		
☐ consultant	n. 顧問，諮詢師	☐ harmony	n. 和諧，協調
☐ tailored	adj. 訂製的	☐ indulge in	phr. 沉浸於，縱情於
☐ compromise on	phr. 妥協於，讓步於	☐ first-come, first-served	adj. 先到先得，先來先服務
☐ showroom	n. 展示廳，陳列室		
☐ be intended for	phr. 用於，為…而設計	☐ unwind	v.（心情）放鬆
☐ premise	n. 前提，場所	☐ refreshments	n. 茶點，便餐，點心
☐ (be) adjacent to	phr. 毗鄰的，鄰近的	☐ unbeatable	adj. 無與倫比的，難以超越的
☐ patron	n. 顧客，贊助者	☐ home essentials	n. 家用必需品
☐ extended	adj. 加長的，延伸的	☐ regular operated hours	n. 正規營業時間
☐ associate	n. 夥伴，同事		
☐ driven	adj. 有上進心的，發憤的	☐ suspension	n. 暫停，中止
☐ proficiency	n. 熟練，精通	☐ valued	adj. 珍貴的，被重視的
☐ job opening	n. 職缺，工作機會	☐ periodic	adj. 定期的，週期性的
☐ graphic designer	n. 平面設計師，圖形設計師	☐ critical thinking	adj. 思辨能力
☐ internship	n. 實習，實習機會	☐ upgrade	n. 升級，提升
☐ influencer	n. 網紅，網路名人	☐ alternative	n. 替代方案
☐ complimentary	adj. 免費的，贈送的	☐ interruption	n. 中斷，干擾

TOEIC 實戰演練　w14_2.mp3

☐ impactful	adj. 有影響力的，震撼的
☐ component	n. 組件，成分
☐ locker	n. 置物櫃，儲物櫃
☐ changing room	n. 更衣室
☐ workout	n. 運動
☐ refrain from	phr. 避免，克制
☐ be held responsible for	phr. 對⋯負責
☐ deposit	v. 存放
☐ valuable	n. 珍貴物品
☐ approach	v. 接近，前往
☐ lost-and-found section	n. 失物招領處

Week 15

出題模式與實用策略　w15_1.mp3

☐ clarification	n. 澄清，說明
☐ collaborate	v. 合作，協作
☐ commend	v. 稱讚，表揚
☐ entanglement	n. 糾纏，牽連
☐ footwear	n. 鞋類
☐ headquarters	n. 總部
☐ improper	adj. 不適當的，不正確的
☐ keep... away from...	phr. 使⋯遠離⋯
☐ loose	adj. 鬆的，不牢固的
☐ observe	v. 遵守
☐ promotional	adj. 宣傳的，促銷的
☐ promptly	adv. 迅速地，立即地
☐ punctually	adv. 準時地，按時地
☐ recreational	adj. 休閒的，娛樂的
☐ renowned	adj. 著名的，享有聲譽的
☐ specified	adj. 指定的，特定的
☐ specify	v. 明確指出
☐ submission	n. 提交，遞交
☐ target audience	n. 目標受眾，目標觀眾
☐ treadmill	n. 跑步機
☐ water aerobics	n. 水中有氧運動
☐ wellness lounge	n. 健康休閒室
☐ well-ventilated	adj. 通風良好的，透氣的
☐ workload	n. 工作量，負擔
☐ accommodate	v. 容納，提供（需求）
☐ catering	n. 餐飲服務，外燴服務
☐ clubhouse	n. 會所，俱樂部會館
☐ customize	v. 客製化，量身定制
☐ disruption	n. 中斷，干擾
☐ expertise	n. 專業知識，專長
☐ glassware	n. 玻璃器皿，玻璃製品
☐ inquiry	n. 詢問

TOEIC 實戰演練　w15_2.mp3

☐ interruption	n. 干擾，打斷
☐ linen	n. 床單，亞麻織品
☐ meadow	n. 草地，牧場
☐ narrative	adj. 敘述的，故事的
☐ premium	adj. 高級的，優質的
☐ prestigious	adj. 有聲望的，享有盛譽的
☐ regardless of	phr. 不論，不管
☐ specialist	n. 專家，專科醫師
☐ tableware	n. 餐具，桌上用品

☐ outage	n.（水，電等的）中斷供應
☐ water billing	n. 水費計費（方式）
☐ incur	v. 招致，引發
☐ (be) subject to	phr. 受…影響，須遵守
☐ cancellation	n. 取消，作廢
☐ toll-free	adj. 免付費的，免費撥打的
☐ refund	n. 退款，退費
☐ in advance	phr. 事先，提前
☐ follow-up	n. 後續，跟進

Week 16

出題模式與實用策略　w16_1.mp3

☐ light fittings	n. 燈具，燈飾
☐ periodical	n. 期刊，定期出版物
☐ (be) geared toward…	phr. 針對…，為…而設
☐ title	n. 書名，標題
☐ gazette	n. 公報，報刊
☐ buff	n.【口】迷，愛好者
☐ culinary	adj. 烹飪的，廚藝的
☐ enthusiast	n. 愛好者，熱衷者
☐ quarterly	adj. 季刊的，每季的
☐ bi-monthly	adj. 雙月刊，每兩個月一次的
☐ symphony	n. 交響樂，交響曲
☐ extension	n. 分機
☐ scheduled	adj. 已排定…（行程）的

☐ take over	phr. 接管，接手
☐ auction	n. 拍賣，競標
☐ bid on	phr. 針對…出價／叫價／投標
☐ on offer	phr. 供應中的
☐ bidding item	n. 供競標的物品，拍賣品
☐ truffle	n. 巧克力糖，松露巧克力
☐ elevate	v. 提升，提高
☐ wardrobe	n. 衣櫥，服裝
☐ with ease	phr. 輕鬆地，毫不費力地
☐ thrilled	adj. 激動的，興奮的
☐ place an order	phr. 下訂單，訂購
☐ qualify for	phr. 符合…資格，具備…條件
☐ outfit	n. 全套服裝，穿搭
☐ complimentary	adj. 免費的，贈送的

☐ accessory	n. 配件，附件	☐ accumulate	v. 累積，積聚

TOEIC 實戰演練　w16_2.mp3

☐ heritage	n. 遺產，傳承	☐ bazaar	n. 市集，集市
☐ manor	n. 莊園，宅邸	☐ auditorium	n. 禮堂，大廳
☐ venue	n. 場地，會場	☐ a wide array of	phr. 各種各樣的，多樣的
☐ family gathering	n. 家庭聚會	☐ troupe	n. 劇團，表演團體
☐ intriguing	adj. 引人入勝的，令人好奇的	☐ raise funds for	phr. 為…籌款
☐ take a guided tour of	phr. 參加…的導覽	☐ displaced	adj. 流離失所的，無家可歸的
☐ furnishings	n. 傢俱，裝飾物	☐ enter into	phr. 簽訂，進入（協議等）
☐ ceramics	n. 陶瓷，瓷器	☐ raffle	n. 抽獎，摸彩
☐ loom weaving	n. 織布機編織，機織工藝	☐ field	n. 空格，填表處
☐ instrument	n. 樂器，工具	☐ name tag	n. 名牌，姓名牌
☐ attendee	n. 參加者，與會者	☐ shelter	n. 庇護所，避難所
☐ stroll through	phr. 漫步於，散步穿過	☐ principal	n. 校長
☐ attraction	n. 景點，吸引人的事物	☐ tidy up	phr. 收拾，整理
☐ scenic spot	n. 風景名勝，景點	☐ staff	v. 給…配備職員

Week 17

出題模式　w17_1.mp3

☐ journalism	n. 新聞業，新聞學	☐ highlight	n. 聚焦，受矚目的人事物
☐ in-depth	adj. 深入的，深層的	☐ inaugural issue	n. 創刊號
☐ analysis	n. 分析，解析	☐ culinary	adj. 烹飪的，廚藝的
☐ promo code	n. 促銷代碼	☐ mastery	n. 精通，掌握

TOEIC 實戰演練　w17_2.mp3

☐ on a regular basis	phr. 定期地、規律地	☐ deduction	n. 扣除，減除
☐ out of service	adj. 停止服務，無法使用	☐ stay informed about	phr. 獲得關於…的資訊
☐ stairwell	n. 樓梯間，樓梯井	☐ forthcoming	adj. 即將到來的，即將發生的
☐ occupant	n. 居住者，佔用者	☐ itinerary	n. 行程，旅行計畫
☐ downstairs	adv. 樓下，下樓	☐ disregard	v. 忽視，不理會
☐ staircase	n. 樓梯，階梯	☐ airport shuttle service	n. 機場接駁服務
☐ order delivery	phr. 叫外送	☐ fetch	v. 接（某人）
☐ get through	phr.（電話）接通	☐ arrivals hall	n. 入境大廳
☐ residential	adj. 住宅用的	☐ non-stop flight	n. 直航
☐ commercial	adj. 商辦的	☐ loyalty program	n. 忠誠計畫
☐ permanent staff	n. 正職員工	☐ get a lift	phr. 搭便車
☐ carry-on	adj. 隨身的	☐ collect	v. 接走（某人）
☐ renovate	v. 翻新，整修	☐ grasp	v. 把握，理解
☐ direct flight	n. 直航，直達班機	☐ capture	v. 捕捉，抓住
☐ debut	adj. 首次亮相的，處女秀的	☐ deliver a speech	phr. 發表演講，發言
☐ benefit from	phr. 受益於…，從…中獲得好處		

Week 18

實用策略　w18_1.mp3

☐ renewable energy	n. 再生能源	☐ academic	n. 學者
☐ carbon offset	n. 碳補償	☐ memorable	adj. 難忘的，令人記憶深刻的
☐ sustainability	n. 永續性，可持續性	☐ briefing	n. 簡報，說明會
☐ policymaker	n. 政策制定者		

☐ clarity	n.（說話）清晰，（事理）明確	☐ rooftop	adj. 屋頂，天台
☐ in line with	phr. 依據…	☐ infinity	n. 無限，無窮
☐ flagship downtown store	n. 位於市區的旗艦店	☐ wellness	n. 健康，健康狀態
☐ coffee lounge	n. 咖啡休息室	☐ getaway	n. 遊玩去處，旅遊的地方
☐ streamlined	adj. 流線型的，優化效率後的	☐ phenomenal	adj. 非凡的，驚人的
		☐ stunning	adj. 令人驚艷的，極美的
☐ self-checkout kiosk	n. 自助式結帳機	☐ finalist	n. 最後角逐者
☐ inaccuracy	n. 不準確，誤差	☐ awards ceremony	n. 頒獎典禮，頒獎儀式
☐ deluxe room	n. 豪華房	☐ in-person meeting	n. 面對面
☐ bistro	n. 小餐館，小酒館	☐ at one's earliest convenience	phr. 煩請某人盡速（處理）

TOEIC 實戰演練 w18_2.mp3

☐ cater to	phr. 迎合，滿足	☐ free access to	phr. 免費使用，自由進入
☐ overwhelming	adj. 壓倒性的，令人難以招架的	☐ festivity	n. 慶典，歡慶活動
		☐ exceptional	adj. 卓越的，傑出的
☐ expansive	adj. 廣闊的，全面的	☐ breathtaking	adj. 令人屏息的，驚人的
☐ showroom	n. 展示廳，陳列室	☐ downtime	n. 停工期，休息時間
☐ gadget	n. 小工具，小配件	☐ make the most of	phr. 充分利用
☐ coverage	n. 報導，覆蓋範圍	☐ rest assured	phr. 放心，安心
☐ timeframe	n. 時間範圍，時程	☐ confidential	adj. 機密的，保密的
☐ finalize	v. 完成，使成定案	☐ courteous	adj. 禮貌的，客氣的
☐ correction	n. 更正，修正版	☐ attentive	adj. 細心呵護的
☐ omit	v. 省略，遺漏	☐ peak hours	n. 高峰時段，尖峰時間
☐ misquote	v. 錯誤引述	☐ lucky draw	n.（幸運）抽獎
☐ executive	n. 高管，主管	☐ hitch a ride	phr. 搭便車，順路搭車
☐ affordability	n. 可負擔性，實惠性		

台灣廣廈 國際出版集團

國家圖書館出版品預行編目（CIP）資料

```
英文閱讀加深加廣／周昱翔 著; -- 初版 -- 新北市：
國際學村, 2025.01
   面；  公分
978-986-454-403-5 (平裝)
1. CST: 英語 . 2. CST: 讀本

805.18                                        113017557
```

國際學村

英文閱讀加深加廣
1週突破1個難關，全面備戰TOEIC等英語檢定考試！

作　　　　者／周昱翔	編輯中心編輯長／伍峻宏・編輯／許加慶
	封面設計／陳沛涓・內頁排版／菩薩蠻數位文化有限公司
	製版・印刷・裝訂／皇甫・秉成

行企研發中心總監／陳冠蒨	線上學習中心總監／陳冠蒨
媒體公關組／陳柔彣	企製開發組／江季珊、張哲剛
綜合業務組／何欣穎	

發　行　人／江媛珍
法 律 顧 問／第一國際法律事務所 余淑杏律師・北辰著作權事務所 蕭雄淋律師
出　　　版／國際學村
發　　　行／台灣廣廈有聲圖書有限公司
　　　　　　地址：新北市235中和區中山路二段359巷7號2樓
　　　　　　電話：（886）2-2225-5777・傳真：（886）2-2225-8052
讀者服務信箱／cs@booknews.com.tw

代理印務・全球總經銷／知遠文化事業有限公司
　　　　　　地址：新北市222深坑區北深路三段155巷25號5樓
　　　　　　電話：（886）2-2664-8800・傳真：（886）2-2664-8801
郵 政 劃 撥／劃撥帳號：18836722
　　　　　　劃撥戶名：知遠文化事業有限公司（※單次購書金額未達1000元，請另付70元郵資。）

■出版日期：2025年01月　　ISBN：978-986-454-403-5
　　　　　　　　　　　　　　版權所有，未經同意不得重製、轉載、翻印。

Complete Copyright © 2025 by Taiwan Mansion Books Group.
All Rights reserved.